ANGLES OF ATTACK

BY MARKO KLOOS

Frontlines

Terms of Enlistment

Lines of Departure

Measures of Absolution (A Frontlines Kindle novella)

Lucky Thirteen (A Frontlines Kindle short story)

ANGLES OF ATTACK

MARKO KLOOS

47NORTH

Published by 47North, Seattle

www.apub.com

ISBN-13: 9781477828311
ISBN-10: 1477828311

Cover design by Marc Simonetti

Library of Congress Control Number: 2014954221

Printed in the United States of America

For Robin—the Halley to my Grayson, the peanut butter to my jelly,
and the center of it all, now and forever.

ANGLES OF ATTACK

PROLOGUE

Earth. I never thought I'd ever miss the place.

Granted, it wasn't much near the end. Little blue ball of dirt and mostly water, in a corner of a small galaxy at the ass end of the universe. Five billion years it spun around in space, and then we managed to fill it up with a hundred billion of our species in just fifty millennia. Spoiled water, lousy air, mostly dead oceans. And what we didn't ruin, we fought over incessantly, killing each other by the millions over the centuries as our technology far outpaced our ability to keep the vestigial lizard parts of our brains in check.

No, Earth wasn't much when I left it. But it was home.

Five years in the corps, hopping all over settled space, dozens of light-years away from my home planet, and I never once felt homesick. That was because somewhere in the back of my mind, I always felt secure in the knowledge that Earth was still out there, back where I left it, still orbiting the sun once every 365 days, still crawling with humans, still sprawling with cities full of life-forms who look and act like I do.

Now I'm not sure anymore.

The Lankies showed up and took Mars, our oldest and biggest colony in space. Most of us on New Svalbard have seen at least some of the combat footage and sensor data. Twenty alien seed ships all in orbit at once, blowing our fleet into debris and landing thousands of colony pods, dozens of Lanky settler-scouts in each. Lanky nerve gas raining down on the cities, dispassionate wholesale extermination, scraping a nuisance species off the new real estate before moving in. Every ship capable of spaceflight loading up refugees and fleeing the planet at full burn, only to get blown to shrapnel by the Lanky blockade and their orbital minefields. Those who could ran, and most of them died. Those who stayed died just the same.

The last five years were just a warm-up for them. They were testing our capabilities, probing our defenses, gauging our reactions. Playing with their food.

No, things are not looking good for humanity. The theoretical worst-case scenario has finally caught up with us. If things don't turn around, we are looking at the extinction of our species within the next year, maybe two.

But we are humans. We are obstinate, stubborn, belligerent, unreasonable. And we are doing what most sentient creatures do when you corner them and leave them no avenue of escape: We bare our claws and our teeth, and we go on the attack.

A combined NAC/SRA refugee force arrived at New Svalbard two weeks ago, with most of their troop complements and drop ships lost in the Battle of Mars and the many skirmishes that took place concurrently all over the solar system. There were two carriers in the refugee fleet—the SRA's *Minsk* and the NAC's *Regulus*. The SRA carrier, normally embarking a full regiment of marines, had a reinforced company left. The *Regulus*, one of the NAC's six supercarriers, hadn't fared much better, having lost most of its regiment of Spaceborne Infantry.

For whatever reason, the Lanky seed ship we destroyed in the Fomalhaut system by flying a water-laden freighter into it never deployed defensive minefields around the SRA colony moon before they set out for New Svalbard. They arrived in orbit, dumped their colony pods onto the surface, and went straight after the single Russian unit in orbit, the hapless cruiser whose futile run and subsequent destruction alerted us to the Lanky presence in the system to begin with. Now the SRA moon is crawling with Lanky settlers, but they have no overhead defenses, and no seed ship in orbit to keep our ships away. We can finally fight them on somewhat even terms, with the airpower and spaceborne artillery we're usually denied on Lanky worlds.

There are survivors all over the SRA colony. The Lankies have been on the surface for less than three weeks, and while they've methodically wrecked the human infrastructure on the moon wherever they went, they didn't use the nerve-gas pods they usually employ when scraping us off one of our colonies. There are protective shelters all over the place where people holed up, and their small garrison of SRA marines has even been able to stage hit-and-run raids on the invaders. Our recon flights just prior to the assault made radio contact with dozens of scattered groups of SRA civilians and military personnel. So the brass from both sides got together and decided to stage a raid. The SRA, short on marines but with plenty of drop ships, would supply most of the ships. The NAC, with many infantry troops but few drop ships, would contribute most of the fighting men and women on the ground. Amazingly, everyone agreed. More amazingly, we were able to plan a combined-arms operation across two blocs in just a week and a half, with no common standards in armament, equipment, or logistics.

So now, two weeks after the refugee fleet showed up above New Svalbard, we are on the way to the SRA moon in the Fomalhaut system, to rescue the surviving SRA settlers and garrison troops, kill as many of the Lankies as we can, and get out before another seed ship pops up in the system.

That's the battle plan, anyway, but after five years of operational clusterfucks and near misses, I know for sure that no plan ever survives first contact with the enemy.

CHAPTER 1

FOMALHAUT B

"You look like insect," Dmitry says from the jump seat across the aisle. "Big, ugly, imperialist insect."

"You people are experts on ugly," I reply, and look around.

I'm in the cargo hold of a Russian Akula-class drop ship, which is a place I never thought I'd find myself, at least not while fully armed and in battle rattle. The weirdness of the last few days has reached new, previously unexplored levels of weird. In the cargo compartment with me is a mixed platoon of SRA marines and NAC Spaceborne Infantry, shoulder to shoulder, everyone armed to the teeth and ready for war. Just a month ago, all of us sharing such tight quarters with so many weapons would have resulted in a short, violent shoot-out and a lot of dead bodies. Now we all ride the battle taxi together, our strange new alliance glued together by sheer necessity.

Our drop-ship designers don't spend much thought on making the Wasps and Dragonflies pretty, but it seems like the Russians go out of their way to avoid any design touch that might be thought of as aesthetically pleasing. Our drop ships look like the utilitarian war machines they are. The Russian bird looks like a crude piece of heavy construction gear. I can't help but marvel at the efficiency of the design, however. Our jump seats have single-point swivel mounts with shock absorbers. Theirs are just strong, free-swinging webbing—just as shock-absorbent as ours and probably twenty times cheaper. And whatever their looks, I know that these Russian drop ships can bring down a world of hurt on whoever is on the wrong end of their guns.

"How much longer to the drop zone?" I ask Dmitry. He checks his display and shrugs.

"Eighteen, nineteen minutes. You lean back, take nap." Then he puts the back of his helmet against the bulkhead behind him, his expression one of mild boredom.

Dmitry is one of my SRA counterparts, a Russian combat controller. We've had a few days to get to know each other on the way to this hot and dusty moon around Fomalhaut b, and Dmitry is not at all like the stereotypical Russian grunt. He's not the size of a battle tank, and he doesn't swill vodka or talk lovingly to his heavy weaponry. He doesn't even have a buzz cut. Instead, Dmitry is a rather short guy, just barely taller than Sergeant Fallon, and he has the square jaw and chiseled good looks of a fashion model. His hair is an unruly mop that would be over regulation length in the SI, and he is soft-spoken instead of loud and boisterous. In short, he's pretty much the polar opposite of the stereotype I had in my head. In the last few weeks, I've had a lot of opportunities to adjust my old preconceptions.

I toggle through my available comms circuits and select the top-level tactical channel.

"*Regulus* TacOps, this is Tailpipe One. Request final comms and telemetry check."

"Tailpipe One, TacOps," the reply comes. "You're five by five on data and comms. Good luck, and good hunting."

"TacOps, copy that." I bring up the data feed from *Regulus*'s TacOps center, where the ground-pounder brass and the carrier's air-group commander are coordinating the NAC assets about to drop onto a Lanky-controlled moon.

The data feed from *Regulus* shows the eight drop ships of the first-wave spearhead in a V-shaped formation, streaking into atmosphere from high orbit without any opposition.

I'm going with the first wave, which is made up of SRA drop ships, and I'm the ground liaison for the NAC strike force because I'm one of only two combat controllers in this system right now.

Our atmospheric entry is marked by the usual bumping and buffeting. The armored marines in the cargo hold sway in their seats a little in time with the shuddering of the drop ship. I do one last check of the tactical situation in orbit, still amazed to see some of our most valuable fleet units flying close formation with ships they would have tried to blow out of space a few weeks ago.

Three minutes before Dmitry's predicted time-on-target, the drop ship banks sharply to the left. A few moments later, I can hear the thumping sound of ordnance leaving the external racks, and then the autocannons on the side of the hull start thundering. The SRA birds have bigger cannons than ours do, but they fire at a slower rate. I can feel the concussions from the muzzle blasts transmit through the hull, something I've never felt in our Wasps or Dragonflies. This is a month for new experiences, it seems.

"Kuzka's mother!"

The shipboard comms blurt out a staccato burst of terse Russian from the pilot that my suit's universal translator software helpfully translates for me. It doesn't do well with idioms. I look at Dmitry and point to my ear.

"It means to teach someone hard lesson," Dmitry says.

All around me, the SRA troopers ready their weapons, so I do likewise. In Bravo kit, I carry the big and heavy M-80 rifle, and twenty-five rounds in quick-release loops on my battle armor. I work the release latch for the M-80's breech and verify that the brass bases of two armor-piercing rounds are capping the chambers. The computer keeps track of my weapon's loading status, of course, but no combat grunt with any experience at all ever fully trusts a silicon brain when it comes to life-and-death matters.

The Russian ship changes course a few times, each turn punctuated by bursts of cannon fire or missile launches. The ordnance on a drop ship is for fire support, and it's not good practice to use most of it up before the grunts hit the dirt, but then the ship tilts sharply upward into a hover, the tail ramp starts opening, and I see why we're coming in shooting.

"*Yóbanny v rot!*" one of the Russian marines next to me says, and I have a good idea what it means even without my translator, which merely renders the statement as "Strong profanity."

Outside, the landing strip for the SRA colony's air base stretches out into the distance behind the drop ship's tail boom, and scattered on and near the dirty gray asphalt are the massive bodies of several Lankies, some still smoldering from whatever hit them. I don't have very much time to observe the scenery as the drop ship puts its skids on the ground and the deployment light over the tail ramp jumps from red to green. We unbuckle, I follow the SRA grunts out of the cargo hold and down the ramp at a run, and I'm back in combat.

"Hurry, hurry, hurry!" the SRA officer in the lead shouts as we thunder down the ramp. In reality, he's saying something in Russian, of course, but my suit is giving me the closest approximate translation.

The SRA marines work like a well-oiled machine of which I am no part. They take up a standard covering formation as the drop ship dusts off again behind us, engines screaming their banshee wail, sixty tons of laminate steel and weaponry put together into a hulking shape that looks like it shouldn't be able to fly at all. The drop ship isn't a hundred meters off the ground when it pivots around and opens fire with its cannon again. Blind without any TacLink information, I have to rely on my own suit's sensors and my eyes and ears. I look downrange to see where the drop ship is firing, but I can't see what they're hitting. I do, however, hear the unearthly wail of a stricken Lanky, a sound that has followed me in many dreams over the last few years. Then I see the Lanky appearing behind a structure two hundred meters away, limbs flailing, trying to get out of the hail pouring from the drop ship's heavy-caliber autocannons. As big and formidable as they are, their size makes them excellent targets for our air support. For the first time, we are fighting them with all the air and space power at our disposal, and that is making all the difference.

Overhead, I hear a missile coming off the ordnance rack of our ride. It streaks across the distance in a flash and tears into the Lanky's midsection, blowing it off its feet in a tangle of spindly limbs. The SRA marines around me holler their approval.

The SRA architecture on the ground is almost as sturdy as the housing in New Longyearbyen, but for different reasons. The SRA moon is a hot, dusty, rocky place, much closer to Fomalhaut's sun than our little ice moon. The squat bunker-like buildings here must be even sturdier than they look, because I can't see much destruction in this settlement despite the fact that the place has been under Lanky management for a few weeks. They usually gas the settlements first and then dismantle the terraforming infrastructure before taking down our settlements. From the data my suit delivers, it looks like they've not even gotten around to step one yet. The atmosphere down here is perfectly normal. No biohazards, no ChemWar alerts. I could pop my helmet off and breathe fresh air if I wanted.

In the distance, on the other side of the settlement, tracers and missile-exhaust trails mark the arrival of the SRA attack birds that have been escorting us into the LZ. I hear the explosions from their ordnance rolling across town, followed by the unnerving wail of stricken Lankies.

The Russians set up a perimeter, guns and rocket launchers at the ready, calling out threat vectors and directions to each other. I fire up all the active stuff in my suit and check the situation. One drop ship overhead, three on the ground, four more about to land. The next NAC unit is claiming a patch of ground on the other side of the garrison town. Each of our SI platoons has at least one SRA marine as a liaison, to make sure that the local defenders don't start blowing away the people that came to rescue them.

"Air-defense network is not active," Dmitry tells me over our top-level comms circuit. "Is out of commission. They broke radar, lidar, everything that puts out radiation."

Our scouting runs from orbit indicated as much, but the brass didn't want to risk a bunch of drop ships getting blown out of the sky by automated defenses primed to shoot at anything without SRA friend-or-foe transponders, which is why the first wave consists solely of SRA drop ships, carrying mostly NAC infantry in their holds. Now that we're on the ground, I can call in the NAC hardware.

"*Regulus* TacOps, Tailpipe One. Boots on the ground, landing zone is crawling with hostiles. Requesting close air support for a sweep north of the LZ."

"Tailpipe One, TacOps. Copy that. Close air inbound, ETA ten minutes. Call sign is Hammer."

"Hammer flight inbound, ETA one-zero minutes," I confirm. The last word almost gets drowned out by the staccato of the machine cannon on the Akula drop ship overhead.

"Dmitry, tell those Akula pilots we have close air incoming. They'll sweep that area over there. Let's not have any incidents."

Dmitry gives me a lazy thumbs-up without stopping his work on the control deck he has set up on a piece of rubble in front of him.

"Don't worry, my man," he says, in what sounds like a mock American surfer-dude accent. "Russian soldiers are trained professionals."

Over by the north end of the airfield, beyond the runway, three Lankies appear, their eighty-foot forms towering over the rocky landscape. The drop ship overhead opens up with its cannons again. I can't feel the concussions of the muzzle blasts through my bug suit, but the dust underneath my boots gets kicked up as the Russian drop ship rakes the incoming Lankies with armor-piercing explosive grenades. One of them falls, then another, both shrieking and wailing. Their vocalizations sound like nothing I've ever heard on Earth. They're sharp and piercing and full of deep, rumbling intensity at the same time.

Above our heads, the drop ship pulls up and ascends away from the airfield. Dmitry shouts something to his troops, who form a double line on the tarmac in front of me. The SRA marines in the front row drop to one knee. All of them aim their rifles at the remaining Lanky, 150 meters away and closing in on us. The Russians have big, powerful anti-Lanky rifles, but theirs aren't twin-barreled like ours. Instead, the SRA equivalents are single-shot breechloaders, with bores that look even bigger than those of the M-80 I carry. The kneeling row of SRA marines fire their rifles at the Lanky to a command I can't hear, and six rifles pound out shots at the same instant, a deep thunderclap that sounds almost like a single report. The breeches on their guns fly open and eject the brass bases of their caseless rounds, and the second row of marines prepare their own guns. I watch as the SRA marines fire three, four, five volleys in rapid succession, each row shooting while the other reloads, like line infantry of the old colonial days on Earth. The advancing Lanky takes six, then twelve, then eighteen impacts to its head and chest, each marked by the small violent puff of a high-explosive armor-piercing round. By the fifth volley, the Lanky stumbles and falls. Then it crashes to the ground, its bulk shaking the earth underneath my boots. The marines' five volleys took maybe eight or nine seconds. Their Lanky-engagement tactics are completely unlike ours, but I'll be damned if they don't work at least as well.

All over the SRA settlement, I hear gunfire, like a discordant martial symphony: the deep booms of our M-80s and SRA anti-Lanky rifles, the pop-whoosh of MARS rocket launchers, the thunderclaps of exploding grenades and rockets, all mixed in with the wailing of Lankies and the din from the cannons of the overhead drop ships. Every bit of aboveground infrastructure here in town is wrecked, and only some of the squat and sturdy settlement buildings are still standing amid the rubble. But there are no Lanky nerve-gas pods littering the ground here, no clusters of dead settlers anywhere. It's like they're fighting with their hands tied behind their backs. Whatever the reason, I'm perfectly happy with this change in our fortunes, however temporary it may be.

As the NAC troops on the ground spot and engage targets, contact icons pop up on my tactical display. I can't see what the Russians are seeing because our tactical networks don't talk to each other, but everything our own troops see and do gets transmitted to my bug suit's computer and the control deck I'm carrying. The human troops are an enclave of blue icons, the Lankies a wide and irregular circle of orange symbols all around us, clustered in groups of three or four at the most.

The SRA base and town sit at the end of a rocky plateau. On one end of the town, there's a gradual drop-off into a craggy valley. The other end of the town, where the SRA base and its military airfield sit, opens out onto the flat and wide plateau beyond. Out there, Lankies are milling about, some advancing in our direction, some going the other way, away from the fight. In every engagement I've had with them before now, they've shown more coordination and aggression than this group does. These seem slower, weaker, almost unsure. Even with all the troops on the ground, the Lankies on the plateau could probably overrun us if they all came our way at once. But they don't, and I don't intend to let them have enough breathing room to change their minds.

Close air support comes in a few minutes later, three flights of Shrikes loaded to design capacity with air-to-ground ordnance. They drop out of orbit and come rushing toward the LZ at full throttle, forming up into a six-abreast formation just a few dozen klicks from the target area. I fire up the comms suite and toggle into the TacAir channel.

"Hammer flight, this is Tailpipe One. You have a target-rich environment down here. The plateau directly to the north of the LZ is crawling with Lankies. Consider it a free-fire zone. All friendlies are south of the airstrip. Uploading target reference-point data. And mind the Russkie drop ships right above the deck."

"Tailpipe One, Hammer One," the pilot of the lead Shrike sends back. "Confirm everything north of the airstrip is clear to engage. ETA one minute."

I send the confirmation codes and look over to Dmitry, who is busy working his own comms kit.

"Air support coming in—sixty seconds," I shout at him. "Tell those drop ships to clear the airspace."

Dmitry gives me a thumbs-up again without taking his eyes off the screen of his control deck. A few moments later, the Akulas circling above the settlement abandon their positions and scurry off to the west and east to get out of the line of fire.

The Shrikes announce their arrival in a spectacular display of long-range guided-munitions firepower. Two dozen missile trails streak in from the south and cross the sky above the SRA settlement in a flash. They descend onto the plateau beyond the town and explode in a short and violent cacophony that makes the rubble bounce even from a kilometer away. In the distance beyond the runway, plumes of dust and smoke rise into the clear sky. Ten seconds later, the Shrikes are overhead, their huge multibarreled assault cannons firing thousands of armor-piercing shells at targets I can't see. I've never seen six of our Shrikes make a coordinated attack run together, and it's nothing short of awe inspiring, the fist of a god coming down on a gathering of hapless sinners. The nearby SRA marines, caught up in the moment, actually cheer the Shrikes as they pass overhead and split up into pairs again once they are past the settlement. The moment is so surreal that I find myself grinning at the absurdity of it. A few weeks ago, cheering would have been the last thing on the minds of these Russian grunts at the sight of a six-abreast formation of the NAC Defense Corps's premier ground-attack spacecraft. The world has gone topsy-turvy, and it's strangely exhilarating.

Through the TacLink data connection, I see what the Shrikes see as they come back around for another gun run on the plateau. The orange icons for Lanky contacts pop up on my map as the Shrikes target the Lankies, and then blink out of existence as the antiarmor cannons and missiles from the Shrikes hit home. The sheer size of the Lankies works against them—they can't hide from our attack craft, and they seem to have no way to shoot back. As big and strong as they are, bereft of their mother ship's defensive umbrella they're no match for spacecraft designed to take on armored vehicles and SRA strongholds.

Of course, they're still more than a match for us mudlegs on the ground, who don't have the benefit of an armored shell that can fly away at eight hundred knots when things get dicey.

"Tailpipe One, Hammer One. We're cleaning the rest of them off that plateau. Be advised there's a group of twenty coming your way from two-seven-zero degrees. We don't have enough ordnance left on the racks to take them all on before they're on top of you."

"Hammer One, copy," I send back. "Keep clear of that area for orbital delivery."

"Copy that," Hammer flight's leader replies.

I switch back to the fleet tactical channel and contact the *Regulus*.

"TacOps, Tailpipe One. Priority fire mission. Request immediate kinetic strike on the following TRP." I upload the data for the target reference point passed on to me by Hammer flight, a ravine three kilometers to our northwest. Pissed-off Lankies can cover three klicks pretty damn fast, and I'd rather not see twenty of them show up on the runway in a few minutes, drop ships overhead or not.

"Tailpipe One, *Regulus*. Copy target data. Package on the way in seven-zero seconds."

I send a "KINETIC STRIKE" warning to all the NAC troops nearby and run over to where Dmitry is hunched over his control deck. He looks up at me as I skid to a stop.

"Tell your guys we're dropping kinetic munitions in a few minutes, three kilometers that way." I indicate the direction of the target zone with my hand. You don't realize how much of an advantage integrated data networks are until you have to coordinate a combined-arms melee with a group of people whose computers can't talk to yours. Voice and hand signals are slow and cost precious time when ten kilotons' worth of impact energy is descending into your neighborhood at twenty times the speed of sound.

Dmitry nods and talks on his comms again, presumably to let the SRA marines know that the Hand of God is about to touch down three klicks away. Kinetic strikes are almost as impressive as low-yield nukes, and having one occur nearby without warning can be a bit startling, to put it mildly.

Nearby, a squad of NAC Spaceborne Infantry bring down a pair of Lanky stragglers with a barrage of MARS rockets, assisted by a squad of SRA marines with their own rocket launchers. Theirs load from the front, ours from the back, but they both serve the same purpose and achieve the same results. One Lanky goes down, hit by several armor-piercing explosive warheads and dozens of rifle rounds. The other soaks up the hits and keeps coming, right into the defensive fire put out by the two squads. I take the M-80 from my shoulder, let the computer take aim for me, and fire both barrels at the approaching Lanky just as it bears down on the mixed squad of human troops. I'm still fifty meters away and in relative safety, but some of the other troopers are not so lucky. The Lanky flings them aside with a huge, spindly arm, and they get tossed through the air like debris in a hurricane. I open the breech of my rifle, pluck two more rounds from my harness, and reload the chambers. By the time I've raised the weapon again, the cumulative fire from the surrounding troopers has brought the Lanky to its knees. It wails its earsplitting cry as rifle rounds and rockets pelt it from all sides. Then it crashes onto the rubble-strewn ground, finally succumbing to the dozens of super-dense penetrators we shot through its hide. They are so large, so thick-skinned, so incredibly hard to kill that whenever we bring one down, it feels like we've felled a god.

The kinetic warheads from the *Avenger* announce their arrival with an unearthly ripping sound overhead. Then the first warhead strikes the ground three kilometers away, at the entrance of the ravine. There's a blinding flash in the distance, and a few seconds later, an earth-shattering bang shakes the ground so violently that I have to regain my footing, and

Dmitry's control deck leaps off its makeshift pedestal and clatters to the ground. A plume of dust and rock shoots into the blue sky. Then a second round hits, and a third, and a fourth. The *Avenger* spaced her shots, put the first one into the mouth of the ravine to plug the Lankies' ingress route, and then walked the other three into the ravine itself to do the killing work. Within thirty seconds, the cloud of rocks and dirt to our northwest towers a thousand feet above the plateau.

Dmitry looks at the fireworks in the distance for a few moments. Then he picks up his control deck, wipes off the dirt, and props it in front of himself again.

"You just committed treaty violation," he says. "Svalbard Accords. We get home to Earth, I file complaint with United Nations war crimes tribunal."

Nukes and kinetic weapons—and all other weapons of mass destruction—are banned for combat use by both sides when fighting each other. Technically, Dmitry is correct—the *Avenger* firing kinetic warheads at an SRA moon is probably a letter violation of that treaty—but I don't think it counts in spirit, because we shot at Lankies and not SRA installations. In any case, I'm pretty sure Dmitry is joking, but I'm still getting used to the particular Russian sense of humor, or maybe just Dmitry's.

"If we ever make it home to Earth, they can put that one on my tab," I tell Dmitry. "I'm already looking at twenty years for mutiny anyway."

Three more flights of drop ships arrive in five-minute intervals, all SRA boats with mostly NAC infantry on board. The mixed battalion of SRA and NAC troops mops up the remaining Lankies in the settlement one by one while the drop ships and Shrikes provide fire support from above. This is the first time I've been in action against the Lankies with a whole combined-arms combat team, with fire support from orbit and all the resources of a proper planetary-assault task force. And we are, for the first time, decisively winning against them on the ground. They're not invincible after all. Too bad that we won't be able to replicate this particular set of circumstances again any time soon.

I spend the next three hours coordinating the close air cover and the conga line of drop ships coming down from the task force to pick up troops and survivors, return to the carriers, refuel, and then make the trip again. Every drop ship in the combined task force, NAC and SRA alike, is in space or in the atmosphere of the moon at the same time, coming in or going out. It's still bizarre to see Shrikes escorting a flight of SRA drop ships, or Wasps and Akulas flying in formation overhead, and no matter where this strange new arrangement is going to take us in the future, I've spent so much time shooting at these people that I doubt I'll ever get fully used to the sight.

When the last drop ship full of SRA civvies and straggler garrison troops is in the air, the colony town is a deserted pile of rubble, littered with broken things and dead Lankies. The mixed platoon on the ground with me gathers our casualties and prepares for egress. Two drop ships are waiting for us on the edge of the old SRA military airfield, tail ramps down and engines running. There are still plenty of Lankies on this rock, but the ones that are spotted from the air by our recon flights are milling around singly or in small groups. After we blasted the approaching Lanky group in the nearby ravine with kinetic warheads, the Lankies have made no more attempts to retake the settlement and stop the evacuation. On the contrary, the ones that are still in the area seem to take pains to steer well clear of us. The Shrikes are still engaging targets of opportunity all over this part of the moon's hemisphere, but there are still hundreds of Lankies scattered all over the moon, and it would take us another month to kill every last one of them from the air. We got what we came for, and now it's time to hotfoot it away from this place before another seed ship shows up in orbit and ruins the party.

The waiting drop ships are a Wasp and an Akula. The Russian part of the platoon boards the Akula, while the NAC troops tromp up the loading ramp of the Wasp. We are returning to our respective bird farms, which don't have docking clamps for the other side's hardware.

"Good luck, Dmitry," I tell my SRA counterpart as we walk over to our rides together.

"Same to you, Andrew," he says. "Maybe we won't kill each other for a while, eh? I see you on the battlefield, I try to wound you instead, maybe."

I'm the last to walk up the Wasp's ramp. When I glance back over the devastation that is the old SRA garrison, I see that Dmitry is over by the tail end of the Akula, watching me as I walk aboard. It's only when my boots are on the steel of the Wasp's ramp that he starts to board his own boat. I sketch a little salute, and he returns it precisely and by the book.

I know why he waited until I was off the moon before he climbed aboard his own ride.

First ones in, last ones out. Our profession makes us the first to put boots on the ground, and the last to leave the dirt at the end of a mission. This was an SRA settlement, so their combat controller made sure he was the last one onto the last ship off this rock. It seems that some traditions translate across our respective military cultures.

I strap into the last available seat on the crowded Wasp and secure my weapon. Behind me, the tail ramp whines as the crew chief seals the hatch for spaceflight. In the space down the centerline of the Wasp between the two rows of seats, I count five body bags. We've done our share today, sweated and bled onto SRA-owned ground to rescue civilians we would have left behind to die just a month or two ago. Maybe we are evolving as a species after all, now that we're facing our extinction.

Maybe the Lankies should have showed up a few thousand years ago.

CHAPTER 2

NEW SVALBARD

I've been in the fleet for five years, hopping ships every six months after combat-controller school, and I've never been on a Navigator-class supercarrier until this week. The Navigators are the pride of the fleet, half again as large by tonnage as the next-biggest class of carrier and easily the most powerful warships anyone has ever put into space. But they're too rare and valuable to shove into the kind of action I've mostly seen in the last few years, so I've never gotten to walk the decks of one until now.

The sheer size of the *Regulus* is exaggerated by the lack of personnel on board. I know the staffing levels of a carrier and the general amount of activity on board, and if I had to guess, I'd say that the *Regulus* is running ops with half her regular crew at the most. She was in for an overhaul and resupply at the Europa fleet yards when the Lankies appeared in the solar system and took Mars, and they pressed her into action with her maintenance crew and whatever personnel they could scrounge up at Europa. The NAC Defense Corps took the worst mauling of its history in the failed defense of Mars, and there isn't much left to scrape out of the barrel. *Regulus* wasn't ready for combat until the Battle of Mars was already over, and all that was left to do for her was to take her escorts and run. For all I know, *Regulus* may be the last of the Navigators by now. For all I know, we humans in the Fomalhaut system may be the last of our species.

The post-mission debriefing in the *Regulus*'s SpecOps detachment's briefing room is an agreeably low-key affair. I was the only NAC combat controller on the ground, and the other fleet SpecOps guys in the room are two Spaceborne Rescuemen and a SEAL team from the *Regulus*, and three teams of SI recon from Camp Frostbite's Spaceborne Infantry garrison. The *Midway* left half her embarked SI regiment at Frostbite when she tucked tail and ran with the rest of the task force.

I walk into the briefing room and take a chair in the back, behind the SEAL team and on the opposite side of the room from the SI recon guys. The short and violent bloodshed during our mutiny on New Svalbard is still fresh in everyone's memory, and some of the SI troopers have given me hostile glances or made unfriendly remarks in the mess hall on our weeklong ride here. Until we're back in orbit above New Svalbard, I'll be doing my best to avoid getting caught in some low-traffic corner of this ship with half a dozen pissed-off space apes between me and the exit hatch.

The SpecOps commander on the *Regulus* is a hard-faced major named Kelly. He has prematurely gray hair and the worn-out, hard-lived look common to veteran fleet SpecOps personnel. Our lifestyle is extremely taxing on our bodies and minds, and most lifers in our branch look at least ten years older than their actual age.

"That was a by-the-book ass-kicking," he says when he starts the debriefing by firing up the holographic display on the wall. "Zero podhead casualties on this one. One hundred seventy-nine confirmed Lanky kills, and another fifty-some likelies."

We all cheer our approval in the appropriate muted and professional fashion. That's by far the highest nonnuclear Lanky body count any unit has ever racked up in a single drop, and we did most of it the old-fashioned way, on the ground, with rifles and rockets and automatic cannons.

"How many SI casualties? And, uh, SRA?" one of the SEALs asks.

"Nineteen KIA, twenty-some wounded," the major replies. "Don't have numbers for the Russians, but they had a lot fewer boots on the ground."

"That's not awful for a drop that size," the lieutenant in charge of the SEAL team says. That is of course a massive understatement. We would have taken at least three times as many SI casualties just going up against an SRA garrison battalion or two. And nobody has ever gone up against the Lankies with an overstrength regiment from orbit, but the last time they showed up while we had a force that size on the ground, they wiped it out almost completely.

"'Not awful' is right," Major Kelly says. "We just handed those skinny bastards a major ass-kicking going toe-to-toe, on their turf. If shit had gone half as well on the colonies the last few years, we'd have them on the run by now."

"They were acting kind of odd," I say, and most of the heads in the room swivel into my direction. "Anyone else notice that? They were nowhere near as aggressive as they usually are. Sluggish, almost."

"Yeah," the SEAL lieutenant says. "Like they were drowsy or something."

"Maybe we got 'em demoralized," one of the SI recon guys offers, and the SEAL lieutenant snorts a brief laugh.

"They were without their mother ship," Major Kelly says. "Which is why they got their asses kicked, of course, but maybe there's something else to that. Maybe they were short on something that went nova with that seed ship. Supplies? Who the fuck knows."

"They didn't have anything set up on the surface," I say. "I went through all the recon data before and after the drop. Not a single Lanky terraformer, or whatever the fuck they call theirs. They didn't even manage to tear down all the SRA stations, and that's usually their first order of business. Two-thirds of the SRA terraforming network is still up and running down there."

"If I had to guess?" Major Kelly says. "We blew up their chow and their building supplies when we took out their ship. There weren't enough Lankies on the ground, either. Not for a colony takeover. There's thousands of those things in a seed ship."

"Those were just the advance recon team or something," someone else in the room suggests. "Ship skips by the moon, dumps the advance team, goes gunning for that SRA cruiser, gets blown to shit by the New Svalbard people."

"Advance team gets stranded without support on the SRA moon," Major Kelly adds. "So we basically kicked their asses because they were underfed and aimless."

The major's statement hangs in the room for a moment like an unwelcome after-lunch fart. Nobody wants to think that our first major military success against the Lankies—heroic rescue of colonists!—was mostly due to the fact that the Lankies may have been too weak to put up a decent fight. Then Major Kelly shrugs and shakes his head.

"Whatever. Don't really give a shit about the why and how. Most of our guys made it back, and most of theirs are full of holes. That's a successful mission right there. Too bad it probably won't make a damn bit of a difference in the long run. Go and relax, people. We have a six-day ride back to New Svalbard. May be the last R and R any of us get for a long time."

Or for good, I think. I check my new loaner PDP for the date. It's April 3, 2116, and I have less than three months to get back home to Earth if I don't want to be late for my own wedding. I don't know if Earth is still there, but I don't even want to contemplate the possibility that Halley may not be there anymore. If this refugee United Nations strike force is going back to the solar system, I'm going, too.

The *Regulus* has state-of-the-art recreational facilities for its crew. I've seen a lot of fleet rec centers in my service—Halley and I usually get together at RecFacs whenever we have leave together, because we're often too far away from Earth to make it back there before our leave time is up—and I can say that this one is the nicest I've seen yet. Still, I can't get any enjoyment out of any of the offerings. It all seems so trite all of a sudden—simulators, canned Network shows bundled for fleet personnel who may be on deployment for a show's entire Earthside run, pool and gaming holotables, and dozens of other ways for stressed-out warfighters to turn off their brains and find some diversion. All this stuff seems pointless now, with most of the fleet gone and the solar system under siege by a near-unbeatable enemy. I realize that I never liked the RecFacs anyway, and that I only ever enjoyed them because they were the only places where I got to spend some alone time with Halley in the private berths.

At least the place has sports facilities for team games and solitary workouts, so I use my downtime to sweat. There's a running track that winds its way through the rec deck of the *Regulus*, and because it's a big ship, it's a long track, two kilometers of black rubberized decking with a fat white line running down the center, snaking through the many compartments. It's quite possibly the height of vanity, considering the overall state of humanity right now, but sitting on New Svalbard, I put on a few extra pounds with the mess-hall chow at Camp Frostbite, and I want to be in the best possible shape when I see my fiancée again. There's a better-than-even chance my once again trim body will be an expanding cloud of superheated debris in a few weeks, long before we get even within sight of Earth, but running is a good thing to do right now. It feels normal, and I can stand some of that at the moment, because everything else doesn't.

I don't belong on this ship. I have a loaner berth and a loaner armor set, but I don't know a soul on the *Regulus*. The SI troopers from the *Midway* who embarked with me on this drop are quartered in the section of the ship that usually hosts the *Regulus*'s own SI regiment. I took a berth in the NCO quarters of the fleet section, well away from the *Midway* grunts, and with the *Regulus* running a skeleton crew, it's a pretty quiet run back to New Svalbard. For the first time in weeks, I don't have access to an all-seeing ship network or external sensor arrays, and I'm just another passenger. I sleep, I eat, I work out, and I go out of my way not to have to talk to anyone except the occasional SEAL or Spaceborne Rescue podhead in line for chow. When we arrive back in orbit over New Svalbard after six days of boring and uneventful interplanetary cruise, I'm so bored that I almost wish we had another Lanky on our tail and just a few days to find a way to kill it.

"You look like you need some of the local rotgut," Sergeant Fallon says by way of greeting when I walk down the ramp of the *Regulus* drop ship that ferried me down to New Svalbard's airfield. The weather has gotten a lot worse in the week I was gone. The snowdrifts by the sides of the squat hangars nearby are four or five meters high, and there's a sixty-knot polar wind blowing across the open space and whipping the snow sideways. Sergeant Fallon is in her battle armor, which is ice-caked, and she only raises her visor briefly when she walks up to me to help me with my gear.

"That's some grade-A shit weather," I say to her. "Shuttle got delayed three hours waiting for a break in the storm."

"This isn't a storm," she says. "This is fucking balmy. You can actually see ahead for more than ten meters. Everything has moved underground. And I mean everything. The whole town. Did you know they have a whole damn recreation district underground?"

"No, I did not know that."

"They call it the Ellipse. Come on, stow your new toys, and I'll take you down to the bar. They have a thing called a Shockfrost cocktail. I don't know what's in it, but it will make you think you can arm-wrestle a Lanky."

The Ellipse is an underground concourse that makes a loop underneath a large chunk of New Svalbard. Sergeant Fallon leads me around like a tour guide. All the bunker-like houses on the surface have secondary subterranean exits that lead to neighborhood tunnels, and all of those tunnels converge on the Ellipse. In the winter months, when nobody can spend much time on the surface in hundred-knot polar winds, life moves underground on New Svalbard.

The tunnel that makes up the Ellipse is twenty meters or more in diameter. I always wondered where the settlers of New Svalbard have their shops and pubs and where social life happens, and now I have my answer. Colonial economies are rough and basic, much like the black markets in the PRC back home, and a lot about the Ellipse and its warrens of shops and vendor stalls reminds me of life back home before I joined the service.

"You going to tell me about the drop with our new pals, or what?" Sergeant Fallon asks as we stride down the concourse, which has many more colonists milling around on it than I've ever seen on the surface streets here in New Longyearbyen. The locals are ice miners, hydroponic farmers, engineers, aviation service crews, and their families. Occasionally, we pass HD troopers from our newly minted New Svalbard Territorial Army, who give us respectful nods or salute Sergeant Fallon outright. Regardless of prior rank structures, we are both part of the small group who was in charge of the mutiny a few weeks ago, when Sergeant Fallon and her exiled Homeworld Defense troopers refused to follow orders to seize colonial assets. The resulting battle with the hardheaded elements of the Spaceborne Infantry cost us nearly forty casualties on both sides, along with several aviation assets we could ill afford to write off, not with so few humans in the Fomalhaut system, most of them dug into a moon with very few military assets of its own.

"Best drop I've ever done, really," I say. "By-the-book planetary assault, few casualties, all mission goals accomplished. You should have been there. Could have gotten some trigger time against the Lankies in. Those Russian marines do not fuck around, let me tell you."

"Oh, I have no doubt. I met a few of them at Dalian during that lovely proxy battle we fought with the SRA. 'Course, they were in sterile uniforms back then. Svalbard Accords and all."

I don't know a lot of Sergeant Fallon's service history before I met her five years ago in the Territorial Army's 365th Autonomous Infantry Battalion, but I do know from my former squad mates that the Battle of Dalian was where she earned her Medal of Honor. I know it was a police action that went south and filled a lot of TA body bags, but the official history is fuzzy on the details, which probably means that we technically or brazenly violated a treaty or three.

"You have to tell me about that one of these days," I say.

Sergeant Fallon just smirks. "Andrew, the level of alcohol I need to drink to start telling details about Dalian pretty much guarantees that I won't be able to recall those details. Speaking of alcohol . . . here we are. Welcome to On the Rocks."

She points to a shop front that takes up about twenty meters of the tunnel wall up ahead on our right. In most other settings, the fake blown-glass windows and the obviously resin-molded knobby tree trunks that decorate the front of the establishment would be tacky, but down here it's a welcome splash of colorful kitsch in a place where most everything else is the color of ice and grimy concrete.

"This," Sergeant Fallon says, "is the best bar in New Longyearbyen. And believe me, I've had lots of time to try them all while you were gone playing Superhero Space Commando."

The interior of the place carries on the design cues from the outside. There's no wood on New Svalbard, so the furniture is sturdy polymer molded to look like it has been carved from weathered driftwood. There are fake tree trunks on the walls, and the spaces between them have been adorned with murals by an artist long on enthusiasm and short on talent. It sort of looks like it's supposed to resemble a medieval tavern, and it falls well short of achieving that goal, but after weeks of looking at steel bulkheads and nonslip flooring, the visual clutter is a welcome distraction.

"I didn't know you drank," I say to Sergeant Fallon when we sit down to claim one of the little round plastic tables in the back of the place.

"I do," she says. "Just not the shitty soy beer they serve back in the RecFacs. That stuff tastes like carbonated piss. I like a good black-market whisky. Real beer, too, but that stuff is too expensive for my pay grade."

"Never had any," I reply. "Just the stuff they sell back home in the PRC. Purple Haze, Orange Crush, Blue Angel." I chuckle at the memory of my first forays into intoxication when I was a teenager. "Positively awful shit. Flavored with the fruity juice powder from the BNA packets, to cover up the taste from whatever piping they used to distill it. Still tasted like battery acid, just like fruit-flavored battery acid."

"Not too long before you joined us at Shughart in the 365th, we had a drop into the 'burbs somewhere in Kentucky," Sergeant Fallon says. "Near the Lexington metroplex. Way out in the gentrified area. Some hood rats jacked a hydrobus and drove out from PRC Lexington to stir some shit and redistribute themselves some wealth. Small drop, just a platoon, to help out the local cops. We flushed the hood rats out of one of the real-currency food stores. They'd eaten as much as they could and got piss drunk, and then they trashed the rest."

She looks over at the fake stained-glass windows that also adorn the interior walls, and her voice trails off as she recalls the memory.

"The middle-class 'burbers, they know how to live. When we had the last of the hood rats hog-tied and packed up for transport to the detention center, I had a look around for leftovers. They had a back stockroom, secured like a damn bank vault. I cracked the lock to check for stragglers, and there was this stash of high-dollar luxury goods in there. For extra-special customers with deep pockets, I'm guessing. Saw a bottle that said 'Single Malt' on it, liberated it, and took it back to Shughart in one of my empty mag pouches."

Sergeant Fallon looks at me, and her expression turns very slightly dreamy for a moment. "You've never had anything like that in your life, Andrew. Proper single malt Scotch, from actual Scotland. Not made from soy or recycled piss or whatever. Aged in a fucking wood barrel for fourteen years, then sat on a shelf in some middle-class asshole's private stash for a few more. So simple and clean, and so complex at the same time. All that work and time, just for someone to sip slowly and enjoy. Pure decadence."

"Did you share any with the rest of the squad?" I ask.

"No, I didn't. I kept it all for myself. Took me a month to finish that bottle. And I have no regrets."

I grin at this casual admission of a court-martial-level offense. Truth is, it doesn't seem that bad anymore, not after what happened since we arrived in the Fomalhaut system a few weeks ago. We've done far more subversive stuff since then, and a stolen bottle of liquor barely makes a dent in the ledger now, even if that bottle probably cost more than I made in my first nine months in the military.

The bar isn't very busy. There are a few locals sitting at tables and chatting, mostly ice miners and engineers clad in blue overalls, waterproof adaptive nanofiber jackets hanging over chair backs. There's music playing at moderate volume, some ancient K-pop tunes that were already oldies when I was in public grade school.

"What's it going to be today?"

The girl that walks up next to our table with an empty tray in one hand and a towel in the other looks to be all of sixteen years old. She's wearing beige overalls and a thermal vest that's a particularly vivid shade of purple.

"Bring us two Shockfrosts, Allie," Sergeant Fallon says. "My friend here hasn't tried one yet."

"Got it," Allie says. She takes a small handheld scanner off her belt. Sergeant Fallon pulls her dog tags out from underneath her uniform tunic and holds them out for Allie, who scans them with a quick and practiced motion. Then Allie wipes down the table perfunctorily and walks off toward the bar.

"Payment system?" I ask, and nod at the dog tags. Sergeant Fallon nods.

"They keep track of who buys what. Normally they run accounts every month when they get a data link via courier. With the network closed, they're probably sitting on two or three months' worth right now. I don't think timely accounting matters much at the moment anyway."

"This is what you've been doing? Trying out all the watering holes in this place and running your government account dry?"

"I wish," Sergeant Fallon says. "Most of my time I've been too busy trying to figure out how to keep two battalions' worth of bored grunts from killing themselves or each other. Flight ops are cut back because of the weather, so we haven't been able to keep up with the rotation. We were going to cycle the platoons at the terraformers through New Longyearbyen every other week, but the puddle jumpers can't fly in this kind of weather. It's a miracle anyone can live in this place at all. We are a hardy species."

"Not as hardy as the Lankies," I say.

"They're just bigger and stronger. But you don't see them trying to colonize places like this. They go for the real estate we've already prepared for them."

"That's true," I admit. "Maybe that makes them smarter, too."

"I can't argue much with that point of view right now," Sergeant Fallon says. She leans back in her chair with a little sigh and stretches out her prosthetic leg underneath the table. "Five years with that thing a part of me, and it still feels like a foreign object at the end of a long day."

Allie returns with our drinks, squat polyplast tumblers full of a light blue liquid. She puts the glasses in front of us with a curt smile and walks off again.

I pick up my glass and smell the contents. "God. It smells like someone dropped sweetener into a pint of aviation fuel."

"Tastes a bit like that, too." Sergeant Fallon smiles. "Watch this."

She takes a lighter out of the arm pocket of her fatigues, turns it on, and holds the little hissing gas flame to the surface of her drink. Blue flames crackle into life. She watches the alcohol fire for a moment and then extinguishes it by putting her hand on top of the tumbler to cut off the oxygen. Then she picks up the glass and takes a long sip.

"You just want to let it heat up the top layer, but not burn long enough to use up too much alcohol," she says. "It's a delicate balance."

She hands me the lighter, and I do like she did. The drink doesn't taste quite as potent as it smells, but I can feel the burn of the alcohol all the way down into my stomach. It tastes of mint and licorice and a few other things I can't identify. All in all, there's a surprising variety of flavor, considering this stuff was probably distilled in a back room down here and aged for days instead of years.

"Not bad," I say.

"Damn straight it ain't. Just don't have more than one, or you won't be able to remember how to latch your battle armor for the next day or two."

She looks past me and raises an eyebrow. I hear steps behind me and turn to see the three SI troopers walking over to us from the other side of the room. By their tense postures and grim facial expressions, I doubt they're coming our way to make a social call. I turn my chair around so I can face the three troopers as they stop in front of our table.

"I think you'd do us all a favor if you and your boys just stayed over there, Master Sergeant," Sergeant Fallon says. "We have no need for company."

"You're the Earthside hero who ran the show for that little mutiny," the SI master sergeant says. His companions are both staff sergeants. All of them have master drop badges and various other infantry credentials on their smocks.

"You have it all wrong, Master Sergeant. What we did wasn't a mutiny. What you guys did was attempted robbery."

The SI sergeant balls his fists and flexes his jaw. "That drop on the admin center, we lost four guys from my unit, you rubble-humping riot cop. One of them was a first sergeant I've dropped with for ten years. You owe me way more than just some ass-hole commentary. Legal or not, that wasn't for you to decide. But you never should have ordered your people to fire on their own troops."

"They didn't fire on their own troops," Sergeant Fallon replies. "They fired on some jacked-up space monkeys taking ille-gal orders from a warmed-up one-star reservist. And don't you fucking start talking about who owes whom 'less you want a list of my casualties to answer for."

"Homeworld Defense," the SI master sergeant replies, pro-nouncing the words like he's describing an unappetizing medical condition. "Those weren't casualties, Sarge. Those were property damage."

I don't see her telegraphing the move at all, but Sergeant Fal-lon's artificial leg shoots out from underneath the table and takes the SI sergeant down at the ankles. He falls sideways with a yelp, and I push my chair backward and scramble to my feet quickly. The SI master sergeant's head hits the edge of the plastic table and takes it down with him, along with our drinks. The other two SI troopers launch themselves at us, and the brawl is on.

My opponent is half a head shorter than I am but looks much more fit than I feel right now. I take advantage of my slightly longer reach and jab him in the face with a quickly thrown left straight, which rocks his head back a little but doesn't slow him down. He hauls off with his right hand and hits my own right fist, which I'd put in front of my face to block his punch, and I end up punching myself in the lip with my own hand. Then we're too close for punches. He grabs me by the tunic and tries to head-butt me. I turn my head slightly and pull my chin to my chest to make his blow land somewhere other than my face. Then I pull back my right leg and knee my opponent as hard as I can. I was aiming for his groin, but due to our height difference, I hit his abdomen instead. He doubles over without letting go of my uniform. I knee him again in the same spot, and he lets go and stumbles back.

Next to me, the third SI trooper is already on the ground, holding his nose. The master sergeant who led the attack is just now getting back to his feet, and I look on as Sergeant Fallon very deliberately cocks her leg and kicks the SI master sergeant in the small of the back. He shouts out in pain and falls backward.

There's a loud and sharp whistle from the door. We all turn to see Chief Constable Guest, the moon's top law-enforcement officer, standing in the doorway and holding the door open with one hand. The barrel-chested constable looks only very slightly less solid than the heavy steel door or the foot-thick concrete wall next to him. His other hand is hovering somewhere in the vicinity of his gun holster and the stun stick on his belt, and his sour expression makes it clear that he is currently thinking about deploying one or the other. He assesses the situation for a few seconds and then points at the SI troopers.

"You three. Out. And don't come back in here. No argument, no debate. Leave now, or I will lock you up in my ice dungeon."

The SI master sergeant looks like he wants to put up an argument anyway, but Constable Guest just shakes his head and removes the stun stick from his belt. Then he points over his shoulder with the crowd-control device, through the door he's holding open with the other hand.

"Now."

The master sergeant turns around and looks at Sergeant Fallon, who returns his gaze impassively.

"We are not done yet," he says to her. Then he picks his beret up off the floor and heads toward the door. His comrades follow him, but not before shooting us hostile glances of their own. When they reach the door, Constable Guest steps aside for them, still holding open the hatch, and they file out one by one. Then he lets go of the door, puts the stun stick back onto his belt, and walks over to where Sergeant Fallon and I are standing. All around us, people haven't even interrupted their conversations. The colonists on New Svalbard are some of the toughest people I've ever met, and our little interservice disagreement hasn't even raised any eyebrows down here.

"You two of all people shouldn't be down here picking fights with other soldiers," he says to us in his laid-back Texas drawl, his tone stern and sorrowful, as if he's lecturing his daughters instead of two hardened combat veterans. "When people get into it down here, I have to come and straighten things out, and then my expensive and hard-to-get hand-pressed coffee gets cold in my office. I don't like it when that happens. It disturbs my peace. Please do not disturb my peace."

"Sorry about that," Sergeant Fallon says. "I would have avoided the whole thing, but those three had a tussle on their minds the minute they decided to walk over to our table. Hard feelings."

"Well, maybe I need to ban Camp Frostbite personnel from town altogether again. Not that I have the manpower to enforce that right now. Or maybe I need to just ban all of you from all the bars in town." He looks around and sighs. "But then you'll have no place to go, and you'll just beat each other up out on the Ellipse somewhere."

"Won't happen again," Sergeant Fallon says. She bends down to pick up the table the SI master sergeant tipped over when he crashed into it. I pick up the plastic tumblers and put them back onto the table when she has righted it.

"See to it that it doesn't," Constable Guest says. "Please. It would go a long way toward restoring my good mood."

Constable Guest is jovial, soft-spoken, and courteous. He's also about the size of a drop-ship tail ramp, and probably roughly as heavy. I've not seen him in a fight since I arrived on New Svalbard for the first time a few weeks ago, but I have little doubt that he could mop the floor with half a squad of infantry grunts if provoked.

"I'll give you a free pass on this one, because they came to hassle you and not the other way around," he says. "But do not make this a habit, or you will get on my bad side. And as much as I respect your valor in the service of our Commonwealth, you do not want to find yourself on my bad side. I know you Earth folks aren't used to being locked up inside for months to ride out the winter, but I cannot have hand-to-hand combat happening in my area of responsibility."

Sergeant Fallon looks slightly embarrassed by Constable Guest's dressing-down, and it's the first time I've ever seen that particular emotion on her face.

"That was my failure," she says. "No excuse. I think I need to hop on one of those snow tractors and drive around in the fresh air for a day or two. This indoor living is starting to cloud my judgment."

I have the taste of blood in my mouth, and my left lower lip is feeling a little puffy. It will probably be fat for the rest of the day. The girl Allie walks over from the bar with her dirty hand towel and starts mopping up the drinks we spilled when the fight started. I step aside to make room for her.

"We have a spell of decent weather coming up in a few hours," Constable Guest says. "Winds down to below fifty, light snow. Good enough for outside pursuits. You may want to consider stretching your legs a bit. Maybe go up to the carrier. We'll be able to run flight ops again for a little while, from what I hear. Take it easy, you two, and don't cause me any more grief than you have to, please."

Constable Guest nods at Allie and turns to walk out of the bar. He has to duck slightly to fit through the door as he leaves.

"Go into orbit to lock myself in an even smaller space," Sergeant Fallon says. "No, thank you. I'm pretty fucking glad I pulled a TA ticket after boot, let me tell you. I don't know how you fleet people can stand it."

We look around, and nobody else in the bar is paying even the slightest bit of attention to us. We could sit back down and order another round of drinks, but I'm still unpleasantly buzzing from the adrenaline jolt, and the laid-back mood from earlier is broken thoroughly.

"Are we still running the show in the ops center?" I ask Sergeant Fallon, and she nods curtly.

"Padded the crew a little. Half civvies, half our HD people. We're not letting any of the Camp Frostbite troops anywhere near the place, and the new troops are just going in and out of Frostbite."

"I'm going to see what's up in orbit, talk to *Indy* for a bit. I've been out of the loop for two weeks."

"Hitting the ground running," Sergeant Fallon says, and shakes her head. "No wonder you made E-6 so fast. You need to learn how to ride out downtime."

"I've had almost two weeks of downtime," I reply. "Twelve days of utter fucking boredom with a six-hour battle in the middle. If they gave out medals for sitting on your ass on a carrier, I'd have ribbons from my collarbone all the way down to my knee."

"The constable would make a killer grunt," I say to Sergeant Fallon as we walk on the Ellipse back toward the ops center. "If we even had battle armor for someone his size."

"No, he wouldn't," she replies. "He's too laid-back and too smart besides."

"Don't think he has it in him to take someone out?"

"Oh, I know he does," she says. "Don't let the guy fool you with that antique pop gun on his belt. I've been in his office a few times. He has a ready pack sitting in the corner. Hardshell laminate armor, all magazine pouches loaded up, and an M-66C in a locked bracket right next to that. It's all dolled up with zero-mag battle optics. And the finish on it is so grungy, I guarantee you it sees plenty of use at the range. Our constable is a bona fide gunfighter."

"Can you imagine him in an infantry squad? He could damn near carry an M-80 in each hand. Biggest hands I've ever . . ."

I trail off as Sergeant Fallon looks over her shoulder. We're not alone on this section of the Ellipse, but the foot traffic is light right now, and I notice the sounds of military boots on concrete behind us just a fraction of a moment later. We turn and see the three SI troopers from the bar coming up quickly behind us, and none of them look like they're in the mood for an amicable chat. They come to a stop maybe five meters away.

"Care to continue our discussion from earlier, Sergeant?" the SI master sergeant says.

"That's Master Sergeant to you," Sergeant Fallon answers coolly. "And you guys better take your candy asses back to Camp Frostbite before someone gets hurt."

"Maybe someone ought to get hurt," one of the staff sergeants says. He reaches under his fatigue tunic and pulls out a knife with a short double-edged blade that has the glossy shine of ceramic to it. "Don't think you get to pull that shit with the roboleg more than once."

I don't see Sergeant Fallon even start to make a move, but in the blink of an eye, there's a pistol in her hands. She holds it at low ready, not aimed at anyone in particular, but I have no doubt that she could cap all three of the SI troopers before they can cover the distance between us. The standard-issue M109 automatic pistol is woefully inadequate for defense against troops in full battle armor, but none of us down here are wearing hardshell right now, and the 4.5-millimeter high-velocity projectiles from a service pistol can do awful things to an unprotected human body at close range.

The three SI troopers freeze on the spot. I get that unwelcome wrenching feeling in the middle of my chest that always wells up when lethal violence is about to happen. I look at Sergeant Fallon's face, and she looks like she is merely deciding where to put the first bullet.

"Whoa," the SI master sergeant says. "Whoa. Take it easy." He holds out his hands slowly. Sergeant Fallon tracks his movement with the muzzle of her pistol, and it never wavers even a fraction of a millimeter.

"Drop the fucking blade," she says to the SI trooper who is still holding his ceramic knife. "I'm not going to tell you twice."

The trooper complies and lets go of his knife. It clatters to the concrete. The SI master sergeant looks back at his man, sees the knife at his feet, and shakes his head slowly in frowning disapproval.

"Back there in the bar, that was harmless fun," Sergeant Fallon says. "This right here is not. I could have shot that idiot the second he pulled his knife. You all want to die in this place, right now?"

"No, ma'am," the now disarmed staff sergeant says. Some colonists pass by, giving us a berth when they see the gun in Sergeant Fallon's hand, but are seemingly unconcerned otherwise.

"Take your men and go back to Frostbite now," Sergeant Fallon tells her SI counterpart. "Do not come back into town while HD is running the show here, or I will shoot you on sight. We clear?"

"Yes, Master Sergeant," the SI master sergeant says. He takes a slow step back, hands still outstretched. Then he turns on his heel and pulls the other two SI troopers with him. Sergeant Fallon keeps the muzzle of her pistol trained on them until they disappear around a bend fifty meters down the concourse. Then she exhales sharply, as if she had been holding her breath the whole time. She lowers the pistol and tucks it back into a holster on her belt. Then she straightens out the tunic to cover the butt of the gun again and picks up the dropped knife. For a long moment, neither of us says anything as we both process what just happened.

"We're not a military anymore," she finally says to me. "Senior NCOs assaulting, pulling weapons on each other. We're just a bunch of armed gangs now."

She nods at me to follow her and starts walking toward the ops center again, a bit more briskly than before. I look over my shoulder to where the SI troopers disappeared around the bend, and follow Sergeant Fallon.

"We need to get off this fucking rock," she says. "If we don't find a sense of purpose again pretty damn soon, we're going to be shooting it out in the streets with each other before too long."

CHAPTER 3

—BALANCING THE SCALES—

I'm still buzzing with adrenaline when Sergeant Fallon and I walk into the ops center a few minutes later. The confrontation down in the Ellipse has turned my mood a bit sour, so I throw myself back into work to get my mind off the event. I sit down in front of the comms console and check our situation overhead while I contact the *Indianapolis* for a status update. The holographic display comes to life and dutifully displays ship icons and hull numbers.

Up in orbit, the strangest collection of warships I have ever seen is circling frozen little New Svalbard. The fleet overhead is nominally split up into three factions at the moment. There's the NAC contingent: the carrier *Regulus* and the battlecruiser *Avenger*. Then there's the SRA contingent that came with them: the assault carrier *Minsk*, the destroyer *Shen Yang*, the frigates *Gomati* and *Neustrashimyy*, and three unarmed supply vessels that are worth their weight in platinum right now. Finally, there's the sole remaining member of the nascent New Svalbard Territorial Army's space arm, Colonel Campbell's little orbital combat ship *Indianapolis*. On paper, we have force parity between the SRA and NAC units, but the *Minsk* and her escorts are all thirty years old at least, and I would bet heavily on the *Regulus* and her bodyguard cruiser in a tussle. Luckily, we're all one big multinational refugee family now.

"Stores are topped off, but that ain't saying much," Colonel Campbell says over the orbital link from the *Indy*'s CIC. "This boat was never meant for extended deep-space operations. There are only so many ration boxes we can cram into our holds. We're good for another month of ops, six weeks if we live lean."

"Anything new on the *Midway*?" I ask. Next to me, Sergeant Fallon's expression darkens at the mention of the carrier whose commanding officer decided to make a grab for New Svalbard's civilian food infrastructure, then tucked tail and ran when it looked like the Lankies were about to wipe us off the ice moon altogether.

"Last we saw them, they were headed into deep space. Got a few long-range infrared blips on the scope over the last few days. I think they're trying to make a very long dogleg back to the Alcubierre chute and get out of Fomalhaut," Colonel Campbell replies. "Either way, I'm not terribly consumed with finding them."

"Be a real fucking blast if they showed up again and started shooting at our new pals," I say.

"Yeah, I wouldn't really want ringside seats to that show, even if that one-star in charge of that bucket is a moron," Sergeant Fallon chimes in. "There are a lot of people on the *Midway* that don't need to be turned into stardust."

"I don't disagree with you on that one in the least," Colonel Campbell says. "I wish them the best of luck in finding safe harbor somewhere."

The ops center is staffed with a near-parity blend of military and civilian personnel. The colony's regular team of administrators and technical-operations people is supplemented by myself, Master Sergeant Fallon, and one of the staff officers from Sergeant Fallon's HD battalion, a Major Frederick. The command structure remains tentatively unorthodox—while the major outranks us both, there's a common understanding that the master sergeant and her inner cadre are in charge down here, and the staff officers of both HD battalions are content to let her run the show in New Longyearbyen. Of course, Sergeant Fallon would rather be dodging bullets and crawling through ChemWar-contaminated mudholes than dealing with the minutiae of everyday military administration for a two-battalion-strong garrison.

"Weather conditions will be good enough for flight ops for maybe another twelve hours," Major Frederick says. "The puddle jumpers are drop-and-go right now to rotate people in and out from the terraformers. No idea when we'll get the next decent window in this frozen shit soup."

"Let's get as many people shuffled through as possible," Sergeant Fallon says. "And any orbital business we have, best get it done in the next half day or so."

There's a holographic display on the wall that currently displays a slowly rotating sphere representing New Svalbard, the sole moon of Fomalhaut c, third planet in the vast and very empty Fomalhaut system. There are sixty-four evenly spaced icons dotting both hemispheres, each of them a state-of-the-art multibillion-dollar terraforming station, powerful fusion reactors with giant atmospheric exchange units attached. Each of them has a garrison platoon of Homeworld Defense troops assigned to it—partially for security reasons and partially because New Longyearbyen doesn't have the infrastructure to support two battalions of soldiers. The terraforming stations have energy and space in abundance, but they are extremely isolated and don't have much in the way of recreational opportunities, so Sergeant Fallon has set up a rotation schedule, which the harsh New Svalbard climate screws up on a regular basis.

"I'm passing along a request from *Regulus* Actual," Colonel Campbell says. "The task force skippers want to have a meeting with all the COs to discuss our plans for getting back into the fight."

"Back into the fight? I could have sworn we're right in the middle of it," I say.

"It's no secret that our supply situation isn't great. We sure as hell don't have the resources to winter in this place, let alone spend the next year or two here and wait for the Lankies to come to us. Without a fleet yard for maintenance, half our hulls will be out of commission before too long anyway. Especially those SRA relics. Those people don't put much emphasis on scheduled service intervals in ideal conditions. I don't feel like towing one of those overarmed garbage scows to the Alcubierre chute and then back to Earth."

"All the COs?" Major Frederick asks. "Theirs and ours?"

"Everyone," Colonel Campbell replies. "Ground commanders, fleet skippers, SRA brass, and our little gang of plucky mutineers."

"Festive," I mutter. "We're like a tiny, fucked-up United Nations now."

"We can pass a unanimous resolution against Lanky invasion," Sergeant Fallon says wryly. "Problem solved."

Strategy meetings are usually hair-pulling affairs just across NAC service branches. The idea of a multibranch, multinational discussion between fleet capital ship commanders, ground pounders, rebellious Earthside garrison troops, and our equivalents from the bloc we've been at war with until just a month ago doesn't fill me with glowing confidence of success. We'll do well not to light off a localized World War V right here in orbit once everyone figures out just how many pairs of boots we have competing for just how few resources. We have water and reactor fuel to keep everyone running indefinitely, but there are no calories in ice and snow, and the hydroponic farms on the surface of New Svalbard are barely sufficient to feed the civvies, much less five thousand combat troops and another two thousand fleet personnel.

"Well, let's schedule it," the major says. "It's not like we have much else to do right now."

"But that better be a conference link in the ops center. No way I'm walking into a room with all those people sitting around one big table, spirit of cooperation or not," Sergeant Fallon says. She leans back in her chair and stretches her biological leg with a grimace. "'Cause I don't know about you people, but I am fucking sick and tired of this light indoor duty. I still don't know what exactly I'm good for, but it ain't answering comms requests and shuffling paperwork from behind a console."

The strangeness of the day continues at 1800 hours Zulu, when we gather back in the ops center to participate in the conference link requested by the *Regulus*'s commanding officer, Colonel Aguilar. The holoscreen at the end of the room divides itself into ever-smaller segments to accommodate the camera feeds of the conference parties as they join the talk. By the time everyone's in the link, there are twelve different heads looking back at us from the holoscreen. There's the commander of the SI garrison at Camp Frostbite, Lieutenant Colonel Reddicker, the captains of every NAC ship in orbit, the commanding officers of both HD battalions on the moon, and the head of the SRA component of our task force, a hard-faced little Korean brigadier general named Park, who looks like he chews bulkheads for breakfast and shits rivets all day.

Colonel Aguilar begins once everyone has joined the link and indicated their readiness.

"The purpose of this meeting is to determine a course of action for the military forces of the Sino-Russian Alliance and North American Commonwealth jointly garrisoning the Fomalhaut system at present. Whatever decision we make at the conclusion of this meeting will be made jointly with input from all parties, both military and civilian."

Colonel Aguilar pauses as people nod and voice assent. I am watching the SRA officers I can see in the lower right quadrant of the screen. The faces of the Korean brigadier and the staff officers sitting on either side of him are void of obvious emotions. Of all the nationalities that make up the SRA forces, the Chinese and Koreans would make the best poker players.

"If I may?" Sergeant Fallon asks the civilian administrator of New Svalbard, who is seated next to her. He nods, and she clears her throat.

"This moon cannot hold out for long," she says. "I'm not just talking in terms of military firepower, although that's an obvious truth either way you slice it. We have a powerful task force, but it's not even close to what they threw against the Lankies at Mars and lost. But our limited military capabilities are not the biggest fly in this particular soy patty. We are using food and other consumables much faster than we can replace them. Barring a change in the supply situation, we'll be down to eating ration packaging and hull plating in another three months. Too many mouths to feed, not enough to feed them with."

"We can take care of our own population, but we can't keep that many troops fed at the same time," the colony administrator says. "Our infrastructure isn't at the point yet where we can sustain a few thousand extra people to keep fed."

"How are the fleet stores looking?" Colonel Campbell asks.

"Oh, we still have rations," Colonel Aguilar replies. "And we have spare parts to keep most of the drop ships flying for a while before we have to start cannibalizing units. But at this rate, and without any resupply, we'll be out of sandwiches in ten, twelve weeks. I can't imagine that our SRA friends are doing any better at this point."

"Worse," Brigadier Park says with just the barest hint of a smile. His English is good, hardly accented at all, and his diction as sharp and precise as the creases in his mottled camouflage jacket. "*Minsk* is an assault carrier, not a fleet carrier like your own *Regulus*. Much smaller, less space for sandwiches." He smiles his tiny smile again at the last word. "Our supply ships have mostly ammunition for planetary assaults, not so much food."

"Can you put that in a number?" Colonel Campbell asks.

"Three weeks, four perhaps," Brigadier Park replies.

"Super," Sergeant Fallon mutters. "Starvation or getting blown out of space. No winner in that bunch of picks."

"If I had to choose just between those, I would much prefer perishing in battle," Brigadier Park says. "But I suggest we find a way to avoid such a limited variety of options."

"I'm with you there, General," Colonel Aguilar says. "Question is, what do we do with all these ships and combat troops if we can't go back the way we came?"

"We can't go anywhere but the solar system," Colonel Campbell says. "There's no other transition point anywhere else in Fomalhaut. Light-hours and light-hours of Not a Damn Thing."

"Our transition point isn't safe. We already had half a dozen seed ships on our tail when we made it through on the way here, and God only knows why they didn't just follow us through and finish the job. We go back that way, we'll run right into the middle of a Lanky proximity bio-minefield. Or worse, six or ten seed ships loitering by the transition point to blow us to shreds as soon as we're out of Alcubierre."

"We can't stand up to multiple seed ships with what we have, not even with *Regulus*," Colonel Campbell concurs. "Forcing the blockade just isn't an option. If we can sneak back into the solar system and get a whiff of things first, we'd have a better grasp on the situation. Maybe they stopped at Mars for now, and the fleet bases in the outer system are still there. The Titan anchorage has a full wartime supply stock. That's a lot of food and ammo sitting in storage. Maybe there are even fleet remnants we can add to the task force."

"That's an awful lot of maybe," Lieutenant Colonel Reddicker says. The stocky infantry officer crosses his arms in front of his chest and leans back in his chair. "We go back that way on the carrier, I'll have almost two thousand grunts camped out on the flight deck, all helpless. They kill that carrier, those men are all going to die without ever getting the chance to fire a shot back at the enemy."

"We will not load up all our troops and transition back blindly," Colonel Aguilar replies. "We'll send a recon team through first."

"Through Alcubierre? You can't shoot pods or drones through the network. Not without sticking your nose out the other end of the chute."

"So we send one ship," Brigadier Park says. "A small ship, with good sensors. Your little spy ship. It has stealth capability, does it not?"

If we were all in the same room, I have the feeling that all heads would be turning toward Colonel Campbell right now. He looks surprised for a moment and then shakes his head.

"*Indy*? Yes, she does, but that's a no-go. I'm tasked with orbital defense by the colonial administrator. If I leave, nobody is covering for the HD grunts from above."

"I'm fairly sure your ship is still an NAC Fleet Arm asset," Colonel Aguilar says.

"And I'm fairly sure I have rank seniority," Colonel Campbell replies. "But even if I didn't, you folks are going to turn blue in the face if you're going to hold your breath waiting for me to leave orbit without civilian authorization."

Several of the other NAC officers chime in, and for a few moments, the conference feed is cluttered with a bunch of staff brass cross-talking in escalating volumes while the SRA officers watch the proceedings silently. Then the colony administrator speaks up, and the military officers fall silent as the tech who runs the feed mutes out their audio.

"Colonel, I do appreciate your willingness to adhere to Commonwealth law," he says. "But if any of those warships decide to take on the colony, we'll be dead meat with or without you." He looks to a spot somewhere offscreen and then shakes his head slowly. "Look, if we don't find a way for you to get back to the solar system, we're all going to bite it anyway. Either when our supplies run out in a few months and we starve to death, or the Lankies show up and gas us all. From where I'm sitting, the best use for your ship is doing exactly what the general proposed, and scout a path for the rest of you all back to Earth. Or at least the outer solar system. You have my authorization to leave orbit and discontinue your current mission."

Brigadier Park nods at the administrator, who returns the nod curtly. Colonel Campbell merely shrugs.

"Fine," the colonel says when the tech restores his audio. "That's settled, then. But I'm still not excited about transitioning back blindly. Even under stealth, they'll shoot *Indy* to shards if they're staking out the Alcubierre node. And you all wouldn't know what happened until we were overdue a few weeks later. At which point you'll have no options left other than a suicide run of your own. And I have to be honest, General: It bugs me to know that you SRA boys and girls will have no skin in the game."

"I am not familiar with that idiom," Brigadier Park says. "What does 'skin in the game' mean?"

"That means you are risking nothing in this operation," Sergeant Fallon supplies.

Brigadier Park looks at the officer next to him and mutes the audio feed on his end. They engage in a short discussion. The general is as calm as he has been since he joined the feed, but whatever they're discussing must make the other officer uncomfortable or upset, because his expression gradually turns from neutral to visibly perturbed. Then it looks like they come to some agreement as the other officer nods and lowers his gaze. Brigadier Park turns back toward the camera and turns his audio feed back on.

"We know that the enemy is aware of the Commonwealth's transition point and is very likely guarding it from the other side," he says. "But we cannot say for sure that the same is true for the transition point controlled by our own Alliance."

"Are you volunteering to send one of your own ships through, then?" Colonel Aguilar asks.

The SRA general allows himself that tiny smile again, one corner of his mouth barely arching upward by a few millimeters. "No," he says. "Your stealth ship will go. None of ours have the ability to stay hidden and conduct clandestine operations."

He pauses for a heartbeat or two. "But we will volunteer the location of the Alliance's transition point, and provide the access codes for successful passage."

There's a moment of shell-shocked silence at this, and then the comms tech has to cut everyone's audio feed again as all the participants save the SRA officers burst into loud and animated discussion at the same time.

The colony administrator lets out a low whistle next to us.

Sergeant Fallon looks at me and raises an eyebrow. Then she folds her arms in front of her chest, leans back, and plops her artificial leg onto the console in front of her with a grunt.

"Well, well, well," she says. "Isn't this shaping up to be an interesting month."

It takes a few moments for the general commotion to die down. Brigadier Park waits out the cross-talking discussion that follows. Finally, Colonel Aguilar takes the reins again and speaks up.

"You will hand us the coordinates of your Alcubierre point and the transition access codes? Just like that?"

Brigadier Park shakes his head. "Not precisely. We will share the location, but we will have to supply personnel to your ship that will be in control of the access codes. Regardless of our current situation, I do not believe that it is wise to give you a way to break our encryption protocols. We may not be at war with each other anymore, but we need to keep some of our secrets."

He smiles curtly and addresses Colonel Campbell. "Does this satisfy you regarding the amount of skin we contribute to this game?"

Colonel Campbell nods slowly. "That's a mighty big secret to give away, though. I don't know if they'll be happy with you back home if they learn that you gave away your number one military-intelligence nugget in Fomalhaut."

"It is of small consequence," Brigadier Park says. "Besides, it is—how does the idiom go—fair turnabout? We already know the location of your transition point, and we have in fact used it alongside your own ships. This way the scales are balanced."

He almost-smiles again, the barest hint of amusement reflecting in the corner of his mouth briefly. "We need your ship to find a safe way back for us. If it does not, then we will all die soon, and there will be very little point in keeping military secrets. We will just have to make new ones if things change back to the old ways."

"How much personnel do you wish to assign to this mission for *Indianapolis*?" Colonel Aguilar asks.

The general considers the question and confers with his staff officer briefly.

"One would be enough," he says. "A communications expert, one of our own battlespace coordinators. That might also be useful if the . . . *Indianapolis* . . . encounters other Alliance fleet units that may not be aware of our current truce."

"Wait up for a moment," Colonel Campbell says. "You want to put an SRA combat controller with advanced comms and data gear on the most advanced electronic-intelligence boat in the fleet? I know this is supposed to be the dawn of a new era of cooperation and all that happy horseshit, but that strikes me as a monumentally unwise idea. You know, just in case we go back to shooting the hell out of each other."

"You can limit access to sensitive areas of your ship," Colonel Aguilar suggests.

Colonel Campbell shakes his head. "Doesn't matter if I lock him in the brig for the trip if he has his ELINT gear right with him. And even if I take away his hardware, I have to give it back to him as soon as we get close to their Alcubierre point. All it takes is three minutes on our network, and they can reverse engineer this ship from master blueprints at the New Dalian fleet yards in six months."

"Well, what do you suggest? There aren't too many other options on the table right now," Colonel Aguilar says. "We need *Indy* to scout, and *Indy* needs the access code for the SRA node, unless you want to take your chances with the NAC node instead."

"I don't like either option," Colonel Campbell says.

I clear my throat and chime in. "Sirs, I can ride herd on that combat controller. Be his minder, make sure he doesn't do stuff he's not supposed to."

I'm the most junior rank in the conference by a fair margin, and the sudden undivided attention from a dozen staff officers is a little unnerving. I shift around in my chair and try to tune out the other officers by pretending I'm just talking to Colonel Campbell alone.

"Are you positive, Mr. Grayson? That trip may be a one-way ticket."

"Yeah, I'm positive," I say. "I know the job, so I know what he should and shouldn't do. And I've worked with their guys on the Fomalhaut b drop, so we have a bit of a working relationship. It'll be fine, I think."

The colonel chews on his lower lip while he considers my reply. I can sense that everyone in the ops center is looking at me, Sergeant Fallon next to me foremost, but I keep my attention on the screen.

"I still don't like either option, but I don't like that one a little less than the other one, if that makes sense."

"Is that acceptable to you, General Park?" Colonel Aguilar asks. "Have your detachment work with Sergeant Grayson here to keep things smooth?"

"It is acceptable," Brigadier Park says in his carefully neutral voice.

"What about you, Colonel Campbell? Does this alleviate your concerns about hosting an SRA combat controller on your ship for the mission?"

"If I can get Mr. Grayson to serve as a chaperone, I'm fine with it. Not ecstatic, but fine. Assuming that the civilian administrator releases him from his current assignment with the New Svalbard Territorial Army."

The NSTA is the fancy title for the mutinous Homeworld Defense troops on New Svalbard, all of which voluntarily subjected themselves to civilian control. Some of the other commanders, especially the officers of the Spaceborne Infantry battalion we fought for control of New Svalbard's scarce food facilities, think that we've committed outright treason and desertion, but Colonel Aguilar was luckily sympathetic to our argument and decided not to force the issue or pry the HD troops out of New Longyearbyen and its terraforming network. I have no doubt that we will all end up in front of a court-martial if things ever get back to the way they were, but I also have no doubt that things won't ever go back to the way they were. Too much has changed way too quickly, and this strange new alliance of necessity has rewritten the rulebook entirely. It's amazing how much stuff you can accomplish when you don't give a shit whether or not it's feasible. We pulled off a large-scale combat mission by integrating military units from two blocs with incompatible hardware and different standards and protocols because we threw out the old manuals and improvised on the spot. Unencumbered by the stupidity of the strategic thinkers at the NAC Defense Corps headquarters, our little slice of the armed forces went from an organization that takes six years to standardize on a new toilet seat to a lean and fast outfit that can prepare and execute a two-regiment interbloc combat drop onto a Lanky-controlled moon in only two weeks. I like the new way of doing things, and I don't want to go back to the old way.

"I have no problem with Sergeant Grayson going with you on the *Indy*," the colony administrator replies. "We have more than enough troops to keep the town and the terraformers secure. That is, if Master Sergeant Fallon is okay with releasing him back to fleet service."

"Oh, hell," Sergeant Fallon says. "Andrew can go wherever he wants to go. For what it's worth, I agree that his time would be better spent getting us all back to Earth. We have enough asses to polish chairs down here already."

"That's settled, then," Colonel Aguilar says. "The *Indianapolis* will use the Alliance transition point to sneak into the solar system and find us a way back. General Park will provide the access codes and control personnel, and Staff Sergeaht Grayson will be our interbloc liaison on the *Indy*. Let's hammer out the details and get your ship ready for that mission, Colonel. And Sergeant Grayson, report to *Indianapolis* as soon as the weather allows."

"Understood, sir," I say, and suppress the urge to snap a salute.

I push my chair back from the conference table and get up to step out of the range of the cameras. It's a terribly selfish conceit, but after I make sure nobody is looking at me for the moment, I take my PDP out of its uniform pocket and check the calendar. I have ten weeks and two days to get back to Earth and make it in time for my wedding. I don't know if Halley is still alive, but I made a promise, and I'll do my best to keep it. Because if I don't, there's not a damn thing left for me in the universe worth fighting for.

CHAPTER 4

FROM FLAME TO FIRE

"What do you figure your chances are to make it back through and to Earth in one piece?" Sergeant Fallon asks.

I take another sip of my drink and pretend to think about it, as if I haven't already considered the odds of the mission many times since I volunteered for it a few hours ago. We're in On the Rocks again for a parting drink while I wait for a break in the weather to have a standby drop ship shuttle me up to *Indianapolis.*

"I'm not a tin-can skipper," I say. "Don't know a lot about spaceborne warfare, to be honest. But that's a really stealthy ship. If she can't make it past a Lanky, we have nowhere left to hide." I turn the glass in my hands and watch the reflections from the overhead lights on the surface of the blue liquid of my drink. "Honestly?

Fifty-fifty, and I wouldn't drop too much money on the spread. Really honestly? I'm scared shitless. Again."

"Figured you'd be used to this business by now," Sergeant Fallon says.

"Well, yeah. I'm always scared before a drop. Aren't you?"

"Little bit," she says with a slight smile. "Anyone who isn't scared at the thought of going into battle is either a moron or a sociopath."

"It's different for this sneaky space shit. On a combat drop, you have lots of stuff to distract you, keep your mind off things.

And you have at least the illusion of control. A rifle, a bunch of ammo, stuff to shoot at. But fleet engagements? You're just sitting at your combat station in a metal tube. Nothing to do but to wait and see if you're going to die."

"Yeah, that shit is for the birds," she says. "I never did have the slightest desire to go fleet. All those idiot nuggets in boot, hoping for a navy slot. Space is awful business."

"It has its moments. First time I looked at Earth from orbit, it damn near blew my mind. The scale of it, you know? And it looked so peaceful. You realize just how stupid it all is. Us, the SRA, the welfare rats, trying to kill each other, when we're all just a bunch of ants hurtling through space on this little piece of rock and water."

"Damn, Andrew." Sergeant Fallon shakes her head and smiles again. "You're too smart by half to be in the soldiering business."

She takes a swig from her drink and makes a grimace.

"But you're a good soldier," she says. "You were a good soldier from day one at Shughart. Scared like the rest of them, but saddling up and doing what you're supposed to. And you've never been a mindless trigger puller. I knew that you were still the same kid who felt awful after Detroit when you threw in your lot with our little rebellion. Maybe that makes you a better soldier than me, because I've mostly lost the ability to feel awful about any of this."

The PDP in my pocket chirps a notification alert. I pull it out and look at the screen.

"MetSat update," I tell Sergeant Fallon. "Fair-weather window in ninety-one minutes. I guess I better get my gear and head over to the airfield."

I push my drink aside and get up. Sergeant Fallon does likewise. She puts one hand on my shoulder and studies me at arm's length. Then she pulls me into a brief but firm one-armed hug and lets me go as quickly as she initiated the contact.

"I'm not going to get all squishy on you, but see that you don't get yourself killed," she says. "World's a shitty place, but it'd be a fair bit shittier without you in it."

I smile at her. "That's by far the squishiest thing you've ever said to me."

We part without further words, without any melodramatic last salutes. I just leave the bar to get my gear, and turn around at the entrance hatch of the bar to look back at my old squad leader. She's sitting down again, one hand on her drink, and she meets my gaze. I raise a hand briefly to give her a casual little two-finger wave. She nods at me, and the expression on her face is her usual facade of mild, detached amusement, but her eyes convey emotions we wouldn't be able to fit into five minutes of extended emotional good-byes.

Fair winds and following seas, my friend.

I return her nod and turn to leave On the Rocks, likely for the last time in my life.

There's a tunnel that leads from the Ellipse straight to the airfield on the other end of New Longyearbyen. It's a kilometer and a half, an easy walk on level ground, and I walk out toward the airfield in no particular hurry. When I am a third of the way down the tunnel, I hear the hum of an electric ATV coming up behind me, and I turn around to see Chief Constable Guest rolling up.

"Saw you on the security feed," he says as he comes to a stop next to me. "Want a ride?"

"Sure," I say. "Thanks."

I take my kit bag off my shoulder and dump it into the cargo basket of the ATV. Then I take the passenger seat behind the constable, and he puts the vehicle back into motion.

"Figured you'd stop by the office to say good-bye," he says over his shoulder.

"I was thinking about it, but I'm already kind of a mess as it is," I say. "There's a lot riding on this mission."

"Tell me about it. I've got two girls and a wife down here on our little frozen paradise. If you don't come back with a road map for all those troops to go home again, we're about to have a very bad winter, and it'll be our very last one."

"I'll do my best to see that it won't be," I say.

"I have no doubt that you will. But it's not entirely up to you, is it?"

"It's not even mostly up to me. I'll just be another little cog in the wheel again."

"Well, be a really good cog, then. I almost envy you in a way, you know."

"How so?" I laugh. "You want to go in my place?"

"I would if I had the expertise. Beats having to wait and watch, and not being able to do anything to influence the outcome."

"What are you going to do if we don't come back?" I ask.

Constable Guest is quiet for a little while. The hum from the electric motor reverberates from the concrete walls, and the fat tires of the ATV whisper on the floor slabs as we trundle through the sparsely lit tunnel at a fast trotting speed.

"I'll hole up with my family," he finally says. "Down here in the tunnels. Stockpile whatever supplies we can, and try to make it stretch. Hoping someone's going to come and resupply us before all the food runs out. As long as I can keep them alive, there's always hope."

I've been to Constable Guest's office a few times, and I remember the pictures of his daughters he keeps on a shelf behind his desk. His girls are still young, in their early teenage years. He told me that they were born on Earth, but they've been here on

New Svalbard since before they could form coherent memories of the old home. This is the only world they've known, and if we fail to find a way home for all those troops that are consuming the resources of the ice moon just to stay alive, then they'll never know anything else. They'll die with their parents, down here in these cheerless tunnels with their bare concrete walls and unpainted laminate steel doors, and the whole town will be buried under ice and forgotten, a very minor footnote in humanity's short history. It's a harsh life in the colonies, but it's their only life, and I feel shame for having contributed to the very likely possibility that these girls and everyone else here will die. I didn't have any influence on the military's decision to come here and dump seven thousand extra mouths to feed onto this world, but I can try to help get them out of here again. It's a much better use for all my training than killing Chinese or Russian marines over yet another untamed piece of rock circling some faraway sun.

We roll through the semidarkness in silence for a while. Then the tunnel ahead comes to an end. There's a concrete staircase leading up into a little vestibule, and a heavy security hatch set into the wall beyond. Constable Guest climbs off the ATV, and I follow suit and grab my kit bag.

He holds out his hand, and I shake it.

"Faithless is he that says farewell when the road darkens," he says.

"Where did you get that?" I ask.

"Oh, an old novel that I like. Orcs and elves and high adventure, that sort of thing."

"Then let's make it 'See you in a few weeks' instead," I say.

"See you in a few weeks, Staff Sergeant Grayson. Thank you for sticking up for us colony roughnecks. And be safe out there."

"You, too, Constable Guest."

He gets back onto his ATV, nods at me, and drives back the way we came, leaving me in the dimly lit tunnel terminus. I watch as the blinking caution light on the back of his vehicle briefly paints the walls of the tunnel red in steady three-second intervals. Then I shoulder my bag again and walk up the stairs into the basement of the airfield's main control center.

The brief lull in the weather isn't very obvious on the surface. It's still snowing, but at least I can see further than a few yards now, and the snow is coming almost straight down instead of whipping across the landscape horizontally. Out on the vast concrete tarmac, tracked vehicles with massive triangular plow blades are pushing snow out of the way. In the already cleared area, three Wasp drop ships, one Dragonfly, and two of the colony's fixed-wing transport aircraft are in various stages of postflight operations, unloading their cargo bays or refueling their tanks from the airfield's automated fuel probes.

I know the pilots of the Dragonfly assigned to the *Indianapolis* by sight, so I walk across the tarmac to where the hulking battle taxi is parked, mindful to stay out of the way of the ground crew and the refueling machinery. The pilots are in the cockpit, running through checklists. As I mill around near the port side of the Dragonfly, the loadmaster tromps down the lowered tail ramp. He spots me and comes walking over to where I stand.

"Sergeant Grayson?" he asks. I turn toward him so he can see my name tag, and raise the face shield of my helmet. The bitingly frigid polar air immediately makes my face numb.

"We ready to go?"

"Almost. We have to wait for some passengers from the *Minsk*. Their birds don't fit into *Indy*'s docking clamps, so they have to switch rides down here."

"Copy that," I say, and lower my face shield to lock out the knife-blade winds again.

A little while later, there's a shrill roar overhead, and two Akula-class drop ships come swooping out of the driving snow overhead. They settle side by side on a landing pad on the far end of the drop-ship tarmac in an impressive display of skillful synchronized shit-weather flying. I think of Halley, probably one of the best drop-ship pilots in the entire fleet, and wonder what her critique of that landing maneuver would be.

I can see why the SRA designers decided to call their creation the "shark." Next to the NAC drop ships, the Sino-Russian birds look more crude, but decidedly more predatory. Their fuselages are more narrow, their cockpits smaller, and the overall shape of the airframes is more streamlined. They're bigger than our Wasps, although not quite as large as the Dragonflies. They do, however, bristle with an almost excessive array of air-to-ground weaponry—a nose turret with two multibarreled guns, large-caliber ground-attack cannons in fixed mounts on either side of the fuselage, and more cannons still in removable pods on the wing pylons. Autocannons are simpler and cheaper than intelligent guided munitions, and the SRA engineers sure used as many of them as they could cram into the design. I've been on the receiving end of Akula attack runs more than once, and those things can put an awful lot of armor-piercing high explosives on target very quickly. No matter how permanent our new alliance of necessity may turn out in the end, I will never lose the feeling of dread that settles in my stomach whenever I see the insectoid, angular shape of an Akula.

I watch as the tail ramps of the SRA drop ships open. From the tail end of the closest Akula, two figures in Alliance battle armor emerge, heavy-looking kit bags slung under each arm. They walk toward us across the expanse of the landing pad. The face shields on the SRA helmets are quite a bit bigger than ours, so it's easier to make out faces. When the two SRA troopers are twenty meters away, I recognize the taller figure on the left. I raise my own face shield again and wave.

"Dmitry," I shout.

Dmitry walks up to me and lightly taps my armor with his gloved fist.

"Andrew," he says. His voice sounds slightly distorted through the speaker system in his helmet. "What are you doing in cold, awful place like this one?"

"We're going up to the *Indianapolis* together. I'll be joining you for this mission."

Dmitry shakes his head with a smile and raps my armor again. "*Iz ognya da v polymya*, eh?"

"What does that mean?"

"We go from flame to fire."

"Out of the frying pan and into the fire," I agree. "Looks that way."

He gestures to the trooper next to him. The face behind the helmet's shield is Asian and very clearly female.

"Sub-Lieutenant Lin. My superior. She is here to make sure I get on Commonwealth ship safely."

Sub-Lieutenant Lin looks at me and snaps a quick and sharp salute, her brown eyes looking into mine unflinchingly. I return the salute. She outranks me, so I should have been the one to offer a salute first, but cross-bloc courtesies are still fairly uncharted territory, and I assume she's conceding that we're on Commonwealth turf and that I am the NAC personnel in charge for this trip into orbit. Dmitry is a *stárshiy serzhánt*, a senior sergeant, which means he outranks me as well, if only by one rank and pay grade.

I gesture over to the open tail ramp of the nearby Dragonfly.

"Let's get upstairs, then. Before the weather turns to shit again."

"Weather is already shit," Dmitry says.

I let Dmitry walk up the ramp first before following him into the cargo hold of the Dragonfly. At the top of the ramp, I take a deep, unfiltered breath of the cold air even though it hurts my lungs and makes my nostrils freeze. It's a harsh and frigid place, and unfit for large-scale human habitation, but I'll be damned if the air here isn't the cleanest I've breathed in the entire settled galaxy.

I take a seat on the left side of the Dragonfly's cargo hold. My SRA counterpart seats himself right across the aisle from me, mirroring our arrangement in the Akula during our planetary assault a week earlier. Five years of fighting these people, and I don't even know what language they use to communicate on joint missions, or whether they just use their comms' automatic translators.

I'm back on an NAC drop ship, so I get permission from the pilot in command to tie into the Dragonfly's data bus. Then I tune out Dmitry and watch the feed from the optical sensors on the outside hull: dorsal, top bow, bottom bow, starboard wingtip, port wingtip, stern. My battle armor's computer can stitch all the video feeds together into a seamless tapestry and project it on the inside of my visor sight. It pans with my head movements, so it almost feels like I *am* the drop ship as we go up through the clouds and above the horrible New Svalbard weather. Finally, at twenty thousand feet, we break through the top of the cloud cover, and the atmospheric bumps go from terrifying to merely teeth jarring.

New Svalbard has a wild, hostile beauty from above. Much of the ice moon's visible hemisphere is covered in thick clouds, but there are clear patches here and there, and the light from the far-off sun glints on the icy mountain ridges and vast frozen glaciers of the surface below. In another fifty or a hundred years, this will be a prime chunk of galactic real estate if the Lankies don't come in and take it all away from us. When I first went into space after joining the fleet, I used to be awed by the majestic, overwhelming beauty of the sight of a planet from orbit, but these days it mostly reminds me of just how unfathomably vast the universe is, and how very tiny and insignificant we are.

We transition from atmospheric to spaceflight a short time later, and the buffeting stops. You can always tell when you're in orbit because your butt gets light in the seat despite the forty pounds of battle armor. I can see all the warships in their different orbital groups on my tactical display, but only *Regulus* and her escort are in visual range, thirty degrees off the port bow and a hundred kilometers away in a higher orbit than ours, position lights blinking and visible even from this range. *Regulus* is a massive ship, over half a kilometer from bow to stern, the largest warship class any of Earth's nation blocs have ever put into space. Because they're so few and so valuable, the Navigator-class carriers have not been used against the Lankies yet, so nobody knows how they would fare in battle with a seed ship, but the fact that most of the fleet got destroyed above Mars makes me think that *Regulus* may well be the last of her class. In any case, I am going up to *Indy* right now to help make sure that the carrier won't have to go toe-to-toe with the Lankies, at least not yet.

We dock with the *Indy* a few minutes later. As before, I don't even see the stealth orbital combat ship until we're almost on top of it, despite the fact that I can plot *Indy*'s position on my display through her active IFF beacon. Most of the technology in the

OCS is still classified, but I know that the same polychromatic camouflage technology used for the Hostile Environment Battle Armor—our bug suits—has found its way into the outer-hull plating of the *Indy.* She doesn't have overwhelming firepower, although she is well armed for a ship her size. She is, however, extremely hard to spot, track, or target. During our little insurrection a few weeks ago, *Indy* was able to successfully play orbital hide-and-seek with the rest of the *Midway* task force. According to Colonel Campbell, they didn't even break a sweat doing it. He also claims he could have nuked *Midway* from stealth successfully, and I have no reason to doubt that claim.

A light shudder goes through the Dragonfly when *Indy*'s docking clamps latch on to the hardpoints at the top of the drop ship's hull. We move through the hangar hatch and into the artificial gravity field of the larger ship, and my armored weight pushes me downward into the seat again. Through the armor plating of the hull, I can hear the low warning klaxon of the automated docking system as it seals the outer hatch and pulls us into the *Indy*'s tiny drop-ship hangar. We come to rest with a final shudder, and the klaxon outside stops. The engines of the Dragonfly steadily decrease their racket, then fall silent altogether.

"Welcome aboard NACS *Indianapolis,*" I tell Dmitry. "Hope you're wearing battle dress uniform underneath that armor, because you need to turn your plate in until we get to the Alcubierre chute. And your admin deck, too."

"You are worried I spy on precious new intelligence boat, eh?"

"I would," I reply, and Dmitry grins.

He starts popping open the latches of his computerized battle armor, strips off the shell segments, and stacks the pieces on the deck. The SRA commander sent him over unarmed, so I won't have to ask for his rifle and sidearm, too. I feel a little stupid asking the man to disarm when just a week ago I fought the Lankies by his side, admin decks and loaded weapons and all, but the agreed-upon rules for this joint mission call for it. And truthfully, I don't know Dmitry well enough yet to know that he won't try to use the situation for all the intelligence gathering he can. Paranoia is one of the defining traits of the experienced combat soldier.

The tail ramp opens to reveal the claustrophobic confines of the *Indy*'s tiny drop-ship hangar. The bulk of the Dragonfly fills it out almost entirely. I collect my bag and walk down the ramp. Before I step on the deck, I salute the North American Commonwealth flag painted on the bulkhead in front of me and address the officer of the deck, who is standing by the exit hatch. There's an SI corporal in battle armor next to him, PDW hanging on his chest from a sling, pistol in a holster on his leg. They don't usually bother with armed security when a surface transport arrives, but those don't usually contain an SRA frontline combat trooper. I salute the officer of the deck.

"I request permission to come aboard. Staff Sergeant Grayson, with SRA guest, to report to the CO as ordered."

The OOD returns my salute.

"Permission granted. The skipper is waiting for you in CIC." His gaze flicks past me to the SRA trooper as Dmitry stops on the ramp just behind me and salutes the NAC colors.

"Crazy-ass new world, I know," I say to the OOD as we walk past him to the exit hatch under the watchful eyes of the armed Spaceborne Infantry corporal.

"Crazy don't cover it, Sarge," he replies.

Colonel Campbell is standing at the holotable in the combat information center when I walk through the armored hatch. Dmitry is behind me in the corridor, and there's a pair of armed

SI troopers guarding the CIC. We may not be shooting at each other anymore, but Colonel Campbell's spirit of cooperation does not yet extend to welcoming SRA soldiers into the nerve center of his ship.

"Good to see you, Mr. Grayson," he says. He returns my salute and then extends his hand. "Fine work on Fomalhaut b with our new pals. I read the mission reports."

"Thank you, sir. I was just along for the ride, mostly. But those SRA marines did all right."

"Yeah, it's amazing what we can blow up when we actually point our guns the same way." He glances at the armored hatch behind me, where the SRA trooper is waiting just on the other side of the clear polyplast viewport.

"And now we're setting out on another joint mission with these folks. This one's going to be fun. And by fun, I mean 'white-knuckled, pants-shitting terror.'"

"We've been there before, sir," I say. "More than once. *Versailles* wasn't exactly a slow day at the office, either."

"No, it wasn't." The shadow of a pained look shows on his face very briefly as he undoubtedly remembers his old command that burned up in the atmosphere above the colony planet Willoughby, after having lost over a third of its crew to Lanky proximity mines. That was five years ago, and it seems like forever and only just yesterday at the same time. Colonel Campbell shakes his head slightly, as if to rid himself of the memory.

"Mr. Grayson, have you ever considered the fact that you seem to be right at the bleeding edge of the shitstorm way too often, considering your pay grade?" he asks.

I can't help but chuckle. "The thought has occurred to me, sir."

"We're finishing up taking on extra supplies and mission personnel. There's chow and ammo stuffed into every corner, and we have a full squad of jarheads embarked as it is, so don't expect a lot of elbow room on this ride. We'll be on our way just as soon as we've secured the extra ordnance we're taking along. Check in with Master Sergeant Bogdan and see if he can find you some rack space somewhere."

"We'll need to quarter our new friend, too," I say, and point over my shoulder.

"Ah, yes," Colonel Campbell says. "I want you very close to him for as long as he's on this ship. I'm not asking you to hot-bunk with him, but see if the master sergeant can find you adjoining quarters. If he's out of his berth, I want you to be with him. Last thing I need is that enemy combat controller finding a quiet corner and a data jack somewhere."

"Understood, sir," I say.

"Take heart, Mr. Grayson," the colonel says. He turns back to his holotable and examines the plot again. "You'll be on the bleeding edge of the shitstorm once again, but at least we'll be doing exactly what this ship was designed to do. Unless they parked a seed ship right across the Alcubierre node on the solar system side, we'll make it through to Earth."

"Yes, sir," I say. I'm not quite as convinced as he is, to put it mildly, but his confident attitude helps to take the edge off my own anxiety a little. Every time I've worked with Colonel Campbell, I've bucked dreadful odds. Either I'll get lucky again, or I'll die a quick death in good company.

Master Sergeant Bogdan finds us two adjoining berths in the mission-personnel module of the ship, which is occupied by the *Indy*'s embarked Spaceborne Infantry squad. All the grunts on this ship have been assigned to the *Indy* since before she last left the solar system, so they were all on the New Svalbard side of the mutiny a few weeks ago. That means I won't have to constantly watch my back when I go to the mess hall or the head, which is a relief. There are ten berthing slots in the personnel module. All the junior enlisted SI grunts are sharing three multibunk berths, one for each of the three fire teams, and the three sergeants and the squad's lieutenant each get their own private berths. Two of the berths are still empty, so Dmitry gets one berth and I get to claim another, continuing the record streak of private berthing spaces I've been able to keep going for at least a year now.

I stash my kit in the locker and the storage drawer under the bunk. I don't have much to tuck away other than the brand-new battle armor and HEBA kit they issued me on *Regulus* two weeks ago. My personal gear is still at Camp Frostbite—maybe in the locker where I placed it, possibly in the trash incinerator—and I've not had the desire to claim it in person. Camp Frostbite is controlled by the Spaceborne Infantry troops that obeyed the *Midway* commander's order to seize the civilian assets on New Svalbard, and we killed about thirty of their number when we fought back. If I show up at Frostbite to pick up my stuff, I am likely to end up in the brig.

When all my kit is secured, I stretch out on the bunk for a bit and watch the viewport on the door, which I have turned on to monitor the corridor outside for my new SRA pal.

Dmitry knocks on the hatch a few minutes later. I get up to answer the knock.

"Does advanced imperialist warship of yours have place to eat of some sort?" he asks when I open the hatch.

"Yes, it does. You may have to make do with a sandwich and some coffee if it's not mealtime right now, though."

"Coffee is *kharasho*," Dmitry says. "Maybe sandwiches will be not shit."

"Well, let's go," I say. "The mess is one deck up."

The NCO mess is mostly empty. One of the tables is occupied by two senior sergeants with a data pad and a pile of paperwork between them. They look up when we walk in, and neither makes an effort to conceal a bit of surprise at the sight of a fleet NCO walking in with an SRA trooper. The camouflage pattern of the SRA battle dress is an irregular collection of brown, green, and black blotches that looks almost reptilian. It's nothing like the regular digital pattern of the NAC battle dress, and the Alliance grunt sticks out on this ship like a peppercorn in a saltshaker.

We get coffees and sandwiches and claim a table in the corner of the mess. The two fleet sergeants return to their paperwork but shoot us curious glances every once in a while.

"Sandwiches are not shit," Dmitry proclaims after his second one. They are standard between-meals fleet chow, bologna and soy cheese with a smidgen of mustard. They're not entirely awful, but they're far from not shit. I've had so many of them over the years that I only eat them when I have no other choice and my stomach is very empty. If Dmitry likes them, they must feed those SRA troopers some pretty awful garbage over in the *Minsk's* NCO mess.

Overhead, the 1MC announcing system comes to life, and Colonel Campbell's voice interrupts my contemplation of relative cross-bloc culinary standards.

"Attention all hands, this is the CO."

Even though the 1MC speaker strands are built into the filament of the ceiling liner and invisible, I still turn my head up out of habit. Dmitry follows suit.

"We have completed replenishment and secured all stores. As soon as we have finished our final neural-net synchronization with the rest of the task force, we will get under way and leave New

Svalbard for the coordinates the Alliance has transmitted to us. We are setting out for the SRA Alcubierre node in this system. From there we will transition back into our solar system and begin our scouting run. There is no doubt in my mind that this ship will fulfill her mission and return to New Svalbard with the intelligence needed by the rest of the task force. This is what this ship was built to do. This is what this crew was trained to do. I will not wish us luck. We won't need luck, because we have skill. Those skinny planet-stealing sons of bitches are the ones who are going to need luck, and lots of it. We're going home. All hands, prepare for departure."

Dmitry nods and turns his attention back to his half-eaten sandwich. "Good speech," he says around a mouthful of food. "*Ochyen kharasho.*"

I take my PDP out of the leg pocket of my battle dress and bring up a picture of Halley. It's the one she sent me after she graduated Combat Flight School, when the world was still in balance and we were still slugging it out with the Chinese and Russians, unaware of the Lankies' existence or the coming two-front war we'd be fighting for the next half decade. I zoom in on her face, that barely contained proud smile that's teasing, gloating, and loving all at the same time. Then I freeze the screen and run the tip of my index finger along her jawline.

We're going home. I repeat the colonel's words in my head. *I'll see you after we run the blockade*. Piece of cake.

CHAPTER 5

— CULTURAL EXCHANGE —

Front sight, press, I remind myself. *Ride the reset. Two shots, change target, two shots.*

The M109 automatic pistol in my hands bucks very slightly with every shot I fire at the troops in the hallway before me. Some are hidden behind makeshift cover, only popping out to return fire sporadically. Every time I am forced to fight with the pistol, it reaffirms my belief that the stupid thing is the most useless weapon in our arsenal, good for nothing but a display of rank.

One of my opponents pops his head up over the storage crate he's using as cover and aims his PDW at me. I put the front sight on his helmet and fire a quick double tap. One round glances off my enemy's helmet, but the other drills right through his lowered face shield. He drops instantly, and his PDW clatters to the deck. I don't have time to celebrate my brief victory—two more enemy troops come around the corridor bend twenty-five meters ahead, and the slide of my weapon is locked back on an empty magazine. I eject the disposable cartridge pack, fish a new one out of a pouch on my harness, and reload with fingers that seem too clumsy and imprecise for the task. I release the pistol's slide and switch the fire selector to salvo fire. Then I hose down the hallway with most of the thirty-round magazine. One of the new soldiers catches a burst to his armor, but the rounds fragment against the hard laminate of his breastplate. Then they return fire together, automatic bursts from two PDWs converging on my hiding spot. The hallway in front of me goes dark.

"Piece of shit," I swear when the lights in the firing range come back on and the simulation resets itself. I unload the training magazine from the pistol and clear the action. "Who programmed these scenarios? Seven against one, and all of them armored and with buzzguns?"

"The lieutenant did," Staff Sergeant Philbrick says. "We're just a squad on this boat. We get boarded, we may have to hold down a corridor with what we have, by ourselves."

"Remind me of that if I ever get the itch to put in for transfer to the SI," I say.

"You did all right for a fleet puke." Staff Sergeant Philbrick pokes at the display of the range computer on the bulkhead behind us. "Three kills. Seven more nonpenetrating hits."

"Those don't count for shit outside the sim."

Staff Sergeant Philbrick is the leader of the embarked Spaceborne Infantry squad's first fire team. The squad is split into three fire teams of four troopers each, twelve combat grunts, with a second lieutenant in command and a sergeant first class as his right hand. Fourteen battle-hardened SI troopers make up the sole ground combat component of the *Indianapolis.* A frigate usually has two squads, sometimes a whole platoon, depending on the mission. A carrier, designed as the centerpiece of a planetary assault force, never has less than a reinforced company on board, and often a regiment. If *Indy* bumps into problems that require infantry surface action or shipboard firefights, fourteen SI troopers won't be able to plug too many corridors, not even on a small ship like this one.

The *Indianapolis* is hauling ass to the coordinates for the SRA's Alcubierre node. We're half a day away, and we went for turnaround and reverse burn almost two days ago after a fun little four-g sprint. Every day we spend in transit means fewer supplies and less food in New Svalbard and on this ship, and Colonel Campbell does not want to waste any time. I've been spending my shipboard time chaperoning Dmitry, and spending most of my downtime with the grunts of the embarked SI squad. Shooting up imaginary enemies is more fun than staring at a bulkhead, and it keeps my mind occupied and off the fact that in less than twelve hours *Indy* will transition into Lanky-occupied space.

"How is the Russkie behaving?" Staff Sergeant Philbrick asks.

"Fine," I say. "He seems all right."

"I'm not sure I'd want to sleep in a berth right next to his."

"What, you think he's going to go commando one night and start slitting throats?" I put the training pistol back into the holding bracket on the rear bulkhead for the next trooper to use. Access to live weapons is limited—you only get to sign them out of the arms locker if you have a pressing reason to go armed on the ship—but the training pistols can't be loaded with live rounds, and they are molded in bright blue polymer for visual clarification.

"Something like that. We're still at war with them out here, after all."

"I'm not sure that's true anymore," I say.

"What do you mean, Grayson?"

"I mean that things have changed. A lot. We know the location of their inbound node for the solar system now, and they know ours. You think we're going to go back to shooting each other any time soon? After trading top-level military secrets and running combat drops together against the Lankies?"

"Hell, I have no clue." He shrugs and takes a training carbine out of the gun rack. Then he checks the action with a practiced motion and steps over to the range computer to call up another scenario for the shooting simulator. "Way above my pay grade. But you're probably right. Be stupid to go back to the way things were. You coming down to Grunt Country for some sparring tonight?"

Grunt Country is the mission-personnel rec area at the back of the modular berthing reserved for attached personnel. It's a big square room, twelve by twelve meters, and probably the only open space on the ship—other than the mess halls or the hangar—that isn't packed to the ceiling with supplies or portable water tanks. The Spaceborne Infantry troopers have set up some improvised exercise equipment and a small boxing ring, to let off some steam and stay in shape while we're in transit.

"Sure, I'll come," I say. "As soon as our Alliance friend is in his berth and I'm done chaperoning for this watch."

"Hell, just bring him with you," Staff Sergeant Philbrick says. "He can watch and learn how the SI does in the hand-to-hand business. It'll be a cultural exchange." He takes a pack of training magazines, loads one into his rifle, and puts the other ones into the pouches on his armor. "'Course, we grunts ain't got much in the way of culture to exchange."

I snort a laugh and leave the staff sergeant to his impending battle with imaginary faceless enemies.

Dmitry doesn't object to joining me down in Grunt Country a little while later. If anything, he seems eager for some variety after days of boredom staring at the bulkhead in a berth the size of a closet.

When I open the hatch to the rec room in the back of the module and step across the threshold, none of the eight or nine grunts in the room take much notice. Some are working out on benches or heavy bags, someone is doing pushups in a corner of the room, and two of the SI troopers are sparring on a square of training mats in the center of the room. When Dmitry walks into the room behind me, however, the moderately busy din in the room dies down gradually as the grunts become aware of the SRA trooper's presence. He has been around at mealtimes and in the corridors of the ship, so his presence isn't a novelty anymore, but I've never brought him down here into the SI's only private sanctum on this ship.

"Grayson," Staff Sergeant Philbrick calls from the back of the room, where he has been doing pushups. He hops to his feet and walks over to us. "Come on in, join the fun."

"Don't mind if we do," I reply. "You've met Senior Sergeant Chistyakov."

"Senior Sergeant." Philbrick nods at Dmitry, who returns the gesture. The SRA trooper looks a little apprehensive, which is understandable. I sure as hell would be if I were in their boots right now.

"Sergeant Chistyakov dropped with me when we did the Fomalhaut b drop last week," I say. "He knows his shit."

"What's a senior sergeant rank?" Philbrick asks Dmitry. "How does it compare to ours? E-5, E-6, what?"

I'm pretty sure that Staff Sergeant Philbrick has a general idea of the rank structure of the SRA military—we learned stuff like that in our OPFOR-recognition classes—but I appreciate his effort to break the ice.

"Senior sergeant is like your master sergeant," Dmitry replies. "Is different, though. In company of garrison, *stárshiy serzhánt* is at desk, helps out company officer. Administration," he says with an expression of strong distaste on his face. "I am battlespace coordinator, not administrator. Drop ship and rifle, not desk and paperwork."

"We speak the same language after all," Sergeant Philbrick says with a grin. "We're just doing some friendly sparring down here. Feel free to hang around."

The SI troopers go up against each other in quick one-minute rounds of contact sparring in protective gear. Staff Sergeant Philbrick is a good fighter because he is tall and lanky and has a lot of reach with those long arms of his. I watch as he goes up against a stockier but stronger-looking dark-haired corporal. The corporal tries to get in underneath Philbrick's defense, but the staff sergeant uses his longer reach to keep his opponent at bay and out of grappling range. At the forty-second mark of the round, the corporal gets a little careless, and Philbrick takes him down with a sweeping kick to the lower legs that sends the corporal crashing onto the mat. The other SI troopers clap and hoot their approval.

"You gotta learn, Nez," Philbrick tells the corporal when he helps him back up onto his feet. "You get too hasty and leave yourself open."

"Yes, Sarge," Corporal Nez replies.

The SI troopers swap gel gloves around, and another pair of troopers step onto the mat for a quick bout. I watch Dmitry as he watches the unfolding fight. Dmitry has his arms folded across his chest and a slight smile on his lips. He looks like a teacher watching a group of first graders playing around at recess.

I pick up a pair of nearby gel gloves and put them on. Then I grab another pair and call Dmitry's name. He looks over to me, and I toss him the gloves. He extends one hand almost lazily and snatches them out of midair.

"You want to go a round? Show the SI how the Russian marines do it?"

Dmitry chuckles. Then he puts the gloves on his fists and pounds one into the other with a muffled thump. They look a lot tighter on him than mine do on me.

"Andrew, my friend," he says, "that may not be best idea you have today."

One minute doesn't seem like a long time when you're doing fun stuff, but on a fighting mat, it's damn near an eternity, especially when you are getting your clock cleaned comprehensively. Dmitry is roughly in my weight class, and he doesn't look much more muscled than I am, but he punches much harder than a guy his size ought to be able to hit. I probe his block with a few left jabs, then follow up with a right cross, which he deflects with both gloves. Then his response combination comes. I block his straights in return, but his cross plows right through my defenses and makes me hit myself hard in the mouth with the side of my own glove. For a moment, I see stars. I throw out a low shin kick to the side of his legs, but it's like kicking a bulkhead. He lands another left-right combination. I lash out blindly with a straight that clips him on the jaw. Twenty seconds into the fight, my skull is ringing, and I feel like I've run a half marathon. At the end of the minute, he has landed three hits for every one of mine, and he's never even tried to use his legs. When the timer sounds its little electronic trill to signal the end of the round, I am thoroughly worn-out, and my mouth tastes like fresh blood. Dmitry looks a little sweaty, but otherwise not half as rumpled as I feel.

"You were right," I tell him when I've caught my breath and we're taking off our gloves again by the side of the mat square. "That wasn't the best idea I've had today. That SRA hand-to-hand training must be something else."

"Is not Alliance training," he says. "I spend six months in military prison once. Other man in cell, he was boxer. Before military, he fight in underworld ring, for money. He teach me how to punch the color out of a man's hair. I go easy on you because I am guest here." He smiles and hands me back his gel gloves. "You are not bad for soft little imperialist tool. We fight every day for six months, you learn to punch better, *da*?"

"*Da*," I agree. "If we're still alive in a week or two."

Overhead, the ascending two-tone whistle of a 1MC announcement sounds, and we all interrupt what we're doing to listen.

"Attention all hands. This is the CO. We are minus two hours and ten minutes from the Alliance transition point. I want everybody suited up and ready to man combat stations. That means everyone, not just the grunts. All hands, prepare for vacsuit ops. Staff Sergeant Grayson, report to CIC with our guest at 0830 Zulu."

The announcement ends with a descending whistle. Staff Sergeant Philbrick looks over at me and purses his lips.

"Vacsuit ops? We're all gonna go EVA and push this thing through the node by hand?"

"Beats me," I reply. "You heard the man. Best we hit the showers and put on hardshell."

"Copy that. Let's go, squad," he addresses his men, and they all gather their kit with the controlled urgency of combat troops switching to battle-alert mode.

I turn toward Dmitry. "Back to the berth, and into your armor. And Dmitry . . . don't turn on the comms and data in your suit until we're in CIC and the colonel gives the order."

"No trust at all," Dmitry says. "Maybe there is hope for you still."

CHAPTER 6

DOORWAY HOME

"Combat stations, combat stations. All hands, prepare for battle. Alcubierre transition in two minutes."

I know that we aren't really going faster than light speed—in an Alcubierre bubble, the ship moves at subluminal speed while the drive shifts the space around it—but it still feels like we've been racing through space for the last few hours. A ship keeps the forward momentum it had when it entered the bubble, and Colonel Campbell hit the node at four gravities of acceleration with the fusion engines going at flank speed. When we pop out of the bubble on the solar system side in a few minutes, we'll be shooting out of the node like a ship-to-ship missile.

"The second we get out of Alcubierre, we go cold on the engines," Colonel Campbell reminds the helmsmen. "Shut it down and coast ballistic. EMCON check, please."

"Everything's cold," the weapons officer says. "All active radiation sources are full EMCON. Once those engines shut down, we'll be a black hole."

"I want this ship to do its best impression of an asteroid. Just a rock, coasting through space. No spaceship at all."

We're all in battle armor (the grunts) or EVA vacsuits (the fleet personnel). Colonel Campbell stands in the center pit of the CIC, watching the consolidated readouts on the screens of the holotable that serves as the hub of the ship. I've never been in a ship's CIC dressed in full combat hardshell, and the feeling is more than a little unnerving. My brain is primed to expect the imminent chance of sudden death or dismemberment whenever I'm in armor, and I'm not used to that expectation right here in the best-protected part of an armored warship. Behind me, Dmitry is holding on to the railing that surrounds the pit, looking supremely out of place in his angular Alliance armor with its mottled paint scheme.

"Alcubierre transition in one minute."

This is the most dangerous part of the mission. We are going to blast out of the Alcubierre node at a few kilometers per second, with everything shut down except for the optical sensors, transitioning back into the solar system blind to whatever may lie in wait for us on the other side. If the Lankies have a seed ship parked right across the inbound node, we are hurtling toward a closed door at a full run, and we will disintegrate and turn into a smear on the hull of a seed ship in a millisecond. At least it will be over so quickly that my brain will never be able to process the nerve impulses from my body before I cease existing.

"On my mark, stand by to kill propulsion. Bring the optics online as soon as we are through. Anyone turns on a thing that puts out active radiation, you are going out the central airlock."

"Standing by for propulsion shutdown," the engineering officer says.

"Alcubierre transition in thirty seconds."

"Don't expect any last speech from me," Colonel Campbell says. "I don't intend to buy it today, and I don't give any of you permission to do so, either."

There's some light chuckling in the CIC. Humans being what we are, I am quite sure that everyone on this ship is thinking about the possibility that we all may have only a handful of seconds left to live, including Colonel Campbell. But I also know that the skipper would rather pet a Lanky than show fear or doubt in front of his crew. If he's making his peace, he has made it privately in his own mind.

"Ten seconds."

I close my eyes and think of Halley. If I am about to end, I want her face to be the last thing on my mind before the lights go out.

"Five. Four. Three. Two. One. Transition."

I feel the momentary dizziness I usually experience after an Alcubierre ride ends, and the low-level discomfort that has been in every part of my body for the last few hours falls away. We're through, and we're not dead. Yet.

"Kill the drive now," Colonel Campbell barks. "Get me optics on the main display."

The thrumming noise from the ship's fusion drive winds down quickly as the engineering officer shuts down the propulsion system. Nothing is shooting us to pieces, and we haven't run into anything solid. *Maybe they left the doorway unguarded*, I think. We're about due for some good luck for a change.

Then the optical feed comes up on the holotable display, and there's a collective intake of breath all over the CIC. Behind me, Dmitry mutters something in Russian that can only be a swear.

Directly underneath *Indianapolis*, the huge glossy bulk of a Lanky seed ship stretches for what seems like miles. The optical sensors under the ship triangulate on the vessel and project a distance readout: 2,491 meters. The distance display changes as we hurtle away from the Alcubierre transition point and into the solar system. The Lanky is on a reciprocal heading, passing below and going the way we came. On the holotable, a polite alarm chirps, and a readout overlay appears on the display: "PROXIMITY ALERT."

Indy is coasting faster than the Lanky is going, but even with our combined separation speeds, it takes *Indy* eight or ten seconds to clear the bulk of the Lanky ship. In that time, nobody in the CIC makes a sound, as if we could draw the Lankies' attention just by making noise. For all I know, we might—no fleet vessel has ever been this close to a seed ship and lived to tell about it.

"Bogey at six o'clock low, moving off at fifty meters per second," the tactical officer says in a low voice.

"Yeah, I can see that," Colonel Campbell replies. "Too damn close. Get me a three-sixty now."

The holotable display changes as feeds from various sensor arrays organize themselves in a semicircular pattern, stitching together a panoramic tapestry of the surrounding space. The Lanky seed ship takes up a disturbingly large section of space below and behind us, even as we are coasting away from the behemoth at hundreds of meters per second.

"There's more of them. Visual on Bogey Two and Bogey Three." The tactical officer reads out a bunch of Euclidean coordinates. The tactical display at the center of the holotable's array of overlapping imagery updates with three orange icons. One of them, slow moving, is almost on top of the blue icon representing *Indianapolis*, only slowly inching away from us. The other two are farther away, but moving faster. One is above and to our starboard, the other below and to our port side. Colonel Campbell shifts some of the holograms around with his hands and expands them until he has a good view of Bogey Two and Three side by side.

"Bogey Three is on a perpendicular, passing to port aft," the tactical officer says. "Bogey Two is closing laterally from our starboard. Bearing five-zero degrees, closing at two hundred meters per second." He looks up from his display and flicks a hologram over to the main tactical readout on the holotable.

"Sir, Bogey Three is on a collision course. If our speed and heading don't change, our paths will intersect in twenty-three seconds."

"Bring propulsion back online," Colonel Campbell orders. "Hold the burn until the last second. We're too damn close as it is. I don't want to light off a signal flare earlier than we have to. Prepare for course change, make your heading zero-five-five by positive zero-four-five. At the last second, helm."

"Aye-aye, sir," the helmsman says.

"Is patrol pattern," Dmitry says behind me. "Like sharks."

"Exactly like sharks," Colonel Campbell says. "They're circling the node, waiting for food. And we're the minnow."

I watch as the orange icons for the Lanky seed ships and the lonely blue icon representing the *Indy* shift around on the plot gradually. One of the orange icons inches closer to our blue one by the second. The computer, ever helpful, has drawn trajectory lines for both ships, and the orange and blue trajectories intersect at a point in space 2,500 kilometers and twelve seconds away.

"Propulsion online," the engineering officer announces. "Standing by for burn."

"Burn in three, two, one," the helmsman says. I swallow hard at the sight of the Lanky ship approaching from starboard, intruding into our section of space like a careless hydrobus driver. "Burn."

The fusion engines come back to life with a thrum, and even with the antigravity deck plating keeping us on our feet, the sense of sudden acceleration is dramatic. The tactical display on the holotable spins as the *Indy* reorients herself to correct her trajectory with the thrust generated by her powerful main propulsion system.

"Come to new bearing, all ahead flank. Get us the hell out of here," Colonel Campbell shouts.

The Lanky ship on the optical sensor feed grows larger and larger on the display. Even with the cameras at minimum optical zoom, the seed ship blocks most of the view to our starboard as the distance between us decreases rapidly. I really do feel like a minnow, but the Lanky ship isn't a shark—it's a whale, and it's about to swallow us without intent, purely by accident of proximity. At this distance, I can make out details on the Lanky ship I've never seen before—elongated bumps, irregular patterns of texture that almost look like bark or wrinkles on wet skin. I know it's a ship—I've seen plenty of recon footage of them deploying seedpods by the hundreds onto colony worlds—but it's not the first time that I find myself thinking it looks like a living, sentient thing.

Indy counter-burns her engines at full thrust to correct her path, then swings around to the new heading, which has us racing alongside the Lanky ship going roughly the same direction. The Lanky is going at a steady two hundred meters per second, but *Indy* is accelerating at maximum gravities, streaking through space like a guided missile. We are so close to the seed ship that it feels like I could open an airlock and touch their hull. Two more seconds of uncorrected trajectory, and we would have shattered against that hull at thousands of meters per second.

"Come to new heading zero-five-zero by negative four-five," Colonel Campbell orders. "Give this asshole some space."

"Aye-aye, sir," the helmsman acknowledges.

Behind me, Dmitry curses in Russian again. We pull away from the Lanky ship—not nearly quickly enough for my taste—and the *Indy* turns slightly, pointing her bow at the space below and to the left of the Lanky. Despite our difference in speed, we are still not completely clear of the seed ship.

"Too close," the tactical officer warns. "They spotted us, I think. I see activity on their port hull."

The camera feed shows the flank of the Lanky from an upside-down angle. I can clearly see movement—not the mechanical opening of missile tubes like on a human warship, but rather dilations, small holes opening in the side of the Lanky ship in a cascading wave of what looks like contractions on the flank of an animal.

"Go active on all sensors," Colonel Campbell shouts. "Weapons, set the CIWS to Condition Red. All hands, brace for incoming."

I turn around and grasp the railing of the CIC pit. More displays come to life as the various stations around the pit have their functions restored, the ship regaining her eyes and ears, and what few teeth she has. The CIWS, the ship's close-in weapons system, is designed to swat enemy missiles out of space before they can reach *Indy* and blow her up. I don't know if they work against Lanky penetrators, which don't show up on radar and move at insane speeds, but anything is better than no defensive measures at all.

"Bogey One and Two are changing course," the tactical officer warns. "They're starting to come about."

"Cat's out of the bag now," Colonel Campbell says. "Get us the hell out of this neighborhood."

"Incoming," the tactical officer shouts. "Visual launch confirmation. Vampire, vampire. All hands, brace for—"

There's a series of thundering bangs, and *Indy* shudders perceptibly. All over the CIC, warning lights and alarms start going off.

"Multiple impacts! Explosive decompression in multiple compartments."

"Roll the ship," Colonel Campbell orders. "Come to new heading one-zero-zero by negative four-five, zig and zag evasive pattern. Weapons, go active on the rail gun and return fire. I'll be damned if I let them shoot holes in my ship without shooting back."

"Aye, sir." The weapons officer activates the ship's rail gun mount. I can't see the control screen, but I can hear the metallic clang of the projectiles transmitting vibration through the hull as they leave the electrified rails of the cannon barrel at Mach 20. Then I see the impacts blooming on the hull of the nearby seed ship. The super-dense penetrators from the rail gun would shear through a fleet frigate from bow to stern at such close range, but as far as I can tell, they're not even scratching the hull as they shatter into stardust on whatever unearthly material the Lankies use for armor plating.

"We took some major hits," the engineering officer says. "Half the damage board is red."

"Collect reports and have damage control stand by. We'll sort this shit out when we're in the clear."

"Incoming," the tactical officer warns, not quite as urgently as before. "They're spraying blind at this point. We're out of their weapons envelope."

"Keep our course and don't let up on the throttle," Colonel Campbell orders. "And go full EMCON again. Visual kit only."

"Aye, sir."

Whatever the Lankies hit, the propulsion system and main reactor are not among the destroyed systems. *Indy* is running from the area around the Alcubierre node as fast as her fusion drive allows, and that's all that matters right now. The Lanky seed ships keep circling around in irregular search patterns, but it's pretty clear from the optical tracking that we've turned invisible to them again. Ten minutes pass, then fifteen. After twenty minutes of sustained maximum acceleration, the seed ships are small enough in the optical feed to not invoke a feeling of imminent demise in me anymore. All around me, there's hectic activity in the CIC as department heads collect reports from their subordinates and issue orders.

"Throttle back, let us coast for a while," Colonel Campbell says. "Damage reports."

The XO consults her display. "Looks like we took two hits. Both penetrators nailed our lower aft starboard side and went right through to the top fore port side. We have decompressed compartments on Alpha, Bravo, and Echo decks, and seven compartments forward of frame twenty-five are open to space."

She scrolls through the data on his display with the flick of a finger.

"Missile tubes one and three are gone. The secondary data bus got shredded. We lost the forward water recyclers and the entire port-side freshwater tank. Officers' mess is gone. And the auxiliary neural-networks cluster is offline. We have four KIA. Would be more if everyone hadn't been in vacsuits."

"That was sort of the point," Colonel Campbell says. "After *Versailles*, I've become a firm believer in vacsuit ops. Have those damage-control teams patch what they can with what we have."

"We'll need a month in a fleet yard just to plug the holes," the engineering officer says.

"Well, ain't none of those nearby. Where the hell are we, anyway? Astrogation, give me a fix. And then I'm going to need a fucking drink after all this excitement."

"More bad news, Skipper," the XO says.

"Well, don't make me wait."

"The number-two parasite fighter bay took a direct hit. The fighter's scrap, and the refueling nodes in number two are shot to shit."

"There goes half our offensive fighter power."

Colonel Campbell sighs loudly and runs a hand through the short stubble of his regulation-length buzz cut.

"Well, I suppose it could have been worse. Welcome back to the solar system, I guess."

The navigation fix places us right on the inner edge of the asteroid belt, two hundred fifty million kilometers away from the sun and sixty million kilometers from Mars. The plot on the CIC holotable updates with the plotted course back to Earth.

"That takes us awfully close to Mars," the XO says. Major Renner looks like she hasn't had any decent sleep in a month. *Indy* is at the limit of her endurance for interstellar deployments, and so is her crew. With the weather the way it is on New Svalbard right now, very few of the crew members actually got to catch some fresh air and a change of scenery while *Indy* played orbital bodyguard to the colony, so most of her crew have been on watch rotation for over three months without a break.

"What about the Titan fleet yards? They're way past the asteroid belt. Maybe they're still around."

"Mars is the way we have to go," Colonel Campbell says. "After that run through half of Fomalhaut, we don't have the fuel left to try for the outer solar system. I wouldn't want to try and take a damaged ship through the belt even if we did."

He looks around in the CIC, where every pair of eyes is fixed on the holotable in the center of the room.

"We're here to scout out the path to Earth, and that's what we will do, folks. If Earth is still in human hands, we can rearm and refuel, get the dents hammered out. And if the Lankies have the place, none of this matters a good goddamn anyway."

He studies the plot again and points to the computer-generated trajectory.

"We'll coast for a bit until we have the worst of the damage patched up. Then we go for a low burn toward Mars, and use the gravity well to dogleg over to Earth. Helm, lay in the course. Tactical, let's keep the active radiation to a bare minimum. It's not like we can spot the bastards on radar, anyway. Optical recon only, and stay sharp. I want a recon bird out on our trajectory as a curb feeler. Maximum telemetry range, passive listen only. Let's get to it, folks."

The CIC crew tend to their new duties in a flurry of activity. I feel a little in the way now in my bulky armor, taking up a good amount of space down here in the pit.

"Sir, what can I do to make myself useful around here?"

Colonel Campbell looks at me and runs his hand through his short hair again.

"Hell, Mr. Grayson, you've been fleet long enough. Never miss an opportunity to grab some rack time if it presents itself. Take our guest with you and get out of armor for now."

He looks at the holographic display in front of him and pokes at our trajectory line with his index finger.

"Mars is occupied space. And I'll eat my collar eagles if the sixty million klicks of space between here and there aren't lousy with Lanky seed ships. If they know where the doorway is, they know which way we have to come. Best keep that armor close, Mr. Grayson. You'll be needing it again soon enough, I think."

"Aye-aye, sir." I turn to leave and signal Dmitry to follow me. The armed SI guard at the hatch opens it for us, and we step out into the corridor in the center of Charlie Deck. It's only when I release my helmet seal and let the cool air of the environmental system replace the stale air in my battle armor that I realize my back is completely sweat-soaked, even though I haven't moved more than a few feet since we got out of Alcubierre.

CHAPTER 7

—PLANETARY GRAVEYARD—

It's strange to be in the inner solar system and not hear any comms chatter at all.

The inner system is usually a busy, noisy place, despite the vast distances even between intersystem planets and moons. We've had a hundred years to put infrastructure into place, and you can place video comms from one of the asteroids in the belt to your family on Earth, provided they allocate you the priority bandwidth and you don't mind holding a conversation with a six-minute delay between replies. But as we coast through the space between the belt and Mars, there's nothing at all on the comms frequencies. *Indy* is a signal-intelligence ship among her other functions, so she has good ears, but nobody out there is talking.

"Got visual on another Lanky," the tactical officer says. "Distance four hundred kilometers. Designate bogey Lima-7. Bearing zero-one-eight by positive one-three-eight. Reciprocal heading, moving at two hundred meters per second steady."

"Stay on course," Colonel Campbell orders. "He'll pass with room to spare. We've dodged closer."

In the past few hours, we've detected and evaded half a dozen Lanky seed ships loitering along our pathway toward Mars. Even with the excellent optical gear on *Indy*, the Lankies are all but invisible until they're almost on top of us, astronomically speaking. We are coasting on our trajectory, using the momentum from our earlier burn that set us on our way, and without radar emissions or engine-exhaust signature, *Indy* is a hole in space, a black cat in a dark room.

"There's no way the rest of the fleet can make this run," the XO says.

"No, there isn't. Even if they make it past that welcoming committee at the transition point, they'll get chewed up before they're halfway to Mars," Colonel Campbell says.

The damage-control crews are still at work patching up the ship's wounds. The penetrator rods fired by the Lanky ships are short ranged, but whatever ends up in their path gets foot-wide holes blown through it at hypersonic speeds. *Indy*'s agility and small size let her avoid most of the salvo from the seed ship, but the two projectiles that hit hurt the ship badly. They blew through *Indy* from our bottom right flank to the top left of the hull, wrecking everything in their path. Still, most of us are alive, the ship is moving, and most of the compartments have air in them.

As we make our way toward the gravity well of Mars, I use one of the CIC data consoles to go through the pictures of the Lanky seed ships we've encountered so far, studying them like an encyclopedia of advanced superpredators, and I realize that for all our struggles with them, all the ass-kickings we have doled out and received over the last five years, we know next to nothing about them.

"They're all different, you know," someone says from behind my right shoulder. I turn around and see the tactical officer looking over my shoulder. He's sipping soy coffee from a mug with the ship's seal on it.

"Different how?" I ask.

"You know whale pods, back on Earth?"

I nod.

"They're all individuals, right? You can listen to them on sonar and tell them apart by voices. When they're on the surface, you can see markings and scars and stuff."

He points at the screen in front of me, which shows two seed ships side by side in profile.

"Those guys? Same thing. We've been cataloguing every one we spot. Speed, size, patrol path, optical profile. They don't have hull numbers like we do, of course. But once you're close enough for optical gear, you can tell them apart. A mark here, a bump there. Ripple in the skin. That sort of thing."

He takes another sip of his coffee.

"Ours all look the same 'cause they all came out of the same fleet yard. Built to the same set of blueprints. These guys? They don't look like they've been built at all."

"They don't look uniform enough," I say.

"Right. Cheery thought, huh? Maybe there's an even bigger mother ship pumping these things out somewhere. Like a whale birthing a calf."

"Cheery thought," I agree.

"Getting some traffic from Mars now," the sergeant manning the signals-intelligence station in CIC says a few hours later. We are well into the second half of our parabolic trajectory that will slingshot us around Mars and toward Earth.

"Anything on fleet channels?" the XO asks.

"Uh, sort of, ma'am. All I'm getting right now is automated traffic on the fleet emergency band."

"Crash buoys," Colonel Campbell says darkly.

"Yes, sir."

As we get closer to Mars and the signals burn through the interplanetary clutter, the plot on the holotable in the center of the CIC updates with the blinking pale blue icons of automatic emergency buoys. The computer assigns ship IDs to the signals as they are identified and sorted out.

"FF-478 *Guadalupe Hidalgo*," the XO reads out loud. "CVA-1033 *Alberta*. Damn, that's one of the Commonwealth-class carriers. CG-759 *Vanguard*. DD-772 *Jorge P. Acosta*. CG-99 *Caledonia*."

"I know the skipper of *Caledonia*," Colonel Campbell says. "Jana Mackay. I went to Fleet Command School with her."

Knew, I think. Past tense, not present. Colonel Campbell knows as well as I do that the automatic emergency buoys don't start sending until they are ejected from their host ship. No fleet skipper would have the emergency buoy jettisoned unless the ship is completely disabled and in the process of ejecting its life pods, and the computer will only release it if the ship is in the process of breaking up. If the *Caledonia*'s crash buoy is out there sending its distress signal, then the ship is almost certainly gone, and all her sailors with her. Then again, both the colonel and I survived the activation of the *Versailles*'s crash buoy some five years ago over the colony planet Willoughby, so maybe hope dies hard even in a seasoned, hard-bitten staff officer. Maybe the crew of *Caledonia* did manage to man life pods and make it down to the surface of Mars, and maybe they're holed up down there waiting for a rescue, just like we were half a decade ago.

"Picking up Alliance beacons, too," the SigInt sergeant says. "Lots of Alliance beacons."

We watch silently as the plot fills with pale blue and red icons, all blinking their pulsing distress signals. We don't know the identities of the SRA ships who released their own distress beacons, but there are—were—a lot of them. Ten, twenty, thirty—I try to count the mass of icons on the display but give up at thirty-five, and every few seconds the computer adds more of them to the holographic sphere hovering above the holotable. The space between our position and Mars is a sea of slowly blinking pale blue and red icons.

"What the hell is left at this point?" Colonel Campbell wonders out loud.

"Still nothing on active fleet comms," the XO says. "We could go active, see if we can get anyone to talk back. There have got to be some surviving units in range somewhere. Ours or theirs."

"That's a negative," Colonel Campbell replies. "If there's Lankies out there in the dark, I sure as shit don't want to broadcast a quarter-million-watt flare for everyone in this corner of space to see. Passive listening gear only, unless we know we have someone to talk to nearby."

"Understood, sir," the XO says. "Remain at full EMCON. Ears only for now."

"Visual contact, Lanky seed ship," the tactical officer calls out. "Bearing zero-nine-zero by positive zero-zero-three. Distance eighteen hundred kilometers, heading one-two-zero relative, speed two hundred meters per second. Designate new bogey Lima-8."

"We'll be passing a little too close for comfort. Correct our course, XO. Nudge us three degrees to port so we pass his stern with some room to spare. Son of a bitch is damn near right across our trajectory."

"Three degrees to port, aye," the XO says. "Helm, give me a two-second burn on the starboard-bow thrusters. On my mark. Three, two, one. Burn."

I watch as the trajectory on the holoscreen simultaneously updates with the position and trajectory of the Lanky bogey catalogued as Lima-8 and that of *Indianapolis* as she fires her bow thrusters, nudging us onto a slightly different course to avoid swapping hull paint with the Lanky patrolling not too far ahead of us. The bow thrusters do their quick, controlled burn, and the line representing our trajectory bends to port very slightly. Physics being what they are, spaceships hurtling along at hundreds or thousands of meters per second can't just turn or stop on a dime when something pops up in front of them. I've never paid enough attention in physics to be able to begin to make sense of conning a ship like *Indy*, but I know that in space, steering and braking require a lot of calculating and planning.

Colonel Campbell watches the plot correction and nods. "Steady as she goes, helm. XO, countercorrect to the original trajectory when we have this bastard at least a thousand kilometers aft of our stern."

"Aye, sir," Major Renner replies.

The more time I spend in fleet CICs, the more I realize that there is no real control in a starship's control center, just an illusion of it, and that we are merely hanging on to an angry dragon by the tip of its tail. I may have even less control as a grunt on the ground, but with a rifle in my hands and a map on the display in front of me, I feel better equipped to determine my own fate than standing on a rubberized deck tile and holding on to a handrail while watching a hologram.

"Have you regretted your desire yet to switch to the navy all those years back, Mr. Grayson?" Colonel Campbell asks when he sees me studying the plot, as if he could read my thoughts.

"Yes, sir," I reply. "Every single payday. This deep-space combat shit—they ought to pay us a ton more. Too hazardous."

Major Renner chuckles softly. "Ain't that the damn truth."

"All Commonwealth units, please respond. This is Camp Webb, emergency shelter Sierra-Five. One hundred thirteen military personnel, seven hundred ninety-five civilians. Low on food and water, oxygen level critical. All Commonwealth units, please respond. This is Camp Webb, emergency shelter Sierra-Five. One hundred thirteen military personnel . . ."

We started receiving the distress call a little while ago, and right now I feel myself wishing Colonel Campbell would just take the repeating message off the speakers in the CIC. Camp Webb is one of the NAC's main military installations on Mars, ten kilometers from Olympus City and its enormous civilian spaceport. It houses the School of Spaceborne Infantry, where SI assignees fresh out of boot camp learn the ropes of off-Earth ground combat.

"Almost eight hundred civvies," Major Renner says. "Christ."

"We can respond on tight-beam for the next four minutes," the comms officer says. "Low power, probably won't even make a blip on the Lankies' radar."

"Give me a link," Colonel Campbell orders. "The second you see a Lanky heading our way, you cut comms, tight-beam and all."

"Aye, sir. You have a link."

"This is NACS *Indianapolis*, in approach to Mars, *Indianapolis* Actual. Broadcasting party, please identify yourself."

There are a few seconds of line static. Then the voice comes over the speakers in CIC again.

"*Indianapolis*, thank God. This is Major Vanderbilt. I am holed up in emergency shelter Sierra-Five with almost a thousand people. The Lankies own the surface. They've taken out most of the infrastructure. They seem to target the radio transmitters and radar stations in particular. We are down to five percent oxygen. They have gassed the base and the city. We need immediate evacuation, Colonel."

Colonel Campbell closes his eyes and exhales slowly before replying.

"Sierra-Five, *Indy* Actual. I'm sorry, but that's a negative. We are in stealth approach for a high-orbit periapsis burn toward Earth. We are just an orbital combat ship, and a damaged one at that. We have one drop ship, and there are multiple Lanky seed ships in orbit. We can't stop. Should have counter-burned seven hours ago for that, and then we'd have no fuel left for the burn to Earth. And even if we could stop on a dime, we can't shuttle nine hundred people up to *Indy* with one drop ship, through the Lanky minefields. I'm sorry, Major," he says again.

There's a long silence on the line. I imagine the major down in the stuffy bunker deep underneath Camp Webb, hope flaring up at a possible last-minute rescue, only to have it snuffed out just a few moments later. Almost a thousand people, and they are about to suffocate, and there's not a damn thing we can do about it.

"A hundred thirteen troops down here, Colonel. Over seven hundred civilians. Almost a hundred of them are children. For the love of God, if there's anything you can do, please do it."

Major Renner curses quietly under her breath. Several of the CIC personnel groan audibly. Colonel Campbell is stone-faced.

"We are minutes from our burn," the colonel says. "We are moving way too fast, Major Vanderbilt. It would take us two days just to counter-burn and reverse our trajectory, and we'd run out of fuel trying. I wish I could help you, but I physically can't. I will relay your coordinates if we make contact with any other Commonwealth units."

There's another long silence on the tight-beam link. Then Major Vanderbilt comes back on, and his voice sounds almost toneless.

"Then give us a kinetic strike directly on our transmitter. Three rounds, sequential. Enough to reach down fifty meters."

Colonel Campbell looks over at the tactical officer, who shakes his head.

"Not at this speed," the tactical officer says. He looks like he's ready to throw up on the console in front of him. "We're too far for the gun, and we'll be past the launch window too quickly. Can't hit a bull's-eye that small going this fast."

"Two minutes until the comms window closes," the communications officer cautions.

We can't even give them the mercy of a quick death, I think. Reversing course would be suicide—hell, this close pass is almost suicidal as it is—and we would never get everyone off the surface even if we had the space and fuel, but speeding by and not being able to do anything for these people is like a physical punch in the gut.

"I'm sorry," Colonel Campbell says. "I'm sorry."

"*Indianapolis*, don't let us suffocate like a bunch of—"

"Cut tight-beam," the colonel says over the transmission from emergency shelter Sierra-Five. "Now."

"Aye, sir. Tight-beam link terminated." The comms officer complies with an ashen face, and Major Vanderbilt's voice cuts off midsentence.

For a few moments, nobody in the CIC says anything, and the only sounds in the room are the soft audio prompts from various consoles and the faint, distant hiss of the environmental system that is pressurizing the room. The mood in the CIC is only slightly more upbeat than a funeral.

"Nothing we can do," Colonel Campbell says into the silence. "Nothing except to push on, or our people back on New Svalbard are going to go the same way. Eyes on the ball, folks."

"Periapsis burn for Earthbound leg in two minutes," the tactical officer announces. The plot on the holotable updates with a time readout. We are going to get as close to Mars as possible before slingshotting around, to take maximum advantage of the planet's gravity. There are much fewer seed ships in orbit than I had expected. We encountered half a dozen of them on the way here; I would have guessed to see many times that number above Mars. But as we hurtle toward our periapsis point a few thousand kilometers above the upper layer of the atmosphere on the currently dark side of the red planet, Tactical has plotted only four of them.

"We won't see the minefields at this speed until we're right in the middle of them," the tactical officer cautions.

"We're giving up the closest approach already," Colonel Campbell says. "We should be far enough away for clearance."

I'm in armor again—the ship is at combat stations for the approach to Mars—but the snug hardshell is less of a comfort than usual. If we run into a Lanky minefield at the speed *Indy* is going, nobody will be able to make the escape pods in time. Even without getting hit by their penetrators, the Lanky proximity mines will tear the ship into a billion fragments if we hit a few of them with *Indy*'s hull.

"Close enough for optical of the surface now," the tactical officer says.

"Bring it up on holo," Colonel Campbell orders.

Three new display windows open on the CIC's central holotable, all displaying various feeds from the *Indy*'s high-powered optical surveillance gear. Mars is shrouded in thick, gray, swirling clouds almost from pole to pole. The Lankies had over two months to set up their terraforming network and flip the atmosphere to suit their preferences. I know that right now, the carbon dioxide levels on Mars are ten times what they used to be before the Lankies got there. If we ever get the place back, it will have to be terraformed all over again.

"Lots of radiation hotspots." The tactical officer highlights a few locations on the holographic orb representing Mars. "One, two, three, four . . . That's half a dozen just in this part of the northern hemisphere. Looks like fifteen-, twenty-kiloton tactical nukes."

"Tried to stop them when they landed," Colonel Campbell says. "Looks like it wasn't enough."

I see the familiar latticework of Lanky towns dotting the landscape below. Their shelters look nothing like human housing. They are interconnected, spreading out from a central point in what looks like a fractal pattern from above. Like everything else the Lankies make, their places look like they're grown, not built—not a straight line or right angle anywhere. A Lanky settlement looks more like a coral reef than anything else. From the number and size of them, it's clear that the Lankies have been busy, but Mars is a big place, and they haven't settled even 10 percent of it yet.

"Maybe their resources are as limited as ours," Major Renner suggests. "I expected more seed ships than this. Maybe they only have so many of them."

"Wish we could pop a few nukes on those Lanky towns on the way past," the colonel says. "Look at that. Ten, fifteen, twenty . . . That's close to thirty settlements on this quarter of the hemisphere already."

"At this rate, they'll have the place settled in a year, maybe two," I say.

"And then it's Earth," Colonel Campbell says darkly.

"Periapsis burn in thirty seconds," Major Renner says. She picks up the handset for the 1MC. "This is the XO. All hands, prepare for slingshot burn." She turns off the 1MC. "Helm, stand by on main engines," she orders. "Full burn, on my mark. Give me a twenty-second burn."

"Standing by on main engines, for twenty-second burn," the helmsman confirms.

"Twenty seconds to burn."

"Tactical, please tell me we still have a clear path ahead," Colonel Campbell says.

"Optical shows clear to the periapsis," the tactical officer replies. "There's a ton of floating wreckage twenty degrees off our starboard bow, but we'll clear it by five kilometers at least."

"Let's hope they don't have any roadblocks stacked up on the other side. XO, take us around."

"Ten seconds to burn," Major Renner announces. "Helm, on my mark. In six . . . five . . . four . . . three . . . two . . . one. Burn."

The hull shudders again as the main engines light off at full thrust. We are trading acceleration with Mars, using the gravity of the planet to bend our trajectory around and toward Earth, and stepping on the accelerator at the same time. The plot curve on the holotable display updates as we reach the periapsis point of our Mars approach. We are just far enough away from the planet's surface to avoid the upper atmosphere and the Lanky minefields that will be scattered in low orbit to catch approaching intruders.

"Five seconds," the XO calls out. "Stay on the throttle. Ten seconds."

"Tactical, I want a full sweep on the active kit once we're out of the parabolic and on our way," Colonel Campbell orders. "We're a huge IR flare right now. If they spot us, they'll spot us, active gear or not."

"Aye, sir," the tactical officer replies. "Warming up the active. Sensor sweep in forty-five seconds."

With *Indy* in the iron grip of physics, there isn't much for anyone to do other than wait and look at the holotable's display. The icon representing *Indy* shoots around Mars at what seems an agonizingly slow pace. I know that we're going much faster than anyone who has done an orbital skip of Mars in at least the last fifty years, but I wish that little blue icon could make its way around the holographic orb much quicker.

"Fifteen seconds," the XO calls. "Coming around the bend. Cut main engines in three . . . two . . . one . . . now. Steady as she goes."

We shoot out from the dark side of Mars and onto our projected course toward Earth. I watch the optical feeds still live on the holotable, which still show mostly swirling cloud cover and the very occasional patch of red Martian soil. I don't know the details of the Lanky takeover, but I doubt they had any more warning than any of the colony planets we have lost over the last five years. That means the pole-to-pole blanket of clouds below is now a funeral shroud for over twenty million people, most of them civilians.

"Sensors online," the tactical officer says. "Active sweep commencing."

The holotable display updates with information. Lanky ships or minefields don't show up on radar, but the optics can spot them at short to medium range. Everything man-made shows up on radar just fine, however. The combined inputs from the optical lenses and *Indy*'s active sensors paints a grim picture on the holographic sphere and shows us just how blind we have been flying these past few minutes.

"Son of a bitch," Colonel Campbell says.

The space around Mars is littered with wreckage parts, dozens of spaceship hulls drifting in the void, some still bleeding air and frozen fluids from their shattered hulls. I've seen the damage the salvos from a Lanky seed ship can do to our fleet, but I've never seen carnage at this scale. The computer collates the information from the sensors and the transmissions from the crash beacons that are wailing their repetitive little distress tunes, and marks each wreck with its name and hull number. The Lankies were equal-opportunity exterminators—the sea of icons before and below us is a mixed cluster of red and blue colors, SRA and NAC ships united in destruction.

"Two bogeys inbound, closing in fast from bearings zero-four-eight and one-one-five. Designate Lima-11 and Lima-13. They're on an intercept course, sir." The tactical officer updates the holotable display, and two orange icons appear on the plot, steadily moving toward our trajectory.

"We're going too fast for them, but let's increase the margins a bit. Helm, full burn on main engines. Make it a five-second burn."

"Five-second burn, aye," the helmsman acknowledges.

The blue icon marked "OCS-1 INDIANAPOLIS" inches away from Mars, and the two orange icons representing the Lanky ships fall behind. We have too much of an acceleration advantage, and they spotted us too late for the seed ships to intercept us on our racetrack loop around Mars. It's a small comfort to know that even their ships have limitations.

"Cut the active gear and go cold on the main engines," Colonel Campbell orders. "Full EMCON. Let's become a fast-moving hole in space again."

"Aye, sir. Going full EMCON."

Fifteen minutes pass, then thirty. The Lanky ships behind us disappear from the plot as *Indy* leaves them behind. Without the active sensors, the contacts marked on the holotable fade from the solid colors of "confirmed" to the progressively paler icons denoting an old contact that can't be updated. Up ahead, the wedge of space before *Indy* is clear as far as the ship's optical sensors can tell. Behind us, Mars recedes into the darkness, along with all the minefields and human wreckage floating in space around it. For a moment, I wonder if Halley was on one of the ships the Lankies destroyed, and the thought is making me almost physically nauseated, but then I dismiss it again. She's at Combat Flight School on Luna, and her tour as instructor isn't supposed to end until early next year. They don't pull flight-school instructors out of the classroom and assign them to active fleet ops at the drop of a hat. But that's a lot of destroyed hulls around Mars, and a small, nagging part of my brain doesn't want to let go of the dreadful suspicion that Halley is out there, lifelessly drifting in a slow orbit around Mars, or still strapped into the pilot seat of a shattered Wasp somewhere on the planet's surface.

An hour after we complete our slingshot maneuver around Mars, there's nothing but empty space in front of us as far as the optical sensors can tell. Behind us, there's the red planet, rotating around its axis twenty-four and a half hours a day just like it always has and always will, not caring which species has temporarily settled on its surface. It occurs to me that I may never see this sight again in person. Maybe no human will ever get close enough again to find out just how many corpses are littering the surface down there now, human and Lanky alike.

"Stand down from combat stations," Colonel Campbell orders.

Major Renner picks up the 1MC handset and passes the order down to the entire ship. She replaces the handset and looks at the plot, where we are inching along a trajectory that has Earth's orbit at its end point.

"One hundred forty-four hours until turnaround burn," she says. "Fastest I've ever done this track."

"We'll be burning what's left of our deuterium for the turnaround," the engineering officer says. "We'll coast into orbit with the reactors sucking recycled air."

"As long as we get within radio range before the propulsion quits," Colonel Campbell says. "I'm sure we'll be able to hail a fleet tug or two to haul this boat back to Gateway. If anyone's left back on Earth, that is."

As I watch the images of Mars receding in our wake, I wonder what we will find when we reach Earth. I'm almost ashamed to realize that I would have a harder time accepting Halley gone and dead than Earth having suffered the same fate as Mars.

CHAPTER 8

— A FROSTY RECEPTION —

It looks like Earth still has humans on it.

A day and a half after we make our close pass of Mars, we get comms chatter on the regular fleet and civvie channels again. We're still coasting along with passive listening gear to avoid broadcasting our presence, but we haven't spotted any Lanky seed ships on our path since Mars. It seems like the Lankies are content with holding the essential strip of space between Mars and our Alcubierre nodes, but that's more than sufficient to blockade all traffic in and out of the solar system. We snuck in through a crack in the door, but we almost lost a bunch of toes doing it.

"Getting long-distance pings off the main comms relay on Luna," the communications officer says. Without much else to do, I am back in CIC to listen in to the far-off radio chatter we've started picking up from the direction of Earth. It's enormously relieving to hear other voices out in the void and know that we're not the only humans left alive in the universe.

"Sons of bitches took out the Mars comms relay and everything beyond," Colonel Campbell says. "That is going to take years to rebuild."

"They must have done something else, too," the communications officer replies. "Even with the Mars relay gone, the Luna relay has plenty of juice to reach anything clear up to the Titan fleet yards. Plenty of lag, sure, but we should have heard them the moment we popped out of Alcubierre. But we got precisely squat on our passive gear until half an hour ago. Which would mean—"

"They're jamming us somehow." Colonel Campbell sighs. "Five years of this shit, and I could write everything we actually know about these things on my thumbnail and have room to spare."

Indy is hurtling toward Earth, or more precisely its turnaround point for reverse burn, at breakneck speed, far faster than I've ever made the Mars-to-Earth trip before. This is the most heavily used intrasystem pathway, the solar system equivalent of a traffic-clogged Main Street. Almost every ship that leaves the system or goes on to the military bases or science posts around the outer planets takes the Mars route because it's the most energy-efficient way to travel. We should have passed dozens of ships going in either direction by now, but as we shoot toward our turnaround point, we're the only thing out here.

"Contact," the tactical officer says. On the holotable, a solid blue icon appears on the extreme range of our awareness bubble. We're still running on passive sensors alone, but the new contact is scanning the space ahead of him with active radar.

"Contact is squawking Commonwealth IFF codes. CG-760, NACS *Aegis*. One of the Hammerhead cruisers."

"Check our wake again," Colonel Campbell orders.

"Clear. No contacts since we got away from the Mars blockade."

"Let's go active, then. Announce that we're coming before they get a whiff on their active gear and start shooting at shadows. Turn on the radar, broadcast our own transponder codes. Let's become visible again."

"Aye, sir. Going active on the sensors and IFF."

With our active gear radiating megawatts out into space and our IFF transponder marking our presence, it doesn't take long for the distant Commonwealth ship to pick up our trace. A little while later, the comms officer announces an incoming transmission.

"They're hailing us on ship-to-ship fleet channel, sir."

"On speaker," Colonel Campbell says. "And open the line for me."

"Aye, sir. You are on."

"This is NACS *Aegis*, to the approaching vessel broadcasting Commonwealth ID. Please identify yourself."

"*Aegis*, this is NACS *Indianapolis*, *Indy* Actual," Colonel Campbell replies. "Good to hear someone else out there. We were starting to think we're the only ship left between Mars and Earth."

Due to the distance between us, we have to wait for *Aegis*'s reply for a few moments.

"*Indianapolis*, *Aegis*. You pretty much are. We are in the outer picket line. What is your status and mission?"

"*Aegis*, we just had one hell of a run past Mars. We are part of a task force that sought refuge in the Fomalhaut system. We reentered the solar system about a hundred hours ago via the Alliance transition node. The space between the belt and Mars is crawling with Lankies. My ship has taken damage, and we are almost out of fuel. En route to Earth for refueling and emergency repairs. If it's still there."

The reply from *Aegis* takes quite a bit longer than what is warranted due to the distance between us.

"*Indianapolis*, affirmative. Earth is still there. You are to decelerate and rendezvous with the picket task force, to proceed to Earth under escort. Do not attempt to cross the picket line without clearance, or we will employ defensive measures. Acknowledge."

Colonel Campbell and Major Renner exchange glances. I get that unwelcome feeling in the pit of my stomach again that sets in every time I see us heading for trouble. This is not the warm welcome I had expected, and judging from the expressions all around me, *Indy*'s CIC crew is just as taken aback as I am.

"*Aegis*, acknowledge receipt of order. Be advised that *Indy* has significant battle damage and is running low on reactor fuel. If I burn to decelerate now, we won't have the juice to get back to Earth, and someone will have to tow us."

The next reply takes even longer to get back to *Indy*. Whoever is in charge in *Aegis*'s CIC apparently has to phone home for orders.

"*Indianapolis*, acknowledged. Go for turnaround and deceleration burn as instructed. We have a supply ship on standby that will rendezvous with us as soon as feasible and refuel your ship. Keep comms traffic to a minimum and do not deviate from your current trajectory. Acknowledge."

"What the hell?" Major Renner says. "We squeeze past the blockade and make it to friendly space, and they're talking to us like we have half a dozen Lankies in the cargo hold."

"We have the acceleration advantage," the tactical officer says. "We can go a few degrees either way, and they'll never catch up to us. They can't burn that hard, not even a Hammerhead."

"We don't know how deep that picket layer is," Colonel Campbell says. "No point in giving them a reason to shoot at us."

He looks at me and smirks.

"Maybe that useless one-star desk pilot and the *Midway* group made it back to Earth, and word of our deeds on New Svalbard has preceded us, Mr. Grayson."

"Maybe," I say. "Can't say I give much of a crap right now."

"Neither do I. We always knew we'd eventually have to face the music on that one." Colonel Campbell signals the comms officer."Open the channel."

"You're on, sir."

"*Aegis*, *Indy* Actual. Copy your orders. We will go for turnaround burn and rendezvous for escort and refuel as instructed. Just make sure you have the fuel truck waiting, 'cause our tanks are dry."

"Acknowledged," comes the terse reply from *Aegis*.

Colonel Campbell studies the plot, our little blue icon slowly moving toward the one marked "CG-760 AEGIS." He exhales slowly and rubs his temples with his fingertips.

"Well, you heard the order. Prepare to flip the ship and go for turnaround burn. Get me a burn calculation and stand by on main engines."

Aegis is true to her word. When we coast into rendezvous position a few hours later, there are three ships waiting for us. One is *Aegis* herself, one of the fleet's advanced Hammerhead cruisers. The other two are the destroyer *Michael P. Murphy* and the fleet supply ship *Portland*.

"Looks like you had a rough day at the office," *Portland*'s boom operator sends when we are alongside to take on reactor fuel. "Those are some holes you have there."

"You have no idea," our comms officer replies. "Nothing but category-five shitstorms all month."

"Yeah, same here."

"*Indianapolis*, keep nonmission chatter to a minimum," *Aegis*'s CIC cuts in. "Finish refueling and prepare for course and burn instructions for Earth transit."

"*Aegis*, *Indy*. Understood." The comms officer looks over at Colonel Campbell. "What has gotten into their underpants this morning?"

"I don't know, but I'm rapidly getting tired of it," the colonel says. "Let's stow the juice. Comms, keep your ears open on the passive gear. I want to know if there's anything weird going on. I don't have a warm and fuzzy feeling about this."

It takes several hours to fill *Indy*'s dry reactor fuel tanks. During the entire procedure, we're connected to *Portland* via her refueling boom stuck into the fuel receptacle on our port side, and *Aegis* is flying formation on our starboard, only a few kilometers in the distance. The Hammerheads are designated as heavy cruisers, the fleet's main offensive space-control units, but everyone calls them "battlecruisers" because of their size. Only the carriers are bigger, and even then, *Aegis* isn't much smaller than an assault carrier or one of the old Intrepid-class bird farms. Her flanks are lined with rows of hatches for her missile-launch system, and there are two batteries of twin rail guns parked on her dorsal armor. I study the immaculately clean, brand-new laminate armor with the fresh paint markings, illuminated by running and position lights from bow to stern. The missiles stowed behind those hatches can punch a hole of half a cubic kilometer into a Lanky minefield, and there are nuclear missiles tucked away in vertical launchers deep in the bow that can turn a small moon into radioactive slag. The Hammerheads are the apex war machines of humanity, all our best destructive tools put into a tough and sleek hull, and so far they've managed to accomplish nothing against the Lanky seed ships.

"Refueling operation complete, sir," the XO reports. "We're back to a hundred percent on main and both aux tanks. At least they're not stingy with their juice."

"Probably not too many ships left to pass the fuel on to, I

imagine," Colonel Campbell says. "Comms, open a channel to *Aegis* and let them know we're standing by for instructions."

"Aye, sir."

Portland retracts the refueling boom back into her hull and fires starboard thrusters briefly to break away from the much smaller *Indy*. I watch through the external camera feed as the big fleet supply ship drifts back into the darkness, position lights marking her progress.

"*Indianapolis*, *Aegis*. Transmitting waypoint data. You are to follow *Murphy* back to Gateway. No course deviations are authorized for any reason. Keep your comms suite cold except for communications with *Murphy*. Acknowledge."

"*Aegis*, *Indy*. Understood. Why the cloak-and-dagger stuff? We don't need a chaperone to find our way back to Gateway." Colonel Campbell sounds a little exasperated.

"*Indy*, there are new security measures in place. Trust me when I tell you that you do not want to get anywhere near the inner defensive perimeter without a chaperone right now. You will follow *Murphy* if you want to make it to Gateway in one piece."

"Affirmative," Colonel Campbell says after a brief pause. "Have *Murphy* lead the way. *Indy* out."

The colonel motions for the comms officer to cut the channel. Then he folds his arms in front of his chest and looks around in the CIC.

"You heard the man. Lay in the course and bring up the reactor."

He turns to me and lowers his voice.

"Mr. Grayson, go check in with our SI detachment. Make sure they're not too far from their armor or weapons when we dock wherever it is they're going to have us dock. In fact, tell Lieutenant Gregory I want the whole SI squad in battle rattle before we arrive."

"Aye, sir." I turn on my heel and head for the CIC's exit hatch.

Meeting up with other surviving fleet units and finding out that Earth is still human real estate should have been a joyous occasion, but the distant dread I've been feeling since that first terse radio contact with *Aegis* has only gotten stronger.

CHAPTER 9

YOU CAN'T GO HOME AGAIN

When *Indy* and her chaperone destroyer are close enough to Earth for the optical gear to pick up our home planet, there are quite a few more people in the CIC than usual. It seems like anyone with even a weak excuse to be in *Indy*'s nerve center right now has chosen this time to do so. Even Dmitry is up here with me, standing by the side of the CIC pit and leaning against the waist-high safety railing.

"There she spins," Major Renner says when the camera feed from *Indy*'s front sensor array shows the familiar blue-and-white sphere, or at least the half of it currently illuminated by the sun. As always, Earth is mostly cloud covered, but there are patches of clear skies. I can spot a chunk of what looks like the eastern coast of Australia and the sunlight reflecting off the South Pacific beyond. We're still too far to spot spaceship traffic, but I can see the space stations in their orbits, each the size of a small city: Independence, Gateway, the SRA's Unity, and the half dozen stations from the Europeans, Africans, and Australians I can't ever tell apart without consulting a recognition manual. I see Luna in the distance as well, and the knowledge that I may be within radio range of Halley again is almost making me forget the anxiety of the strange reception.

"*Indianapolis*, contact Independence control for approach handoff," *Murphy*'s CIC sends. Our comms officer sends back his acknowledgment to *Murphy*, which hasn't exchanged ten words with us other than navigational instructions since we teamed up for the run back to Earth.

"And good riddance," Major Renner says. "Comms, hail Independence and put them on speaker."

"Aye. You're on for Independence."

"Independence Control, this is NACS *Indianapolis* on Earthbound approach. Request vectors and permission to dock."

"*Indianapolis*, Independence Control. Decelerate to seven kilometers per second and enter approach pattern three-one-three Alpha. Stand by for terminal docking guidance."

"Independence, decelerate to seven K per sec and enter three-one-three Alpha," Major Renner confirms. Then she picks up the handset for the 1MC.

"Attention all hands, this is the XO. All departments, prepare the ship for docking. We are in the pattern. Arrival in nine-zero minutes."

To our starboard, NACS *Murphy* keeps pace with us, as if they want to make sure we're not going to skip the prescribed course at the last moment and go romping around unsupervised in our home space. Whatever the reason for the front-door escort, it's pretty clear that our unexpected appearance in the solar system hasn't exactly overjoyed whoever is left in charge here.

I step to the back of the CIC, away from the holotable everyone in here is watching intently, and take out my borrowed PDP. We have line of sight to the big comms relay above Luna that serves as the hub for most military data traffic from and to Earth, and I am anxious to let the system synchronize my device and maybe catch up on three months' worth of backlogged messages from Halley and my mother. But as I get onto MilNet, the connection just hangs. My PDP can see the network, but the update operation goes at the speed of a pedestrian stroll in the middle of a New Svalbard winter. I've never seen the data synchronization take more than a minute, not even from the far side of the asteroid belt, but after several minutes of furtive checking, the progress bar on my PDP screen has barely moved. Finally, after what seems like the tenth time I've pulled the PDP out of the pocket to look at the display, it reads "TIMEOUT ERROR—CONSULT NN ADMIN." I suppress the urge to throw the useless little device against the armored bulkhead with great force.

No network, I think. I've never been in this part of the solar system—in visual range of Earth—without a good and solid MilNet link. It's the communications lifeline of everyone in uniform. If MilNet doesn't even work in Earth orbit, our comms infrastructure is profoundly screwed up.

The holotable plot updates with every minute we get closer to Independence. There are ships in orbit, but not nearly as many as usual. Several NAC and SRA fleet units are patrolling the space between Luna and Earth, but they're tiny little task groups—pairs of frigates, lone destroyers, a gaggle of orbital-patrol craft. I don't see any capital ships at all—no cruisers, no carriers, nothing bigger than the Blue-class destroyer that's still shadowing us to our starboard. If this is what's left to defend Earth, we're not just scraping the bottom of the barrel. We've turned the barrel over and shaken out all the old crap inside.

Luna isn't quite close enough for me to see the structures on the nearly airless surface, but I could shine the laser designator of my M-66C carbine and bounce the beam off the retroreflectors they planted on the surface when the old United States first stepped onto the surface a hundred and fifty years ago.

So close, I think. *So damn close.*

"All those empty docking berths," Major Renner says. We're in the approach pattern to our assigned berth, coasting parallel with Independence Station. "I've never seen it this bare."

"Wonder if it's the same over at Gateway," I say. "There's not much military traffic in orbit."

"Not much, but some," Colonel Campbell says. "But go ahead and find me any civilian traffic at all on the plot right now."

I check the plot again and realize that Colonel Campbell is absolutely correct. Every ship in our scanner range right now is broadcasting a military ID. Most of the ships are NAC or SRA fleet units, but I also see a few EU ships, two or three African Commonwealth units, and a corvette from the SAU. I don't see any civilian traffic at all—no corporate transports or refinery ships shuttling ore and personnel back and forth between Earth and the colonies, no research ships heading out for deep-space exploration, not even low-orbit passenger flights.

"*Indianapolis*, you are cleared for docking at Foxtrot Three-Niner. Be advised that quarantine protocol is in effect. Your personnel are not authorized to depart *Indianapolis* upon arrival. Execute docking procedure and stand by for further instructions."

"Independence, copy clearance for docking Foxtrot Three-Niner under quarantine protocol," Major Renner replies.

I've docked at Independence Station a few times on military ships. Independence is the civilian station, and the military only uses it on occasion. The last time I docked here was when I returned from the disastrous Sirius Ad drop. The Lankies interrupted a battle between our NAC task force and the SRA garrison, and we lost half a dozen ships and ten thousand troopers and sailors in just a few hours of laughably one-sided battle. I got a ride home on the frigate *Nassau*, one of the very few survivors of that battle. We docked at Independence when we got back to Earth, and then we spent the next several days in what seemed like an endless chain of debriefings.

"Foxtrot Three-Niner," Colonel Campbell says as he checks the approach plates for Independence on the holotable. "If this station had an ass end, F39 would be the docking port closest to it."

Above and slightly behind us, the destroyer *Murphy* creeps along the rows of empty docking berths on this side of Independence with us, less than a kilometer off our starboard side.

"Are they going to follow us all the way into the docking clamps?" Major Renner grumbles.

For the next few minutes, we coast down the Foxtrot extension of Independence, passing berth after berth, our position lights reflecting off the titanium-white outer skin of the station.

"There's the beam," the helmsman says. "Engaging autodock sequence. On the beam for Foxtrot Three-Niner."

The navigation computer takes over *Indy*'s conning and rotates the ship with the fine-tuned control of a silicon brain. *Indy*'s bulk turns and slows as the thrusters fire in sequence to get us into the docking berth at the prescribed approach speed. The berth is spacious enough for a destroyer or a cruiser; *Indy* looks almost lost in the large U-shaped berthing spot.

The arrestor clamps latch onto *Indy* from the port side and pull the ship into mooring position. Then the service and maintenance hoses attach themselves to our side, and finally the docking collar slides into position over *Indy*'s external airlock and latches into place.

"Confirm hard seal on the collar," Major Renner says. "Cut all propulsion and switch the reactor to standby power."

"Not exactly a warm welcome home," I say.

Colonel Campbell rubs his chin with the palm of his hand.

"No, it isn't," he says. "Let's not take off our boots and get comfortable just yet. I don't like this quarantine business one bit."

I don't have any pressing business by the ship's main airlock, but I am curious, so I go down there anyway. Sergeant Philbrick and Corporal DeLuca are shipside security on our side of the docking collar. The collar is a thirty-meter length of flexible lamellar steel that connects the station to our ship.

"This is some bullshit," Staff Sergeant Philbrick says to me when I walk up to the open hatch, Dmitry in tow.

"What's that, Philbrick?"

"Nobody's allowed off the ship. They won't let anyone through the collar."

On the far side, over on Independence, four armed guards control access to the only way onto or off *Indy.* They're not SI troopers, but civilian security police wearing night-blue uniforms and white body armor. Philbrick and Corporal DeLuca are in armor, too, and they look a lot more menacing in their full SI hardshell than those cops in theirs. The SI troopers are carrying M-66 carbines, sidearms, and a full combat load of magazines on their harnesses. Complete battle rattle is usually overkill for guard duty on friendly installations, but the way my stomach has been twisting for the last few hours, I'm kind of glad for the excessive show of force.

"That is bullshit," I agree. A month on this little tub, and we don't even get to stretch our legs. And I really don't care to be treated like a goddamn POW.

"Look at those assholes." Philbrick nods over at the other side of the docking collar. "Blocking the airlock with that clown show over there. I could crack that fruity eggshell armor of theirs with my dog tags. That's almost worse than leaving the hatch unguarded."

"Is not military armor," Dmitry says. "Too light. Is not for fighting, just for—how do you say? Show?"

"They're civilian police," I explain. "Independence isn't a military station."

"Civilian police," Dmitry repeats with a smirk, like he's somehow insulted that the Commonwealth is trying to keep him on this ship with just a handful of lightly armed noncombatants.

"Anyone come over from their side yet?" I ask Staff Sergeant Philbrick.

"Yeah. Hour and a half ago. Three civvies, a handful of medics, two staff officers. A major and a light colonel." Staff Sergeant Philbrick shifts the weight of his carbine in his arms. The polymer shell of the weapon makes a soft rasping sound against the laminate of his battle armor.

"What branch?"

"Fleet," Corporal DeLuca answers. "But no unit patches. Kinda weird. Didn't say shit to us, either. Barely returned our salutes."

I look over to the far side of the docking collar again. The civilian SPs are standing in pairs, two on either side of the hatch, PDWs slung across their chests. Beyond them, behind the station airlock, there are rec and medical facilities, mess halls with fresh food, and MilNet terminals for access by military personnel. If we had permission to leave *Indy*, I could grab some chow and a long shower and then call Halley, to tell her that I kept my promise and made it back to Earth in one piece and in time for our wedding. Being this close to her without a way to contact her is worse than the anxiety I feel before a combat drop. I've made it past Lankies and across thirty light-years of space, and now the only thing between me and a way to talk to her is this group of lightly armed SPs. Part of me wants to go below, put on combat armor, get my carbine from the armory, and see if they have the guts to do something about me walking right through them. The combined refugee force waiting for our return at New Svalbard is running lower on supplies every day, and we are playing protocol games with whoever is left in charge here.

"Staff Sergeant Grayson, report to the NCO mess. Staff Sergeant Grayson, report to the NCO mess."

I feel a little jolt of anxiety when I hear my name over the shipboard announcement system. I pull my PDP out of the leg pocket of my fatigues and check the screen again. This close to Independence, I should have unrestricted access to MilNet at full network speed, but the synchronization still hangs up with an error message. I've had my PDP locked out of MilNet on purpose before, but this is different. It's like the network is overloaded.

"Gotta go," I say to Staff Sergeant Philbrick. "Don't get complacent. There's some weird shit going on right now."

"Oh, I have the same feeling," Philbrick replies. "We've had the squad comms running since we docked. You be careful, too."

"Come on, Dmitry," I say. "I gotta drop you off at your berth before I go down there."

Dmitry shrugs and turns to follow me.

We leave the SI troopers behind and walk down the passageway toward the elevator. For a moment, I feel like turning back and asking Staff Sergeant Philbrick for his sidearm. I'm exhausted and anxious, and I've never felt less prepared for trouble than I do right now.

CHAPTER 10

— THE TOUGHEST GUY ON — THE BLOCK

When I step through the hatch of the NCO mess, the room is largely empty except for the two strangers that are sitting at the table closest to the food counter. One of them is a civilian, a slightly round-faced man with a balding head and old-fashioned eyeglasses. Everything about him screams "bureaucrat." He's wearing blue overalls like the civilian yard apes do, but his look like they just came out of the bag at the issue station. Underneath, he's wearing a dark red high-collared suit, the kind fashionable among Earthside government functionaries and newscasters.

The man next to him is a military officer, and he looks nothing like a bureaucrat. He's in standard fleet-issue CDU fatigues, the new blue-and-gray camouflage pattern they started issuing only last year. He's wearing the shoulder boards of a major, a silver oak wreath with one four-sided star in it, and a name tape that identifies him as "CARTER." He studies me with hard gray eyes as I step into the room, and I take an instant dislike to him. I stop in front of the table where the two are sitting and render a cursory salute just barely on the right side of insubordination. These people are intruders on this ship. They don't belong to the crew with whom I've risked my life for the last month, and I don't like seeing them holding court in the one spot on the ship where the noncoms can relax and socialize occasionally.

"Staff Sergeant Grayson reporting as ordered," I say to the major, ignoring the civilian entirely. The major nods to an empty chair in front of the table.

"Sit, Staff Sergeant."

I sit down and study the major's uniform as the civilian next to him starts to tap away on a data pad in his hands. The uniform is correct, technically speaking—clean CDUs, proper rank sleeves, a midnight-blue fleet beret tucked underneath the left shoulder board, everything crisp and sharp and according to dress regs. But there's only a name tape on his chest above the right breast pocket. There's no specialty badge, no combat drop wings, nothing at all that lets me deduce the major's service branch within the fleet. The spots on the upper arms where the unit and organizational patches ought to be are just blank stickythread squares. The major sitting in front of me is as generic a fleet staff officer as it gets.

"This meeting is classified," the civilian says without preamble or introduction. "You are not authorized to share any details of this conversation with anyone not in the room at present. Please place your PDP on the table before we proceed."

"May I ask who you are?" I ask the civilian. "I don't see any ID or rank sleeves on you."

"Place your PDP on the table as requested," the major says. "You see my rank sleeves, don't you?"

"I do," I confirm. "And I don't know who you are, either, sir. What fleet branch are you? I see no unit patch."

The major looks at me and then flashes a curt and humorless smile.

"Logistics," he says. "But it's not me you need to play nice with. It's this gentleman over here."

The civilian takes a credentials folder out of his overalls without looking away from his data pad screen. He flips it open and flashes a holographic badge and ID card at me.

"I am Special Agent Green. I'm with the Commonwealth Security Service. Please comply with my requests without delay, or things are going to get unfriendly."

I look at his credentials. I've never seen a CSS badge before, so for all I know he could be showing me a merchandise voucher for the government commissary in Halifax, but it looks authentic enough.

"CSS is civilian. This is a military ship. You have no jurisdiction here. You got a beef with me, I should be talking to the master-at-arms or Fleet Investigative Service."

Special Agent Green exchanges a look with Major Carter and smiles thinly. "Oh, boy," he says. "Another latrine lawyer." He nods over to the nearest bulkhead. "You are docked at Independence Station. Independence is a civilian facility. I can assure you that we have jurisdiction on civilian facilities. But I didn't call you down here to debate the coarse points of Commonwealth law with an E-6."

He looks at his data pad again and flicks through a few screens with his finger. "When *Indianapolis* did its slingshot burn around Mars, were you in armor, Sergeant Grayson?"

"Well, let's think about this," I say. "Periapsis approach to a Lanky-held world, right past several Lanky seed ships. Of course I was wearing armor. Everyone was in a vacsuit."

"Yes or no would be sufficient, Staff Sergeant Grayson." Special Agent Green looks up from his data pad again and gives me a thin-lipped smile. "Go ahead and assume that you don't need to impress me with your cleverness or your toughness."

"I don't feel the need to impress you," I say. "I'm just a lowly E-6. You said it yourself. Why are you talking to me right now?

We just ran the blockade past Mars. There's a hundred shipwrecks floating out there. Did the skipper tell you we have thirty thousand people waiting for us to get back to Fomalhaut and show them a way back home?"

"Fomalhaut," Agent Green says. "Yeah, I read the logs. That's why you're sitting here."

He consults his data pad again. I suppress the sudden urge to rip it out of his hands and cram it down his throat. A hundred of our ships gone, millions dead on Mars, tens of thousands waiting for news on New Svalbard. Why are we wasting time with this right now?

"You took part in a bona fide mutiny on New Svalbard. You disobeyed direct orders from the task force commander and shot it out with fellow troops. I'm still sifting through the details, but from where I'm sitting, I've already tallied up twenty-five years in Leavenworth, Staff Sergeant Grayson."

"They were illegal orders," I say.

"Not your call to make. You're an E-6. You're a combat grunt, not a JAG officer."

"That was my call to make," I say. "First thing you learn in NCO school is to never give an order that you know won't be followed. Second thing you learn is that you have the right to refuse illegal orders. The task force commander had no right to use us to claim civilian assets by force."

"Be sure to bring that up at your court-martial," Major Carter says.

"I will," I say. "And I'll also bring up how you people exiled two battalions of Earthside grunts on a colony with almost no resources, and then turned off the FTL network."

Agent Green gives me his brief, thin-lipped smile again. "Two battalions," he says, aping my tone of voice. "Five thousand troops."

"And the colonists."

"And the colonists," he replies. "How many people live on that frozen ball of shit again?"

"Ten, fifteen thousand," Major Carter supplies. "It's a pretty new colony. Ten years tops."

"Twenty thousand people at the most, then." Agent Green sighs. "A quarter of them insubordinate rabble-rousers who thought their oath of service was more of a loose suggestion."

"And three-quarters of them civilians."

Agent Green sighs again and puts his data pad onto the table in front of him. "Do you know how many civilians have died on Lanky-invaded colonies, Sergeant?"

"I have a rough idea," I say. "I've done four years of combat drops. Seen an awful lot of dead bodies."

"Eight hundred fifty thousand," Agent Green says. "Give or take a few ten thousand. And that count was from two months ago. Mars blew it all to hell. Call it twenty, twenty-one million now. But you know what? That number is a weak piss in a lake compared to the number of people that are going to die when the Lankies show up in Earth orbit."

I look at the Earth bureaucrat with his neat suit underneath the borrowed overalls, with that badge in his pocket and the data pad in front of him, acting like any of this still matters.

"We have a few weeks," I say. "Maybe a few months. There are a dozen Lanky ships patrolling between Mars and the asteroid belt. When they're done settling Mars, they're going to head this way. Way things stand, I don't think Leavenworth is going to be a problem for me."

"Well, aren't you just the toughest guy on the block," Agent Green says. "I am, of course, duly awed. Where is your berth, Staff Sergeant?"

"I can't seem to recall just now. Maybe I'll remember by the time you get me some JAG counsel in here. I don't think I should be saying anything else right now."

Agent Green shakes his head, a mildly irritated look on his face. Then he picks up his data pad again and taps the screen.

"Have the master-at-arms find and unlock Staff Sergeant Grayson's berth. Secure the data module from his armor and report back to the docking collar as soon as complete. And secure the SRA prisoner."

"He's not a POW," I interject. "He's the liaison for the Alliance task force we joined up with in Fomalhaut. I thought you debriefed the skipper?"

"And I thought you were done talking without JAG counsel," Agent Green says.

"We need the Russian to get back through the Alliance node for Fomalhaut," I say. "He has the access code."

"This ship is going precisely nowhere right now, Sergeant. Once we have untangled the personnel situation, *Indianapolis* is going to join the defense of Earth. You may have noticed that we're down a few ships right now."

"If we don't go back to Fomalhaut, thirty thousand people are going to die," I say. "They're waiting for us to get back and tell them the way home. It's what we came back for. We're the scouting mission for a twenty-ship task force. They can't make the transition blind without our intel. What the hell is wrong with you?"

"If you go back to Fomalhaut, billions are going to die," Agent Green replies. "You'd never make it anyway. It's amazing that you made it all the way here to begin with." He pushes the chair back from the table and looks at Major Carter. "Let's gather our things and get off this bucket. Call the SPs in to take Sergeant Grayson into custody for now."

I don't know why, but they will not let us leave, and they sure as hell won't let me get off the ship and talk to Halley or anyone else. For some reason, they want to keep us all quiet. If they replace the command crew and take the ship, we all risked our lives for nothing, and Sergeant Fallon and everyone on New Svalbard are going to be dead in a few months.

I look at Agent Green, who returns my glance with a slight, self-assured smile that makes me instantly furious. Whatever his priorities are, he couldn't care less that my friends are going to die if he gets his way. If I am about to get locked in a brig for the rest of humanity's final chapter, I'll at least get a last lick in, to wipe that smirk off this bureaucrat's face. It's not like I have much to lose anymore.

The bubble of barely contained rage that has been floating just below the surface of my consciousness pops, and I let the anger take over. I seize my PDP and throw it at Agent Green. He sees it coming and raises his data pad to deflect my throw, but he's just a fraction of a second too late. The hard polymer shell of my loaner PDP hits him in the face, right on the bridge of his nose. He yelps and drops his data pad, which lands on the table with a dull clatter.

The major is already out of his seat when I lunge across the table. I grab the front of his uniform tunic and pull hard. He pulls back with force to resist getting pulled across the table. I give it half a second and then turn the pull into a push, letting go of his uniform and shoving him against the chest with both hands. He flies back and stumbles to the floor. The serving counter is too close behind him for clearance, and he crashes into it, arms and legs flailing.

"SP detail to the NCO mess," Agent Green shouts. The blood is pouring freely from his nose. He backs away when I come around the table. When I am close enough for contact, he hauls off and shoots a surprisingly competent left straight against my cheekbone. I am so full of anger and adrenaline that I barely register the hit. I return the favor with a left straight of my own, which he blocks with his lower arm. Then I follow up with a right cross, and I put all my weight and force behind it. My fist hits him on the nose, almost exactly in the same spot my PDP nailed him just a moment ago. He collapses with a strangled-sounding little grunt.

Behind me, I hear the unmistakable sound of a pistol's slide cycling and slamming home. I turn around to see Major Carter pointing a gun at me from his slightly crumpled position on the floor. He is aiming with one hand. The muzzle of the pistol wavers more than just a little, but at this range, he doesn't have to be good, just lucky, and there are thirty rounds in his magazine.

"Move another centimeter," he says. "Please."

I freeze in place and hold my hands away from my body. Then I turn sideways, very slowly, until I offer him the smallest possible target.

"You are a logistics guy," I say. "Carrying with an empty chamber."

Behind us, the entrance hatch of the NCO mess slams open, and four civilian SPs pile into the room, PDWs at low ready. To my right, Special Agent Green sits up with a groan. He has his hand over his face, and there's blood seeping out from between his fingers.

"Put this asshole in cuffs," he says, his voice muffled.

With five guns pointed at me, I do my best to impersonate a piece of furniture. The SPs surround me, and one of them aims his PDW at my head.

"Hands behind your back. You make a move, I'll hose you down."

I do as instructed and put my hands behind my back. Immediately, someone else grabs me by the uniform and yanks me back roughly. Then I feel the hard plastic of a set of flex cuffs closing around my wrists.

Agent Green gets up from the deck and steadies himself. He wipes the blood out of his face with the back of his hand. The front of his loaner overalls is stained with red splotches. The high collar of his suit underneath has blood spatters on it as well. He looks at me with narrow eyes. Then he walks up to where the SPs are tightening the cuffs and patting me down. Without a word, he hauls off and punches me in the face, a solid right cross that cracks into my cheekbone and makes me see stars. My knees buckle, but the SPs on either side of me keep me from falling down. Agent Green takes a step back and observes me as I sway. The side of my face is numb, but I know that the numbness will turn into throbbing pain in a few moments.

"Toughest guy on the block, huh?" I say.

He doesn't even try to make his next shot a surprise. It's a hard punch thrown wide from the shoulder, and his fist slams into the bridge of my nose, right in the spot where I hit him just a few moments ago. This time, my vision goes red, then black. The sudden sharp pain between my eyes tells me that my nose is broken. I fall backwards, and the SPs just let go of my arms and let me crash to the deck. Warm blood runs down my upper lip and then into my mouth, and I cough. Agent Green has a good, solid punch for a bureaucrat.

"Now we're even," he says to me. I open my eyes and look up at him. He wipes his own bloody nose on the sleeve of his overalls, leaving a dark red streak on the fabric.

"Take Staff Sergeant Grayson out of here and move him to the detention area on Foxtrot concourse. If he tries any tough-guy shit, shoot him in the spine and leave him for the cleanup robots."

The SPs march me through *Indy*'s corridors and over to the docking collar. Two of them are behind me, weapons across their chests, and two are on either side of me, guiding me by the shoulders. When we reach the main airlock, Staff Sergeant Philbrick and Corporal DeLuca aren't at their posts anymore. Instead, there's a pair of SPs guarding *Indy*'s side of the docking collar.

When we pass through *Indy*'s main airlock and step out into the flexible collar connecting us to the station, it occurs to me that I may never step onto a spaceship again. I don't have any personal gear left in my berth, but I've lived and fought with the people on that ship for a few tense months now, and not being able to say good-bye to them as I get hauled off *Indy* like a bag of refuse hurts a lot more than the broken nose or the sore and puffy cheekbone.

The corridors of Foxtrot concourse are nearly deserted. There are a few civilian techs scurrying about, but they give us wide berths. I've never seen a space station this empty. The impression is compounded by the fact that Independence is bigger and roomier than Gateway, which is always packed to the bulkheads with military personnel and materials in transit. Of all the sights I've seen since the Lankies arrived in the solar system, seeing one of the NAC's two major space hubs almost devoid of people is possibly the most apocalyptic.

The civilian security police march me down the length of Foxtrot concourse, which is a long hike down the central corridor. At the main junction that connects the concourse to the central part of the station, there's a security booth next to a wide airlock. The lead cop swipes his security tag at the door. Inside, there's a duty desk and two more civilian police, both in regular black police fatigues with sidearms on their duty belts.

The SPs pat me down again. One of them runs a scanner up and down my body.

"Clean. Give the guy something for his nose. He'll bleed all over the detention unit."

One of the SPs uncuffs me, then another behind the desk produces a rolled-up bandage pad and tosses it over to me. I catch it and press it against my nose. The blood on my face is fairly well clotted now, and I do my best to clean some of the sticky mess, with limited success. The bridge of my nose hurts like hell, and I have a massive headache now, but I don't want to ask the SPs for pain meds. I don't want to ask them for any favors at all. They remind me too much of the casually brutal riot cops I met last time I went down to Earth a few months ago.

"I'm going to take the cuffs off," the cop to my right says. "No funny shit, or that bloody nose will be the least of your problems today. Understood?"

"Understood," I say.

The cop releases the flex cuffs, which were tight enough on my wrists to leave deep red marks.

"This way," he says. "Nice and easy."

He leads me to a door at the back of the security station and opens it with his ID tag. We walk through the door into a detention berth. It's a room maybe five meters wide and long, with stainless steel benches along the walls that are bolted to the floor. There's a toilet in the corner of the room, and a holoscreen high up on one wall near the ceiling. It's showing Network news with the sound muted.

"Have a seat and relax for a little while until the MPs come and pick you up."

"Relax," I say. The wad of bandage I'm pressing against my face is now tinted in various shades of red, and my head hurts enough to make my eyes water. "That's just what I'll do. Thanks."

The cop leaves the room and closes the door behind him. I walk over to one of the benches lining the walls and lie down on it. I've not been in a detention cell in five years of service, but from the look of things, I'm going to have to get used to this sort of environment.

I close my eyes and try to ignore the pain enough to take a nap, without great success.

A little while later, the door of the detention berth opens again. I sit up, expecting the MP detail that will haul me off to the shuttle down to the fleet brig in Norfolk. But the newcomers aren't military police. The civvie cop walks in, followed by Dmitry and Colonel Campbell.

"Have a seat, gentlemen," the cop says.

Colonel Campbell nods at me and sits down on the bench nearby.

Dmitry rubs his wrists and looks around the room. Then he looks at me and shakes his head slightly. "Andrew, my friend," he says. "You look like garbage. Have you had not-good ideas again?"

"*Iz ognya da v polymya,*" I agree.

CHAPTER 11

EXECUTING ORDERS

"Why did you have to go and pick a fight with those CSS goons?" Colonel Campbell asks.

I'm lying down on my bench again because it's easier to keep the blood in my head that way. Dmitry is sitting leaned back against the stark white wall of the detention berth, arms folded, watching the muted Network screen with a slightly bored expression. Colonel Campbell is pacing around in what little space there is, hands in the pockets of his CDU fatigues.

"Oh, I don't know," I say. "I guess since they were hauling me off to the brig anyway, I figured I ought to make it worth my while."

"I guess in the grand scheme of things it doesn't matter much. You're just lucky they didn't stitch you with fléchettes."

"That major was about five pounds of trigger pull away from it," I say. "Couldn't help myself. Told the CSS agent that we had to go back to Fomalhaut, or thirty thousand people are going to bite it. And he just shrugs and goes, 'Too bad.'"

I sit up with a grunt and look at the bandage in my hand. At least my nose has stopped bleeding, but the headache is still there.

"They're not going to let us leave," I say.

"Oh, I know," Colonel Campbell says. "I have been relieved of command. They're going to replace the department heads and senior personnel, and then they're going to attach *Indy* to what's left of the fleet here around Earth."

"That's nuts. *Indy*'s damaged. She's not going to make fuck-all of a difference when the Lankies come calling. No offense, Colonel."

"None taken. And you're right. She needs a month in the fleet yard and six weeks of shore leave for the crew to get back into fighting shape."

He straightens out his uniform tunic and sits down across from me.

"None of this is right," he says. "You don't send civvie cops to arrest mutineers. You send military police. What business does a CSS agent have on a warship? And chucking Sergeant Chistyakov here into the brig with us? That's a straight-up treaty violation. He should have been put on a shuttle and ferried over to Unity Station."

"That major who was with the CSS agent wasn't right, either," I say. "No unit patches. No specialty badge. Just a name tag and a pair of rank sleeves."

"I noticed that," Colonel Campbell says. "Shit ain't right. Hasn't been since we made contact with that picket force. They've locked out all comms on *Indy*. Full EMCON. We can only talk with the station via hard line."

"That explains why my PDP couldn't connect to MilNet." I want to throw away the blood-soaked bandage roll in my hand, but there's no trash container here in the lockup, so I reluctantly hold on to it.

"They're keeping a lid on us," the colonel concludes. "Making sure we don't talk to anyone."

"About what? Fomalhaut? Or Mars? You think they're trying to keep Mars a secret?"

"I don't see how that's possible," he says. "Event of that magnitude, that close to Earth? There's people calling their relatives on Mars every day. They probably knew about the invasion down on Earth about twelve and a half minutes after the first Lanky ship showed up in Mars orbit."

"So why keep us isolated?"

"Beats me," Colonel Campbell says. "But if *Indy* doesn't get to leave in the next day or three and hightail it back to Fomalhaut . . ."

He doesn't finish the sentence, but I know what he means. Even without the Lankies, the colonists and soldiers crammed onto the little ice moon won't live through the coming hard winter. I was hungry a lot when I grew up, and there's very little you won't do for some extra calories when the hunger is gnawing at the back of your rib cage. I know that I'd rather go out fighting the Lankies than by wasting away in an underground city while the temperature outside is low enough to shock-freeze exposed skin instantly.

"You want to make breakout, perhaps?" Dmitry says sleepily from his corner. "Might be next un-good idea you have. Maybe this time you can get bullet wound."

"I'm not fighting a bunch of armed cops hand to hand," I say. "But it's not me we need to get back to *Indy*. It's you."

Dmitry raises an eyebrow and tears his attention away from the Network screen. "How is this?"

"Without the access code for the Alliance node, *Indy* can't go back through to Fomalhaut. They sure as hell can't use the Commonwealth node. We gotta go back the way we came."

"Where is your armor, Sergeant Chistyakov?" Colonel Campbell asks.

"Is in berth, on spy ship of yours. They come take me off, do not ask about armor. I decide not to tell them."

"If they remember to ask, tell them we gave you one of our vacsuits for the trip," Colonel Campbell says. "Just in case."

"In case of what?" I ask. "Major Renner stealing *Indy* out of the dock and making the run back to Fomalhaut by herself?"

Colonel Campbell leans back with a sigh and stretches his legs.

"They're replacing the whole command crew," he says. "Major Renner is just running the boat until they hand it over to a new skipper and XO. *Indy* isn't going anywhere right now."

He shrugs and flashes a brief smile, which makes the wrinkles in the corners of his eyes look a little craggy in the harsh LED light from overhead.

"But you never know what kind of weird shit can happen in a hurry, Mr. Grayson."

We don't have to wait long for our pickup. Not thirty minutes after Colonel Campbell and Dmitry join me in the detention berth, the door opens again, and one of the cops sticks his head into the room.

"Get up," he says. "Military police is here to pick you up."

We stand up as instructed. Dmitry yawns and stretches. He still looks like our predicament is boring him to tears, but I can tell that he is sizing up the cop in the door with a quick glance. Colonel Campbell just looks pissed off.

The cop in the door steps out of the way, and four MPs walk into the room. One stands by the door, hand on his holstered sidearm. The other three each step up to one of us.

"Let's go, folks," the MP by the door says. His rank sleeves identify him as a sergeant. The other MPs are a corporal and two privates first class.

"I'm not 'folks,'" Colonel Campbell says. "I'm a colonel and the captain of a fleet ship. I don't give a shit who sent you or where you are taking us, but you will address me as sir." He gestures at Dmitry and me. "For that matter, every one of us outranks every one of you."

"You know rank means nothing in a detention berth," the MP sergeant replies. "Sir," he adds after a moment.

The MPs put flex cuffs on our wrists. When they get to Dmitry, he flexes his shoulder muscles just a bit, and the PFC putting the cuffs on him takes an involuntary step back. The sergeant at the door tightens his grip on his pistol.

"Boo," Dmitry says. He cracks a smile in my direction, and I can't help but return it. The man is nominally my enemy, and two months ago we may have faced each other on the battlefield, but I like him. I also think he may be just a little bit nuts, or maybe I'm just not used to Russian attitudes yet.

"What exactly are your orders, Sergeant?" Colonel Campbell asks.

"I am to get you on the shuttle and deliver you to the receiving brig at Norfolk. You can talk over the legal stuff with them down there. I'm just a sergeant. Sir."

Colonel Campbell nods toward the door. "Let's not waste time, then. After you, Sergeant."

The MPs march us out of the security booth and through the large airlock that separates Foxtrot concourse from the rest of the station. Out in the main part of Independence, there's a bit more activity than in the concourse behind us, where *Indy*'s berth is the only occupied one. The civilian yard techs and shuttle jocks going about their business on the main concourse look at us as we pass by, two fleet sailors and an SRA noncom handcuffed and flanked by four armed military police officers.

We walk down the concourse about a hundred meters when the MPs direct us to another concourse to our right.

"Echo," the sergeant in charge says. "We're this way."

"You know that Sergeant Chistyakov here isn't subject to the UCMJ, right?" I say. "He's not a POW. The Alliance is going to be pissed when they find out that you crapped all over the treaty."

"The Alliance can kiss my ass right now," the sergeant says. "I am just executing orders. Not my circus, not my monkey."

"You call me monkey, I take electric stick off belt of yours and stick it up your big ass," Dmitry says matter-of-factly from behind the sergeant.

The MP sergeant stops and turns toward Dmitry, who looks at him with an unconcerned little smile on his face.

"You don't shut the fuck up and march, I'll flush your ass out the nearest airlock, Russkie."

I tense and prepare to jump into the tussle that's sure to break out any second now. We are cuffed and unarmed, but I bet I can get at least this blustering asshole on the ground before they take us down with their stun sticks.

Behind us, there's a minor commotion in the main part of the station. I hear the tromping of armored boots on the nonslip deck around the corner. We all turn to look back at the airlock we just passed through, not ten meters behind us.

Two SI troopers in full battle armor come around the corner and train their rifles at us—or more precisely, at the MPs surrounding Dmitry, Colonel Campbell, and me. Their targeting lasers paint green streaks across the light armor shells of the MP uniforms, which look pitifully inadequate compared to what the SI troopers are wearing.

"Hands off the weapons," an amplified voice booms. I recognize it as Staff Sergeant Philbrick's. "Away from the fleet guys and on your knees. Do it now."

Dmitry moves away from the MP escorting him. The MP grabs his flex cuffs and tries to pull him back, and Dmitry reverses direction and butts the MP corporal aside with his shoulder. The corporal is almost a head taller than Dmitry and in light armor besides, but he stumbles aside as if he has been hit by an opening airlock hatch.

Next to me, the MP sergeant draws his pistol from the holster by his side and raises it toward Dmitry. He sees the muzzle swing toward him and dashes forward, but there are five meters between them, and there's no way Dmitry can outrun the MP's trigger finger. I am much closer, and I act on reflex.

I hurl myself at the MP sergeant and bring my cuffed hands down on his pistol as it comes up. My left hand hits the top of the weapon's slide near the muzzle end. I grab the front of it and push it aside, away from Dmitry and me. The gun raps out a three-shot burst that's shockingly loud so close to my face. There's a sudden searing pain in my left hand that makes the headache I've been nursing for the last hour seem laughably mild in comparison. I scream and tighten my grip on the gun with the other hand, but my fingers slip off the now blood-slick polymer, and I drop to my knees. Then Dmitry is in front of me, and he plows into the MP sergeant and sends him flying backwards. I look to my right and see two green targeting lasers converging on his chest armor.

"DROP THE GUN," Sergeant Philbrick's voice thunders on maximum amplification, loud enough to make the nearby bulkhead shake with the sonic energy.

The MP sergeant looks up, his expression that of a panicked, remorseful kid whose prank has hurt someone. He drops his gun to the deck, where it lands with a dull thud. Then he raises his hands and pulls his head low between his shoulders. The two green targeting markers on his chest never waver.

The other MPs decide that freezing in place is an eminently wise course of action. Behind Philbrick and his fellow trooper, two more SI troopers in battle armor appear in the airlock opening, rifles at the ready.

"You fucking imbecile," Sergeant Philbrick says when he steps between us and picks up the MP's pistol. "Look what you've done. Nez, hand me a trauma pack."

"Yes, Sarge." The SI trooper next to Sergeant Philbrick lowers his rifle and reaches into his medkit pouch.

My left hand feels like it has been split in half with an axe, and it doesn't look much better. I cradle it to my chest, look at it to assess the damage, and immediately wish I hadn't. There's a chunk of my hand missing, along with two fingers. Where my pinky and ring fingers used to be, there's nothing left but powder-burned shredded meat. I must have had my finger right in front of the muzzle, and the expanding gases from the blast did as much damage as the three armor-piercing rounds that preceded them. It hurts so much that I can't even scream, even though I want to.

"Hang on, Grayson."

Staff Sergeant Philbrick takes the trauma pack Corporal Nez hands him. He peels the cover off with his teeth and slaps the whole thing onto my hand, mercifully covering the mess from sight. He kneads the pack into place to shape it to the wound area. I feel instant relief as the medication cocktail baked into the pack simultaneously numbs my hand and releases the fast-acting local painkiller.

"Shackle these assholes and let's move," Philbrick says to Corporal Nez. "That gunfire's gonna draw attention. We'll have a tactical team on our asses in a minute."

"Copy that," Corporal Nez says.

The SI troopers round up the MPs and use their own flex cuffs to shackle them together. When the troopers are done, the MPs are standing in a circle, attached by the wrists, with one of the station's vertical support struts in their middle. The SI troopers take all the sidearms off the MPs, unload them, and throw them into a nearby garbage chute.

"Let's move out. Back to the Foxtrot terminus. I'll take lead. Nez, bring up the rear. Put Grayson and the others between us. You okay to move, Grayson?"

"Yeah," I confirm. "Let's go."

When we move back to the airlock to the main concourse, I look back at the gaggle of MPs. The sergeant who blew off two of my fingers is just staring ahead at the support beam in front of him, as if he doesn't want to meet anyone's gaze for fear of inviting retaliation.

Just executing orders, I think. Ain't that always our fucking absolution.

CHAPTER 12

FULL SPEED ASTERN

It's a hundred meters from the terminus of Echo concourse to the airlock at the end of Foxtrot concourse. We haven't covered half that distance when the security alarm overhead goes off, an annoying two-tone trilling sound. Most of the civilians in the concourse have scattered already at the sight of the fully armed and armored SI troopers with combat demeanor, so we have this section of the concourse mostly to ourselves.

"This is a level-five security alert. All personnel, shelter in place and secure airlocks."

Staff Sergeant Philbrick clears the corridor ahead with the muzzle of his rifle before waving us on. "Fifty meters. Let's hustle."

My hand is now pleasantly numb, and the painkillers have started kicking in, but I know that the pain will return before too long. For now, I run behind Sergeant Philbrick and next to Dmitry and Colonel Campbell, glad for the concentration of chemicals in my bloodstream that keeps that razor-sharp agony from registering in my brain.

"Major Renner sends her regards," Sergeant Philbrick shouts over his shoulder toward Colonel Campbell. "She's warming up the fusion plant right now. Ship's at combat stations."

"What about those SPs all over the ship?"

“Third Squad took care of ’em,” Sergeant Philbrick shouts. “Disarmed and secured in a storage room out on Foxtrot.”

We reach the airlock for Foxtrot concourse, which is a laminate hatch six meters wide. Sergeant Philbrick motions us to a halt. Then he waves Corporal Nez forward, and both of them check the concourse beyond in quick and efficient fashion.

“Clear,” Philbrick says. “Let’s move. Second Squad, we’re coming your way. Get ready to fall back to *Indy*.”

On the way back to the ship, Foxtrot concourse seems about three times longer than I remember it from the way into the station, despite the fact that we’re moving a lot more quickly for the return trip. I count the bulkheads we’re passing through—one, two, three, four, five. There were twenty-five of them on the way up from *Indy*.

Before Sergeant Philbrick reaches bulkhead number six, the airlock comes down from the top of the bulkhead almost silently and slams into place, barring our way to the far end of the concourse.

“Contact rear!” the private bringing up the tail end shouts. I see red and green targeting lasers bouncing off the walls of the concourse, and a second or two later, figures in dark blue armor rushing down the concourse behind us from the direction of the main part of the station.

“Into the corner,” Sergeant Philbrick orders. He uses his armored bulk to nudge Dmitry and the colonel toward me and behind one of the support beams just in front of the bulkhead. His squad fans out and takes firing positions, aiming their rifles back up the way we came just moments ago.

“Security police,” a magnified voice booms in the corridor behind us. “Drop your weapons, or we will employ lethal force.”

Improbably, Corporal Nez chuckles. “‘Employ lethal force’? Who the hell talks like that?”

"Don't kill anyone 'less you have to," Philbrick orders. "They shoot first, we take 'em down."

The sheltered space between the support truss and the nearby bulkhead is pitifully small. I am keenly aware of the fact that I am in an enclosed space with a bunch of troopers about to shoot at each other, and that I am not wearing battle armor.

"Keep the Russian safe," I say. "He goes down, nobody's going back through to Fomalhaut."

Philbrick removes the sidearm from his holster and hands it to me butt-first. I take it and check the chamber.

"Drop your weapons," the voice in the corridor shouts again.

"Not a chance," Philbrick shouts back. "You shoot at us, you die."

I chance a look around the support beam that is shielding me inadequately. The cops in the corridor behind us—I count at least four—are wearing heavier armor than the SPs who arrested us earlier, and they're carrying PDWs. The four SI troopers with us outgun them by a fair margin, and they're seasoned combat troops besides, but there isn't much space in the narrow confines of this space station corridor. If both sides open fire, it'll be a bloody mess.

"All the airlocks on this concourse are sealed," the cop shouts. "No way out but through us. Tactical response team is going to be here any second. Don't be stupid, jarhead. Put 'em down."

Staff Sergeant Philbrick exhales slowly. Then he shakes his head. "We don't have time for this shit. Watch your target markers. Low bursts. On my mark."

He looks at each of the SPs in turn, and I know that he is using his suit's targeting computer to send priority target data to his fire team through the TacLink.

"One, two, fire."

The SI troopers raise their rifles as one, and four trigger fingers tighten to execute the order. One of the SPs sees that the balloon is about to go up, and he flinches back and fires a burst from his PDW. The high-pitched rattling of the PDW's report rings through the concourse. The projectiles hit Corporal Nez in the chest and side, and he jerks back in turn.

Then four M-66 rifles hammer out simultaneous bursts. The two nearest cops are cut down instantly, swept off their feet by the impact of dozens of tungsten fléchettes their light armor has no hope of stopping. Sergeant Philbrick gives a signal, and the two privates get up from their crouching position and advance on the two remaining cops. One of them sticks his PDW out from behind the support strut he's using as cover and starts pouring bursts down the corridor blindly. I pull back behind my own cover and try to meld with the wall.

There are two more bursts of rifle fire, and then there's silence.

"Clear," Philbrick shouts.

Corporal Nez gets up from the rubberized deck and checks his armor. The small, high-velocity rounds from the cops' PDWs have left silver-gray smear marks on his hardshell plate. I see that the SI troopers chose to go heavy—their armor is fitted with the optional add-on ballistic plating we only wear when we expect to do a lot of heavy close-quarters battle. It adds twenty pounds to an armor suit that's already one weighty bitch of a load to carry, but the heavy kit can shrug off anything short of an armor-piercing shell from an autocannon.

The four SPs are on the ground, all motionless. Sergeant Philbrick stands over them, kicks their PDWs aside, and shakes his head again.

"Dumb shits," he says. "Civvie cops against combat troops."

I check myself for extra holes and don't find any. Colonel

Campbell and Dmitry are unscathed as well, although the vertical support strut we were hiding behind shows evidence of bullet impacts not ten inches from where my head was just a few moments earlier.

"We need to get the airlock open," I say. "Tac team's going to have bigger guns and better armor."

"No shit." Philbrick waves us over. "Skipper, over here. We need to use the master key for that hatch. Crouch in the corner and cover your ears. Nez, Watson, load HEAT."

He plucks a grenade from his harness and sticks it into the open breech of his underbarrel grenade launcher. I can see the color code on the base of the shell: red, white, red. The high-explosive antiarmor rounds for our grenade launchers are fairly useless against vehicles clad in modern armor, but they do a number on steel airlocks and walls, which is precisely why we use them for breaching fortified positions.

Dmitry sees what the SI troopers are about to do, and he doesn't need to be told to retreat to the nearest corner and cover his ears. I do likewise and take up position next to the Russian.

"Aimpoint is dead center. On three. One, two, fire."

Three underbarrel launchers thump, and the dull but authoritative explosion of hollow-shaped charges pounds my eardrums and knocks me off balance. I get back to my feet and turn toward the airlock, which now has a half-meter hole in its center. Overhead, the smoke alarm goes off, a wailing trill that's even more annoying than the security alert.

"Go, go, go," Sergeant Philbrick urges. "Ship's waiting."

We clear the next four compartments one blown airlock at a time.

"How many HEAT grenades did you bring?" I ask Philbrick after I follow him through the third hole the SI troopers have shot into inch-thick composite hatches.

"Enough to go through every airlock in this fucking place twice," he says. "Figured they may not let us leave quietly."

"Thinking like an NCO," I say, and he flashes a grin.

The last airlock on Foxtrot concourse falls to four more HEAT grenades. Despite the hands I've cupped over my ears for every salvo, I hear a sharp ringing now that feels like it will never go away again.

The SI troopers usher the skipper and Dmitry through the new provisional access hatch in the middle of the airlock. When I climb through, the edges of the hole are still hot and glowing. I help Private Watson through, and then Corporal Nez brings up the rear.

When the corporal is halfway through the hole, there's a sudden fusillade of gunfire on the other side of the damaged airlock. I can hear projectiles smacking into the high-strength laminate from the other side, and I reflexively drop to the ground and scramble away from the airlock. Corporal Nez yells and stumbles, then lets himself drop through the hole made by the grenades. He falls to the floor in an ungraceful heap.

"Contact rear!" he shouts, quite unnecessarily. Then he crawls to the other side of the hallway, away from me. More gunfire clatters against the airlock. Private Watson steps up to the side of the hole, sticks his rifle around the corner, and fires a long burst through the opening.

"Tac team's here," he shouts. "Seven, eight guys. Maybe more. We have got to go."

The airlock connecting the station with *Indy* is just twenty meters away. Several armored SI troopers come running out of the docking collar and into the concourse, weapons at the ready.

"Second Squad, lend a hand," Staff Sergeant Philbrick shouts. "Seven-plus bad guys on the other side of that hatch."

Corporal Nez takes a grenade out of his harness and pops the safety cap. He smacks the fuse end against his armor to activate the charge and chucks the grenade through the opening.

Then the airlock starts to open with a slight mechanical whine.

"Uh-oh," Corporal Nez says.

The lower edge of the airlock is maybe ten centimeters off the ground when the grenade detonates in the corridor beyond. The shock wave makes the laminate ring like a muffled gong. The airlock crawls up another ten centimeters, then twenty, then thirty. When the ragged top of the hole we made reaches the bulkhead above, the upward motion stops with a shrill and tortured metallic shriek.

"Get them into the ship," Sergeant Philbrick shouts, and points at Dmitry and me. The skipper is already halfway to the docking collar, shielded by Private Bennett, who is directly behind him to keep the bulk of his armor between the colonel and the gunfire. Two members of Second Squad dart over to where we are to provide the same service to Dmitry and me. Together, we make a rapid and highly awkward procession to the docking collar as the other SI troopers start pouring fire through the crack at the bottom of the airlock to cover our retreat. One of the tactical cops on the other side of the airlock takes a chapter out of Corporal Nez's playbook and rolls a grenade through the opening, but Staff Sergeant Philbrick stops it with his armored boot and kicks it back through. It explodes just barely on the other side of the airlock, which shudders violently with the explosion and then slams back down rapidly without any restraints. All over the corridor, multiple alarms are blaring, blending with the gunfire in a discordant crescendo.

The SI troopers usher us into the docking collar. Behind us, First Squad holds the line, falling back in turn while keeping up a covering fire aimed at the hole in the airlock. I don't even want to think about what's going to happen if one of the tactical cops decides to fire a grenade launcher down the concourse and into the docking collar while we're between the station and the ship.

Then I'm back on *Indy*, past the main airlock and inside the ship's main port-to-starboard passageway. A few moments later, the rest of First Squad come running up the docking collar and through the airlock.

"Secure the airlock," Staff Sergeant Philbrick shouts. Corporal Nez runs over to the side of the passageway and hits the emergency-lock button with the butt of his rifle. A warning klaxon blares sharply, and the airlock slides down and out into its recess in the ship's armor belt. The noise from the outside of the ship instantly cuts off.

"Seal your suits and guard this airlock," Colonel Campbell shouts over to Sergeant Philbrick. "Nothing in or out. Tell CIC I am on my way. Mr. Grayson, with me."

The combat information center is already abuzz with activity when Colonel Campbell and I step through the hatch. The colonel strides into the middle of the CIC pit. I step up to my accustomed spot on the pit rail and grasp it with both hands to steady myself.

"Sitrep," the colonel barks.

"Reactor is at full output. Propulsion online," Major Renner replies. "All personnel accounted for."

"Get us loose from the station now."

"They're not releasing the clamps, sir. We've initiated undock sequence, but they've locked us down."

"Blow the emergency locks on the docking clamps. Blow 'em off," Colonel Campbell orders.

The engineering officer hesitates for just a second before flicking to a different screen on his control panel and punching several controls in sequence.

"Aye, sir. Emergency release initiated."

A shudder goes through the hull as explosive charges blow out *Indy*'s docking receptacles and eject them from her hull. This is an emergency measure that I've not seen used in five years of fleet service. Once the mating points for the standard docking clamps are torn from the hull, *Indy* won't be able to dock with any station again. Fitting new receptacles to the hull requires a fleet yard visit and a complete hull overhaul.

"Helm, set thrusters full speed astern. Tear us loose."

"Full astern, aye," the helmsman acknowledges.

Major Renner brings up the tactical orb on the holotable. With the station taking up all the space in front of us, our field of view is limited to the hemisphere behind us.

"*Murphy* is moving into intercept position, sir."

The blue icon representing the destroyer is less than three kilometers astern and above us. Their acceleration is slow, but at this range, they don't have to go hard on the throttle to be on top of us in a minute, and there's not a weapon on the *Murphy* that can't reach us even from three klicks away.

"*Indianapolis*, power down your propulsion and your active sensors and return to your berthing spot immediately, or we will open fire."

"Testy," Colonel Campbell says. "No reply, comms. Crank up all the active gear."

"Distance from station fifty meters," the helmsman calls out. "Seventy-five. One hundred."

"As soon as we are clear, go to negative zero-four-five by zero-zero and hit the burners," Colonel Campbell orders.

"Active fire control radar," the tactical officer warns. A warning sound chirps on his console. "They are locking on to us. *Murphy* is opening forward missile tubes, sir."

"Fucking maniacs," Major Renner says. "We're too close. To them and the station."

"Go hot on the jammers and the CIWS," Colonel Campbell shouts.

"Missile launch! Vampire, vampire. Two birds—"

On the tactical display, two inverted V shapes detach from *Murphy*'s icon and race toward the center of the plot. The flight time is ludicrously short. I don't even have time to swallow hard before both missiles have covered the distance. One of them disappears just a fraction of a second before it reaches the center of the plot. The other streaks past *Indy*. I can't hear the explosion in front of the ship, but the blast's shock wave jolts the ship backwards.

"They hit the station," the tactical officer shouts. "Impact on Independence. CIWS got the other one."

"Give me a forward view. Guns, get a firing solution with the rail gun."

"Target acquired," the gunnery officer says. "They're rolling ship to bring their own rail gun to bear."

"Don't let 'em. Weapons free. Hit the sensor array in the bow, make 'em blind. If they roll around enough to unmask their gun mount, you shoot it right off that shit bucket."

"Aye, sir. Weapons free."

Murphy is shadowing us from behind and above, which means that her dorsal gun mount is on the wrong side of the ship to engage us. *Indy*'s gunnery officer takes ruthless advantage of that mistake. As *Murphy* rolls around and coasts toward us, *Indy*'s rail gun pumps out three rapid shots in one-second intervals. The tactical officer brings up the optical feed just in time for us to see the kinetic projectiles tear into the nose of the aging destroyer, sending armor shards flying. *Murphy* shudders visibly under the hammer blows. Rail guns aren't useful at longer ranges or against heavily armored ships, but not even the titanium hull plating of the destroyer can stand up to kinetic shot at point-blank range.

"Ship is clear of the berth!"

"Come to new heading negative zero-four-five by zero-zero, ahead flank," the colonel orders. "Hang on to something, everyone."

I don't need the invitation. I renew my death grip on the rail with my good hand as *Indy*'s bow thrusters fire and pitch her nose sharply downward. The thrum-thrum-thrum of the fusion propulsion system going from idle to full thrust reverberates through the hull. *Murphy* is halfway through her 180-degree roll to give her rail gun a field of fire, and our gunnery officer fires three more shells. One goes over *Murphy*'s hull and screams off into space. The second hits the side of the hull at a steep angle, and the projectile ricochets off the armor. The third round hammers right into the armored rail gun mount. There's the puff of an impact and then a soundlessly expanding cloud of metal debris. Then the mass of the station intersperses itself between the optical sensor and *Murphy* as we pass underneath Independence.

"Good shooting, Guns," Colonel Campbell says. "Keep the jammers running. Let's keep the station between us and them for as long as we can. Tactical, give me a plot."

The tactical officer expands the scan range of the holotable display. There are a handful of blue icons around Independence, most of them sitting still in station berths. Other than *Indy* and *Murphy*, three more ships are under way in the vicinity, but none are on an intercept course.

"Helm, make your new course positive zero-four-zero by negative zero-zero-three. Follow the spine of the station. Stay on the throttle."

"Let's hope nobody backs out of their parking spot in a hurry," Major Renner says.

"We need to be clear and in the black before *Murphy* catches up and blows us into stardust," the colonel says. "We got exceedingly lucky with that exchange. If they had been below us instead of above, we'd be an expanding cloud of debris right now."

"Not bad, though," Major Renner grins. "Punching a destroyer in the nose, with a little OCS."

"No, not bad at all," Colonel Campbell agrees. "But we probably killed a dozen sailors on that destroyer just now. I'm not going to feel proud about that any time soon."

Murphy coasts to the underside of Independence Station and onto our tactical display again a few minutes later, but they're not pulling military acceleration.

"They're trailing debris," the tactical officer says. "We hurt 'em good."

"Four kinetic hits at knife-fight range. Wouldn't be surprised if those went halfway from bow to stern," Major Renner says.

We are well away from the station, coasting ballistically with all the active sensors turned off again, doing what *Indy* does best. With every passing minute, we're putting more and more empty space between us and *Murphy*, Independence Station, and Earth.

"Anything on active?" Colonel Campbell asks.

"Some short-range ship-to-ship comms. Nothing directed our way, though."

"We just stole an OCS out of the docking clamps and shot it out with a fleet destroyer," Major Renner muses. "Why isn't half the remaining fleet looking for us with all their active sensors running?"

"Good question. This whole thing stinks from top to bottom." Colonel Campbell reaches into the holographic plot display and draws a trajectory with his finger.

"Do a corrective boost, and bring us around the other side of Independence. I want to get a better idea of what's going on. Passive sensors only."

"Aye, sir." The XO reads off the new course data to the helmsman.

"Three-second burn, on my mark."

"Three-second burn, aye."

The pleasant numbness wrapped around my left hand is slowly giving way to a decidedly uncomfortable throbbing ache that gets sharper by the minute. The meds in the trauma pack are wearing off. I stick my left hand underneath my right armpit and grimace at the pressure. I didn't spend much time yet thinking about what's underneath that trauma pack—or rather, what isn't there anymore—and I don't really care to.

"Mr. Grayson," Colonel Campbell says.

"Sir?"

"You look like absolute hell. Go to sick bay and have the medical officer look at that. You're bleeding all over my CIC, son."

I manage to muster a half-cocked grin. "Yes, sir. Sorry, sir."

I turn and walk toward the CIC hatch, leaving *Indy*'s command crew to their work. Now that it looks like we won't blow up in the next few seconds or minutes, I suppose I have the luxury of seeing to my own battle damage.

When I step through the hatch and into the passageway beyond, the tension goes out of me like the oxygen from a decompressing airlock, and I just feel drained. We made it through to Earth, against all odds. I should be in a fleet mess right now, eating fresh food and catching up on messages from Halley and my mother. Instead I am in a battle-weary warship again, on the run from our own people, and on my way to see how much of my left hand I'll get to keep. Right now I very much wish I had stayed on New Svalbard with Sergeant Fallon and her fellow HD grunts.

Not the best idea you have this week, I think, and the voice in my head has a heavy Russian accent.

CHAPTER 13

WE TAKE WHAT WE'RE SERVED

Indy's medical specialist is a female corpsman named Randall. She's an E-6, a staff sergeant like me, and I've seen her in the NCO mess often, but we've not had any interactions other than me picking up some no-go pills from sick bay a few times on our trip from New Svalbard.

"The broken nose I can fix in about five minutes," she says when she has examined my various defects. "Won't even leave a mark. That hand, though. How'd you manage that?"

"Reached in front of a muzzle. I think the blast did more damage than the bullets."

"Oh, they both did their share," she says. "Trauma pack meds wearing off yet?"

I nod and grimace in reply. She scoots back her examination chair and gets up. *Indy*'s sick bay is tiny, just a little room about twice the size of my berth, and much of it is taken up by the treatment and surgery chair. There are lockers lined up in front of one of the bulkheads, and she opens one and takes out an injector unit. I try to ignore the searing pain in my left hand while she draws up a dose of whatever it is she's about to give me.

"This will take the edge off. I don't think you're a dope seeker."

She winks at me and scoots back over to the treatment chair. "Annnnd . . . here we go."

I feel the pinprick of the needle in the hollow of my left arm. Almost instantly, I feel a wave of dizziness and nausea flooding my brain at an alarming speed.

"Hang in there for a second, and it will pass," Corpsman Randall says. "Feels bad at first, but it gets better."

"It gets better" is a massive understatement. A few moments after the initial feeling of intense nausea that almost makes me throw up, a massive wave of relaxation and relief washes over me. The pain in my hand goes from almost unbearable to nonexistent in just a few seconds. I let my head tilt back against the headrest of the chair and let out a loud sigh.

"Not bad, huh? Modern pharmaceutics are magic in a syringe."

"Dark, delicious magic," I murmur, and she laughs.

"I'm going to immobilize your left arm for a bit and clean up this mess. Try not to look at it. Take a nap if you want. I don't mind."

"Not really in the mood for a nap," I say, but my eyelids are getting heavy as I say it. Whatever she put into my bloodstream not only took away all the pain, it also put me into a very relaxed mood. I could almost forget the fact that I am on a damaged warship in the middle of what is now a three-front war. Compared to the way I've been feeling since we left Earth to be stranded in the Fomalhaut system, this is damn near euphoria. I close my eyes and listen to the ever-present humming of the ship's environmental and life-support systems.

"How did you end up on *Indy*?" Randall asks. "I've seen you around since New Svalbard, but I never asked."

"I'm a combat controller," I mumble. "I'm babysitting the Russian sergeant who has the access codes to the SRA Alcubierre node. Which is a tightly guarded secret, by the way."

"I won't tell," she says.

My left arm is numb now, and I only feel anything from that part of my body when Corpsman Randall tugs on my hand hard enough to move the arm in its shoulder joint. I remember her advice and keep my eyes closed and away from whatever mess she's stitching up.

"I served under the skipper once," I say. "Five years ago, on *Versailles.* At first contact with the Lankies."

"You were there, huh? I was just out of boot when that happened."

"Where'd you go to boot?" I ask.

"NACRD Orem. January to March '08."

"No shit? Me, too. Which platoon?"

"1068."

"I was 1066," I say. "Corpsman Randall, it looks like our boots churned some of the same dust."

"At the same time," she says. "Small world."

"Getting smaller all the time," I say. I wonder how many graduates of our respective boot camp platoons have been killed in action. There were a whole lot of destroyed hulls in orbit around Mars—dozens of ships, thousands of sailors.

"You made staff sergeant pretty fast," I say. "I thought I got to E-6 quickly."

"Yeah, well. Corpsman billet means you're always in demand. Same as you, I imagine. You're doing good, by the way, all things considered. This shouldn't be too much of a bother."

"Whatever you gave me, I'm not sure I'd mind if you started sawing that arm off."

"I don't think it's going to come to that," she says. "Although you got yourself pretty mangled, Staff Sergeant."

"Andrew," I say. "We're the same rank. Same time in service."

"Nancy," she says. "Now use this opportunity to take a nap while I stitch you up and fix that broken nose. We may be the same rank, but you're in my sick bay, and you will follow the orders of your medical professional."

"Yes, ma'am."

I do as ordered and let the medication and the ambient noise of *Indy*'s distant business lull me into a warm and easy sleep.

When Corpsman Randall wakes me up again, the warm and pleasant feeling from the medication is mostly gone. My left arm is still numb, but my brain is no longer fuzzy, and even if there had been any of the slight euphoria left, it would have dissipated the moment I opened my eyes and looked down at my hand. It looks asymmetrical, off balance, more like a claw than the appendage I've been using to manipulate my environment for the last quarter century. Where before the edge of my hand flared out into a slight fleshy curve, now there's a straight line going from my wrist to the base of my middle finger, which is now the outmost digit. The wound is dressed in new adhesive bandage, so I can't see what the damage looks like after the corpsman's cleanup job, but it looks like there's an awful lot of substance gone.

"How are you feeling?" she asks.

"Like I had too much lousy soy beer last night," I reply without taking my eyes off the bandage. "What's the verdict on the hand?"

"The bad news is that your guitar-playing days are over."

"I never learned to play an instrument. Guess I won't be starting, either."

"They'll fit you for new fingers at Great Lakes," Randall says. "We've come a long way in the medical cybernetics field. Won't be your old fingers, but they'll work just as well."

"Yeah, they can do magic now," I say. "Friend of mine has a new lower leg courtesy of the Medical Corps. She says it's much better than the old one. Says she wouldn't mind having another to match the set."

"I cleaned everything up and removed all the bone shards. Whatever hit your hand pulverized both your MCP joints on the outer two fingers."

"The what?"

"Metacarpophalangeal joints," she says, and holds up her hand. She taps the knuckle joints at the base of her fingers. "Those right there. That's going to be a bitch to fix. And they'll need to do it soon if they want to reconnect those nerve endings."

"How soon?"

"The sooner, the better," Randall says. "I just cleared up the worst of the mess and fused you up a bit. That hand needs a lot more attention than I am qualified to give. You need to see a fleet physician, and soon."

"That may be a problem." I sit up and wince. "I don't think we're on speaking terms with the fleet right now."

She turns to her medicine cabinets again and takes out a medication cylinder. She pops it open, verifies the contents, and closes it again. Then she hands it to me. I take it with my good hand.

"I'm not going to put a DNA lock on those. Take for pain as needed. No more than two every four hours, though, or you'll be shitting bricks for a month straight. And don't operate a starship or heavy ordnance-loading gear. There's a fair chance these won't do the job completely for the sort of pain you'll have soon. If it gets too much, come to me and I'll shoot you up with something stronger."

"Thanks." I put the cylinder into the chest pocket of my CDU blouse, which is still stained with the blood from my nose. "What if I can't get this hand seen by a navy doc for a month or two?"

"Then you may have to retrain how to tie your boots with a hand and a half," Corpsman Randall says.

The combat information center is back to its usual level of focused activity when I walk through the hatch again. *Indy*'s supply sergeant issued me a new set of fatigues, and the blood is gone from my face, but the thick adhesive bandage pack on my hand keeps me from feeling restored.

"Mr. Grayson," the colonel says when he sees me. "How's the hand?"

"What's left of it seems fine," I say. "Two fingers still gone, though."

Colonel Campbell grimaces when he sees my wrapped hand. "Those stupid, trigger-happy SP morons."

"He didn't mean to shoot me. He meant to put one into Dmitry."

"Yeah, I saw that. If it's any consolation at all, your fingers bought us our return trip to Fomalhaut. XO?"

"Yes, sir," Major Renner says.

"Get Sergeant Chistyakov down to CIC."

"Aye, sir." Major Renner picks up the handset on the console in front of her.

Colonel Campbell walks over to the holotable in the middle of the CIC pit. I follow him down and look at the plot. We are making a racetrack pattern between Earth and Luna. There are small clusters of pale blue and red icons dotting the plot, NAC and SRA ships in small task groups or by themselves, docking at their respective coalitions' space stations or patrolling in orbit.

"We're in stealth mode," the colonel says. "Nobody's actively looking for us right now, but we're staying low-profile because we don't have the time to sort out just what exactly is going on around here." He nods to the date and time display on the CIC bulkhead. "We've burned up two weeks just getting here, and the return trip is going to take longer."

"Fuel tanks are full at least. Good thing we ran out of fuel when we did," Major Renner says.

"How are we on chow and drinking water?"

"We have enough rations in storage to make the return trip. Water's more iffy. I started replenishment with the station on a hunch when we docked, but we had to cut short due to our, uh, rushed departure. We're half-full on the potable."

"Should be okay if we don't all take long showers every day."

"Yes, sir. We'll manage."

I look at the plot and exhale slowly. We are so close to Luna, closer than I've been since I visited Halley at Drop Ship U. I've made it back, just like I promised, but I have no way to tell her that I'm here, no way to let her know that I made it close enough to see the above-surface structures of Fleet School through the optical feed without any magnification. I'm here, and now I have to leave again, and I may not come back. This ship is tired, her crew is worn-out, and we've dodged almost-certain death too many times now for the odds to stay on our side. I've used up all my luck and a bunch of other grunts' besides: Stratton's, Paterson's, that of the SI troopers who bought it on the Sirius Ad drop, that of the HD mudlegs who burned up or got ripped to shreds by Shrike cannon fire in New Longyearbyen, and God knows how many others who have fought and died near me when I had the luck to make it back onto the drop ship and back to the carrier every time. Feeling a crushing sense of disappointment and despair because I won't get to see my fiancée again after all seems petty and selfish, but it's what I feel nonetheless, and I can't help it.

Behind me, the main CIC hatch opens, and Dmitry walks in, escorted by Corporal Nez. I nod at him, and he returns the nod.

Colonel Campbell picks up the receiver on the console in front of him.

"1MC, all-ship announcement," he says to the comms officer.

"1MC, all hands," the comms officer confirms.

The colonel takes a long, slow breath. Then he puts the receiver against his ear and presses the transmit bar on the side.

"All hands, this is the CO. Listen up. We are in stealth, about fifty thousand kilometers from Luna, and the XO is preparing the ship for our return trip to Fomalhaut. I know you've all been manning your duty stations for far longer than any of us had anticipated when we set out for this cruise. Our little ship wasn't made for deep-space combat ops, but that's what we've been doing for the last two months straight. I know you're all tired, and if it were up to me, I'd give you all a few weeks of leave right now and hand this boat over to a relief crew. But that is not what we're about to do.

"What we have done—what we are doing right now—is flat-out mutiny. We have resisted arrest, fought military police officers, engaged in a gun battle with civilian police, and we have stolen this ship out of the dock against orders. We have engaged another fleet unit in self-defense and damaged them, probably killed a few of their crew. If another fleet ship catches us here in the solar system, we will probably end up directly in the high-risk ward at Leavenworth if they don't blow us out of space instantly. This is not a legal gray area like our refusal to follow orders above New Svalbard. They ordered this ship's command staff relieved, and *Indy* to join the defense of Earth. We not only disobeyed those orders; we resisted with force of arms.

"But I chose this course of action because we have a task force and thirty thousand people waiting for our return in Fomalhaut. We need to let them know how to get home because they will not transition back blindly. This is our mission, and we will fulfill it. I am not about to sacrifice that many lives to add what is ultimately an insignificant amount of firepower to Earth's defensive picket. You've all seen what the Lankies can do; if they show up here, our presence isn't going to make a bit of a difference.

"Anyone who is having second thoughts: I cannot in good conscience disobey my orders and expect you all to follow the ones I am giving. If you want off this ship, report to the NCO mess within the next fifteen minutes. We will fly you out with the drop ship and deliver you to the nearest fleet facility on this side of Luna. I repeat: fifteen minutes. CO out."

Colonel Campbell puts the handset back into its receptacle and closes his eyes for a moment. Then he looks over to the holotable display and straightens out his uniform tunic, which wasn't at all rumpled.

"XO," he says.

"Sir." Major Renner steps up next to him.

"Have the drop-ship pilot prep his bird and put it on standby. Then go down to the NCO mess and collect whoever wants off this boat. Execute."

"Aye, sir." Major Renner picks up the comms handset and turns away.

"I can't make you the same offer, Sergeant Chistyakov," Colonel Campbell says to Dmitry. "We need you to open the door for us again, or your comrades over New Svalbard will have a bad month. Unless you want to give us the code and leave your suit with us. In that case, I'd have the drop ship take you to Luna with the others and deliver you to the nearest SRA military post."

"Cannot give code." Dmitry smiles and shakes his head slightly.

"Then I guess you're staying with us for the ride back. Sorry."

"I have orders to come back to *Minsk* with little imperialist spy ship of yours." Dmitry shrugs. "I follow orders. Friends in

144th Spaceborne Assault Regiment will be very mad if they die because I do not come back."

Colonel Campbell smiles the tiniest of smiles. "Glad to hear it, Sergeant." Then he looks at me. "What about you, Mr. Grayson?"

"What about me, sir?" I ask.

"You're badly wounded. That hand of yours needs to be seen by a surgeon, in a proper medical facility. You want to take the ship to Luna, I will not think any less of you." He nods at my bandaged hand. "There's no glory in losing that when you don't have to. I don't think we need to worry about Sergeant Chistyakov on the ride back. Take that seat on the drop ship."

The sudden wild hope I feel is almost like a living animal trying to work its way out of my rib cage. I look from Colonel Campbell to Dmitry and back to the colonel.

"They'll arrest me the second I set foot onto Luna, sir."

"They probably will. Maybe not, if word hasn't gotten to them yet. In either case, they'll send you to a medical center to get fixed. We'll all end up in the brig anyway if we make it back. Either way, you'll be ahead of the game."

"May I consult with the corpsman, sir?"

"Of course you may," Colonel Campbell says. "You have"—he checks the clock on the bulkhead—"eleven minutes to decide before I have the drop ship warmed up. Go ahead and make your choice."

"Yes, sir."

I leave the pit and walk over to the CIC's hatch. When I reach the threshold, I glance back. Colonel Campbell is over by the holotable sketching on the plot with a light pen. Dmitry is over on the edge of the CIC pit, hands folded in front of his chest, watching the activity around him with the usual relaxed amusement on his face, like someone who is listening to a friend telling a familiar joke to someone else. He sees me looking over at him and inclines his head in my direction. I return his nod and walk out.

Corpsman Randall is in the passageway in front of the sick-bay berth when I get down to her deck. She's securing the hatch when she sees me coming down the passageway, and she pauses with her hand on the locking lever.

"Back so soon? Meds not doing the job?"

"Meds are fine," I say. Then I notice that she has a small pack slung across her shoulder. "Are you going over to Luna?"

She frowns and shakes her head curtly. "That's a negative. I'm the only medical specialist on this ship. If I leave, nobody's going to get any care that doesn't come out of a bottle."

"Don't you have family on Earth? You don't sound like a colony brat."

"Yeah, I have family." Her eyes narrow a little. "I have a little girl who's seven and a husband who's a civil servant. Down there, in Virginia." She nods at the nearby bulkhead. "I haven't seen them in eleven months. And right now I am making my peace with the idea of never seeing them again. So if you wouldn't mind making your business quick, I would be much obliged."

"Sorry," I say. "Didn't mean to rub it in."

She looks down at the arti-grav tiles on the deck. "It's not like you don't have people on Earth," she says after a moment. "We all do, right?"

"My mom," I say. "Down in Boston, in the ritzy part of PRC-7. And my fiancée, over on Luna."

"What did you want to see me about just now?"

"The skipper says I should take the ride to Luna. If I don't get this hand treated for another month maybe—"

"You should go," she says immediately. "I'm no neurosurgeon, but I know that a day or even a week is much better than a month when it comes to cybernetic implants. You want to use those fingers for more than cosmetic purposes."

"Thanks for the advice," I say.

"Luna, huh?" Corpsman Randall says when I turn to leave.

"Yeah. Stone's throw away. Told her I'd be back in time for our wedding."

"You should keep your promise," she says. "Marriage is great. Make your own joy. God knows the universe doesn't throw much our way right now."

She gives me a curt smile and finishes securing the sick-bay hatch.

"Whatever you decide to do, best of luck, Andrew."

"You, too, Nancy," I say. I watch as she walks down the passageway and disappears at the next intersection.

I check my chrono. Five minutes to report to the NCO mess for a ride to Luna.

I could see Halley again today. We could get married tomorrow. And if we all die, at least we'll die together. The world is about to end. What does it all matter in the end?

There's Halley, and Mom. Then there's Sergeant Fallon, Constable Guest, Dr. Stewart, Corpsman Randall. If I go, I get to—maybe—spend some more time with Halley before it all goes to shit. Is it going to make a difference if I stay on *Indy* and make the trip back to Fomalhaut, risk getting stranded in space and starving or suffocating, or getting blotted out by a Lanky ship? If I don't stay on *Indy*, and they get into a bind where my presence could make the tiniest bit of a difference—

Not that I'd ever know in the end.

I check my chrono again. Four minutes, ticking down.

I walk down the passageway to the next intersection. Left: the way to the staircase below, where the NCO mess is. Right: the connector to the main passageway that leads back up to CIC.

I look at my bandaged hand. It has a vaguely triangular shape to it now, like a crustacean claw. This is not what I want to look at for the rest of my life.

Then I hear the voice of Sergeant Burke in my head. My boot camp instructor sounds as clear as if he were standing right next to me in this narrow passageway.

Nobody gives a shit what we want. We take what we're served, and we ask for seconds, and that's the way it goes.

We take what we're served, I think. But sometimes there's a menu, and we get to pick. Shitty choices, but choices.

I know which way to go, of course. I've known it since I left CIC a few minutes ago. I'm already hating myself for it, but I would hate myself for the other choice, too, and maybe just a little more.

I turn left, toward the NCO mess. I'll have to go to my berth and fetch a few things first.

The NCO mess is empty when I step through the hatch a little while later. I check my chrono to see that I've missed the fifteen-minute window by three minutes. I turn on my heels and race down the passageway to the staircase that leads below.

On the flight deck, the engines of *Indy*'s solitary drop ship are growling in standby. The tail hatch is open, and there are several people in the cargo hold, getting situated in the jump seats. Major Renner is standing at the bottom of the ramp. I trot down to the tail end of the ship, and she turns around when she hears my boots on the hard deck.

"Staff Sergeant Grayson," she says. "You almost missed your ride."

"I'm not going, ma'am."

She raises an eyebrow. "Didn't the skipper order you to go and get that hand fixed?"

"He didn't order, ma'am. He strongly suggested."

"So you're staying with us for the ride back."

"Yes, ma'am. I suppose I am."

I hold up the two small standard mail containers I prepared hastily in my berth just a few minutes ago.

"I was hoping to pass these on for someone to deliver to Luna, drop 'em in a mail tube for me."

Major Renner looks at the two sealed plastic envelopes, mild surprise on her face. Then she inclines her head toward the open cargo bay of the drop ship behind her.

"Hurry up," she says.

I trudge up the tail ramp and look around in the interior. There are six sailors in the jump seats to my left and right. I don't know any of them except by occasional sight in the ship's passageways, but they are all wearing bandages or flexcasts, which means they are the sailors who were wounded when the Lankies shot up *Indy* a few days ago. There are four dark green body bags in the middle aisle—the KIA we suffered in the same attack. All of the fleet sailors are junior enlisted, and despite the fact that I'm in a hurry, I don't feel comfortable entrusting any of them with what I carry. I wrote a letter to Halley and one to my mother, old-fashioned handwritten mail that will have to do in the absence of MilNet access. I can't leave the system again without at least some attempt to say a few last things to the two people who mean the most to me.

The drop ship's crew chief sits in his usual jump seat by the forward bulkhead, in a nook behind the onboard armory next to the narrow passage that leads to the cockpit. Outside, the noise level increases tenfold as the pilot revs the engines up to operational thrust.

The crew chief is an E-7 named Williamson. He wears a barely regulation mustache, and he has a rather large knife strapped to his flight suit's chest armor upside down. I've exchanged a few words with him in the NCO mess on occasion. He looks up at me expectantly as I approach his jump seat.

"Would you drop something into the mail chute for me when you do the turnaround at Luna?" I ask. "I'll talk the Russian out of some hooch to share if you do."

Williamson smirks and holds out his hand. "You don't need to bribe me, but I won't turn it down, either," he says.

I hand him the two envelopes, and he stuffs them into the chest pocket of his armor without looking at them.

"I'll send 'em off for you, Staff Sergeant. Now get off this thing if you're not coming along. You're holding up traffic."

I nod my thanks and get off Sergeant First Class Williamson's drop ship. I've been with a drop-ship jock for long enough to know the true and proper ownership status of the ship—the crew chief owns it, and the pilots get to take it out for a spin every once in a while.

Major Renner is already up by the flight deck hatch. I jog up the stairs of the flight deck's gallery to catch up with her. Behind me, the drop ship's tail ramp rises with a hydraulic hum, and then locks in place. The orange warning light on the Wasp's tail starts flashing.

"Clear the deck for flight operations," an automated overhead announcement says. "Secure the flight deck hatch."

I follow Major Renner out into the passageway, and the flight deck hatch closes and locks behind us.

Major Renner walks over to a comms unit on the bulkhead and picks up the handset. "CIC, XO. The bird is departing." She listens to a reply I can't hear this far away from the handset. "Six, sir. All the walking wounded. Plus the four KIA. Nobody else showed." She pauses to listen for the reply. "Aye, sir."

Major Renner replaces the headset. "And that's that," she says to me. "Last ride off this party cruise just left."

She goes up the passageway toward the junction that leads to the topside ladder. I watch her leave while I listen to the sounds of the drop ship spinning up its engines to full power behind the flight deck hatch.

Some party.

Indy doesn't have any exterior windows. With optical sensors all over the outer hull, there's no need for holes in the ship's skin that would reduce its stealth and compromise hull integrity. There is no observation lounge, no way for me to look at Earth and Luna as we prepare to leave the system again. I can't even go back to my berth and put on my armor to patch into the ship's optical feed because I don't have administrative access to the neural network. All I can do is to climb down to the lowest deck and go aft, where the auxiliary network cluster was before the Lankies shot a penetrator through it. The damage-control teams have patched the holes in the hull and put a mobile airlock in front of the torn-up section of the passageway.

I walk up to the bulkhead and put my hand against it. Right now, only a few dozen centimeters of laminate armor, neural wiring, insulation, and spall liner separate me from the vacuum of space beyond. Luna is on the other side of that vacuum, five thousand kilometers away.

"I'm sorry," I say into the quiet, down here where there's only the faint hum of machinery and the distant thrumming of the propulsion system. *Indy* is the quietest warship I've ever been on, so silent you can hear yourself think when no one else is around.

I don't want to say good-bye. I don't want to believe that this is the closest I'll ever be to Halley again—to home—because if I end up giving in to that dread, I fear that I will just pop the seals on this mobile airlock and step out into space for a quick and very final glimpse of Earth. But there are close to a hundred people on this ship, and every last one of them would love to be off this thing and home with whomever they left behind, and I don't have the first right to feel sorry for myself.

CHAPTER 14

SKIRTING THE PICKET

Colonel Campbell looks up from the holotable plot when I walk back into the CIC. "I thought you were taking the shuttle to Luna, Mr. Grayson."

"Didn't want to run the risk of getting arrested or shot, sir," I say.

"Bullshit," he replies. There's the tiniest hint of a smile showing in the corners of his mouth.

"I'm a combat controller, and I'm neural-networks qualified, sir. There's a lot of stuff I can help fix if it breaks on the way back."

"I appreciate that," he says. "And I'm not just saying that. We're running a short crew now. I'm down six more enlisted, and the XO is having to spread around what's left. We're so far out of our design mission that it's getting ludicrous. A little OCS doing detached duty as a deep-space recon unit."

I look at the plot display, which doesn't look much different from the way it did a little while ago—small groups of ships from the various coalitions in orbital-patrol patterns. Blue for NAC, red for SRA, green for EU, even a few purple icons representing ships from the South American Union. The SAU ships used to have dark yellow assigned to them in our computers, but it looked too much like the orange they picked for Lanky ships, and spotting that color on a plot generally causes a great deal of anxiety in CICs all over the fleet, so they changed the SAU color code to purple. Other than the SRA and the NAC, none of the world's fleets are deep space, which means a force that can conduct and sustain interstellar operations. The Euros and the South Americans are content to mine the solar system resources and limit their defense budgets to local defense units. After the destruction of the bulk of the SRA and NAC fleets around Mars, maybe we've been demoted to local defense capabilities as well.

"Sir, the *Murphy* is separating from Independence," the tactical officer says. "Looks like they're departing. They're moving off at ten meters per, and accelerating."

"Really," Colonel Campbell says. He reaches into the plot display and pans and zooms the scale until the icon for Independence Station is in the center of the screen segment. A pale blue icon labeled "DD-770 MURPHY" is inching away from the station slowly but steadily.

"ETA on the drop ship?"

"Nineteen minutes, sir," the XO says. "They've just finished unloading."

"Tell them to expedite, skip the window-cleaning. Tactical, keep a really close eye on *Murphy*."

"Aye, sir."

"Think they know where we are?" Major Renner asks.

"*Indy*? No. We haven't gotten anything on our active warning kit. We're a hundred thousand kilometers away, and their passive gear is shit. But maybe they saw the drop ship pop up when the pilot lit the burners. We'll see. Let's be ready to hit the throttle if they come our way."

"Aye, sir," the XO confirms.

"The passive kit on this boat is the best I've ever seen," I say. "We don't even need radar with optics like that."

"It's the best in the fleet," Colonel Campbell says. "We should have built a hundred more of these things instead of those stupid big-ass hundred-thousand-ton carriers."

"Those are what makes a deep-space navy, aren't they?"

"They're too big and too damn expensive, and they're one-trick ponies. They're good for leading planetary assaults, and that's it. This ship weighs five percent of that and has a tenth the firepower, and we managed to get past the Lankies when nobody else did. It sucks at offensive ops, but maybe that's not where our focus should have been all these years. Look where it got us."

"Where the hell is he going?" the tactical officer wonders out loud a little while later. The icon for the *Murphy* is moving away from the space station, but her new trajectory points right toward open space.

"He's trailing air and debris, but he's not making for Gateway or the fleet yard," the XO says. "Where the hell is he going with that damaged ship?"

The tactical officer extends the current trajectory of *Murphy* on the central plot. "Nothing there. No fleet yard, no space stations, not even a mining outpost."

"Well, I'm sure he's not taking a ship full of holes for a little joyride around the inner solar system for the hell of it." Colonel Campbell taps his fingers on the edge of the holotable.

"Track him. As soon as the drop ship is secure, we follow him at a safe distance. Just for a little while. I'm curious why they wanted us on such a short leash."

The drop ship returns to *Indy* fifteen minutes later. While *Indy* is a stealth ship, the drop ship is not, and if they're going to pinpoint the location of the OCS, the docking sequence is our most vulnerable phase. But no active radars light us up, and there's no contact on the tactical display suddenly changing course to come gunning for us.

"Bird's back in the barn," the XO says a little while later.

"Take us out and shadow that destroyer," Colonel Campbell orders. "Mind your distance and stay on their stern. Make it ten thousand klicks."

"There hasn't been a lick of active radiation from them since we popped them in the snout," Major Renner says.

"We took out their front array, which is probably why we're still afloat. But let's not take chances. The second it looks like they've spotted us, we're turning about and going full burn. No point pushing our luck."

We've been pushing our luck since we set out for Fomalhaut, I think, and look at the spot where my two missing fingers used to be. I can feel the pain throbbing underneath the chemical layer of fuzzy bliss from the painkillers, and I'm very thankful for modern chemistry right now.

Murphy leaves Earth and Luna behind, and *Indy* follows.

The destroyer pulls low acceleration, probably because of the damage we inflicted. The Blue-class destroyers are large ships, almost three times the size of *Indy* and much better armored and armed, but they are deep-space combatants and not even slightly stealthy. We are following in their wake, where the noise from their own engines make their passive sensors as good as blind.

We are under way and on *Murphy*'s tail for just a little under four hours when the tactical officer perks up and updates the holotable display.

"We have some active radar sweeps ahead. Two—make that three sources."

On the holotable, three pale blue icons appear on the edge of our scanning range. They have three-dimensional lozenge-shaped zones projected around them. Our passive gear is picking up the radar transmitters, but it hasn't pinpointed the exact locations of the sources yet, so the lozenges mark the zones where the contacts are likely to be.

"Source?" Colonel Campbell asks.

"Military, definitely Commonwealth units. ELINT is sorting out the profiles right now," the tactical officer replies. "Stand by."

"There's precisely squat out here according to the charts," Major Renner says. "This is not even a travel lane. Military or civilian."

"Let's see what we have here," the colonel says. "Just keep an eye on those active sources. We come even close to detection, we break off and leave them be."

It takes the computer and the electronic-intelligence suite of *Indy* another twenty minutes to sort out the radar transmissions in front of us. One by one, the contact icons on the tactical display change from "UNKNOWN PRESUMED FRIENDLY" to actual class designations. The wedges that mark the location of the transmitting ships shrink with every second we spend in pursuit of *Murphy*.

"It's another picket," the XO says. "A frigate, Treaty-class. Another frigate, unknown class. And a Hammerhead cruiser."

"All new stuff," Colonel Campbell says. "Why are they a million klicks from Earth instead of in orbit?"

"Pretty sure *Murphy* is talking to them. I'm getting burst transmission noise," the electronic-warfare officer says from his console.

"They're talking on tight-beam."

"Not tight-beam, sir. It's encrypted ship to ship, but it's not a fleet key. At least none we have in the computer."

"Private conversation. Interesting." Colonel Campbell leans over the holotable and rests his palms on the glass surface. His fingertips poke through the holographic orb of the tactical display, which re-forms itself around his hand.

"Change course to negative zero-two-zero by zero-four-five. Hold that for ten minutes and then return to the old heading, go parallel to *Murphy* again. And deploy the passive arrays, too."

Over the next hour, the plot slowly shifts as *Murphy* approaches the picket line of unknown Commonwealth ships and we trail behind and below. The picket ships are in a patrol pattern, sweeping the space in front of them with active radar. *Indy* has to make several course corrections to avoid the invisible searchlights of the radar transmitters, and each turn takes us a little more off course from wherever *Murphy* is going.

"That's about as far as we'll be able to sneak in without getting lit up, I think," Colonel Campbell says after the radar-warning-threat meter pegs from green into yellow twice in the span of a minute. "Bring her about and coast ballistic. Make your new heading positive one-two-zero by two-one-zero."

"Hang on," the tactical officer chimes in. "Multiple contacts on passive, bearing positive twenty degrees. Five . . . seven . . . ten . . . Sir, I have at least a dozen distinct contacts popping up on optical."

"Go for magnification and verify," the colonel says. Everyone in the CIC looks over at the holotable, where a cluster of pale blue icons has popped into existence on the far upper edge of our situational-awareness bubble. The picket ships are keeping us at bay, but *Murphy* is passing through the picket and heading right for that new cluster of contacts.

"Any of them squawking ID?"

"I'm getting IFF from the picket ships. The Hammerhead is the *Phalanx*. The frigates are *Lausanne* and . . . *Acheron*?" He looks over at the colonel with a slightly bewildered expression on his face. "Sir, I've never heard of a frigate named *Acheron* in the fleet."

"There is no *Acheron*," Major Renner says.

On the holotable, the closest blue icons update with ship names and hull numbers: "CG-761 PHALANX," "FF-481 LAUSANNE." Putting lie to the XO's statement, the letters on the third icon change from "UNKNOWN" to "FF-901 ACHERON."

"What the hell is an *Acheron*?" our weapons officer says.

"A river," I reply. "A river in the Greek underworld. Mythology."

Colonel Campbell gives me a curt smile that looks slightly amused and a little approving. "Wonder if we'll bump into *Styx* and *Lethe* out here, too," he says.

The weapons officer's look is blank, and the colonel sighs ever so slightly.

"Rivers," he says. "More rivers in the Greek underworld."

"Yes, sir."

"Let's just hope that whoever named that thing just has a hard-on for the classics," the colonel says. "That name's a shitty omen otherwise."

"Why is that, sir?" the weapons officer asks.

"Acheron's the river the souls of the dead must cross to get to the underworld," I supply.

The frigates and the cruiser are performing competent patrol patterns, with interlocking sensor coverage and tight execution. *Indy* maps out the area kilometer by kilometer, coasting on a parabolic trajectory just at the edge of the picket force's detection range. Minute by minute, we close the distance a little, and our passive sensors yield more data bit by bit. One active sweep of *Indy*'s radar would map out our entire awareness bubble to the meter and centimeter and tell us the location of every scrap of metal bigger than a trash can in this part of space, but that would be like a thief in a dark building strapping a ten-thousand-watt flashlight to his head.

"There's a lot of ships out here," Major Renner says. The cluster of blue icons on the edge of our sensor range is growing bigger—every few minutes, the computer adds an icon or two to the group as we get closer and the passive arrays sniff out more radiation sources and visual contacts.

"Eight, then, twelve . . . fourteen. They have a big-ass task force assembling in the middle of nowhere."

"Something else, too." The tactical officer brings up a window on the holographic plot and increases the size and scan range. "Too big for a ship, too small for a station. And it's right in the middle of all that traffic."

Colonel Campbell studies the image from *Indy*'s optical array. The ships we've plotted are mere specks on the screen, all clustered around an asymmetrical white-gray structure.

"It's an anchorage," he says. "They have a deep-space anchorage out here. Maybe a small fleet yard. Look at that. There's the outriggers—that's the central part right there." He pokes at the display with his index finger and pans the image by moving his hand clockwise.

"Whatever they're doing out there, they're keeping really tight EMCON," the tactical officer says.

"Yeah, I'm sure they are. How many recon drones do we have left on the ship?"

"Fourteen, sir. We used up half our loadout in Fomalhaut." Major Renner looks over to the ELINT officer, who confirms the statement with a nod.

"Prep them for launch. I want to make a box with them all around this anchorage." The colonel points at the display and starts marking locations on the plot.

"They're picketing right here, and whatever they're assembling is on the other side of that anchorage. Put four birds on the near side—here, here, here, and here. Then four more on the far side at these coordinates." He marks the spots by poking them with his finger. "We'll bracket the whole area, box 'em in. I want to keep tabs on every ship that comes or goes."

"Aye, sir. Weps, let's get those birds into the tubes and warmed up."

Indy's autonomous stealth drones are like miniature starships. They have propulsion, guidance systems, sensor packages, and a comms suite. I don't know half the technological voodoo that goes into them because they're superclassified secret tech, but I know from my Neural Networks days that a recon ship with the new drones tied into its sensor network is worth a whole squadron of the old ships that don't have the drones and the new datalink infrastructure they require.

"Recon birds are ready in tubes two, four, five, and six," the weapons officer says when the loading procedure is complete. The drones are sized to fit and launch from *Indy*'s standard ship-to-ship missile tubes—*Indy* lacks external launchers, so everything that leaves the ship has to go through the main airlock, the hangar bay, or the launcher tubes.

"Flight One ready to launch," the XO confirms. "Float 'em out, minimal noise. Go for quarter-g acceleration once they're at least ten kilometers away."

"Aye, sir." The weapons officer flips the safety covers off the hardware launch buttons on his console. Then he toggles them in sequence.

"Launching Two. Launching Four. Launching Five. Launching Six. Birds away, sir."

"Confirm separation," the tactical officer says. "Drones are coasting passive and ballistic."

On the plot, the four drones we just launched appear as blue inverted V shapes. They slowly crawl away from *Indy*, fanning out very slightly as they go.

"We have good data link."

"Prep Flight Two and launch when ready," Major Renner says.

Almost as soon as the recon drones are away from the ship, our sensor input markedly increases in quality and resolution. The tactical plot does sort of a blip as it updates the holographic orb with new data, and ship icons shift around a bit to reflect the new data from the remote drones.

"They don't have enough ships for a decent picket," Colonel Campbell says after he watches the plot change for a few minutes. "Not for a chunk of space like this. They have those three right there"—he points at the picket force we just evaded—"and they're walling off the likely approach from Earth and Luna."

"Not meant to be airtight, just to keep nosy neighbors away," Major Renner agrees.

"Well, it's not like there's a lot of traffic left around Earth."

The drones coast out from *Indy*'s trajectory powered only by the magnetic acceleration imparted by the launch-tube system. Ten thousand meters away, and with *Indy* already a few dozen kilometers away from the launch point, they activate their own propulsion systems, and they speed off on their respective trajectories. *Indy* is sending out four more sets of eyes and ears on a very long leash, doing exactly what she was built for in the first place.

"Flight Two is going into the tubes right now," the weapons officer announces. "Three minutes for prelaunch warm-up."

When the second flight of recon drones launches, the first flight is already hundreds of kilometers away, making a fuel-efficient and stealthy path to their assigned positions. Flight Two separates from the ship, and the drones coast out to their activation points and shoot off to their own preprogrammed coordinates. Within two hours, the drones are roughly where we want them: above, below, and to either side of this uncharted deep-space anchorage. *Indy* has made a long, curved detour around the picket screen, which is now above and off our starboard stern. The anchorage is off our starboard bow, half a million kilometers away.

"Correct our trajectory," Colonel Campbell orders. "Helm, nudge her fifteen degrees to port, neutral pitch. Let's reduce our aspect a little. Just in case their sensors are as good as ours."

We creep closer to the anchorage, like thieves staking out a mark on the dark streets of a PRC past midnight while the cops are patrolling nearby. There's an anchorage out here, all right, and the combined sensor feed from *Indy*'s passive gear and the eight stealth drones that are bracketing this sector of space paint a clearer picture of its surroundings every minute we close the distance.

"Eighteen ships," the XO counts. "Dang, that's a respectable task force."

"There are at least two more," the tactical officer says. He highlights the anchorage on the screen above the holotable. "Right here, in the docking berths. And they're big ships. I'd say carrier sized."

"Any ID on them?"

"No, sir. I'm not getting anything from them at all, not even IFF."

The cluster of ships on the far side of the anchorage gives up the identities of its members bit by bit. The drone network and *Indy*'s computer compare the electronic signatures of the ships and assign hull numbers or class IDs to the assembled fleet one by one as we get closer.

"There's another carrier," the XO points out. The ID tag on the contact icon reads "CV-2153 POLLUX."

"A cruiser. Two more frigates. That right there is a fleet supply ship. Looks like the *Hampton Beach*. Another one. And another one." Major Renner looks at Colonel Campbell and chuckles. "You were on the money, sir. With those frigate names."

She points to the icons for the frigates, which are in a formation with the cruiser and escorting the carrier. The ID tags have changed from "UNKNOWN" to "FF-902 LETHE" and "FF-900 STYX." The colonel smiles a curt, humorless smile.

Then the IDs for the bulk of the ships in the middle of the group get updated, and Colonel Campbell lets out a quiet whistle.

"Twelve auxiliary fleet freighters."

"What kind of strike force needs that much cargo space?" the XO wonders out loud. "That's almost a million tons of bulk cargo."

"That's not a strike force," I say.

Colonel Campbell shakes his head. "No, Mr. Grayson, it is not."

He puts the palms of his hands on the edge of the holotable and leans forward a little, his eyes on the central cluster of icons on the tactical orb. The hologram reflects in his eyes with a blue tinge.

"Seven fighting ships, three fleet supply ships, and a dozen Alcubierre-capable deep-space bulk freighters. That right there is an evacuation fleet. We are looking at an exodus."

CHAPTER 15

— LIKE IN OLD CAPITALIST — MILITARY FILM

"Maybe they're assembling a relief force for Mars," Major Renner says. The discussion in CIC has been going on for a while, and it's clear that the XO is trying to look for an explanation for the situation that doesn't involve command betrayal on a grand scale.

"What are they doing with almost a quarter of the merchant fleet out here?" I ask. "They're not flying them to Mars. Might as well blow them up right here and save the reactor fuel."

"Hell, I don't know. Ground troops? A few armor regiments? You don't really believe that we're running from the Lankies. Leaving Earth undefended. How many people can you even put on those freighters?" says Major Renner.

"Lots," the engineering chief says. "You convert one of those bulk beasts to passenger use, you can stuff damn near ten thousand people into one. More if they're not picky about accommodations."

"Still, that's—what, a hundred, hundred and fifty thousand? That's barely two fifth-gen public-housing blocks. It makes no sense at all."

"I don't think they're evacuating the PRCs," I say.

Major Renner gives me a look that tells me she finds the suggestion uncomfortable.

"I think Mr. Grayson is correct," Colonel Campbell says. "I think whatever protocol they have in place here doesn't involve a wholesale evacuation of the civilian population. We all know that's a logistical impossibility. All the tonnage in the fleet couldn't hold more than a fraction of a percent of the civvies down there." He taps his fingers on the glass of the holotable. "If anyone's getting ready to evacuate, they're not getting out the rabble, that's for sure."

"We're getting some better top-down footage of the anchorage from Drone Five," the electronic-warfare officer says. "You may want to look at this, sir."

"Bring it up on the plot," Colonel Campbell orders.

The EW officer flicks the footage over to the holotable, where a window pops up above the tactical orb and its slowly moving confederation of pale blue icons.

"What in the fuck are those?" Major Renner says.

The optical feed from the drone shows the anchorage from "above," giving us a snapshot of the whole thing in its lateral configuration. It's not as big as a proper space station, but much more sizable than any of the deep-space anchorages I've ever seen. There are six outriggers with docking points attached to a central spine. Three of the docking stations are occupied. One holds the familiar silhouette of a Blue-class fleet destroyer—the damaged *Murphy*, in the process of docking. The other two ships are something I've never seen before. With *Murphy* nearby providing a handy scale for reference, I gauge that the two ships on the opposite side of the anchorage are enormous, over twice the length of the destroyer and considerably wider.

Colonel Campbell studies the image. He reaches out and zooms in with his fingers, then pans the picture left and right.

"That is nothing you'll find in the fleet database," he says. "They look like carriers, but they're not. I mean, they're big enough—what's your guess, XO? Hundred, hundred and ten thousand tons?"

"Hard to guess without knowing what's inside the hull," Major Renner says. "A hundred thousand, if half the interior volume is flight deck. If it's not a bird farm, a hundred and fifty, easy."

The tactical officer lets out a low whistle. "That's a huge fucking hull."

I look at the image of the two unknown ships sitting side by side in their berths. They don't quite look like carriers to me. They look different, denser somehow, more aggressive, like a Hammerhead cruiser flattened out and blown up to almost twice its original size. Whatever they are, I have no doubt that I'm looking at a pair of warships, meant to get close to dangerous things and take them apart.

"They're not finished," the chief engineer says.

"What?" Major Renner leans forward a little and peers at the image more closely.

"See that lamellar pattern on the hull?" The engineering officer leans in and does his own pan-and-zoom. "Pretty sure that's standoff armor plating. Maybe that new reactive stuff they were trying out a year or two back at the proving grounds. See how it's mounted in slats, like here?" He points at a section of the picture. All I see are shadows on the hull that make a sort of crosshatched pattern, but I nod anyway.

"But it doesn't go all the way from bow to stern. It goes to right here on this ship, about one-third of the way down the hull. A little further on the other one. Look at the stern sections. Those are lateral bulkhead frame supports, open to space. Unless they meant to build those things with only their bow sections armored, they're not finished."

He zooms out the image a little and pans over to the berth outriggers between the ships. Then he taps the hologram with a finger.

"They're still welding the hull together. You can see the laser arms here and here. Those ships are under construction. I'd say they're about two-thirds done, maybe a little more."

"But what are they for?" Colonel Campbell wonders out loud. "What the hell are they building out here, out of sight and off the books?" He flicks the image over to the edge of the tactical display and looks at the plot. "Can we get Number Five drone a little closer to that anchorage? I want to get better footage of those hulls, maybe an ELINT profile if they have any of their sensor gear installed and running already. Hull that size, you don't wait until all the armor's on before you put in the radios."

"Aye, sir. I can go in another few hundred K."

"Just as far as you can go without pegging any meters over there. If they find a recon drone, they'll know someone's eavesdropping, and then they'll comb the neighborhood."

I've been in the CIC since our hasty departure from Independence Station almost eight hours ago, and I am tired to the bone. Colonel Campbell looks as worn-out as I feel. The wrinkles in the corners of his eyes seem to have gotten quite a bit deeper overnight. He stifles a yawn and looks over at the time-and-date display on the back bulkhead of the CIC. The ship time is 0230 Zulu, half past two in the small hours of the morning, when human reaction times are at their worst. In a starship, that number is as arbitrary and meaningless as any other, but somehow knowing that it's the middle of what would be the night watch on Earth just adds to the sense of fatigue I am feeling. None of us has gotten any rack time in at least fourteen hours.

The colonel catches me glancing at the clock as well and gives me a tired little smile.

"No rest for the weary, Mr. Grayson."

He closes the recon picture windows on the holotable and pans out the scale of the plot until *Indy* and all the ships around the clandestine anchorage are just little blue dots right near the center. I see the blue-and-green orb representing Earth, and the smaller gray one for Luna beyond.

"Staff Sergeant Grayson, please fetch our Alliance guest and have him join us in briefing room Delta. XO, come along and bring the department heads. Tactical, you have the deck and the conn."

"I have the deck and the conn," the tactical officer confirms.

"We are going to figure out just what the hell we are going to do next," the colonel says. "And then we're going to take some rack time in shifts before this crew collapses from exhaustion."

Dmitry is asleep in his berth when I come to fetch him, but he seems to sleep in his battle dress uniform, because he's dressed and ready to go not sixty seconds after I rap on the hatch of his berth.

The briefing room on Delta Deck is one of the larger spaces on *Indy*. It's not quite as spacious as the enlisted or NCO mess berths, but it's bigger than the CIC pit. Most importantly, it has about twenty chairs bolted into the deck, all facing the forward bulkhead, which holds a single large holographic display that goes from the top of the bulkhead all the way to the bottom.

Dmitry and I walk into the briefing room to find half the chairs in the room full already. Most of the department heads are here, including the lieutenant in command of the embarked SI squad. He gives me a nod when he sees me stepping through the hatch, and I return it. Everyone in this room looks in need of a daylong appointment with their racks and then a month of R & R.

"Philbrick told me about the hand," the lieutenant says when I sit down in the chair next to him. "Doc couldn't stitch 'em back on?"

I shake my head curtly. "Those fingers are all over the deck liner on the concourse," I say. "Nothing left to stitch back on. I'll never talk smack about those shitty little cop buzzguns again."

"At least it's not your gun hand," he says.

"Yeah, I lucked out, huh?"

The hatch opens again, and Colonel Campbell and Major Renner walk in. The XO takes one of the empty chairs while the colonel walks to the front of the room and turns on the holoscreen with a gesture. It comes to life and shows a tactical orb, a mirror image of the situational display in the CIC. The group of auxiliary fleet freighters is sitting in space, flanked by the small group of warships in attendance. Well off past our starboard stern, the picket force is doing its patrol, lighting up the tactical display with occasional flares of active radar energy as they shine a light into the black to flush out intruders. *Indy* is like a burglar listening in to a family meeting in the living room after having snuck past the armed guards at the neighborhood gate.

"Situation," Colonel Campbell says. "We are in deep space a million kilometers from Earth, in optical sensor range of an uncharted installation that is very clearly military in nature. There is a sizable civilian cargo fleet nearby, and some very powerful deep-space combatants escorting them. That includes three frigates that aren't even listed in the fleet register, and two warships under construction that are bigger than anything we have in the fleet right now."

He turns around and marks the respective icons on the screen. The icon for *Indy* is coasting away from the station and the picket force again slowly, but the eight stealth drones are keeping station all around the anchorage and the assembled fleet.

"Based on our reception when we got back to the solar system unexpectedly, I am convinced that this anchorage and the ships all around it aren't common knowledge back at Earth. They tried hard to keep a lid on our arrival, and they were perfectly willing to blow us out of space to keep us from leaving again. It's clear that they are up to something they don't want to become general knowledge. The question is, what do we do with this intel now?"

"Go back to Earth, send the coordinates of this little party to every ship we see, and then down to the civvie networks for good measure," Major Renner says.

"To what end?" our tactical officer says. "That's a bad idea, ma'am. No offense."

"Elaborate, Captain Freeman," the colonel says.

Captain Freeman probably only has ten years on me, but at the moment, he looks like he's pushing fifty. He's haggard and tired, with deep rings under his eyes. I haven't looked in a mirror in a while, but I suspect I'm not looking all that youthful and fresh anymore myself.

"Well, that force sitting there obviously doesn't want to be discovered," the tactical officer says. "And they're the only task force close to Earth right now. Anybody goes checking out the coordinates we give them, they'll get the shit shot out of them."

"So we'll send the info down to the civilians," Major Renner says. "Let the Networks run with it. Story of the century, right?"

"And then what?" I ask. "The civvies find out that the fleet is tucking tail and evacuating? You'd cause a riot from coast to coast." Then I have a nasty, unwelcome thought. "If the authorities even let the Networks air that sort of thing. All those civvie freighters? I'm sure they don't just hold military assets. Hell, I'd be shocked if they don't have mostly 'burbers and government employees on them."

"Now that's a cheerful prospect," Lieutenant Shirley murmurs next to me. "The rats leaving the sinking ship."

"The well-connected rats," I correct, and he smiles weakly.

"So what do we do?" Major Renner asks. "Run off and leave them be? They're fixing to leave with most of the combat power on this side of the blockade. Maybe on both sides. Who knows what's left out there?"

"That's precisely what we should do," Colonel Campbell replies.

"You can't be serious, sir," the XO says.

"I can." Colonel Campbell brings up the date-and-time window of the tactical display mirrored on the screen.

"We've been away from Fomalhaut coming on fifteen days now. We don't have time to sit here and keep an eye on this happy assembly out here. This detour has cost us enough time and fuel already. Let them pack up and leave the system—I don't give a shit right now. We have thirty thousand people waiting for us to come back to New Svalbard and tell them where the Lankies are lying in wait. We'll leave the drones on station. If we ever get back, we can collect them and download the recon data." He looks around in the briefing room. "Does anyone present disagree in any particular aspect?"

Major Renner doesn't look happy, but she shakes her head curtly.

"I want to hear if anyone dissents," the colonel says. "I am serious, people. You've all put your head into the noose with me when you decided to spring me out of the detention berth. You've earned the right to a choice here."

There's silence in the room except for the faint rustling of uniforms as people shift in their seats a bit. Then Major Renner clears her throat.

"We don't go back and complete our mission, none of this is going to be worth the court-martial, sir," she says. "They won't risk the task force on a blind transition into the solar system, especially if we go missing."

All over the room, there's murmured agreement.

Colonel Campbell nods. Then he exhales slowly and pinches the bridge of his nose with thumb and forefinger. "Very well. Then let's figure out how to get back to Fomalhaut, and then get the hell out of here."

"Two options," the XO says back in CIC. "And you won't like either one."

She highlights two different trajectories on the hologram in front of her. The display table shows a long-scale three-dimensional map of the inner solar system, or at least the slice of it that stretches from Earth to the asteroid belt beyond Mars.

"Option one," she says, and the first trajectory lights up briefly in pale yellow. "We go back the way we came, through the blockade and around Mars. We'd do another slingshot burn and hope we get lucky again. If we make it past, we'll stealth to the Alliance transition point again, wait for a gap in the Lanky patrol pattern, and slip through into Fomalhaut. Same run we took in, only in reverse. Ten days, little less if we manage to use Earth's gravity well for a nice push."

She highlights the second trajectory, which lights up in pale green.

"Option two, we go the long way. With the current alignment, we can take the deep-space route here, but there won't be anything to slingshot around. It would take a lot more time and energy."

"How much longer?" the colonel asks.

"If we want to have any juice left in the tanks after we get to Fomalhaut, we can't go full-out burn on that leg. Thirty-five days at one-g sustained for both legs of the burn, and I wouldn't advise going any faster, or we'll be coasting through the transition point with vacuum in the tanks."

Colonel Campbell studies the map while rubbing his chin. There's gray stubble on his face that makes him look uncharacteristically untidy.

"I like fast," he says. "Thirty-five days is more time than we can spare. But the fleet back at Fomalhaut can't make the run past Mars."

He reaches into the display and zooms in on the area around the Alliance's Alcubierre node. The two alternate trajectories converge or separate here, depending on your perspective and starting point, and he flips the map around a bit as he follows both tracks with his finger.

"We go the deep-space route, we may find a different way back from the node to Earth. Could be they don't patrol that stretch of space as heavily."

"Or at all," Major Renner says.

"God knows there's precisely fuck-all between here and the node on that route. If we get stuck out there, we're truly stuck. Not even a comms relay in that area, never mind a depot or a mining outpost. But thirty-five days."

I watch the exchange with some anxiety. I don't know which fills me with more dread: the prospect of doing the death ride around Mars again in reverse and rolling the dice on those fifty-fifty odds one more time, or spending over a month in this ship scouting out the middle of nowhere.

Then Dmitry, who has been standing next to me and politely observing the exchange, clears his throat, and everyone in the CIC pit turns to look at him.

"Is not fuck-awl between here and node," he says.

"Excuse me, Sergeant?" Colonel Campbell says with a raised eyebrow.

Dmitry steps up to the holotable and pokes the pale green option-two route with his finger. "You go this way. Is not just empty space. We call this *Krasnyy Marshrut Odin*. Red Route One. Like in old capitalist military film. There is anchorage for refuel and supply." He taps a point halfway on the trajectory. "We use this sometimes when we have new ship to keep secret. Or for specialist operation. Black ops," he adds, in his best version of an American accent.

"Whoa," Major Renner says. All around, there is some incredulous chuckling and tittering in the CIC. "You are telling us that the SRA has a secret supply point for refueling Special Forces units. That sits near the trajectory we have to take to get to the SRA transition point."

"*Da*," Dmitry says agreeably.

"And you are volunteering this information. As if it isn't a major military secret."

"*Da*," Dmitry says again.

"Why would you do that?" Colonel Campbell asks.

"Is best way to get back. Not quick like go around Mars again, but more safe. You go faster burn, use more fuel, fill up again at Alliance anchorage. Can get food, too, but I would not recommend."

"You have the coordinates for this anchorage," the XO says.

"Is in suit, in computer."

"And they'll let us refuel there? Think you can convince them to refuel a Commonwealth ship? That's mighty risky."

"Nobody there," Dmitry says. "Is automated."

"They'll throw you into military prison and throw away the access card when they learn that you gave away a major military secret, Sergeant Chistyakov," the colonel says.

"Then you will not tell," Dmitry says with a wry little smile.

"Assume we can get there at full burn, fuel consumption be damned. How much time would we need if we can top off the tanks at the Alliance anchorage?" Colonel Campbell asks the XO.

Major Renner consults her PDP and taps around on the screen for a few moments. "Seventeen days, sir."

"To the anchorage or the turnaround point?"

"To the transition point, sir. The whole run."

Colonel Campbell looks at the major, then me, then Dmitry, and then he shakes his head with a smile.

"What weird and wonderful times we're living in, people."

"*Khorosho?*" Dmitry asks. "Is good?"

"*Ochyen khorosho,*" the colonel replies. "Very good. XO, lay in the trajectory for option two and prep the ship for departure. We're going the long way in a hurry. And let's hope there's light traffic along the way."

CHAPTER 16

LITTLE COGS IN THE GRINDER

I don't want to be awake when we pass Earth again for our ride back to Fomalhaut. I don't want to see my home planet and Luna through the optical feed, close enough to make out continents on Earth and man-made structures on the moon, because I don't want to be tempted to just jump into one of the escape pods and shoot myself Earthward. Luckily, I am so fatigued that knocking myself out completely takes no effort at all.

Back in my berth, I take twice the instructed dosage of the pain meds that Corpsman Randall gave me. Then I lie down on my rack, close my eyes, and wait for the warm and fuzzy sensation of the narcotics to flood my brain.

When I wake up again, my body seems to have lost all desire for independent locomotion. With the privacy curtain drawn, I'm in a little box that feels comforting and predictable. It lets me pretend that there isn't a larger world beyond that curtain, tedious days spent standing the watch on a ship hurtling through the hostile vacuum of space, always just one major hull breach away from oblivion, in a galaxy full of genocidal aliens and a human race that isn't much better in the ethics department.

I check my chronometer to find that I've slept for thirteen hours. I should be rested, and the overwhelming fatigue is no longer weighing on my brain, but instead of refreshed I just feel drained.

I get up and put on a fresh set of CDU fatigues. The ones I am wearing right now are from the supply chain of the carrier *Regulus*, as is my armor set hanging in its spot in the wall locker nearby. I've attached a name tape and rank insignia, but no unit patches. I'm not sure where I belong at this point. The fleet? The New Svalbard militia? The rebellious HD battalions? The crew of *Indy*? It doesn't feel proper to declare membership in one of those groups above any of the others, so I claim no affiliation at all on my uniform right now.

I don't want to go back to CIC and stare at a holographic globe for hours on end that shows me to the tenth of a kilometer just how far I am away from Halley and Earth again, and how fast I'm going the other way. Instead, I fasten the locks on my boots and wash up one-handed in the bathroom nook of my berth. Then I step out of the hatch and turn left, toward the NCO mess.

I am intimately familiar with *Indy*'s limited menu selections. There are two kinds of sandwiches: the standard service bologna, which is only half soy and actually has some meat content, and peanut butter and jelly, which doesn't. Even considering all the gross combinations and throwing in a slice of soy cheese, there are only seven or eight ways to recombine the selection. Then there are standard field-ration packages, reheated in the galley. Those come in six different entree options, all of which are just half a degree more edible than the standard Basic Nutritional Allowance rations I used to choke down in the PRC back home.

We haven't had anything other than the prepackaged-ration stuff for weeks now, and it's amazing how much the lack of food variety can drag down the general morale of grunts and sailors. The pain meds suppress whatever appetite I may have had left, but I can feel my stomach rumbling, so I grab a meal tray despite my lack of gusto and put a bologna sandwich and a cup of coffee on it.

I'm halfway through the coffee and two bites into the mealy sandwich when Dmitry walks into the NCO mess. He sees me sitting by myself in a corner of the room and crosses the mess hall. There's a bottle in his hand, and he puts it down on the table in front of me as he sits down.

"Present," he says. "From distillery on *Kiev*."

"What is it?" I ask. The stuff in the bottle looks clear and innocent, like tap water.

"Is distilled fermentation," he says.

"Fermented what, exactly?"

"Is best not to ask," Dmitry replies. He pops the plastic seal of the bottle open with his thumb and pours a bit of it into my coffee before I can yank the mug away.

"You try. Is not so bad."

"Your assault carrier actually has a distillery."

"Is Russian ship. You will not find Russian ship anywhere in SRA fleet without engineer who knows how to make proper drink in secret."

"And here I thought all my preconceptions about Russians were wrong," I say. "You get twenty pounds of personal gear to bring with you, and you take along alcohol?"

Dmitry shrugs. "Is useful sometimes, no? Better than box of medals or playthings."

I bring the mug up to my nose and take a smell. The familiar, slightly sour scent of the standard fleet soybean coffee substitute now has a slightly acrid quality to it. I take a sip, expecting to gag on the spiked blend, but it actually has a tolerable flavor, and I enjoy the slight burn on my palate.

"Not bad," I say, and take another sip. Dmitry smiles and pushes the bottle all the way to my side of the table.

"You take. Keep for useful purposes."

"This is serious trade currency, Dmitry. You can probably trade that to the galley cooks for a week of field-ration picks."

"I pay you for what I owe," he says. Then he nods at my bandaged hand. "You trade hand of yours for enemy battlespace coordinator."

I open my mouth to tell Dmitry that that isn't quite the case, but he waves me off impatiently.

"Yes, yes. I have codes for transition point. Was not personal favor. You save yourself and ship so we can go back to Fomalhaut." He pronounces the system's name with a *-ch* sound in the middle. "But is no matter why. You still lose fingers, and I still put air in lungs. Maybe—if things do not go all shit again—I go home one day. Because you hold hand in front of gun and make shots go down and not here." He taps at his forehead and chest.

"You got anyone at home? Family?"

He blinks, as if my question has thrown him off a little. Then he reaches into the pocket of his lizard-pattern fatigues and fishes out a little personal document pouch. The SRA version looks much like the ones we carry around, just a tiny waterproof sleeve big enough for a handful of ID chips and maybe a letter hard copy or two. Dmitry reaches into his pouch and takes out a print image. He puts it in front of me almost gingerly.

"Maksim," he says. "Husband. Big, dumb, but good heart."

The image shows a soldier about my age. He has an aggressive buzz cut, and he's dressed in the same lizard-pattern SRA battle dress tunic Dmitry is wearing. The undershirt is striped horizontally in alternating white and blue, and the beret under his shoulder board is sky blue.

"He's a marine, too?" I ask.

"Like I say. Big and dumb."

I grin and hand his picture back to him. Dmitry takes it and slips it back into his document pouch carefully.

That kind of personal disclosure requires a tit for tat. I take my own personal pouch out of my leg pocket and open it. It has my military ID in it, the last letter I got from Mom, and two pictures of Halley. I take out the one of her in her flight suit, the one I've been carrying around since she sent it to me back before I even joined what was still the navy back then.

Looking at her smile and that rugged short haircut of hers gives me a momentary ache that's far worse than what I'm feeling from my healing nose or the bandaged hand. I give the picture to Dmitry, who raises an eyebrow and nods in appreciation.

"She is pilot," he says. "Good pilot?"

"Good pilot," I confirm. "Instructor at Combat Flight School."

"What is she pilot of? Big piece of *govno* with big gun for shooting Russian marines? What do you call, Shrike?"

"Not a Shrike. Wasp and Dragonfly drop ships. Small piece of *govno* with smaller guns for shooting Russian marines."

Dmitry chuckles, his eyes still on the picture of Halley. "Show me other one."

I hand over the second picture, which is one of Halley and me at a fleet rec facility two years ago. We're both wearing dress blues, and Halley's fruit salad of medal ribbons is slightly but noticeably bigger than mine.

"Girlfriend? Wife?"

"Fiancée," I say.

"What is fiancée?"

"We're getting married," I reply. "Once I get back. If we get back."

Dmitry reaches into a different pocket and produces a small metal object, which he holds up and turns slowly with his fingertips. It's a stylized eagle holding a wreath in its talons. The wreath has the Roman numeral *III* in its center. The eagle's wings are stretched out behind it, a raptor in the middle of a high-speed dive for its prey.

"Another present," he says. "I have these for fifteen years. Now I give to you."

He hands the eagle badge to me. I put it on my palm and look at it.

"Are these jump wings?"

"I get at spaceborne training course. Is for dress uniform, to look pretty. Not for battle dress. You keep, maybe give to fiancée. You can tell her you took off body of dead Russian."

"I can't take your damn jump wings, Dmitry." I put the eagle badge on the table and carefully slide it over to him. If the Sino-Russian marines put half as much value on their original set of jump wings from their version of a School of Spaceborne Infantry as our own SI troopers do, he just gave me the most sentimental thing he owns aside from the picture of Maksim.

"You take, or I punch color from your hair again, Andrew," he says without smiling, and his expression makes it pretty clear that he won't brook an argument. "Is poor trade for left hand, I know. But you take anyway."

He pushes the eagle back across the table. It certainly looks like it has been worn for fifteen years. The gold enamel on the wreath in the eagle's talons is rubbed off in spots, and all the high points of the relief stamping are worn smooth. I wonder if that little set of jump wings has been on a contested planet with its owner while I traded shots with him at some point.

"Fine," I say. "Now shut up about the whole thing. Like you said, I was just making sure our ticket back didn't get yanked."

I open Dmitry's bottle again and put another splash into my coffee. Then I hand the bottle to Dmitry, who accepts it without hesitation before taking a long swig. Then he caps the bottle and puts it back on the table.

"We are same, you and I. Both *duraky*. Fools. Idiots. They tell us, 'Go here, shoot this man, call missile on this building,' and we do. Shoot at each other for many years, kill each other's comrades, and get little pieces of metal with colorful ribbon. We should not be here. We should be home, you and I. Back home with Maksim and . . . what is name of your fiancée?" He pronounces the new word deliberately.

"Halley," I say. "Her first name is Diana, but she hates it, so she's just Halley to everyone."

"Halley," Dmitry repeats. With his Russian accent, it sounds like "Challey."

It almost seems like a cliché from an old war movie, I think. Enemies get together, have a drink, exchange trinkets, and show off pictures of each other's sweethearts, and then they realize that they have so much in common that they don't want to fight each other anymore. The futility of war, young men and women ordered from above to kill each other for stupid reasons, and all that. But I don't feel ennobled or enlightened by any of this. Mostly, I just feel like I've wasted most of the last five years of my life killing people who didn't need or want to be killed, as part of a big stupid machine that has been chewing up the very assets we needed to fight the Lankies, the real threat. A little numbered cog in the meat grinder, ready to turn on command. And now the same people who pulled the handle on that grinder over and over are probably getting ready to walk away from the mess, hands clean, to leave the rest of us to our fates.

"*Duraky*," I say.

Dmitry smiles sadly and gets up from his chair. "I will go sleep now, or maybe learn more secrets of fancy imperialist spy ship. Enjoy distilled fermentation," he says.

I watch as he walks out of the NCO mess, which is now once again empty except for me and the bottle of Russian contraband ethanol on the table.

I eat the rest of my sandwich without much enthusiasm. My hand has started hurting again, so I pull out the bottle of pain meds and open the cap. Then I pop two of the little white pills into my mouth and wash them down with a swig of my spiked coffee. If I am going to check out of reality for a while, might as well do the job all the way.

The mess hatch opens, and two of the SI troopers walk in, Corporal DeLuca and Sergeant Acosta. I quickly take Dmitry's bottle and stick it into the leg pocket of my jeans. Every second we move along on Red Route One toward the transition point means another few thousand kilometers of vacuum between me and Halley again. I know I made the right decision, but right now every passing hour increases my resentment of myself, and I need to take the edge off a bit. I nod at the newcomers and vacate the table to head back to my berth for some more warm and fuzzy narcotics-assisted alone time.

CHAPTER 17

RED ROUTE ONE

"Goddammit, easy on the stern thrusters. Half a degree more positive angle. Keep the bow up."

The XO is in the middle of the CIC pit, the center of the room with the big holotable that is the brain of the ship, coordinating the docking attempt like a conductor in charge of a small orchestra. Everyone is tense, none more so than the helmsman, who is in charge of keeping *Indy*'s four thousand tons in perfect synchronicity with the SRA anchorage not thirty meters off our port side. This is docking attempt number four in as many hours, and what was supposed to be a two-hour affair from start to finish is turning into an all-day event.

"There we go. Now counter-burn on the bow for half a second at ten percent. A mouse fart of a burn."

Indy has no docking arrestors anymore, having shed them like a bee losing a stinger when we fled Independence eight days ago. Even if we did still have something for the docking clamps to grab, the SRA docking system is not compatible with ours, so we have to fly in a very precise formation and perform what the fleet calls a floating link—a flexible docking collar from airlock to airlock, and nothing to keep things from coming apart except the formation-flying skills of the helmsman.

"You got it now," Major Renner says. "But don't slack off. We lose the collar, we won't be replenishing squat."

Dmitry and I are in armor again. The padding on my left hand makes the armored glove uncomfortably tight, but I luckily still fit into battle armor without having to leave off one glove and rendering the whole system compromised. We stand by as the CIC personnel do their rendezvous dance for the docking maneuver. Almost a month of seeing an Alliance sergeant in battle rattle standing in the middle of a Commonwealth warship's CIC has completely blunted the novelty of the sight for the rest of the crew.

"Extend the docking collar," the XO says. "Nice and easy. Half a meter per second."

The holotable has half a dozen windows open, all showing the docking operation from as many different camera angles, with the numerical data readouts from the navigation computer overlaid on top of everything: closing rates, relative velocities, elapsed mission time, radar distances. *Indy* has her own flexible docking collar for ship-to-ship docking actions, and we watch as it extends out of the hull and starts to stretch across the twenty-five and a half meters to one of the auxiliary airlocks of the unmanned Sino-Russian deep-space anchorage Luzhōu-19.

"Hard lock achieved," the chief engineer says from his station. "Divergence rate one-quarter centimeter and steady. We are go for transfer ops."

Major Renner looks over to Dmitry and me. "Your turn, Sergeants. Go over there and open sesame."

We go down to the main airlock, where the SI squad's fire team Charlie are all already waiting for us in full combat gear:

Sergeant Humphrey, Corporal DeLuca, and Privates Andrews and Pulaski.

"Ready for a field trip?" Sergeant Humphrey asks when we connect to the fire team's comms circuit. She readies her M-66 carbine and bounces the targeting laser off the nearest bulkhead to make sure it works.

"Anything to get to step out for a few minutes," I reply. There's a PDW slung across my chest instead of my usual issue M-66. I tested my marksmanship with the carbine on *Indy*'s range a few days ago, and the two missing fingers on my left hand make it a little awkward to maneuver the short but heavy weapon. The PDW is a strictly short-range affair, but it weighs about half of what the rifle does and is less than half as long, much easier to handle with a hand and a half.

Dmitry is in battle armor, but unarmed. He looks at the handful of combat-ready troops in front of the airlock and shakes his head.

"Station is automated," he says. "No personnel. Nobody to fight. You can leave weapons."

Sergeant Humphrey grins without humor. "I don't care how many lunches you've had with the skipper. I'm not going to break into an SRA installation unarmed."

She walks over to the control screen for the main airlock and punches in the access code. The inner airlock door opens, and we file into the lock.

"Verify hard seal on the docking collar," Sergeant Humphrey says into the shipboard comms panel.

"Hard seal verified," the reply from CIC comes.

We all lower our helmet face shields and let the suits take over the life support.

Sergeant Humphrey seals the inner lock and cycles the outer hatch. The air rushes out of the lock—not the violent decompression of a compartment venting into vacuum, but the relatively slow release of air into a low-pressure environment. Beyond the open main hatch, there's the twenty-five-meter stretch of flexible alloy tube connecting us to the auxiliary hatch. The outer surface of Luzhōu-19 looks like nobody has bothered to refresh the paint job or scrub the hull down since they assembled the anchorage.

"Let's go," Sergeant Humphrey says. "Moving out."

We make our way across slowly and carefully, mindful of the minor up-and-down and side-to-side movements of the tube, which is the only thing connecting *Indy* to the station, a rather inconsequential and easily torn umbilical. It won't be a disaster if it breaks while we're in it because our suits are vac-sealed and we can EVA our way back to the airlock, but we are sandwiched between *Indy*'s four thousand tons and the larger mass of the anchorage. A slight nudge in the wrong direction on the helm controls in CIC, and we'll be adding to the layer of grime on the outside of the SRA facility.

"Sergeant Red Star, you're up." Sergeant Humphrey points at the auxiliary hatch and the bulge for the wireless network receiver next to it.

Dmitry nods and turns away as he accesses his suit's computer to ferret out the access codes. A few moments later, the auxiliary hatch unlocks with a loud thunk and a vibration that makes the skin of the flexible docking collar ripple slightly. Sergeant Humphrey brings up her M-66 and turns on the weapon light to illuminate the hatch. It slides into a recess in the hull, and lights come on in the airlock and passageway beyond.

We make our way through the docking collar and onto Luzhōu-19, with Sergeant Humphrey taking point and the rest of us close behind. The inside of the anchorage is almost as grimy as the outside. I don't know when they put this pit stop on Red Route One, but from the worn deck lining and the myriad of scuffs and paint streaks on the passageway bulkheads, it looks like SRA starships have been filling up and resupplying here for many decades.

The anchorage is roughly cross-shaped, with a big central hub and four smaller docking spokes branching out from the central section. When Sergeant Humphrey has satisfied herself that there isn't a platoon of SRA marines looking to jump out of dark corners and ambush us, she lets Dmitry take the lead. He guides us to the anchorage's main control booth in the central cargo transfer area of the station, where he starts turning on displays and flicking switches.

"Made ready freight lifters and fuel system," he says. "Anchorage has fuel for twenty little imperialist spy ships."

"*Indy*, Delta Six," Sergeant Humphrey says into the comms circuit. "All clear on the inside. Our Russian friend says there's plenty of juice."

"Delta Six, *Indy*. Splendid news," the XO replies. "We're sending over the engineering team. In the meantime, secure the place top to bottom. And see if you can find us some variety for the galley. Maybe the Alliance has field rations that aren't altogether awful."

Either Dmitry has super-acute hearing good enough to have picked up the reply from Sergeant Humphrey's helmet comms, or he has found a way to hack into our protected tactical comms circuit.

"Another not-great idea," he says to me. "You drop Russian food on floor, it will eat hole in hull of weak Commonwealth ship."

The replenishment takes about four times longer than the most tedious underway refueling I've ever witnessed. The SRA refueling probes and cowlings aren't compatible with ours, so it takes the engineering crew several hours and half a dozen EVA trips along the outside of *Indy*'s hull to rig up a field-improvised adapter system.

While the techies are busy trying to get the SRA's deuterium into our reactor fuel tanks, we grunts go through the anchorage's storage berths to look for other useful things to claim. The station has eight large cargo holds, each big enough to hold a thousand tons or so of palleted supplies. There's small-arms ammunition that's incompatible with our fléchette rifles, heavy ordnance for shipboard weapons we don't have, and spare parts for drop ships we don't use. Finally, Private Pulaski finds the section that has the palleted chow, and we converge on it to take stock of what's there.

"My Russian and Chinese skills are really rusty beyond 'Put down your fucking weapons,'" Sergeant Humphrey says. "What is this stuff?"

Dmitry peels back the olive-green wrap on one of the pallets and looks at the stack of ration containers. Then he points at several of the boxes in turn.

"Type A is lentil stew. Type B, soy beef with tomato. Type C, goulash, also soy. Type D is barley porridge."

"Sounds delightful," Corporal DeLuca says. "Let's steal some."

Dmitry shrugs. "Is your burial."

We manage to haul half a pallet of SRA field rations back through the docking collar and onto the ship before the engineers have hooked up the station's refueling system to *Indy*. Once the deuterium-tritium pellet matrix is pouring from the SRA station's tanks into *Indy*'s, we look around for other replenishment opportunities, but the pickings are sparse, at least for consumables that are used by human bodies instead of fusion reactors or weapon mounts. At least we get to top off our water tanks from Luzhōu-19's supply as well.

"Refueling ops completing in one-zero minutes," the XO calls out from CIC. "Finish whatever you're doing and return to *Indy* for departure."

"Aye, ma'am. Returning to the ship," Sergeant Humphrey responds. "You heard the woman. Everyone back to the docking collar. Anyone gets left behind, it may be a long wait until the next ride off this thing."

We detach from the SRA deep-space anchorage eight hours after our initial docking approach with full deuterium and water tanks. In regular fleet operations, even a tricky refuel while under way shouldn't take longer than an hour and a half at the most, but considering that we tapped a supply infrastructure that was never designed to interface with our ship, it was a reasonably short stop. We're almost half a day behind on our high-speed run back to the Alliance node, but now we have the fuel to get there as fast as *Indy* can go, which is plenty hasty. If we die trying to get through, we'll die warm, clean, and reasonably well fed.

CHAPTER 18

—MINNOWS AND SHARKS—

"Combat stations, combat stations. All hands, combat stations. This is not a drill. I repeat . . ."

I'm already in vacsuit when the combat-stations alert trills overhead. I knew it was coming, but after two weeks of deeply uneventful cruising the backwater of the inner solar system, it's still a bit of a jolt back into reality: This is a warship, and we are hurtling toward the enemy again.

I pick up my helmet and leave the berth. As I step through the hatch, I almost collide with Dmitry and Staff Sergeant Philbrick, who are squeezing through the passage outside just as I step out.

"Here we go," Philbrick says. His combat station is outside the CIC with his fire team in case we get boarded—a very unlikely event when going up against Lankies, but shipboard protocol is what it is. Dmitry's spot is in the CIC pit because he has to open the door for us once again, and my spot is right beside him to make sure that's all he does while he's patched into *Indy*'s silicon brain.

We rush down the passageway and up the staircase to the CIC deck with measured haste. All around us, *Indy*'s crew perform the well-practiced choreography of a fleet ship getting ready for battle.

"Good luck," Philbrick says when we get to the armored CIC hatch, and he veers off to join his fire team on the outside of the vestibule.

"You, too," I say. If things go pear-shaped, he'll be closer to the escape pods than the CIC crew, but there won't be any rescue out here for any of us if it comes to that.

Colonel Campbell and Major Renner are in their usual spots in the CIC pit. Dmitry and I take our positions by the handrail. The plot on the holotable isn't very busy. It has just three icons on it, but two of them are the signal orange of positively identified Lanky contacts.

"Bogey One, bearing two-seven-zero by positive zero-one-three, moving laterally at ten meters per second, designate Lima-20. Bogey Two, bearing two-niner-zero by negative one-five-zero, moving laterally on reciprocal heading at fifteen meters per second, designate Lima-21." The tactical officer marks the target icons with their assigned designations.

The plot shows us fifty thousand kilometers from the Alcubierre transition point. The two Lanky ships are slowly cruising through the slice of space in front of it. We are in a wide elliptical trajectory, coasting ballistic with only our passive sensors, the exact way we have been evading the Lankies since we almost traded hull plating with them when we popped out of this transition point almost a month ago.

"They're just crawling along," the XO says.

"They don't have to be fast," Colonel Campbell replies. "They just have to be in the way. But where is the third one? We had three seed ships in front of us when we transitioned in."

"No sign of anything but Lima-20 and 21 as far as our optical gear can look, sir."

"Sons of bitches are damn near invisible even this close. The other guy could be fifty thousand klicks further out, and we wouldn't even see him unless we knew exactly where to look. How the hell do they manage to hide something that big so well?"

On the optical feed, the Lanky ships are slow-moving blotches against the background of deep, dark space. Their hulls don't reflect light the way our metal alloy hulls do. They've always reminded me more of bug carapaces than spaceship armor. *Indy* is stealthy because she is small and because she is crammed to the gunwales with the very latest in stealth technology. Nobody knows yet why the Lanky ships are so damn stealthy that they don't even show up on radar, thermal imaging, or gamma-ray scopes. It's hard to study something that will blow you full of holes when you get close enough to spot it.

"How many drones left in the racks?" Colonel Campbell asks.

"Six, sir."

"Get four of them into the tubes and warm 'em up. I want to have eyes on this from all angles before we try and make our dash."

The flight of stealth recon drones launches five minutes later. At this range, less than fifty thousand kilometers away, their propulsion systems only need to burn for acceleration a few seconds. They spread out from the icon marking *Indy*'s location and rush toward the Lanky ships.

"They give the slightest hint that they spotted us, we're reversing course and going for full burn back the way we came," Colonel Campbell says.

"Tickling the dragon's tail." Major Renner watches the little blue icons on the plot closing the distance with the larger orange ones. "All fun and games until the dragon turns and bites you in the ass."

The drones are on their run for thirty minutes when the Lankies change course, both seemingly at the same time.

"Lima-20 turning to bear negative ten degrees relative. Fifteen degrees. Twenty."

The icon for Lima-20 shows the Lanky making a sweeping turn, but he's not turning toward us or the drone that is now within a thousand kilometers off his port side. He's turning away from us. At the same time, the icon for Lima-21 changes direction as well, going in the same direction but with hundreds of kilometers of space between them. We now have stern-aspect views of both Lanky ships.

"They're circling the transition point," the colonel muses. "Remember when we came in? Like sharks searching for prey."

The data from the drones bears out the colonel's observation. We watch as the Lanky ships execute another leg in their pattern, then change course again. Their elapsed track on the plot begins to form an elliptical racetrack pattern, with both ships at opposite ends of the ellipse from each other, and the transition point in the center of the racetrack.

"Surely they're not that dumb," the XO says when we're five or six turns into the pattern.

"What's that, Major?"

"What's the first rule of planning and executing a patrol route?" Major Renner asks nobody in particular.

"You make patrol random," Dmitry says. "So enemy cannot predict."

The XO and Colonel Campbell look at Dmitry with a mix of mild surprise and amusement.

"Ten points to our Russian guest," the XO says. "That's precisely it. But it's not what these guys are doing. Wait for the next turn." She points at one of the icons on the plot.

"Lima-20 will turn to relative one-seven-five in ninety seconds. Lima-21 will turn to relative three-zero-zero five or six seconds later. Watch."

I divide my attention between the plot and the chronometer readout on the CIC bulkhead. Sure enough, a minute and a half after the XO's prediction, the icons change direction on the plot again, exactly the way she predicted. Major Renner picks up the marker pen from the holotable and clicks a trajectory onto the plot.

"There's the patrol pattern, and it's entirely predictable, down to five seconds and a kilometer or two."

"That's weapons-grade stupid," the tactical officer says.

"By our standards, sure." Colonel Campbell pans the map around and changes the scale to get a better spatial sense of the Lanky patrol pattern relative to our position. "But they're not human. We don't have a clue how they think. If they think. They could be acting on instinct alone. Think of the shark analogy. Does a shark have to care whether it's predictable or not?"

"Maybe they know as little about us as we do about them," I say.

"Maybe. Problem is, they don't have to give a shit about figuring us out. Sharks and minnows and all that."

Colonel Campbell taps the plot again to reset the range scale. "We'll observe their pattern for a little while, make sure it stays constant. I want a best-time trajectory to the transition point, calculated for the precise moment when both those ships are as far away from the node as their pattern takes them. We're going to have to loop around and burn for speed."

"What about creating a little diversion?" the XO asks. "Just to be on the safe side."

"What do you have in mind?"

"Well, we can use the parasite fighter we have left. Load it with tactical nukes, coast it in from the far side, and stick a few megatons into the nearest Lanky."

"We can launch, then have the bird drop stealth and run the opposite way," the tactical officer suggests. "Maybe the Lanky will give chase. But even if not, we'll have the background noise from a few nukes to keep their eyes off us. It'll at least get their attention."

"We'd be giving up the rest of our offensive fighter power to do the space-warfare equivalent of throwing a rock down an alley." Colonel Campbell chews on his lower lip in thought. "That's a mighty expensive distraction."

"May be worth it just to increase the margin of error."

The colonel mulls the idea for a few moments and then shrugs. "Let's do it. Cheaper than losing the ship because we made the node three seconds too late."

It takes another hour to prep and load *Indy*'s remaining parasite fighter. They are small and stealthy, and like the drones, the parasite fighters are remote-controlled from the weapons station in *Indy*'s CIC. Unlike the drones, however, they are designed for combat, to give *Indy* stealthy standoff capabilities for sneak attacks. They have ordnance bays for missiles, and while the weapons officer is prepping the ship's guidance and targeting systems for launch, the flight deck crew loads four tactical nuclear antiship missiles onto the hardpoints.

"Bird's prepped and ready for launch. Nuke yield is dialed in at five hundred kilotons per."

"They'll make a pretty light show at least," the XO says.

"Next burn window for max clearance transition is coming

up in seven minutes." The tactical officer puts the corresponding countdown marker on the holotable display.

"Launch the fighter," Colonel Campbell orders. "Prepare for acceleration burn and Alcubierre transition. We have one shot at this. Let's not fuck it up."

Indy does a sequence of short burns to extend the parabolic curve of her path and swing her around to gain speed for the transition. Then we reach the apex of our path and swing around in a wide arc to aim straight for the node, which means we are also aiming right for the spot between the two Lanky ships. The detached stealth fighter is five thousand kilometers off our starboard bow and heading straight for the closest Lanky seed ship, a mosquito taking on an elephant.

"Fifteen seconds on the burn, five-g sustained," Major Renner announces.

"Thirty seconds to weapon release. Requesting authorization for nuclear fire mission."

"Authorize nuclear release, commanding officer, 0437 Zulu shipboard time," Colonel Campbell replies.

"Confirm authorization for nuclear release," the weapons officer says. Everything we say and do in CIC gets recorded by the computer and logged in the ship's data banks. If we live through this and the crew gets hauled in front of a court-martial tribunal, the log will undoubtedly serve as evidence.

"Two minutes and forty-five seconds to transition," the XO says. I look at Dmitry, who watches the proceedings with his usual stoic expression, but I know him well enough by now to tell that he is as anxious as any of us.

"Ten seconds to weapons release. Five seconds. Three. Two. One. Birds away, birds away."

On the plot, four little inverted V shapes pop into existence just ahead of the icon for the stealth fighter and shoot toward the nearest Lanky ship at an acceleration that would turn us all into pudding if *Indy* could pull it.

"All four birds tracking optically. Time to impact: forty-five seconds."

The combined destructive power of two million tons of conventional explosives is hurtling toward the Lanky ship. For even our biggest warships, a two-megaton direct hit would mean catastrophic damage if not outright destruction, but after seeing an entire task force launch hundreds of megatons against a lone seed ship without effect, I have no hope of seeing the Lanky blotted from the plot by our missile fire.

"Thirty seconds to impact. One minute forty-five seconds to transition."

"Sergeant Chistyakov," Colonel Campbell says. "Stand by to transmit access code at the thirty-second mark."

"Thirty-second mark," Dmitry confirms. He walks over to the comms officer and brings up a holoscreen on the console. "Standing by for transmit."

"Twenty seconds to missile impact."

The gap between the two Lanky ships is close to a hundred kilometers, as wide as it will get on their predicted patrol pattern. Both are moving away from the transition point. I know that their ship-to-ship penetrators are strictly a short-range affair and that the seed ships are too massive to just turn on a dime to get into our path if they detect us at the last minute, but intentionally racing *Indy* between two of those monster ships is still the scariest, dumbest thing I've been a part of in my life. So much is riding on a second or two and the fraction of a kilometer. We are not just tickling the dragon's tail; we are timing a flyby through its open jaws while it is yawning.

"Ten seconds to missile impact. Five seconds. Three . . . two . . . one . . . impact. We have nuclear impacts on bogey Lima-21."

The optical feed shows the blindingly bright miniature suns of four atomic detonations in vacuum, perfect spheres of light and heat and deadly radiation. Then the Lanky seed ship bulls its way through the nuclear fire, trailing superheated particles behind it as it shrugs off the hits.

"Turn the fighter around and go active on the decoy transmitters," Major Renner orders. "Give the son of a bitch something to chase."

The unmanned stealth fighter makes a brutally sharp twenty-g turn under full acceleration and races back the way it came, toward the section of space where *Indy* started her run for the transition point. On the plot, the icon for the fighter changes in size as the electronic-warfare decoy module on the little ship pumps out megawatts of radio energy to match the ELINT signature of a frigate. To an SRA unit, the fleeing fighter would look like a much bigger ship, and hopefully the Lanky will find it worthy of pursuit.

"Lima-21 is changing course to twenty degrees starboard relative. Son of a bitch took the bait." The tactical officer sounds almost jubilant.

"One minute to transition. Stand by, Sergeant Chistyakov."

"Standing," Dmitry says.

"Lima-20 is coming about! Course change for Lima-20, turning through two-seven-zero relative. He is accelerating. Ten meters per second. Thirty. Fifty."

"Not fast enough," Colonel Campbell says. He is staring grimly at the plot, where the second seed ship has started a ponderous 180-degree turn toward our trajectory. "Looks like size isn't everything, huh?"

Off in the distance to our starboard, the stealth fighter is racing into the black, flashing its fake ID card, with seed ship Lima-20 in pursuit. We are racing for the doorway at top speed, sixty humans in a little alloy shell against two almost-invulnerable planet destroyers.

"Lima-20 is going for the bait, too. I don't think he spotted us, sir."

"Works for me," the colonel says, jaw muscles flexing.

"Transition in thirty seconds."

"Sergeant Chistyakov," the XO says, just a few decibels below a shout. "Now, if you please."

Dmitry's fingers fly across the display in front of him. He's using *Indy*'s comms suite as an amplifier for his own suit's communications gear, sending the SRA access code with the ship's transmitting power instead of that of his armor. Still, at this speed we will be in transmission range for only a few seconds, and if we miss our window, we'll just coast right through the Alcubierre point and remain in local space instead of shooting off toward Fomalhaut at superluminal speed.

"Is done," he says.

"I show positive lock on the beam," the helmsman confirms. "Automatic transit lock enabled. Transition in fifteen seconds."

The XO picks up the handset for the 1MC. "All hands, prepare for Alcubierre transition in minus-ten. Hang on, people."

"Distance to Lima-20 now ninety thousand. Eighty thousand. Seventy thousand and closing."

"Three, two, one. Engage."

The icons on the plot wink out of existence. I feel the familiar low-level ache in my bones that sets in whenever I enter an Alcubierre transit bubble, and I've never welcomed the feeling until this very moment.

CHAPTER 19

CATCHING UP

NACS *Indianapolis* coasts back into orbit around Fomalhaut c's moon, the colony called New Svalbard, twenty-nine days after our departure. We arrive with almost-empty deuterium tanks, 25 percent of drinking water remaining, and most of our food stores gone except for the truly unpalatable SRA rations we held back for eat-or-starve emergency chow. On the personal side of the ledger, I arrive without my fiancée, and I am missing two fingers on my left hand. I've also lost whatever idealism I may have had left after five years of getting fucked by the brass, and any desire to stick my neck out for anyone above the rank of colonel ever again.

"Look at this, sir," the XO says from the holotable. Colonel Campbell walks up from the CIC hatch, where he just had a conversation with the commanding officer of the embarked SI squad, Lieutenant Shirley.

"What is it?"

Major Renner points at the plot and highlights a few of the ship icons that have popped up on our radar since we turned the bend for our orbital capture. She points out a small cluster of blue icons slightly away from the main task force.

Colonel Campbell laughs out loud. "Well, I'll be dipped in shit. The wayward carrier has returned to the fold."

I walk over to the pit and look at the plot. The ships Major Renner pointed out are labeled "CV-233 MIDWAY," "FF-471 TRIPOLI," and "CG-97 LONG BEACH," our wayward carrier task force 230.7, which tucked tail and ran when the Lankies came calling a little over two months ago.

"Amazing what empty freshwater tanks can do for one's memory," Major Renner says wryly. "The general remembered there was a colony moon to defend out here in the sticks."

We've been in radio contact with the combined SRA/NAC task force since shortly after we shot out of the Alcubierre chute and back into the Fomalhaut system, but the presence of the *Midway* is a major surprise. I see it as a good sign that we are in touch with the same command crew that was in charge when we left—an ad hoc council of senior SRA and NAC commanders—which means that the wayward general in command of TF230.7 did not manage to claim authority over the entire fleet by virtue of rank.

"*Regulus*, *Indy* Actual. Request permission to come alongside one of the supply ships as soon as we've completed our orbital capture. We are out of everything, and *Indy*'s full of holes."

"*Indy* Actual, this is *Regulus*. Permission granted. Complete orbital capture and contact *Portsmouth* for approach vectors. You guys look like you've had a journey."

"*Regulus*, you have absolutely no idea," Colonel Campbell sends back.

We burn to enter the orbital trajectory that will get *Indy* into New Svalbard orbit in just one pass, using the top layers of the moon's atmosphere to slow the ship down to orbital maneuvering speeds. Someone in CIC put a large window with the external planetside camera feed onto the holotable next to the tactical orb, and I get to see the ice moon and the massive gas giant behind it in ultrahigh resolution at this range. New Svalbard's cloud cover is almost complete as usual, but there are stretches of clear skies along the temperate belt around the moon's equator. It's a harsh world, but a beautiful one, clean and cold and unspoiled.

"Weather report for New Longyearbyen says they're go for flight ops as long as we don't mind a bit of chop," Colonel Campbell says to me. "I'm pretty sure that you're good and ready to get down to the surface. Stretch your legs after almost a month in this little barge."

"Colonel," I say, "I think that this ship is the finest unit in the fleet, and I would gladly go into battle with this crew again any time, against anyone. But don't take it personally when I tell you that I've never wanted to get off a spaceship as much as I want to get off this one right now."

Major Renner chuckles, and Colonel Campbell smiles curtly and shakes his head.

"God knows you've earned yourself a bit of fresh air," the colonel says. He glances at my still-bandaged hand. "They'll want you around for the debriefing, but you can join that from down there. And I wouldn't wait too long to have that looked at by a surgeon."

Dmitry and I are alone again for the ride in the drop ship. He sits across the aisle from me, his gear bag between his feet and strapped to the cargo eyelets that are recessed into the floor in regular intervals. The other personnel on *Indy* will transfer to other ships in the task force directly if needed, but Dmitry needs to switch rides on the surface because the SRA drop ships don't fit into NAC docking clamps. If this shaky new alliance of necessity is going to continue, we will need a whole new level of standardization across both fleets—or what's left of them at this point.

The drop ship detaches from the docking clamp, and I turn on the networked feed in my suit and tap into the outside cameras the way I like to do whenever I am along as a passenger and not doing a combat drop. We drop free from *Indy*, and the pilot takes us into a gentle descending turn to port.

"Holy hell," I say out loud when I see the battle damage on *Indy*'s hull with my own eyes for the first time. The holes in the forward port section are each at least two meters across, and the exit hole closest to the bow section caused a lot of ancillary damage. Two of *Indy*'s missile-launch-tube covers are gone, and several square meters of hull plating around the open tubes are torn and buckled from the sudden high-velocity passage of the Lanky penetrators. Such a simple weapon, and so effective against a species that needs to ride in air-filled shells to survive out in space.

I watch *Indy* recede on my helmet display until all I can see of the stealthy OCS is a cluster of flashing navigation lights approaching the much bigger bulk of the fleet supply ship *Portsmouth*. Her streamlined little hull looks tiny against the backdrop of the gas giant behind New Svalbard and the vastness of the space beyond.

The atmospheric part of the ride is less serene than the space phase. We get bumped around a bit as the shearing winds in New Svalbard's atmosphere buffet the drop ship left and right, up and down. After a month of smooth zero-gravity ops, it's a little jarring to get tossed around again like a pebble in a can. I keep my helmet display active and do my usual all-aspect feed from every camera at once, which cuts down on the motion sickness.

Twenty thousand feet above New Longyearbyen and fifteen kilometers away, the cloud cover breaks and gives way to a pale blue sky. Below us, the white expanses of the snow-covered tundra belt stretch as far as I can see, all the way to the distant mountain ranges to our north and south. To our starboard, a white exhaust plume rising from a large flat building marks the location of one of the moon's sixty-four terraforming stations, which are strung along the tundra belt like a girdle, one every hundred and fifty kilometers.

The drop-ship pilot makes a low pass over the town as we come in for a landing at the airfield. I look down at the bunker-like colony housing, each a windowless ferroconcrete dome thick enough to withstand two-hundred-kilometer winds and several meters of snow load. The streets down here are laid out in a way that minimizes alleys for the driving winter winds to funnel through, so New Longyearbyen looks a little bit like a fractal pattern from above. I see several of the colony's tracked snow-movers out on the streets, and even a few people bundled up in hostile environment garb. I know the outside temperature is low enough to shock-freeze exposed flesh in just a few seconds, but after a month in a tiny OCS, I am looking forward to walking in a continuous straight line for a few minutes without having to step across bulkhead thresholds or change directions at gangway intersections every twenty-five meters.

The drop ship touches down on the airfield's vertical landing pad a few minutes later. The tail ramp lowers to reveal a busy stretch of tarmac. There are several rows of drop ships parked in front of the nearby hangars, NAC Wasps and Dragonflies shoulder to shoulder with SRA Akulas. A Dragonfly and an Akula are standing nearby on the VSTOL pad, with the engines running and navigation lights blinking.

Dmitry and I walk down the ramp and onto solid ground for the first time in almost a month. I suppress the urge to kneel down and kiss the frigid concrete, which would probably cost me my lips. Dmitry shoulders his kit bag and nods at me.

"Good luck, Andrew. I do not think I will see you again."

I hold out my good hand, and he shakes it firmly.

"Good luck, Dmitry," I say. "See you on the battlefield some day. Hopefully on the same side."

"Is not likely. But I will not forget what you did. You come defect to Alliance, I put in good word for you. Maybe even make you senior sergeant."

"I'll think about it."

"*Do svidaniya*," he says. Then he turns to walk toward the waiting Akula parked across the landing pad.

There's plenty of activity on the airfield, but I don't see any familiar faces here to meet me. I walk into the control building and down to the access tunnel that leads to the Ellipse, a kilometer and a half away, and start walking, grateful for the solitude and the opportunity to stretch my legs.

The Ellipse is as busy as it was when I left New Longyearbyen a month ago. Civilian ice miners and their families are mingling with soldiers in Homeworld Defense uniforms and the occasional Spaceborne Infantry smock. There's music coming from some of the vendor stalls, and I can smell fried food in the air down here, a scent that makes my stomach lurch. Food vendors down here either mean that the supply situation isn't desperate yet, or the official supply is bad enough to spur black-market demand. I know a thing or two about economics in a shortage zone from my formative years trading stolen shit in the PRC back home.

I make my way through the foot traffic, feeling vaguely out of place in my bulky hardshell battle armor, and head for the admin center, which is naturally almost at the opposite end of the Ellipse from the terminus of the airfield access tunnel.

Chief Constable Guest's office is one of the first rooms beyond the entry vestibule of the admin center. The door is open, and when I peek inside, the constable is behind his desk. He has his humongous boots propped up on the desk, and there's a data pad on his lap. He sees me in the doorway and does a little double take.

"How do you even get boots in that size?" I ask. "I swear, I've seen armored vehicles with narrower tracks."

"Special order. Takes six months to get a pair from Earth. Well, used to, anyway." Constable Guest puts down his data pad and swings his legs off the desktop. Then he gets out of his chair and comes over to the door.

"Good to see you back," he says. "I knew *Indy* was entering orbit, but I figured it'd be another three or four hours before they send a drop ship down." He looks at my bandaged hand and raises an eyebrow. "That doesn't look too good."

"It's not great," I say. "I'll have to take my boots off in the future whenever I have to count to ten."

"See a doc about that yet?"

"We sort of had to leave Gateway in a hurry. I've had the corpsman on *Indy* look at it."

"You still need to go and have one of our docs fix you up. The clinic is down here on the ground floor, at the end of Hallway C and to the right."

"I'll go see 'em soon enough," I say. "No hurry. Fingers are gone, no going back on that. Have you seen Sergeant Fallon around?" I ask, partially to change the subject.

Constable Guest scratches the top of his head. "Check the ops center. If she's not there, she's probably either up in the science section with Dr. Stewart, or over at On the Rocks. Also with Dr. Stewart."

"What is Master Sergeant Fallon doing with the head of your science mission? Is she getting some schooling in astrophysics?"

Constable Guest smiles and shakes his head. "I think their mutual interests are more in the field of chemistry. Distillation, to be specific."

I leave my armor in a corner of Constable Guest's office next to the rack holding his well-worn M-66 carbine in its DNA-locked safety clamp. Then I walk over to the ops center and stick my head into the room, but it's mostly empty except for three civvies and two troopers in HD uniforms I don't know. Dr. Stewart's office in the science section is empty as well except for an impressive amount of clutter on her desk that looks like a scientific experiment on the limits of static design. I jog down the staircase to the underground passage into the Ellipse, eager to catch up with my friend and former squad leader.

On the Rocks is noisy and a bit raucous. There are tables and chairs on the outside of the bar taking up space on the Ellipse, and people are drinking and talking out here at a volume that can be heard fifty meters beyond the nearest bend. I make my way through the little maze of tables and walk into the bar, which is packed to the last table. The people here are mostly civilian workers. A few of the tables have soldiers sitting at them, most in Homeworld Defense uniforms. The soldier and civvie tables are segregated except for one table in the corner of the room. Sergeant Fallon sits with her back to the wall, facing the door, engrossed in conversation with Dr. Stewart. I walk up to the table, and she looks up when she notices my presence.

"Andrew," she says. Then she gets up from her chair and gives me a fierce one-armed hug that squeezes the air out of my lungs. "I am ridiculously glad that you aren't dead."

"That makes two of us," I say, and she laughs. From the way she has to steady herself very slightly before letting go of me tells me that whatever distillation-related business she has been practicing with Dr. Stewart has been going on for a little while already.

"Sit, and have a goddamn drink, Staff Sergeant Grayson. That's an order."

She sits back down and pushes back a chair for me. Dr. Stewart watches our little glad-you're-back exchange with wry amusement.

"Janet," I say. "Good to see you again."

"And you, Andrew. How was the trip to Earth?"

"I've had more fun," I say. Then I sit down on the offered chair and hold up my bandaged hand. "But we got it done. In a fashion."

"Never doubted it," Sergeant Fallon says. "What happened to the hand?"

"Civilian security cop on Independence shot off two fingers. It's a long story."

"Well, we have nothing but time," Sergeant Fallon says. She gets up from her chair again and pats my shoulder as she squeezes past me. "Talk amongst yourselves while I go and get us another round. And then you'll tell me what went down on that mission."

The first Shockfrost cocktail goes down smoothly and quickly, so I chase it with another. My hand is aching again, that unpleasant deep and painful throbbing that comes with deep tissue damage, and I use the last third of the second glass to wash down a pair of Corpsman Randall's little chemical helpers. Then I run Sergeant Fallon and Dr. Stewart through the events of the mission from my perspective. By the time I am finished, the alcohol has warmed me up considerably, and the painkillers have started to deliver the goods.

"We got the big picture from the post-op briefings your skipper sent back. They've had a bunch of meetings about it already. My God, so much talking. And it's all like a snake biting its own tail. Never gets anywhere." Sergeant Fallon takes a sip from her own drink.

"What's the story on *Midway*? When did they rejoin the party?"

Sergeant Fallon's expression darkens. "That chickenshit fuckstick of a reservist," she says. "We sent them messages constantly after you left. They were all the way in deep space, trying to map a sublight path back to Earth, as if they had thirty years' worth of reactor fuel with them. Week or so ago, they came limping back with dry water tanks. And get this: The task force CO tries to claim command. Of all the Commonwealth units in the system. Because he has a golden wreath and a star on his shoulder boards, see."

"Bet that went over well," I say.

"Oh, yeah. *Regulus* Actual told him to go piss up a rope. Not in so many words, of course. Turns out the general spent three weeks in his cabin, never once stepped into the CIC. Had the surgeon write him a chit and claimed health issues. He had the XO bring him his meals to the flag cabin. Personally. His XO relieved him of command and locked him in his cabin for good. No word on whether he got a spanking or two on top of that."

I don't want to laugh—the one-star jackass in question cost us several drop ships and thirty lives with his orders—but the mental image of the reservist general with his CDU pants around his ankles getting his ass beaten by the senior NCO makes me crack up nonetheless.

"Anyway, they came back and rejoined the orbital parade, and we've all just been a big, happy, dysfunctional family ever since," Sergeant Fallon says. "Nothing too exciting. Nothing like what you guys went through."

"So who's in charge now?"

"We do shit by committee right now. The COs of the HD battalions are in command down here. We get together on videoconference with all the COs in orbit once a day to chitchat. Patrol assignments, replenishments, that sort of thing. Bores me to tears. But I guess talking's better than shooting at each other."

"Anything's better than shooting at each other," I say, and look at my bandaged hand.

"Don't worry too much about that," Sergeant Fallon says. "They can do miracles with body-replacement cybernetics these days. Ask me how I know."

I don't really want to talk about our brief stay near Earth anymore, because every time I think about it, I have to consider just how close I was to getting off *Indy* and over to Luna. Just one drop-ship ride, ten minutes of transit, and I would have been breathing the same air as Halley. Instead, I am back here at the ass end of the settled universe, in a crummy little bar on a frigid little moon, and there are once again twenty-eight light-years and God knows how many Lanky ships between me and her. But I don't want to tell my companions that this is what's on my mind. I don't know Dr. Stewart well enough to share these personal concerns, and bitching about not having seen my fiancée and missing a few fingers would seem like self-indulgent whining sitting next to a woman who lost her leg in combat and who got stranded here by her own command, exiled from Earth altogether. So I do the only prudent thing left to do for someone in my place at this point in time, with the resources at my disposal.

I hold up my empty glass and turn it in my hand. "You think I can get another one of these, maybe?"

CHAPTER 20

EXODUS

When I wake up the next morning, it feels like someone clubbed me in the head with a rifle butt last night.

I'm in a bunk, and I'm still wearing my fatigues, but the room around me is absolutely unfamiliar. I sit up—slowly—and try to orient myself while the room around me is not only spinning slightly, but also drifting in and out of focus.

My boots are by the side of the bunk, neatly parked side by side, and my fatigue tunic is neatly draped over the back of a nearby chair. The room I'm in is pretty austere, almost as sterile as a shipboard berth on a fleet vessel. There's an open door on one wall that leads into a small bathroom, and I heave myself out of the bunk to do my morning business and restore some of my cognitive and sensory functions.

I'm in the middle of washing up when the door on the other side opens, and Master Sergeant Fallon walks in.

"Good morning," she says when she sees me swaying in front of the sink in the bathroom. "How are you feeling?"

"Like hammered shit," I croak.

"You wouldn't listen when I told you that the fifth Shockfrost cocktail was a bad idea. You're quite a bit heavier than you look, by the way."

"Did you drag me here all by yourself?" I grab a towel from a nearby rack and start blotting my face dry. "Where is 'here,' anyway?"

"My quarters," she says. "You didn't have assigned quarters yet, and you were in no shape to request them from the civvies. Looks like you came straight to the bar from the landing pad. I can appreciate a soldier who has his priorities so clearly in order."

"Well, I stopped by the ops center first," I say. "Left my armor with the constable." I look over at the bunk, which is a standard military folding cot. "Wait. If I slept on that, where did you sleep?"

"Next to you, dipshit. Floor's too fucking hard." She chuckles when she sees my surprised and mildly embarrassed expression. "Don't worry, lightweight. I was pretty drunk myself. There was no funny business. You were a booze corpse, and I don't poach among the junior NCOs anyway. Especially not the almost-married ones."

She picks up my tunic and throws it in my direction.

"Get dressed and pop some headache meds," she says. "Conference with the CO committee in fifteen. Looks like we're going home soon."

The conference call takes place in the admin center's meeting rooms. From the efficient and routine way everything gets set up and prepared, it's pretty clear that everyone involved has had plenty of practice since *Indy* set out for Earth. I take a seat on the long side of the big conference table in the room, next to Sergeant Fallon. The COs of the two HD battalions, Lieutenant Colonels Decker and Kemp, are sitting across from me, along with their senior NCOs. On our side of the meeting, the civilian administrator and Dr. Stewart round out the group. The far wall of the room is set up with a large holoscreen that is split ten ways to show the feeds from all the other participants. I see Colonel Campbell on one of the screen segments, standing in the well-familiar CIC pit on *Indy*, with Major Renner by his side and slightly behind him, and I feel a vague sense of abandonment.

"Let me open by stating that if there's still a military administration when we get back to Earth, I am recommending you for the Medal of Honor, Colonel Campbell," Colonel Aguilar says over the feed from *Regulus*'s CIC. "You and your crew have pulled off an impossible mission, and we are all indebted to *Indianapolis* for your skill and bravery."

"I appreciate the sentiment, Colonel Aguilar. But we scouted out the solar system as ordered, no more and no less. And considering the way we left, they may give me a firing squad before they hang that medal around my neck."

"We will sort out that situation when we show up in Earth orbit with a three-carrier strike force," Colonel Aguilar replies.

"Our supply situation is critical," the senior SRA officer says. General Park looks tired, and the shadows on his face make his angular features even more prominent. "Our fuel is not so bad, but our rations are low. We are at fifteen percent of reserves. That is a week and a half at best."

"We aren't doing any better," Colonel Aguilar responds. "Ten thousand troops to feed on the ground every day without bleeding the colony dry. We're down to sweeping up the crumbs over on *Portsmouth*. A week at the most. Then we're down to emergency rations."

"Then it is in our best interest to set the agreed-upon plan in motion as soon as feasible."

"We agree, General Park. If you have no objections, we will prepare for departure and initiate the return to the solar system via the Alliance node within twenty-four hours. If you wish, we can level out the supply situation prior to departure and redistribute whatever is left among the Alliance and Commonwealth ships as needed."

"That would be most appreciated," General Park replies.

A new spirit of cooperation and courtesy, I think. Amazing how civilized we can be when there's nothing left to shoot each other over.

"With the airlift capabilities we have left, we'll need six to eight hours to get all the SD troops off the terraformers and onto the carrier," Lieutenant Colonel Decker chimes in. "And that's if the weather doesn't shut down flight ops."

"Then get those birds in the air as soon as you can," Colonel Aguilar says.

"I want to unload my Homeworld Defense troopers on *Regulus*, sir. I know we came here on *Midway*, but they'll need their space for the Spaceborne Infantry regiment from Camp Frostbite. I think it's best if we don't camp out on the same flight deck with the SI boys, considering what happened before you got here."

"I have no issue with that. *Regulus* has the bigger flight deck anyway, and we're short on drop ships. You'll have lots of elbow room."

"What about you, Administrator?" Colonel Campbell asks. "How many civilians are you sending home with us?"

"Any that want to go. But I'll tell you that it won't be very many. We're sort of set in our ways down here."

"If the Lankies find you again, you may regret having passed up the chance."

"If the Lankies find us again, we are going to ground and hope they'll find the place too cold for their taste. From what info you brought back from Earth, I'd say we wouldn't be any better off there right now."

"That's your decision to make, and we have no right to try to tell you otherwise. Make sure that any evacuees are ready for airlift up to the carriers by 1800 tonight at the latest," Colonel Aguilar says.

"Understood," the colony administrator says. "They'll be there on time, whoever's going."

The commanding officers hash out details of our departure while I listen and try to ignore the throbbing pain in my temples. Apparently, the brass have started planning our return while *Indy* was still on her return leg to New Svalbard, but I have no idea how they're planning to get past the seed ships on the other side of the Alliance node, and it's not my place to ask in this particular meeting. All I know right now is that we are leaving for good within forty-eight hours, and that we are heading for unfriendly space again.

"You can stay, you know," Sergeant Fallon says to me when we leave the conference room and walk back down to the ops center.

"Here? On New Svalbard?"

"The COs are giving the Homeworld Defense grunts the option to stay here and be a permanent part of the defense. Way we see it, the Commonwealth dumped them here for good. They have the right to decide for themselves."

"What about you? Are you staying?"

"I thought about it," she says. "Briefly. Very briefly."

"But no."

"But no," she confirms. "None of my guys want to stay here on Ice Station Bumfuck, and I'm not going to leave my troops. Besides, I'd run out of shit to do here really fucking fast."

"The recreational opportunities are limited," I agree.

"It has its good sides. Clean air, lovely scenery. Peace and quiet, if you're into that sort of thing." Her tone makes it clear that she isn't into that sort of thing, as if I needed the clarification.

"You've not been on a spaceship when the Lankies are nearby," I say. "Down here, you get to hold a rifle and shoot at them. Run, hide, fight. Up there, you have nothing. All you can do is hold on to the nearest handrail and hope that the people in command know what the hell they're doing. Most scared I've ever been in my life, and that's no lie."

Sergeant Fallon says nothing for a few moments. We walk up to the ops center door, and she puts one hand on the door handle.

"You're scared because you still have something to lose," she says. "That's the main difference between us. And I really hope that we make it back through again. So you get to marry your sweetheart and stop sticking your idealistic neck out for the greater good. You don't want to keep doing this soldiering shit and then find one day that you're not scared of dying anymore."

"You got no fear of dying, you got nothing to live for, either," I say.

She rolls her eyes at me and shakes her head. "Spare me the motivational-calendar quotes, Andrew. Every time I think you've learned a thing or two, you get all un-jaded on me again. You are such a babe." She wrenches the ops center door open. "T-minus eight," she says. "Pack your shit and enjoy that clean white snow one last time. I'll see you at the airfield at 1800 Zulu."

"Yes, ma'am," I say. "See you there."

I walk up to Dr. Stewart's office to find it an even bigger mess than usual. Janet is going through the drawer of her desk and tossing things into a pair of open shipping containers in the middle of the office floor. She looks up when I step into the open doorway.

"It's the most intoxicated soldier in the world," she says. "From a science point of view, I am surprised you are walking around."

"With some difficulty," I say. "Packing for something?"

She looks around at the mess all around her. "Four years of research in this place. You'd figure I would have had some time to get some sort of organization into place. It's not like there are a lot of distractions around here."

"Ever heard of digital storage?"

"Yeah, yeah," she says with a dismissive wave of her hand. "I'm old-fashioned. I like to mark up my pages while drinking coffee. It's how my brain works best. Most of it is scanned and in the data banks."

"So I'm guessing you are evacuating with us tonight."

"Damn right I am." She pulls a small notebook out of a stack of loose printouts and tosses it into the nearest transport bin. The stack loses its cohesion, and papers slide onto the floor. Janet pushes them aside with her foot.

"I've been here for forty-seven months. I've not seen my family in well over a year. I don't have any kids that were born here. My family's back on Earth, in Pennsylvania. I'm already six months past my original contract commitment. You bet your ass I'm taking the last ride out of here. I don't think there'll be much need of astrophysics research here in the future."

"They're at Mars," I say. "The Lankies. They've wiped out the colony. I saw it when we flew by. No telling when they'll move on Earth, but they will."

"Then that's all the more reason to get home. I'd much rather die with my husband and my kids than out here by myself." She picks up another small stack of notebooks and flings them into the bin next to her. "Piece of advice, Andrew. If you ever get married and have kids, and they offer you a job that will take you thirty fucking light-years away from home, tell them to smooch your taint. Even if they offer a hundred percent monthly bonus. You can't read good-night stories to your bank account, or brush its hair, or teach it how to ride a bike for the first time."

I don't have anything to pack except for the set of battle armor I left in Constable Guest's office. The tall chief constable is behind his desk when I walk in. Unlike Dr. Stewart's environment, his is orderly and neat, and he is not in the process of packing up things.

"Staying here," I say, not a question but a statement of fact.

"Of course I'm staying here," he says. "This is my home."

I don't even consider trying to talk him out of his decision because I know I would get precisely nowhere. He has lived here for ten years by choice, both his daughters grew up here, and he's an essential member of this community. If things are about to end for humanity, they will end right here in this place for him, and he is perfectly fine with that prospect.

"I don't think we'll see each other in a few weeks," I say. "So I guess this time it's a genuine farewell."

"In the classic, literal sense," he says. Then he gets out of his chair and extends his hand. "May you fare well, Sergeant Grayson. Not just for the trip, I mean. With whatever comes after for you."

I shake his hand, which is about twice the size of mine.

"And you, Constable Guest."

I gather my armor and leave the office. Constable Guest sits down again and returns to whatever paperwork he was working on when I walked in, steady and predictable as the sunrise.

I spend the rest of the day taking one last walk on the Ellipse and letting the chrono tick down to 1800 hours. On the Rocks is as busy as it was yesterday, but this time I give the place a wide berth. Just the sight of the little plastic tumblers they use to serve their drinks is making me feel queasy again.

In the midafternoon, I run out of places to walk. I'm anxious the way I always am before a really big event—shipping out for boot camp, or preparing for a combat drop. I put on my armor in the admin center and stroll out through the surface doors into the sunlit and snow-packed streets of New Longyearbyen. We fought a battle here against our own allies, a little over two months ago. I walk over to the corner where we had one of our autocannon emplacements set up. The concrete barriers we used for cover have long since been removed, but I can still remember exactly where I stood and what I did when the SI troopers tried to force a landing here in front of the admin center. On the thick walls of the building behind me, deep craters still bear witness to the strafing runs from the *Midway*'s Shrikes. On the other corner just to my left, we lost half a dozen HD troopers to that cannon fire. I've never been able to revisit a site where I fought a battle before, and it's a strange, detached feeling. That building behind me is so solid that it will survive this generation, and the next one, and then the one after that. It will even survive a Lanky attack if they come and take this place. In a hundred years, those marks left by the armor-piercing grenades from the Shrikes will still be in that wall, long after everyone who has fought in this battle is dead and forgotten, and nobody knows about the little skirmish that took place here, a minor footnote in a very short chapter of colonial history.

We're in one of New Svalbard's perennial daylight phases, so when I get to the airfield for the last batch of pickup flights, it's still bright and sunny outside. The cold is tolerable enough that I am not wearing my helmet. Overall, it feels a lot like the day I set foot onto this moon a few months ago when we arrived on *Midway*, before all the local trouble started.

There are fewer drop ships on the ground than when I arrived this morning. A flight of four Wasps is standing on the VSTOL pad in a single row, tail ramps down, with refueling probes in their fuel receptacles. I can still see the hastily repaired damage on the tarmac where the missiles from *Midway*'s Shrikes blew up the underground aviation fuel tank. The drop ships are refueling from mobile bowsers on tank-like treads.

There are maybe fifty civilians waiting in the nearby main building that houses the control tower. Some are families with children. All have luggage with them, standard cargo boxes and a motley assortment of personal bags and polyplast suitcases. Considering the civilian population of New Svalbard, which is somewhere between ten and fifteen thousand, I had expected more takers for the evacuation offer.

Standing in the group is Dr. Stewart, looking a little lost in her oversized cold-weather clothing. She has a wheeled tote next to her, and she is fidgeting with a PDP in her hands. Then she looks up and spots me, and I give her a smile and a nod that I hope to be reassuring. If I feel anxious at the prospect of running a Lanky blockade, I can't imagine how these civilians must feel.

Outside, three of the colony's large six-wheeled snow tractors pull up on the tarmac. The rear doors open, and a bunch of HD troopers come filing out, each with a rifle slung across the chest and carrying a personal kit duffle. I recognize a bunch of them from our earlier defense of the colony. This is Sergeant Fallon's inner core of 330th AIB Spartans, the NCOs and pilots who had key positions during our little rebellion. Sure enough, the last people to disembark from the last tractor in the line are Sergeant Fallon herself and the CO of the battalion, Lieutenant Colonel Kemp. I walk over to the door and step outside to join them.

"Let's get the hell out of this place," Sergeant Fallon says when

I walk up to her and the lieutenant colonel. "Let's give these people their little moon back."

"How many of ours are staying?"

"Thirty from the 309th," Colonel Kemp says. "Eleven from the 330th."

"We put them under the administrator and Constable Guest," Sergeant Fallon says. "Camp Frostbite is keeping a garrison in place, too. One reinforced company of SI."

"They know nobody's going to relieve them again if things go to shit?"

"They do. Figure they'll take the devil they know over the devil they don't."

"That's it, then," I say, and look across the windswept tarmac toward the waiting drop ships.

"That's it," Sergeant Fallon confirms. "Now let's get those civvies strapped in and ready for dustoff. I never was a big fan of garrison duty. Too much idle time."

We board the drop ships in mostly segregated fashion. The Homeworld Defense troopers claim one of the drop ships, and the crew chiefs load the civilians on the other three. Some of the smaller kids fuss and cry when they are led up the ramp of the forbidding-looking war machines, and it occurs to me that they are young enough never to have been on a spaceship despite being colony-born.

I get on the ship with the civvies just so they have someone else in battle armor on their ship other than the loadmaster if things go wobbly. Atmospheric flight in a drop ship can be alarmingly shaky even when you're not on an ice moon with a volatile atmosphere, and my presence may give some reassurance.

We leave the ground at precisely 1800 hours Zulu time and begin our ascent. I don't bother putting on my helmet and asking the flight deck for data-link permission for my usual external-view sightseeing. I've seen enough snow and ice down here to last me for a few years at least.

Good luck, Constable, I think. *May you live a long and uneventful life with your family down there.*

The flight deck on the *Regulus* is huge and very empty. Our four Wasps are the only drop ships on the deck when we depart New Svalbard orbit. There are three Shrikes parked on the other side of the flight deck, and a whole lot of bare deck in between. A Navigator-class carrier, built for housing a planetary-assault task force, usually has thirty-two drop ships, enough to launch two full battalions of Spaceborne Infantry, but *Regulus* was in the dock for refits when the Lankies arrived, and her usual complement of Shrikes and Dragonflies was either assigned to other ships or lost in the Mars battle. On the plus side, we have more than enough elbow room for the civilians and the almost three thousand troops of the 309th and 330th Autonomous Infantry Battalions who are already busy erecting makeshift privacy walls and rows of collapsible cots on the flight deck.

As a fleet NCO, I have the right to claim whatever open berthing space they have on this ship, but it wouldn't feel right to run off and leave the HD troopers I've fought with against my own command, so I go and find Sergeant Fallon to stay close to her gang of rogues.

"We're claiming those drop ships," she says to me when I get to where the command section of the 330th is milling around and supervising the construction of their section of Tent City.

"Claiming them for what?" I ask.

"Command posts. One ship for the 309th, one for the 330th, one to store all the emergency rations so we can supervise the distribution. They're taking up space on the deck anyway. Might as well use them for temporary berthing. They're big enough inside."

"Might as well," I concur.

Overhead, the 1MC trills its ascending two-tone signal for the beginning of an all-ship announcement.

"Now hear this: All hands, prepare for departure. Repeat, all hands prepare for departure. Secure all docking collars."

"Well," Sergeant Fallon says after the end-of-announcement trill. "It's all or nothing now. Earth or bust."

"Earth or bust," I agree, but without enthusiasm. I've seen too many times what it looks like when a warship in space goes bust.

CHAPTER 21

—CLEARED FOR TRANSITION—

We decelerate for the transition point four days later in deep space way out in the Fomalhaut system, the strangest and most colorful task force I've ever been a part of.

We have three carriers: *Regulus*, *Minsk*, and *Midway*. *Regulus* is as large by displacement as the much older *Minsk* and *Midway* put together, but they are still three carriers in close formation, and I've never seen that many together in one spot. There are the two cruisers, *Avenger* and *Long Beach*. One destroyer—the Chinese *Shen Yang*—and three frigates. With the three SRA supply ships and our own *Portsmouth* fast fleet oiler, there are thirteen ships from two different navies and four separate nations in battle-group formation in front of the SRA transition point. Dmitry is undoubtedly back on *Minsk* with his marine comrades, and I imagine their flight deck is probably even more crowded than ours.

"Commencing resupply operation," the refueling operator on *Portsmouth* says as *Avenger* comes alongside to take on reactor fuel.

I'm in the cargo hold of the Wasp drop ship serving as the command post for the 330th AIB. As a fairly junior NCO, I have no business in the carrier's CIC, but I don't want to stay out of the loop and stare at a flight deck ceiling while we are in the middle of combat ops. So I've used my data access as a combat controller to patch into the nonsensitive parts of *Regulus*'s shipboard tactical network. We liberated a holographic projector, and the forward bulkhead of the drop ship is serving as a display screen, showing the feed from the drop-ship computers that are talking to the tactical network. It's a nonregulation setup, but the *Regulus* crew either haven't discovered it yet or simply don't care. I put the ship-to-ship channel on the overhead speakers, and the screen is showing the feed from multiple external cameras on the *Regulus.* All around the carrier, ships are coasting into and out of formations. We are refueling all the ships in the task force from the supply ships before accelerating through the Alcubierre node and into the solar system.

"God, what a shitload of steel," Sergeant Fallon says from behind my left shoulder. She waves a half-eaten emergency ration bar at the screen. "You want to know why the welfare civvies are eating shit, there's your answer. That's where all the money went." She takes another bite from the bar and makes a face. "Speaking of eating shit. This is awful. It tastes like a chunk of boot sole that someone marinated in sweat for a week. I thought the fleet ate better than the mudlegs."

"Those are emergency rations," I reply. "Once you're down to those, you don't care much about flavor. One thousand calories per bar."

"Give me your unadulterated fleet-trained, combat-experienced opinion, Andrew. How good is this battle plan they cooked up?"

I think about it for a moment—not that I haven't played out the scenario in my head a hundred times since the briefing earlier today. I'm no longer invited to the all-brass conferences, but the COs of the HD battalions were, and they were courteous enough to brief their senior NCOs.

"It's actually pretty damn smart," I say. "The little Korean brigadier cooked it up. Sly son of a bitch. I'd hate to fight a battle against him."

Indy will play scout again. They combed through all the data we brought back from our scouting run and came up with an algorithm for the predictable patrol pattern of the Lanky seed ships. In another forty-five minutes, *Indy* will accelerate and transition back to the solar system by herself, and if the algorithm is on the money, she will pop out of the node at a moment when the Lanky ships are at the far ends of their patrol ellipse. Seven minutes later, the now-empty supply ships will follow *Indy* and play bait before the rest of the task force comes through at maximum safe-transit velocity. The crews of *Indy* and the supply ships will be stripped to their bare minimum. The remaining crew members have all volunteered for what is dreadfully close to a suicide run. If all goes well, the Lankies will give chase to the empty supply ships and make way for the rest of the task force to come through the node seven minutes later.

"What if they mined the exit after you guys went through right between them?"

"Then the supply ships are going to be minesweepers," I say. "Nonreusable ones."

"Damn." Sergeant Fallon wraps up her emergency ration bar again and sticks it into the chest pocket of her tunic. "Don't ever let me say again that fleet deck moppers have no balls."

We watch the resupply ballet as the smaller combatants take their turns on both sides of the *Portsmouth*. There's nothing left on the supply ships but reactor fuel and drinking water. We used up the last of the packaged rations and New Svalbard bring-alongs yesterday, and now we're down to emergency bars. They'll keep us alive until we get back—if we get back—but they take all the fun out of chow time. Under normal circumstances, I would get bored watching frigates refueling from a fleet oiler, but right now I wouldn't mind the whole process taking longer, because when it's over, we are jumping back into the shark tank again. Everyone on this flight deck is nervous and anxious, and we're all trying to pretend that we're not.

When the refueling queue is finally serviced, the supply ships break formation and take up position in front of the task group and slightly above. I don't see *Indy* on the optical feed at all—it's difficult to spot the stealth ship unless you know exactly where to point the lens, even at short range—but I know she's out there right now, swinging around the task group to gather speed for the transition. I feel guilty for not being in her CIC right now, even though there's absolutely no good I can do over there on this mission. All nonessential personnel have been transferred off *Indy*, which would have included me anyway, but it doesn't ease the feeling of letting Colonel Campbell and Major Renner down, irrational as it is.

"Combat stations, combat stations. All hands, combat stations. This is not a drill. I repeat: combat stations, combat stations."

The combat-stations alert sounds a lot louder in the cavernous flight deck than it did in *Indy*'s CIC. We will be on alert for the entire Alcubierre transition back, because we know that as soon as we come out on the solar system side, we will be fighting and running for our lives.

Then the 1MC comes to life again.

"Attention all hands: This is the CO. We are cleared for transition in T-minus twenty-one. Stand to and man your stations. *Regulus* goes to battle."

Out in the distance toward the transition point, a set of position lights glows briefly, as if in salute.

"*Indianapolis*, you are cleared for transition in one minute. Good luck, and Godspeed."

I listen to the radio chatter on the ship-to-ship channels as all the ships in the task force send their own salutes to *Indy.*

If you don't make it through, I hope you make a bright comet, I think.

"Transition in thirty. Beam lock confirmed. See you on the other side. *Indianapolis* out," Major Renner's voice comes over the speakers. She doesn't sound anxious in the least.

"Twenty seconds," *Regulus*'s tactical control says. "Ten seconds. Five . . . four . . . three . . . two . . . one. *Indy* has transitioned out."

"T-minus seven for Flight Two. Flight Two, advance to your transit positions."

Time ticks away as we wait for the supply ships to maneuver into position. *Indy* went through the node at slow speed, to maximize her stealth when she came through on the other side. The supply ships, going through exactly seven minutes after *Indy*, are transitioning while going at full acceleration. When they are through, they will shoot out of the Alcubierre node at five hundred meters per second, to play the hares that give the foxes something to chase. The supply ships swing wide around the task force and accelerate toward the node. Then they are gone in a blink, off at superluminal speed and away to a point twenty-seven light-years in the distance.

"T-minus seven for Flight Three. Flight Three, advance formation to transit positions and keep queue order."

The three-carrier formation and its escort spread out and line up for the transition. Then we are under way at maximum acceleration, which we will keep for seven minutes. By the time we hit the node, we will be going almost as fast as the supply ships that went before us.

Regulus is the fastest of the carriers, so she gets to take the lead in the queue. The knot in my stomach grows bigger with every minute we accelerate toward the Alcubierre node. Once we are engaged, there's no putting on the brakes or turning back.

"One minute to transition . . . Thirty seconds to transition . . . Ten. Nine. Eight. Seven. Six . . ."

Next to me, Sergeant Fallon takes the ration bar out of her pocket again and sticks out her tongue. "You know what? If this ends up being the last thing I get to eat before we all buy the farm, I'm going to be really fucking pissed."

CHAPTER 22

BATTLE PLAN ROMEO

"All hands, prepare for transition. In ten. In five, four, three, two, one. Transition."

Regulus's hundred thousand tons and three thousand souls blink back into normal space with barely a hull vibration, the smoothest Alcubierre transition I have ever experienced in any fleet ship.

"Oh, fuck me," Sergeant Fallon says next to me when the display on the bulkhead comes back to life. Her voice is a little muffled by the battle-armor helmet she's wearing with raised visor.

"All units, all units. Execute Battle Plan Romeo."

We are back in normal space. Ahead of us and above our trajectory, there's the unmistakable bulk of a Lanky seed ship, but it's in the distance and heading away from us at a thirty-degree angle. I can't quite get a grip on the situation as well as I would if I had a three-dimensional tactical display in front of me instead of overlapping camera feeds, but I can see that the plan has worked at least partially—the Lanky is moving away from the Alcubierre node, and we have at least fifty kilometers of open space between us and him.

Regulus swings hard to port to clear space for the ships that popped through the node right behind us, and the ship-to-ship channels erupt in terse combat chatter.

"Contact at zero-four-five relative, positive zero-three-zero!"

"Get behind *Regulus*. Come to new heading three-four-one by negative thirty. Expedite, goddammit."

"Get me a targeting solution on that huge son of a bitch."

"Hold all missile fire. Repeat, hold all missile fire. Unmask rail gun batteries and link for barrage fire."

I try to open up as many camera-feed windows on the display as I can to capture the scope of the action that's unfolding. *Regulus* is leading the breakout charge through the node, and all the other ships are behind us in a staggered battle line. We are forming a V with the Lanky ship, with the Alcubierre point at its tip, and the legs of the V slowly diverging as we accelerate away from the seed ship as fast as we can.

"All units, open fire. Weapons free, weapons free."

We watch the fireworks on the camera feeds in slack-jawed awe. Nine capital warships open fire simultaneously with all their rail gun batteries. Hundreds of tons of kinetic warheads streak toward the Lanky ship, salvo after salvo. They cover the fifty-kilometer distance between the ships in just a few seconds and shatter against the hull of the Lanky ship in spectacular thermal blooms. This concentrated barrage would be enough to take apart any ship ever put into space by us or the SRA, but the Lanky seed ship's hull shrugs the kinetic rounds off like an animal swatting aside angry wasps.

"Bogey is coming around! Bearing change to zero-four-five relative."

The seed ship seems annoyed enough with the barrage to break off pursuit of whoever managed to lure it away from the transition point, or maybe whatever entity controls it has decided to pursue the more numerous targets that just popped out of nowhere behind it. But we have a slight speed advantage, and our task group is accelerating as fast as our ships can burn. Whatever cosmic fates have set us on a collision course with this species, at least they're still beholden to the laws of physics, even if they have ships that can withstand millions of joules of kinetic energy.

The task force ships fire another barrage. The lights on the flight deck dim momentarily as the power output of the ship's fusion reactors is almost completely eaten up by a propulsion system going at emergency power and a battery of electromagnetic artillery firing from all tubes. We are increasing the distance meter by meter, and trying to slow the Lanky seed ship down by throwing spit wads at their hull, pure defiance and desperation.

Our formation is rapidly pulling apart. Every ship is making its own best acceleration, and some of the older units are falling behind a little. *Regulus* was leading the charge out of the Alcubierre node, but even with the ten-second head start we had, the frigate *Tripoli* is pulling ahead of us. The heavy cruiser *Avenger*, *Regulus*'s bodyguard unit, could probably outrun us easily, but she is just off our stern and to our starboard, faithfully and doggedly shielding her charge.

"Incoming fire! Vampire, vampire. We have incoming ordnance from the Lanky."

Overhead, the forceful voice of the *Regulus*'s CO comes over the 1MC.

"All hands, brace for impact."

This time I can actually see the Lanky missiles. One of the cameras is angled just right, and against the backdrop of the rail gun impacts in the distance, there are dart-like objects crossing the space between us in a flurry of movement.

This is it, I think. A hit to propulsion or the reactors, we slow down, and then the Lanky closes in for the kill.

But *Regulus* must be just outside the reach of the Lanky's weapons envelope, because there are no impacts on our hull, no holes in the flight deck and screams of panic and anguish. Instead, we keep accelerating away from the Lanky ship, which is still in the middle of its wide and ponderous turn to port.

Behind us, one of the task force ships is not so lucky. There's a soundless explosion blotting out one of the camera feeds and blinding the optical sensor briefly. When the feed returns, it shows a rapidly expanding field of flame and debris, a ship hull losing integrity at full acceleration, getting torn apart by the same forces it had harnessed just moments ago.

"Good God," Lieutenant Colonel Kemp says, ashen-faced behind the half-lowered shield of his helmet.

"We just lost the *Long Beach*," someone says on the ship-to-ship channel.

The escort cruiser to the *Midway* must have taken a direct hit to the fusion plant or into a launch-ready nuclear warhead. Ten thousand tons of steel and alloy, and five hundred men and women, cease to exist as a cohesive unit in the blink of an eye, the most rapid catastrophic failure I've ever seen. Nobody on that ship had time to get into an escape capsule. Nobody on that ship probably even knew what hit them. Just like that, the cruiser CG-97 *Long Beach* and her crew are gone.

"*Shen Yang* is falling out of line," someone else sends.

Our stern camera feed shows the Chinese destroyer. It's still intact, but there's obviously something wrong, because they are slowing down and veering off to starboard. As they turn away from the main body of our task force degree by degree, I can see that they're trailing debris and frozen air from their stern section.

"Oh, no," I hear myself saying. "No, no, no, no."

Shen Yang turns into the trajectory of the Lanky seed ship, which looks massive even at this distance, a streamlined and yet strangely asymmetric matte black shape that has wormed its way into my nightmares years ago. There are only sixty or seventy kilometers between us and the Lanky, and *Shen Yang*'s speed adds to that of the seed ship as she closes the distance rapidly. I know what the Chinese skipper is about to do, but I can't avert my eyes, and from the gasps among the 330th grunts in the cargo hold, I know that they are aware of what's about to happen.

As the Lanky ship rushes out to meet her, the *Shen Yang* starts launching missiles. The covers for the bow launchers fly open, and ship-to-ship ordnance streaks from the launchers, first singly and then in pairs. The rail gun mount on the dorsal line of the destroyer never stops firing at the Lanky. The missiles stream toward the seed ship and explode against its hull, huge white-hot fireballs that blot out the optical feed momentarily when they hit. There are still missiles coming from her launch tubes when the Chinese destroyer rams the seed ship head-on and instantly disappears in a violently expanding cloud of debris.

So close, I think. They were so close. Already we're increasing the distance, and it's clear that the Lanky ship with its millions of tons of mass can't match our acceleration rate. Twenty seconds more and *Shen Yang* would have been out of the seed ship's reach.

All protocols of station-holding and battle-group formation are suspended as every remaining ship in the task force makes maximum acceleration along the same general bearing, away from the Lanky seed ship. We are running for our lives, and we are slowly pulling ahead kilometer by kilometer, but the price we paid is staggering. Between the two ships we lost in the span of three minutes, a thousand sailors, marines, and Spaceborne Infantry troopers are dead, all men and women who had survived the Battle of Mars and the assault on Fomalhaut b.

Thirty minutes later, we are still alive, and still running away. The Lanky seed ship is ten thousand kilometers behind the task force, still pursuing but falling behind more every minute. On the optical feeds, I count only seven other ships of our task force remaining, rushing along at full burn in a procession that stretches for a hundred kilometers.

The infantry soldiers in the cargo hold of the drop ship all seem more than a little shell-shocked by what they just witnessed on the makeshift situational display projected against the bulkhead. Outside, beyond the open cargo ramp, there's a sort of tense calm among the troops on the flight deck, who know that we are in battle but blissfully unaware of just how close we all came to dying a few minutes ago, and how many people did die.

"All units, proceed to assembly point Alpha at best speed," *Regulus* sends over the task force's tactical channel. One by one, the remaining ships radio in their acknowledgment of the order: *Midway. Avenger. Neustrashimyy. Minsk. Gomati. Tripoli. Portsmouth.*

Then, after a long delay of maybe ten seconds during which I hold my breath, Major Renner's voice comes over the channel to acknowledge for her ship.

"*Regulus, Indy.* Proceeding to assembly point Alpha."

I let out a long and very shaky breath.

The sudden relief I am feeling doesn't last very long. A few moments later, someone else chimes in on the ship-to-ship channel. The voice has a heavy Russian accent.

"Supply ship *Ivan Donskoi* has been destroyed also. Total loss, none survived."

Two cruisers and a supply ship gone. One hell of an admission fee to get back into the solar system. But the *Minsk* made it, which means that Dmitry is still alive.

Battle Plan Romeo was a success, tactically speaking. Most of the task force got past the Lanky guarding the transition node, including all three of the valuable carriers with their flight decks packed full of people. But their escorts have taken a brutal mauling doing the jobs they were designed to do: shielding the carriers. Of the three cruiser escorts, two were destroyed. Only *Regulus*'s bodyguard cruiser, the *Avenger*, is still with us. In terms of tonnage, we lost less than a tenth of our task force, but it sure doesn't feel like we got off lightly. *Long Beach* was an older design, not as heavily automated as the new cruiser classes, and half a thousand souls went with her when she blew up. We've been trading slaps with the SRA for decades, but the casualty counts were small in comparison—an infantry platoon here, a frigate there. Against the Lankies, we lose people at a far more prodigious rate, and in much shorter engagements.

"Are we in the clear?" Lieutenant Colonel Kemp asks.

"For now," I say. "He can't keep up with us because we can accelerate just a little faster. Unless there's another seed ship lurking on Red Route One somewhere, we should have a clear shot home."

"But we don't want to stop and smell the flowers," Sergeant Fallon says.

"No, we don't. It was a smart idea to fill everyone up before the transition. We won't have time to slow down for refueling ops. Not if we don't want to get overtaken. You saw what kind of life span our ships have against theirs."

Sergeant Fallon takes her helmet off and puts it on the dropship deck by her feet. Her forehead is shiny with sweat.

"I used to think we grunts had the dirtiest, most dangerous job in the service," she says. "After today, I gotta say I'm pretty fucking glad I'm a ground pounder."

CHAPTER 23

— THIS MAY BE THE DAY —

I can already see Earth through *Regulus*'s high-magnification optics when we encounter the first picket ships. We are less than a million kilometers out from the lunar orbit when we get swept with search radar and pinged with an IFF interrogation.

"Approaching vessels, this is Captain Vigdis Magnusdottir of ICGV *Odinn*. Identify yourselves, or you will be fired upon."

"ICGV?" Sergeant Fallon asks.

"Icelandic Coast Guard vessel," I supply.

"Iceland? I never knew they even had a space-going fleet."

"They don't, really. They have two or three orbital-patrol boats. Nothing that can even make Alcubierre."

"And she's threatening us with that little tin can," Sergeant Fallon says with a wry smile. "I like her pluck."

"Oh, the Icelanders are hard warriors," I say. "Vikings to the core. I have no doubt she'll start shooting if we don't answer the challenge."

Luckily, our acting task force commander isn't taking any unnecessary chances.

"*Odinn*, this is NACS *Regulus*, flagship of Task Force Fomalhaut, coming home to Earth with six Commonwealth ships. We have five SRA units with us as well. It's very good to see you."

"Affirmative," Captain Magnusdottir replies. "It is very good to see you, *Regulus*. Our picket is a bit thin, you see."

If anything, the *Odinn*'s captain has understated the defensive situation around Earth. We pass the picket force, which consists of *Odinn* and one other ship, the South American Union corvette *Barroso*. Together, the two picket ships have maybe two thousand tons of displacement between them, less than half that of the oldest and smallest frigate in our battle group. But as Task Force Fomalhaut coasts into the space between Luna and Earth a few hours later, there isn't much else out there. I see even fewer ships than we did when we had our brief pit stop at Independence a month ago. Almost all the military vessels patrolling the Earth defensive perimeter are from smaller nations and coalitions: South American, European Union, African Commonwealth. Only a handful are SRA or NAC fleet units, and none are larger than a corvette or frigate.

I take control of one of the external camera arrays and point it toward Independence Station as soon as we have a clear line of sight to it. There's not a single ship on any of the docking outriggers, military or otherwise. The section where *Indy* tore loose, the docking berth that took a direct hit from the destroyer *Murphy*'s missile fire, is half-obscured by the bulk of the station, but I can see buckled and torn hull plating and long streaks of scorch marks around them.

"Something isn't right with the comms," I say to no one in particular.

"Why is that, Sergeant?" Lieutenant Colonel Kemp asks.

"Do you have a connection on your PDP, sir?"

The CO of the 330th looks puzzled for a moment, as if he has a hard time remembering just what exactly I am referring to. Then he takes his PDP out of the gear pouch on his leg armor and turns it on.

"Connection, yes." He taps the screen with the thumb of his armored glove. "But I am not getting any updates. Not even the time sync."

Sergeant Fallon takes her own device out and tries it. "Same here."

"I had that problem when we got here a month ago," I say. "Network's up, but it's like it's throttled to death. And I get a ton of comms chatter from a hundred different sources, but I'm not getting shit from the main comms relay. The one above Luna." I point in the general direction of the relay, invisible at this distance in its orbit over the optical sensors. "That thing and the one above Mars route every scrap of comms and data in the inner solar system. We know the Lankies blew the other one up. If this one's gone, too, comms are going to be all kinds of fucked up from here to Titan."

"HD command staff, to the flag briefing room. Command staff, to the flag briefing room," the announcement comes over the 1MC outside.

"I guess we'll find out what's going on," Sergeant Fallon says, and gets up from her seat. "Nice of them to think to keep us in the loop."

"May I come along?" I ask. "I know I'm not part of the command section, but . . ."

"Do come along, Staff Sergeant," Lieutenant Colonel Kemp says. "Least we can do after you rigged us up with eyes and ears down here."

I shut down the display and get out of my chair. Outside on the flight deck, dozens of troopers look over with interest as the senior battalion staff come tromping down the cargo ramp and start the long walk to the access hatch in the flight deck's forward bulkhead.

"The situation is a gigantic Charlie Foxtrot," Colonel Aguilar says, his Spanish accent putting a little trill into the *r*'s. "Nobody—and I mean nobody—is in charge. I've contacted Gateway Control, Fleet Command down in Norfolk, and the orbital-ops center, and they are all giving me different instructions."

The briefing room isn't as spacious as I had expected for a ship the size of *Regulus*, but it's more than big enough for the four NCOs and two staff officers that make up the senior command staff and—in my case—hangers-on. Colonel Aguilar has his XO with him, a tense-looking female major named Archer.

"Truth be told, I'd just as soon ignore everyone right now," the colonel continues. "*Midway* has started to load up her drop ships, but we have no place to unload troops. Can't put them all into Gateway, and planetside . . . Well, take a look."

He gestures to Major Archer, who picks up a controller and turns on the holoscreen on the bulkhead. We're treated to a panoramic high-definition camera feed of the northern hemisphere. It's mostly cloud-covered right now, but there are enough clear spots down by the Gulf of Mexico and the southern part of the Eastern Seaboard to know we're looking at most of North America.

"Goddamn," Sergeant Fallon says. "That's a lot of heat."

Even through the cloud covers, we can see the ember-like glow of multiple massive conflagrations in several spots on the continent. The NAC's metroplexes have finally erupted on a grand scale.

"Half the PRCs down there are ablaze. We have riots from California to Florida down in the South, and halfway up the East Coast. Looks like New York–Boston and the northern cities are fairly quiet, but the South and West look like they're in the middle of World War Four right now."

"Bet you they had a bit of time to regret that they shipped off two full battalions of trained riot troops to the asshole of the galaxy," Sergeant Fallon says dryly. "Looks like what was left wasn't enough to keep a lid on."

"I don't know about that," Lieutenant Colonel Kemp says. "We're looking at the apocalypse. I don't think we ever had much of a chance keeping a lid on that."

"What about the task force we spotted at that deep-space anchorage?" I ask Colonel Aguilar. "All those cargo ships?"

"I think Colonel Campbell was correct," the *Regulus*'s CO says with a resigned shrug. "I think whoever put that fleet together is already gone. So they won't have to deal with that." He nods at the holoscreen. "I sent *Indianapolis* ahead to scout out the anchorage again. Colonel Campbell says he left something behind, and he wants to collect it."

"The recon drones," I say. Sergeant Fallon looks at me quizzically.

"We left a mess of stealth drones at that anchorage," I explain. "We left them on station and with their drives shut down."

"What are we supposed to do now?" Lieutenant Colonel Decker asks. "Between us and Colonel Kemp's troops, we have three thousand people sitting on their asses on the flight deck while that is going on." He nods at the display, the clouds-and-fire tapestry of our home continent spinning slowly in space a hundred thousand kilometers in the distance.

"You want to have them jump into that?" Sergeant Fallon asks. "Be like trying to piss out a million-acre wildfire."

"We can land at—" Lieutenant Colonel Decker begins, but then the lighting in the room switches from white to crimson, and the alert begins to trill.

"Combat stations, combat stations. All hands, combat stations. This is not a drill. I repeat: combat stations, combat stations. Commander to CIC immediately."

Colonel Aguilar dashes to the hatch with a speed that belies his stocky build. We almost fall over each other getting out of our chairs, and follow him at a run.

"Status report," Colonel Aguilar barks when we reach the CIC. "What the hell is going on?"

The tactical officer by *Regulus*'s situation table is white as a bedsheet. "Sir, we got an emergency signal from the picket we passed on the way in."

I know precisely what the tactical officer is about to say, and from Colonel Aguilar's pained little groan, I know that he does, too.

"*Barroso* is destroyed. *Odinn* is damaged and on the way back to Earth. Sir, they have Lankies on their tail. They must have followed us all the way from the transition point."

"How much time do we have before that seed ship gets here?" Colonel Aguilar asks.

"Four hours, thirty-five minutes."

"How the hell did we not see them in our wake?" Lieutenant Colonel Decker asks. He looks like he wants to either punch something or throw up, possibly both at the same time. The *Regulus*'s CIC is awash in conversation at a noise level that is unusually undisciplined for a carrier's nerve center, but considering the circumstances, I'm surprised it's not complete chaos in here.

"Because they're stealthy sons of bitches who don't show up on radar. Because you can only pick them up on optics at short range if you know just where to look. Because we were hauling ass at full burn and blinded our own wakes," Major Archer says. "Doesn't matter right now, does it? They're here."

"Or they will be," Colonel Aguilar says, and looks at his chrono. "In four and a half hours."

"We need to get all the troops and civvies off the flight deck and down to Earth," Lieutenant Colonel Decker says.

"They have little chance on the ground against those things," I say.

"They have no chance at all sitting in that hangar while those things shoot us to pieces, Sergeant," he says sharply.

"We have four drop ships in that hangar," Sergeant Fallon interjects. "Get 'em warmed up and start hauling people down to Earth, right?"

"A round-trip from orbit takes a Wasp seventy minutes under ideal conditions," Colonel Aguilar says. "Thirty people at a time. Forty or maybe fifty if we ignore every single safety regulation and risk a few broken bones. With only four ships—"

"We'll get less than a third of them out of here," Major Archer finishes.

The lightbulb that goes off in my brain is about the size and brightness of a tactical nuclear explosion. I have to restrain myself from bouncing up and down in a very undignified manner, but the idea that just popped up in my head makes for a better sudden high than a whole tube of Corpsman Randall's magic painkillers swallowed all at once.

"How many drop ships can *Regulus* receive and launch at the same time?" I ask.

"She's built for large-scale planetary assault, son," Colonel Aguilar replies. "We can launch thirty-two drop ships simultaneously.

But we don't have those. *Midway* is already using hers for evacuating her own regiment. They'll never be done on time."

"I know where we can get a whole bunch of drop ships," I say.

"Admit it," Sergeant Fallon says in a low voice as we stand a way from the CIC pit to give the command crew space at the comms consoles. "You just came up with that so you can boff your cute little fiancée one last time before the world ends."

"Shut the fuck up," I reply. "No disrespect intended, ma'am."

"No reply from Luna Control, sir," the comms officer says. "It's like nobody's picking up. What the hell is going on over there?"

"I'm getting zip from the relay. Anyone know what kind of network the Combat Flight School birds are tied into?" the comms officer says.

Colonel Aguilar curses softly.

"We're running out of time," Major Archer says.

"XO, call flight ops," the colonel says. "Tell them to get one of the Wasps ready. And tell them to do the fastest preflight they've ever done in their lives if they want to see another sunrise over Earth."

Then he turns toward us.

"You," he says to Sergeant Fallon. "*Héroe de guerra*. Take the staff sergeant here and a platoon of good troops. Race over to Luna and claim every single drop ship in the Flight School hangar on my authority as the acting commander of what's left of the fleet. Anyone tries to stop you, shoot them twice."

"Aye-aye, sir." Sergeant Fallon grins.

The deck crews have already hauled the empty Wasp out of its parking spot and over to the refueling station when Sergeant Fallon and I arrive back on the flight deck at a run. Two thousand sets of eyes are on us when we come through the access hatch, with the older and slower staff officers a little behind us, still catching up in the passageway.

"Sergeant Benoit!" Sergeant Fallon shouts, and one of the NCOs standing near the tail ramp of our repurposed headquarters Wasp snaps to attention.

"Yes, ma'am!"

"Get first platoon of Alpha ready on the triple, full battle rattle. Two minutes," she shouts.

"Yes, ma'am," he shouts back. Behind him, in the nearby makeshift berthing area, the troopers of First Platoon, Alpha Company, are already springing into action without having to have the order relayed to them.

Behind us, the deck crew are pumping fuel into the Wasp as fast as the refueling unit will let them. I have a brief but intense flashback to another hasty refueling, this one on the flight deck of the doomed *Versailles* five years ago, shot full of holes and careening into the atmosphere of the colony planet Willoughby, Halley running through all the preflight motions with grim and focused efficiency.

The grunts are ready in a minute and a half. They assemble on the flight deck in front of Sergeant Fallon, armor sealed, helmets on their heads, rifles slung in front of their chests.

"Not bad for a shifty bunch of fucking slackers," she says. "Now get on board. We have a few dozen drop ships to steal."

The pilot wastes no time getting up to full throttle right out of the docking clamp. He banks the ship to port even before we're all the way out of *Regulus*'s artificial-gravity field, and the troopers in the back hoot and holler like we're on the way to some long-anticipated sporting event.

Outside, in the stretch of space between Luna and Earth, our task force has begun to segregate. The SRA ships have assumed their own formation around the carrier *Minsk*, and the NAC ships have taken protective positions around *Regulus* and *Midway*. Our drop ship banks again, this time to starboard, to avoid running into the hull of the frigate *Tripoli,* which has taken up station in the shadow of *Regulus*'s hull.

"ETA eleven minutes," the pilot says into the ship's intercom. "Still no reply from Luna Control."

Next to me, Sergeant Fallon holds up her wrist and shows me the chronometer she has strapped to the outside of her armor. The little screen shows "04:21:33."

"Four hours, twenty minutes until the end of the world, Andrew," she says. "This may well be the day we both cash in our chips for good."

"You believe in an afterlife?" I ask, and she laughs.

"Nice thought, but no. Although there are some I wouldn't mind. That Viking shit. Valhalla?"

"Where the brave go when they die," I say. "Fight all day, feast all night."

"That doesn't sound so bad. Hope they sort me into that one, not the flaming purgatory shit."

"I think you have the entrance requirements licked for Valhalla," I say, and outline an imaginary medal ribbon around my neck.

"That stupid thing," she says. "I didn't get that for being braver than everyone else that day. I got it for not being dead like everyone else."

We coast over the huge fleet complex on Luna's surface at a speed that's most definitely well above regulation. Combat Flight School has its own little spaceport facility, with hangars for their training ships, and it's as large as the main spaceport on New Svalbard. Our pilot comes in hot over the base's large VSTOL pad, puts the skids down, and initiates the automated docking sequence, all without bothering to ask for air/space traffic-control clearance. We rumble through the airlock into the cavernous drop-ship hangar of the fleet's Combat Flight School, where every aspiring pilot of any combat spacecraft learns the ropes. Inside, there are rows and rows of ships in different sections: Wasps, Shrikes, a few Dragonflies, and two or three designs that are either too old or too new for me to know, because I've never seen them in the fleet.

There are maintenance crews milling about on the hangar deck, and some of them look rather alarmed when the tail ramp of our drop ship opens to disgorge thirty HD troopers in battle armor and with weapons slung across their chests. Some of the deck hands hurry out through the nearest access hatches as Sergeant Fallon's troops spread out around the drop ship.

"Well, there's no shortage of rides here," Sergeant Fallon says.

"You," I holler to a pair of deck personnel in mechanics' overalls standing nearby and looking indecisive at this unusual display. "Go and get whoever's in charge here. And hurry the fuck up."

A very short time later, a group of officers in flight suits come running into the hangar from one of the access hatches. All of them have pilot wings on their suits. The officer in the lead is a soft-around-the-edges major who looks like he sits in a chair much more often than in a cockpit these days.

"This facility is not open for regular flight ops," he says as the group approaches us. "What are you doing here in full combat gear, people?"

"Getting ready for combat, obviously," Sergeant Fallon says. "We're going to need every last drop ship in this hangar and enough pilots to fly them out of here."

"Those are training ships," the major says. "They're out of the regular fleet rotation. I couldn't sign those out to you even if you had the authority to ask."

"Training is over. We have a Lanky seed ship inbound. They'll be here in four hours. There's a carrier with three thousand troops in need of a lift. If you want to start playing protocol games, I will shoot your ass and ask the next ranking officer in this place."

The major looks from Sergeant Fallon to me, the only person in the group who is wearing fleet instead of Homeworld Defense armor. "Is this a joke?"

"I wish it were, Major," I say. "I really do."

"You are now part of what's left of the global defense," Sergeant Fallon says to the group of pilots. "Authority of Colonel Aguilar. He's in charge of that big carrier floating in space nine hundred kilometers that way. How many pilots can you get on deck in the next fifteen minutes?"

"We have twelve instructors left on duty," one of the officers behind the major says. He's wearing the three stars of a captain. "We'll be lucky if we can find all of them right now. It's 2100 hours."

"Get whoever can fly a drop ship," Sergeant Fallon says. "What about the flight students?"

"None of them are qualified yet," the major says. "The senior flight have solo hours, but they haven't graduated. It's still a month away."

"They don't need to fly combat," I say. "Gear up whoever can get a Wasp out of a docking clamp and ferry it down to Earth. Tell the rest to take shelter. This is the big one, sir."

"Sweet mother of God," the major says in a shaky voice. Then he turns to the captain behind him. "Full alert, all hands on deck. Pull the qualified Shrike instructors, too. And all the flight deck crews you can find. Have the senior flight students assemble in the mess hall. Move it."

The captain and two of the other officers dash off without even a salute. A few heartbeats after they're gone, the base alarm sounds.

"Sir." I catch the major by the sleeve of his flight suit as he turns away. "I need to find one of your instructors. First Lieutenant Halley."

The major gives me a puzzled look. For just a heartbeat or two, I am convinced he'll tell me that Halley was ordered off to active duty, or that she's on leave down on Earth, or that he has no fucking idea who I am talking about.

Then the major looks over to one of the other flight suits, this one a first sergeant with a steel-gray buzz cut.

"Where's Lieutenant Halley right now, First Sergeant?"

"Pretty sure she booked the last simulator slot for her class," the first sergeant replies. "They're in the simulator berth on sublevel three."

I am past them and running for the hangar's access hatch before he has finished speaking his sentence.

It takes me a little while to find the staircase to the lower levels. I take the steps four, five, and six at a time. I have no idea which room down here is the simulator berth, so I look into every open hatch as I run down the hallway. Overhead, the base alarm starts warbling, and the lights flicker once and then shift from white to amber.

A door opens down the hallway, and people in flight suits start pouring out of a room to my right and twenty meters ahead. They rush toward me, but I'm wearing battle armor and carry a PDW slung across my chest, and the group parts like water against a ship's bow when I rush through them to go the other way. I reach the room with the open door and step inside.

The simulator berth is at least twice as large as even the generous CIC on *Regulus*. There are simulator cockpits set up in rows along both walls, and there's an instructor platform with a control station on an elevated platform in the middle of the room. Over by the last simulator in the left row, Halley is helping a student out of the cockpit of his fake drop ship, unbuckling fasteners and undoing straps. She turns and sees me, and the expression on her face is equal parts irritation and concern. I notice that she has put her hand on the shoulder of the student who was just about to climb out of the simulator.

"What the hell is going on?" she shouts from the back of the room over the noise of the alert klaxon.

I realize that she doesn't recognize me even with my visor raised. I pop the fast-release locks on my helmet and pull it off my head.

"I'm early," I shout back, feeling relieved and happy enough to burst, and more than just a little smug and heroic. "Told you I'd be back on time."

Halley exhales with a shaky cry when she sees me, and I can see the tears welling up in her eyes. She covers the distance between us at a quick walk.

Then she slugs me in the face, hard.

The hit is such a surprise that I can't even think about blocking it. Her fist connects with my cheekbone, and I see stars for a moment.

"You asshole!" she shouts.

Then she grabs me by the straps of my armor, pulls me toward her, and kisses me on the mouth, roughly and with intensity.

"What the fuck," I say when she lets go.

"I thought you were dead," she shouts, and moves her arm to punch me again. This time I raise my armored glove to be ready to deflect, and she doesn't follow through with the punch. Behind her, the flight student still in the simulator looks at us as if we've started growing tentacles from our foreheads.

"I sent you a letter!" I protest. "A month ago!"

"That's why I thought you were dead," she shouts. "What the fuck, Andrew? You said good-bye to me in that letter. Why the hell would you do that if you were planning on showing up here and being alive? Did you know I grieved for you?"

She raises both fists and holds them up, as if she can't decide whether to punch me, herself, or the nearby bulkhead. Then she lets out a very angry-sounding sob, reaches for my harness again, and kisses me, even more roughly than the first time, a salty and wet kiss that feels like she wants to drain the life from me.

Behind us, the flight student has decided to continue his climb out of the cockpit after all. Halley disengages from me.

"Can't you hear that noise, Stillson? That means alert stations. Get the fuck out of here and topside, will you?"

"Yes, ma'am," flight cadet Stillson says. He unfolds himself out of the cockpit and rushes past us and out the door.

"We need to go," I say. "Things are really bad. The Lankies are coming to Earth."

"After you," Halley replies.

We rush for the door. My cheekbone is throbbing, but I'm happier right now than I've been since I left Gateway in that shit-bucket *Midway* over four months ago, even if the whole world is coming apart around us.

"Give me the short version," Halley shouts from behind as we run up the corridor to the staircase.

"We'll all be dead by midnight," I shout back.

The Combat Flight School's hangar deck is noisy with frenzied activity when Halley and I arrive. At least a dozen Wasps are already lined up on the deck facing the hangar doors, and more are being shuttled into ready spots by half-dressed deckhands and pilots working together. Sergeant Fallon is over by the tail ramp of the *Regulus*'s drop ship, speaking into her helmet headset and pacing. She sees Halley and me as we come trotting across the hangar, and gives me a slight eye roll and a gentle shake of her head. Several of the flight instructors spot Halley and come running toward us.

"Who's here?" Halley asks one of the pilots when they've all gathered around us.

"Everyone but Ricardelli, Carini, and Horner," the pilot replies. "And the major is putting on a vacsuit, too."

"God help us all," Halley says, and several of the pilots chuckle.

"We have a dozen of the senior flight suiting up. I don't feel good about putting them into the command seats, but we have way more birds than pilots."

"They'll be fine," Halley says. "It'll be a milk run. Okay, here's what we'll do."

She points to the ships on the flight line in turn.

"The instructors take the four Dragonflies and half those Wasps. Garner, you take Whisky Nine. She's a bit twitchy when she's cold, so watch the lateral boosters. We don't want to give her to a cadet. The other cadets get the Wasps starting with Whisky Thirteen. The boss can pick from whatever's left. No shortage of ships tonight."

"Please tell me you have pilots for every last one of those ships." Sergeant Fallon comes trotting up, rifle bouncing against the chest plate of her armor.

"We can get twenty-four off the ground," Halley replies. "We have thirty-six Wasps, but six are grounded for maintenance, and I'm flat out of qualified pilots for the rest."

"I thought this was Flight School?" Sergeant Fallon asks.

"I'm not putting cadets with ten solo hours behind the stick for a combat drop," Halley says. "And you don't want to be in the back of the bus with one, trust me."

"First Lieutenant Halley, Master Sergeant Fallon," I interject. "Master Sergeant Fallon, this is my fiancée."

"Don't worry, I won't break her," Sergeant Fallon says. "Pleasure, ma'am. Now let's get these birds in the air. We have three hours and fifty minutes until we are in the middle of a planetary-level shitstorm. Excuse me."

She walks off again, listening to whatever transmission just got her attention in her helmet's headset. Halley looks at me and raises an eyebrow.

"My old squad leader," I say. "Combative is her default setting."

The HD troopers are gathering at the tail ramp of the *Regulus* drop ship for boarding. I look over to the ride in which I arrived, but Halley sees me and shakes her head.

"You are coming with me, mister. You think I'll let you skip town again out of my sight, you are mistaken. Come and watch the door while I change into my vacsuit." She points to one of the Dragonflies the ground crews are rolling into position on the flight line.

"Yes, ma'am," I reply. "It's the apocalypse, and you are worried about propriety? Just change on the flight deck."

"I don't care if it's the apocalypse, Andrew. I'm not about to bare my ass in front of my students, even if the world ends in three hours."

CHAPTER 24

THE BATTLE OF EARTH

For only the second time in my military career, I am riding in the copilot seat of a drop ship, with Halley behind the controls. There's nobody else to claim the second seat in the cockpit, and the cargo compartment behind us is empty. We have seventy tons of spacecraft all to ourselves.

"Remember *Versailles*?" I ask. "You were barely out of Flight School then."

"And you were a green network-console jock," she says. "Yeah, I remember *Versailles*. The good old days."

We're in formation behind the *Regulus*'s Wasp, and there's a chain of twenty-three more drop ships behind us, all empty except for one pilot. Ahead, the position lights of the Fomalhaut joint battle group are blinking in the distance. Earth is a mostly cloud-covered half sphere to our starboard.

All these people down there, and nobody knows what's coming, I think. When I sent my letters off to Mom and Halley a month ago with Sergeant Williamson, I told my mother to get the hell out of the PRC and into the countryside somehow, but I suspect she didn't need the encouragement.

"Do you regret anything?" Halley asks me. "I mean, now that we're looking at the end of it all. Anything you wish you hadn't done?"

I think about her question for a good while and look out at Earth and the stars beyond.

"No, I don't," I say. "Got off Earth. Got to see what's out there. Got to be with you. I wish we could have spent more time together. But I wouldn't undo anything."

"Not even Detroit?"

"Not even Detroit," I say. "Well, maybe I would check the color code on that fucking MARS rocket if I had to do it all again. How about you?"

"Nothing," she says without hesitation. "I wouldn't have changed a thing. Except maybe proposed marriage a few years earlier."

"Sorry," I say. "Looks like we're not going to make the six-month waiting period."

"One last time the military gets to fuck us over and ruin our plans," Halley says, and we both laugh.

We dock at *Regulus* fifteen minutes later, two drop-ship wings hitting the clamps at the same time and getting hoisted into the flight deck simultaneously, a feat that only a Navigator-class supercarrier can pull off.

Halley turns off her engines as we pass through the airlock and get deposited on the flight deck. In front of us, Tent City is mostly gone, and two full battalions of Homeworld Defense soldiers are standing in battle order, waiting for the command to board their rides home.

"Refuel, load up, turn around," she says. "Figure we have thirty minutes."

We step out onto the flight deck to stretch our legs. A few rows down the deck, the *Regulus*'s drop ship settles in, and the tail ramp lowers onto the flight deck.

"Come with me," Halley says. "I have a dumb idea."

"I'm a sucker for those," I say, and follow her across the flight deck and toward the exit hatch.

"First Lieutenant," Colonel Aguilar says sternly. He takes Halley by the arm and walks her over into a corner of the CIC.

"We are three hours away from the biggest battle any of us will ever fight," he says. "And you want me to dedicate some of my limited remaining time to what?"

"You're the CO of a fleet warship," Halley says, unflinchingly. "You have the legal authority. It's not going to take you more than five minutes."

Colonel Aguilar rubs his forehead. "Don't you think that the situation calls for you to have a different set of priorities, Lieutenant? Is this of any importance right now? I mean, look around you."

Halley meets the colonel's gaze with a firm expression, and I've never admired her more than right this moment.

"Sir, I have my priorities straight. I'll go and fight and die tonight just like everyone else. But let us have at least this before we do, please." She nods over to the screen on the bulkhead, which shows the external camera feed from nearby Earth.

"If that's not important, none of it is," she says. "That's why we're up here and not down there, right? For them, not for us."

The colonel looks over his shoulder at the screen. Then he sighs, and his shoulders droop a little. He holds up his left hand and looks at the gold ring on his finger for a moment.

"All right," he says. "*De acuerdo*. Flag briefing room, five minutes."

"Thank you, sir," Halley says, relief in her voice.

Instead of our dress blues, we are wearing flight suit (the bride) and CDU fatigues (the groom). Instead of family and friends, our witnesses are one of the *Regulus*'s SI guards—momentarily pulled off guard duty from in front of the CIC—and a Neural Networks sergeant who just happened to walk past the flag briefing room at the right moment. Our officiant is the very cranky commanding officer of the ship, and we don't have flowers or rice or any of the stuff you're supposed to have. As far as wedding ceremonies go, it's as haphazard and informal as it gets. But Halley and I are here together, and that makes it as perfect as it gets.

"We are gathered here to join Staff Sergeant Andrew Grayson and First Lieutenant Diana Halley in their union," Colonel Aguilar says. "Staff Sergeant Grayson, will you take First Lieutenant Halley to be your wife and legal partner?"

"I will," I say.

"First Lieutenant Halley, will you take Staff Sergeant Grayson to be your husband and legal partner?"

"I will," Halley says, and squeezes my hand lightly.

Colonel Aguilar hands us a pair of rings. They're unadorned, plain aluminum, and they look more like washers than wedding bands.

"Part of the captain's supply chain," he says. "Never needed any until today."

I hold up my still-bandaged hand. "We may have a problem here."

Halley touches my injured hand with hers and lowers it gently.

"We'll just use our right hands," she says. "I hear the Euros do it that way, anyway."

We slip the rings onto each other's fingers. They're the same size, so mine is too tight on me while Halley's is too loose on hers.

"By the authority vested in me by the North American Commonwealth, and as the master and commander of this ship, I now join you in a civil marriage," Colonel Aguilar concludes.

He doesn't say anything about kissing the bride, but I do anyway, and she kisses me back.

"Congratulations," Colonel Aguilar says.

The buzzing of the shipboard comms panel puts an unromantic end to the affair. Colonel Aguilar walks over to the panel and picks up the receiver.

"CO," he says. "Go ahead."

He listens for a few seconds, acknowledges tersely, and hangs up.

"Back to work," he says to us. "The Lanky ship is in visual range now. They didn't decelerate as predicted. They are coming in under steam. We have less than an hour."

"Combat stations, combat stations. All hands, combat stations. This is not a drill. I repeat: combat stations, combat stations."

I am back in my armor, with my helmet on my head. My new wedding band is already gone from my finger because the armored glove won't fit over it. I have it tucked into my personal document pouch, to put back on afterward if there is an after to this. Halley is in her flight suit, and we're back in the cockpit of Dragonfly Delta Five. Behind us, the cargo hold is filling up with troops, and when I look back through the passage past the rear bulkhead, I see that it's Sergeant Fallon and her inner circle, her platoon of Spartans.

"Our ride is on the way to the surface with a load of civvies," she explains when I patch into her channel. "Hope your girlfriend is a crack pilot."

"She's my wife," I say. "And she is a crack pilot."

"When did this happen?" Sergeant Fallon asks.

"Five minutes ago," I say. "She managed to rope the CO into doing the deed."

Sergeant Fallon laughs. "Well, congratulations to the both of you. Of course, this may set a record as one of the shortest marriages ever."

"Attention, all hands." Colonel Aguilar's voice comes booming over the 1MC.

"The Lankies have changed our battle plan for us. The cruisers and escorts will shield the carriers while we move to the rear, to gain time for the drop-ship launches. Once the drop ships are away, the carriers will join the fight. Stand fast, and do your duty. When they land, do not give them a meter. We are the last line, the captains of the gate."

Overhead, the warning klaxons sound, and a dozen docking clamps swivel into position above our row of drop ships.

"'To every man upon this earth, death cometh soon or late; and how can man die better than facing fearful odds, for the ashes of his fathers, and the temples of his Gods?'"

The clamps come down and lock onto our ship. The tail ramp whines shut and seals itself. Next to me, Halley is putting on the Dragonfly like a suit of armor, merging with her systems and letting the ship become an extension of her.

"Wonderful speech," Sergeant Fallon says from the cargo hold. I look over my shoulder through the passageway, and she nods at me and puts two fingers to the browridge of her helmet in a jaunty little salute. She looks like she's having the time of her life.

"Front-row seats to the end of the world," Halley says when we've reached launch position at the bottom of the hull. There is nothing below us but the dirty blue-green sphere of our home world, and nothing in front of us but the darkness of space. *Regulus* is in a long starboard turn, and as we swing around, the other ships of the task force come into sight. They are forming a battle line between the carriers and the Lanky ship, nose to tail and tightly spaced, to concentrate their point-defense fire against incoming ordnance. Halley puts the fleet ship-to-ship channel on the comms and pipes the output through the speakers.

"Now with soundtrack," she says. "I really wish we had some music."

"Twenty Taiwanese Synth-Pop Hits to Die To," I say, and she laughs.

"Attention, all units in Earth orbit," Colonel Aguilar announces over the emergency channel. "This is Colonel Fernando Aguilar, NACS *Regulus.* I am taking command of all military units. All units, proceed to grid two-eight-seven by one-one-five and establish a blocking position against the incoming Lanky ship. Whatever we have left, now is the time to bring it and to use it."

"We are passing into the launch drop window in seven minutes," Halley says. "Once we are loose, I'm flooring it for the deck, so you mudlegs back there make sure you have all your toys strapped in."

One by one, the remaining ships of Earth's orbital-defense patrols climb into higher orbits and come to join the blockade position. Halley has a tactical display on the center console of the Dragonfly, and I count the icons parading slowly across the hemisphere to join our cluster of defenders. A South American frigate, an African Commonwealth corvette, some patrol boats from the Oceanians. They're not enough to blunt the hammer that's about to descend upon us, and their crews know it, but they have decided that dying in a shield wall is better than dying on the run.

"We have visual on the bogey," *Regulus* sends. "Contact, bearing three-five-zero by positive zero-zero-one, two hundred meters per second, CBDR. Distance one hundred thousand and decreasing. All units, unmask batteries and prepare for barrage fire."

With all the task force ships networked, the information from *Regulus*'s CIC instantly pops up on all the tactical screens in every other ship. On the screen between me and Halley, an inverted V shape in blaze orange appears on the very edge of the scan range.

"Weapons free," Colonel Aguilar sends. "All units, engage. Fire at will."

We are too far for the rail guns, but most of the task force ships have held back their missile armaments, and now they're unleashing everything they have in the magazines. Dozens of missile trails streak toward the incoming Lanky, still tens of thousands of kilometers away and increasing the range of our missiles by its own rush toward our effective weapon envelopes.

"Five minutes to launch window," Halley says. "I'll drop early if I have to."

The missile barrage takes no more than two or three minutes. Then the ship-to-ship tubes of the task force ships are spent. I watch the tactical display as dozens of little inverted blue V shapes rush toward the big orange icon and then disappear one by one.

"Missile fire ineffective," *Regulus* sends. "Stand by on rail gun batteries."

"Belay that," a new voice comes on the emergency channel. "All units, hold rail gun fire. This is *Indianapolis.* We are in terminal approach at T-minus sixty. You don't want to mess up our run right now."

I can hear the abandon-ship alert in the background of the transmission, and there's a sudden ball of lead materializing in the center of my abdomen.

"No, no, no," I say. Halley catches on at the same time and shouts a curse against the windshield.

"*Indianapolis*, abort. That is an order. You will abort your attack run immediately," Colonel Aguilar sends.

"Negative, *Regulus*. Get out of the way and make the best of what comes after. It's been an honor serving with you all. Take care to pick up the escape pods we left behind, please. Campbell out."

There's a blip on the display, coming in from the opposite end of the screen from the Lanky intruder, who is now fifty thousand kilometers out and driving on undeterred.

"All units, cease fire! Weapons hold! Weapons hold!"

Indy is moving at full burn, and judging by her insane speed, she must have been burning her main engines at full power for a while. The little OCS is nowhere near as heavy or as fast as the freighter we used to destroy the Lanky ship in the Fomalhaut system, however. I'm not an ace in physics, but even I can do the math involved. Our last-ditch freighter missile at Fomalhaut needed days of constant acceleration to get up to Lanky-killing speed. *Indy* has had only a few hours to accelerate, and there's no way she's going fast enough to destroy a seed ship by ramming it. Colonel Campbell is about to throw *Indy* against the Lanky ship for nothing, and there's not a thing we can do about it. The orbital combat ship has turned itself into a guided kinetic missile that is hurling itself into the jaws of the shark at tens of thousands of meters per second. She crosses our sensor threshold and streaks across it in mere seconds.

I want to close my eyes. I don't want to be witness to the death of *Indy* and however many of her crew that decided to forsake the escape pods and steer the ship toward its target. But I can't tear my eyes away from the display.

Then there's a small new sun hanging in the blackness of space fifty kilometers away.

"*Indy* is—Jesus, *Indy* has hit the Lanky. At fifty K per second."

For just a moment, the universe freezes in place.

Then, through the white-hot bloom of the impact, the Lanky reappears.

"Goddammit," I shout, and pound the dashboard of the Dragonfly with my bandaged hand, an action I instantly regret.

"Lanky ship now at forty-eight thousand, three-five-two by positive zero-zero-one," *Regulus*'s tactical officer sends, and it sounds like he's reading the names off a headstone.

"Aspect change, aspect change on the Lanky," someone else says. "He's ejecting something. Second contact, same bearing."

Something breaks loose from the Lanky ship and gets flung aside into its own trajectory at hundreds of meters per second. Then another object follows, and then it's a constant stream, things of irregular shapes and sizes leaving the ship and forming a trail behind the approaching ship.

"He's damaged. Holy shit, the Lanky is damaged. *Indy* took a piece out of him."

The hull of the approaching ship is no longer the smooth, organic-looking solid thing I'm used to seeing. Instead, the front end of the Lanky ship has a huge chunk missing from it, a scar that extends from the bow of the thing halfway down one side. As I train the camera on it at maximum magnification, I can see matter tearing loose from the wound and tumbling off into space. The hole in the Lanky ship has a strange, fibrous appearance.

"All units, weapons free. Aim for the hole in that hull. Whatever you have left, let the son of a bitch have it."

A dozen ships open up with their rail guns. The barrage fire peppers the undamaged portion of the Lanky's hull without effect, but the hole in the hull seems to absorb the cannon fire instead of deflecting it. Some of the ships have missiles left, and they add them to the shooting-range frenzy that has seized the gunnery officers on every task force vessel.

"Nuclear fire mission," *Regulus* announces. "Firing tubes one through eight. All units, prepare for impact effects."

Eight more missile trails streak toward the Lanky, now forty thousand kilometers out and closing rapidly.

"Get clear! All units, evasive action. Get out of his way!"

There's a mad scramble as a dozen ships go in a dozen different directions to avoid colliding with the kilometers-long behemoth hurtling toward the battle group. The first of *Regulus*'s nukes goes wide and streaks past the Lanky. The second shatters against the undamaged front section and expends itself in a short-lived fission bloom. Then the rest arrive and seemingly hit the hull all at once. At least three of *Regulus*'s nukes disappear into the wound on the side of the Lanky ship.

The side of the Lanky seed ship bows out like the gills of a breathing shark. Then a much bigger section of the hull blows off the Lanky and disintegrates, and this time there is blindingly bright nuclear fire behind it. The seed ship shudders from bow to stern.

"Multiple direct hits! Multiple hits with secondaries!"

"Got you, you son of a bitch," Halley shouts next to me.

The Lanky ship's flight path becomes unstable. The long cigar shape from hell starts to wobble on its trajectory, like an oscillating tuning fork. The stern starts swinging out of line, and the Lanky careens sideways, still on the same bearing but with the bow pointing forty-five degrees off course. The battle group's rail guns and ship-to-ship missiles keep raking the massive hull. Much of the ordnance bounces off the undamaged hull the way it always has, but almost as much is pouring into the open flank of the seed ship.

Our formation is in disarray, each ship evading the Lanky and firing its weapons as fast as it can bring them to bear. It's a brutal short-ranged exchange, and even though the seed ship is clearly mortally wounded, it's not dead yet. From the undamaged side of the hull, penetrator rods spray into space, blindly but in large numbers. We are not in the line of fire, but two of the task force ships are less lucky. *Tripoli* takes a broadside that tears her up all the way from bow to stern, and she starts spinning out of control, bleeding frozen air and shrapnel. One of the smaller corvettes that joined us at the last minute simply blows apart under the hits, shattered alloy and steel hurtling in all directions. Then the Lanky is past the task force, hurtling toward Earth sideways and shedding enormous pieces of itself.

"He's going to hit atmo," someone sends. "My God, what if he doesn't break up?"

"Multiple separations on the Lanky ship," *Minsk* announces.

The camera feed shows smaller objects ejecting from the undamaged side of the hull. They come out in spurts, like the arterial blood of a wounded animal.

"Oh, God," I say. "He's tossing out his seedpods. There's a dozen or more of those bastards in each of those."

"All units, move in and track the debris," *Regulus* orders. "Fire at will."

Avenger still has air/space defense missiles in her magazines. She starts launching salvos of them, fast and angry fireflies that race out to intercept the seedpods before they can make it into the atmosphere and release their cargo onto Earth. But it's too little, too late. Some of the missiles smash into the seedpods, but each of them is the size of a destroyer and seemingly just as hard-shelled as its mother ship. Most missiles fail to track or don't catch up with the seedpods as they hurtle into the upper layer of Earth's atmosphere, trailing bright plasma flares.

"Multiple incursions. Tracking twenty-plus pods in the atmosphere," says *Regulus*.

I don't need a camera to see what's happening right outside our cockpit windows. We are in high orbit above the North American continent, and right now there are hundreds of twenty-meter-tall and hard-to-kill Lankies falling down to Earth in their resilient settlement pods.

"All drop ships, this is *Regulus.* Initiate drop sequence and follow the seedpods down, wherever they fall. Follow them down and kill those sons of bitches. All drop ships, initiate drop sequence," says the *Regulus* tactical officer.

"You don't have to tell me twice," Halley says. She seizes her throttle lever and puts her thumb on the launch button.

"Whisky and Delta wings, follow me," she says. "We'll assign targets on the way down. Dropping in three, two, one. Drop."

She punches the launch button, and the Dragonfly drops away from the *Regulus.* Halley opens up the throttles and brings the nose around and down with a satisfied little shout.

"Tallyho. Lock and load back there, folks. You'll be in the dirt and killing shit in fifteen."

CHAPTER 25

—THE SECOND BATTLE OF— DETROIT

"This is going to be a mess on the ground," Halley says.

We are streaking through the upper layer of the atmosphere, and as far as my field of view through the armored cockpit windows reaches, I can see seedpods falling toward Earth, dozens of them bleeding off speed and trailing long streams of superheated plasma. It's almost misleading to call them "pods" like we've been doing all along, when all we saw of them were the husks on conquered colony worlds after Lanky landings. They're huge and cylindrical, like blunt miniature versions of their host ship, but even in miniature they are hundreds of meters long. It's like an entire fleet of capital ships falling out of the sky over North America.

The computer maps the descending seedpods and projects their trajectories on the navigation map.

"Everyone pick a pod to follow down," Halley sends to the rest of the drop-ship flight. "Whoever's in range. Tag yourselves on TacLink when you claim your target so we don't double up by accident."

There are three pods careening through the atmosphere more or less in front of Halley's Delta Five. Her hand does a rapid dance on the navigation screen.

"Labrador, the Minneapolis metroplex, or Detroit," she says. "Where do you want to party tonight?"

"Anything but Detroit," I say.

"That one's the easiest trajectory for me to follow," she says. "Detroit it is. Sorry."

She assigns her ship to the middle contact and toggles into her flight channel again.

"Everyone, pursue them right down to the deck. Their retardation mechanisms will deploy at twenty thousand, and they'll slow down for the landing. Hit them right when they land. Don't give them a chance to disperse."

She flicks the display to a different screen and checks her stores. "Goddamn, do I wish we had some missiles on this thing."

"We're unarmed?"

"Not totally. We have the cannons. But these are training ships, Andrew. We do flight instruction and systems familiarization with them. Not much of a call for leaving rocket pods on the wing pylons."

"Please tell me the armory is full," I say.

"It's always full," she replies. "Takes too long to get them back to alert status otherwise."

"Best news of the day," I say.

We chase the Lanky into the atmosphere above the northern continent. The Lanky is falling ballistically, and Halley can't follow in the same way because the drop ship would burn to ashes from the generated heat, so by the time we're passing through the troposphere, the Lanky is several hundred kilometers ahead of us and still increasing distance. Once the worst of the buffeting stops, I unbuckle my harness and make my way into the cargo compartment.

"You got some instruction on these when they trained you for the Fomalhaut deployment," I shout. Every pair of eyes in the cargo hold is on me as I hold up one of the M-80 Lanky zappers from the drop ship's armory. "Don't bother with the fléchette rifles unless that's all you have left. Takes too long to make a dent with those. Aim for the joints at the knees and the arms, and the spot where the necks would be if those sons of bitches had any. And take every rocket for the MARS launchers we have. Shoot the armor-piercing first, then HEAT, then thermobaric. Leave the dual-purpose shit for last when you've run out of everything else. Point-blank, they'll do a Lanky in just fine. Use 'em in pairs."

"How many of those things have you killed?" one of the sergeants yells.

"Hundreds," I say. "Thousands. With my radio. They're plenty hard to kill, but you can kill them just fine."

Three of the other sergeants get out of their jump seats to help out, and we start emptying the armory, handing out rocket launchers and heavy anti-Lanky rifles to the platoon. I wish we had a week to give these HD troopers some more training on these things, and I wish we had three times as much ammo in the armory as we do, but this is what we have right now, and all the time we have to prepare.

At five thousand feet, we break out of the cloud cover. The hundreds of square miles of Detroit are spread out below us, the old city ringed by neat clusters of hundred-story PRC blocks, row after row of towers. The part of Detroit I dropped into five years ago and almost got killed in was toward the old part of town, in the old first- and second-generation PRCs that still resembled a regular city somewhat. The part of Detroit we are descending into now has a whole different feel to it. The scale of these fifth-gen

PRCs is overwhelming, each block a self-contained unit of four towers that reach one hundred floors into the night sky, over a thousand vertical feet.

"Try to make contact with whatever HD battalion is closest," I say. "The 365th out of Dayton, maybe. Tell them we need everyone out here who can hold a rifle. And tell them what's coming their way, if they don't know already."

When the Lanky seedpod hits the ground, it's like the finger of a grumpy god reaching out and shaking things up for the mortals. The pod slams into the dirt maybe a hundred meters from the outer perimeter of a fifth-generation housing block, four hundred-floor towers forming a square with ten-meter-tall concrete walls on the outside. We hear the concussion of the impact from several kilometers away and through the multilayered polyplast of the cockpit.

"We have footfall," Halley sends back to *Regulus*. "Lanky seedpod touched down at forty-two degrees, nineteen minutes fifty-three seconds north, eighty-three degrees, zero-two minutes, forty-two seconds west, 1119 Zulu local time."

The Lanky ship hits nose-first. It's much squatter and shorter relative to the shape of its mother ship, so it doesn't stay standing on end for long. The whole thing totters and then begins to lean over in what feels like slow motion. Then the end that was pointing skyward falls toward the nearby PRC towers and crashes down. The Lanky pod is longer than the distance between the outer walls of the PRC block and the impact point, and the mass of the pod bulls into the junction between the wall and the closest PRC tower. There's a thunderclap that sounds like a fuel-air bomb just went off, and the area is obscured by an expanding cloud of concrete dust and flying debris. Halley puts the Dragonfly into a shallow dive and streaks toward the crash site.

When the dust clears a little, the front third of the seedpod is buried in the corner of the residence tower. Thirty meters of concrete wall are pulverized underneath the mass of the pod. Halley switches on the searchlights at the front of the drop ship's nose. They cut through the dusty darkness to reveal three Lankies stalking away from the wreck, into the space between the tower blocks.

"Contact," Halley calls out. "Three hostiles on the ground. They are in the middle of a civilian residential area. I am engaging."

Halley pulls the drop ship into a hover maybe three hundred meters from the crashed pod and the ruined barrier wall of the PRC block. She flicks on the searchlights on the nose of the drop ship, which instantly pierce the dusty darkness with blindingly white fingers of light. The Lankies have skin the color of eggshells. Under the glare of the Dragonfly's lights, they are as obvious as buildings.

"Motherfuckers are *big*," Halley says. All I can do is grunt my agreement.

I've seen many Lankies, and while these appear no different from those I've seen in the past, the human habitat surrounding them gives them a whole new terrifying sense of scale. Two of them are walking away from the wreckage of their pod with brisk, long strides, and the tops of their cranial shields are six stories off the ground.

"Hold on to something back there," Halley shouts over the intercom to the grunts in the back of the Dragonfly. Then she guns the engines and accelerates at full throttle. She swings the nose of the ship to the left, past the nearest undamaged residence tower, and loops back around into the plaza between the buildings. She flips a few overhead switches, and when she starts talking again, her voice is booming out of the speakers for the external public-address system of the drop ship, amplified a few thousand times.

"Seek shelter. Get indoors and away from the windows. Go to the upper floors. Get out of the plaza!"

The scene below is utter pandemonium. The plaza between the four towers is a big square of maybe two hundred meters on each side, and it's packed with people who are retreating from the sight of the Lankies like a swift ebb pulling away from a shoreline. I see the muzzle flashes of gunfire, the sounds too distant and the cockpit glass too thick for me to hear them, as some of the people in the crowd open fire with whatever weapons they have on hand.

Halley pulls the Dragonfly into a hover again between the two nearest residence towers, each reaching three hundred meters into the night sky, a hundred floors of tiny apartments stacked on top of each other. We are close enough that I can see people in the windows staring at us wide-eyed, the position strobes of the drop ship illuminating the scene in regular sharp flashes of red and orange.

Halley pops the safety cover off the launch button on her flight stick.

"Let's rock," she says.

The heavy antiarmor cannons on the underside of the Dragonfly rap out a thundering staccato: boom-boom-boom. The reports echo in the artificial canyon between the buildings and reverberate off the concrete surfaces all around us until it sounds like an entire wing of drop ships just opened fire. Tracers shoot across the plaza and smack into the nearest Lanky in a shower of sparks and flying shrapnel. I realize that Halley made her loop around the towers to get a clear shot at the Lankies, to minimize the risk of these heavy cannon shells hitting the buildings instead. She works her trigger like a musician timing a beat.

The Lanky shrieks that unearthly wail that has chased me through many dreams in the last few years. In this place, it sounds utterly foreign. The sound is so earsplittingly loud that it almost drowns out the thunder from the Dragonfly's weapons. It flails its long, spindly limbs and ducks from the hail of gunfire pouring from Halley's autocannons. Halley doesn't give it any reprieve. She keeps up a methodic staccato of bursts that rake the Lanky's head and torso. Several cannon shells ricochet off the cranial shield that makes the Lankies look a little like old Earth dinosaurs. The tracers careen into the darkness and explode against unseen obstacles in brilliant little bursts of white-hot sparks.

The Lanky turns around and strides away from the cannon fire in long, halting steps. Halley shifts her fire and sends a stream of tracer shells into its lower body. The Lanky stumbles, and its own momentum carries it forward. It flails wildly as it crashes to the concrete of the plaza. Its head hits the wall of the nearby residence tower and tears a three-meter gash into the concrete facade. When the Lanky hits the ground, a cloud of concrete dust billows up around it.

The two other Lankies are crossing the plaza in long, thundering strides, away from the drop ship and its lethal cannon fire. Halley fires another burst into the Lanky on the ground and then swings the nose of the Dragonfly around. The spindly bastards can move amazingly fast for something that large. Not twenty seconds have passed since Halley first opened fire, and one of the remaining pair of Lankies is already all the way across the plaza and disappearing behind another one of the residence towers. The other is right in the middle of the plaza, stalking after its companion in the biggest hurry I've ever seen one move. Halley puts the thumb down on her flight stick button, and the cannons spit out their hail of red-hot fire and death again.

The shells pepper the Lanky's torso and the backs of its legs. Its stride falters, and the huge alien stumbles and falls to the ground with a dull and resonant concussion. Halley keeps up her fire—short, deadly accurate bursts of two or three shells at a time, using the entire ship to aim the guns. There's a cluster of small one-story buildings where the Lanky fell—food-distribution booths or vendor stalls maybe—and the Lanky's enormous mass flattens them as if they were empty ration boxes. It tries to scramble to its feet in the rubble, but Halley rakes its legs with another burst, and it crashes back down to the ground, wailing its shaky and warbling cry at deafening volume. The unearthly sound reverberates from the concrete canyons nearby. I've always wondered what that noise would sound like in the middle of a major city, and now I don't have to wonder anymore. It sounds like something from an old monster feature on the Networks.

"Goddammit," Halley shouts. "Will you just fucking *die* already?"

But the Lanky doesn't do us the favor. Instead, it rights itself once more and scoops up what looks like half a ton of random debris with a long and spindly arm. Then it flings the load of shattered bits of concrete wall and corrugated roofing at us from maybe fifty meters away.

"*Whoa*," Halley says. She ceases her cannon fire and pulls up the nose of the Dragonfly sharply. The engines increase the pitch of their noise, and then we are flying backwards. For a moment, I see the tops of the nearest two residence towers through the windshield of the drop ship, and the dirty night sky beyond. I am keenly aware that we are between two of those towers, with very little clearance for maneuvering. I look to my right and see windows, and faces staring back at me. Then a bunch of debris noisily hits the armored underside of the drop ship. The Dragonfly shakes with the impacts. From the cargo bay in the back of the ship, I can hear some concerned shouts from the grunts, who are undoubtedly hanging on for dear life as Halley yanks our ship's nose almost straight up into the sky and hurls us backward and upward, away from the immediate danger.

I hold my breath as the Dragonfly hurtles backwards on the tip of its tail for what seems entirely too long considering how close we are to the ground and the buildings on either side of us. Then we are clear of the towers, and Halley gooses the throttle and pivots the ship to the left and downward in one swift, stomach-lurching move. When the nose of the drop ship tilts down again, we are so close to the ground that I could hop out of the cockpit and jump onto the concrete below without hurting myself.

"Testy little fucker," Halley says almost conversationally, as if she had just done nothing more exciting than duck away from a swing. She turns the nose of the drop ship to the left and accelerates the ship. We are flying alongside one of the residence towers now, this time with a little more clearance than before, but we're still much closer than I want to be to that much unyielding concrete and steel when I'm hurtling through the night air at over a hundred knots.

When we swing back around the tower and point the nose of the ship back toward the plaza again, the Lanky is no longer there.

"Where'd he go?" she says. She rotates the Dragonfly around its dorsal axis and skids into the plaza sideways, like she's drifting a hydrocar around a corner. In five years of frequent passenger status on drop ships, I've never seen a pilot handle one like Halley is flying hers.

"There he is." I point to our starboard. At twenty-five meters in height, Lankies can't hide all that well even in their own environments, much less in a place built for beings a tenth their size. The Lanky is crouching in the entrance vestibule of one of the residence towers, hammering away at the concrete of the tall archway with its head.

"Shoot him," I urge. "Shoot his ass."

"I can't," Halley replies. "Not with the big guns. I'll hit the building."

She switches to the smaller-caliber multibarreled cannon mounted in the chin turret. This one has a much higher rate of fire than the big antiarmor cannons on the side of the fuselage. Halley mashes down on her trigger button, and a rapid-fire hail of smaller tracers streaks over to the Lanky. They ricochet off into every direction, kicking up little puffs of concrete dust wherever they hit the walls and ground all around the Lanky. The archway of the atrium entrance is four floors tall, at least forty feet, and with another violent push, the Lanky dislodges a few meters of reinforced concrete from the top of the archway and breaks through, away from Halley's relentless gunfire. The Lanky disappears into the atrium beyond with a long and tortured-sounding wail, leaving a cloud of concrete dust and falling debris in its wake.

"I can't get to him in there," Halley says. "Not without guided munitions. Goddamn, I wish I had some missiles on these wings."

"Put us on the ground," I say. "I'll take a squad inside and smoke the Lanky out. You take the other squads down the street and hunt down the other one that got away."

Halley nods and swings the nose of the Dragonfly around for a landing on the plaza below.

"Get them ready," she says. "I don't want to spend more than a second and a half with the skids on the ground in this place—do you understand?"

I push the release for the seat harness and toggle the switch for the Dragonfly's intercom.

"Fallon, Grayson. Get a squad onto the tail ramp. We are going hunting."

"Affirmative," the answer comes from the cargo hold.

"Your show down there, but call in the guns if you need help," Halley says to me. "Don't you dare get yourself killed."

"This is what I do," I say, and peel myself out of the seat to go aft. "Honey."

She flinches a little and then flips me the bird without taking her eyes off the Dragonfly's instrument screen.

"Have fun, but be back for dinner," she says.

I rush down the passageway aft. In the cargo compartment, the HD troopers are gearing up, distributing rocket launchers from the armory's magazine and stacking a bunch of them on the tail ramp.

"We land, you kick all the shit we can't carry out of here and leave it in a pile on the ground," I yell into the din of clanking gear and pre-battle banter. "We'll come back for that stuff later. We go inside and after the Lanky. Second and Third Squads go with Halley. She'll drop them off on the far side of the next residence block to run down the other Lanky."

"Only two of them left?" Sergeant Fallon asks.

"Be glad," I say. "Fuckers don't drop easy."

The drop ship swerves and rotates around its dorsal axis. The red caution light comes on over the tail hatch, and the ramp starts to lower while we are still in the air. Outside, there's the plaza between the four residence towers that make up this block, acres of dirty concrete and a collection of some booths and shacks over to one side.

Then the ship's skids touch down on the plaza with a solid thud.

"Let's go, let's go," Sergeant Fallon shouts. "Kick out the gear. First Squad, off the bus!"

We file out of the drop ship at a run. I am carrying entirely too much hardware—an M-66 fléchette carbine for human targets, an M-80 for Lankies, ammunition for both, and a pistol. If I stumble, I may be stuck on my back like a turtle.

Behind us, Second and Third Squads are tossing out our spare MARS rockets. Then Halley gooses her engines again and lifts off, not even bothering to close the tail ramp. She pitches the nose down slightly and swings the ship around. She thunders across the plaza at low level, so close to us that I can almost read the name tag taped to the browridge of her flight helmet. As she flies by, she gives me a quick thumbs-up, and the Dragonfly disappears from sight behind one of the nearby residence towers.

I turn and follow the squad into the ruined vestibule. Ahead of us, inside the atrium, the Lanky wails again, a sound only slightly less intense than an explosion.

The new fifth-gen residence towers are massive things, a hundred floors of apartments and facilities arranged around a large hollow core for ventilation. The atrium on the ground floor is a big plaza, fifty meters on each side. We rush in through the crumbling archway of the vestibule, weapons at the ready. The Lanky is impossible to miss even in the huge atrium. It has retreated into a corner of the plaza, and the shield-like protrusion on the back of its head is brushing the balcony of the sixth-floor concourse.

"MARS rockets," Sergeant Fallon shouts. Four of the troopers with us take the launcher tubes they brought off their shoulders.

"Go armor-piercing," I say. "Remember—joints and the neck nape. And if it comes for us, you get your ass to cover."

We spread out and seek cover underneath the overhang of the second-floor concourse above. The atrium level has balcony ceilings that are at least triple the height of those on the floors above. The concourse levels open to the central core, are noisy with yells and shouts from hundreds of civilians with premium seats to the fight that is about to unfold. Then there's some small-arms fire coming down from the higher levels, armed civvies unwilling to just be spectators. The rifle and pistol bullets splash off the tough hide of the Lanky, as effective as thrown pebbles.

"Two left, two right," Sergeant Fallon orders. "On my mark."

The troopers with the rocket launchers take position on either flank of our short firing line. I raise my M-80 rifle and aim it at the neck nape of the Lanky. If anything, the alien looks like it really doesn't want to be here. It tries to merge with the corner of the atrium, letting out its sharp, earsplitting wails in irregular intervals. I almost feel sorry for the thing—it looks out of place, maybe even scared, as if it just wants to get away. It's stranded on a strange world, surrounded by things that want to kill it, and separated from its own. But my empathy only goes so far. They chose to come here and bring this fight to us, and because they did, many of my friends are dead.

Sergeant Fallon turns up the public-address system of her suit, and her voice thunders through the atrium and echoes off the concrete chasm that stretches a hundred floors over our heads.

"Heads down, people! Get away from the atrium and cover your ears. Fire in the hole!"

The Lanky turns its head toward the new sound and responds with a drawn-out wail that hurts my ears even through the hearing protection. For a moment, all the gunfire from the upper floors ceases completely.

"Launchers One and Two. Fire!"

Two MARS launchers pop-whoosh, and four missile trails shoot across the atrium in the blink of an eye. The Lanky lowers its head toward the incoming fire at the last fraction of a second. One of the missiles clips the shield on its skull, and the armor-piercing warhead glances off with a dull, sickening thud and buries itself in the concrete of the sixth-floor overhang. It explodes out of the floor and blows out twenty feet of balcony floor in a cloud of debris. The second warhead bores into the Lanky's side and knocks it back into the wall in a tangle of ungainly flailing limbs. The alien shrieks again, at a volume I've never thought possible. Out in the open, it would be earsplitting. In the confines of a hundred-story concrete box, it's like standing in front of a starship's fusion-rocket nozzles at full thrust. My helmet's hearing protection kicks in and makes me deaf for my own safety, but I can feel the sonic energy of the Lanky's scream slamming against my chest like a physical push. All over the lower floors, windows shatter, and when my hearing returns after a few moments, I can hear people screaming in agony and fear on the concourse levels right above us.

Then the Lanky scrambles to its feet on the other side of the atrium, unfolds its limbs again, and rises out of the dust. It plants a massive three-toed foot onto the concrete and swings its head toward us. Lankies have no eyes in their odd, elongated skulls, but I could swear an oath that if they can see at all, this one is looking right at us.

"Fire at will," Sergeant Fallon shouts.

I yank the M-80 rifle to my shoulder and put the targeting reticle in the middle of the Lanky's chest. Then I pull the triggers for both barrels. The recoil slams the stock of the gun violently against my armor. To my left and right, more rifles thunder their deep, sonorous reports. The Lanky takes half a dozen rounds to its chest and midsection, and for a moment it looks like it is going to falter and fall back into the debris. Then it puts one foot in front of the other and steps toward us. Whenever it puts its foot down on the surface of the atrium, I can feel the vibration through the soles of my boots.

We manage one more volley of rifle fire before the Lanky is already halfway across the expanse of the atrium, moving faster than I have ever seen one move, despite the very obvious still-smoldering hole that our MARS tore into its side.

"Get to cover!" I shout into the squad channel. Nobody needs the encouragement. We retreat from the atrium and dash underneath the overhang and toward the nearest hallway. Even with the equipment strapped to my armor, I am making what feels like personal record time for the fifty-meter dash. Behind us, the Lanky thunders across the atrium and toward the position we just abandoned in a hurry.

We're into the hallway maybe twenty meters when the Lanky hits the overhang behind us with a thundering crash. I get swept off my feet and hit the floor hard. My M-80 skitters down the hallway in front of me. Then it feels like the entire building is coming down on top of us. I curl up and cover my head with my armored hands and arms as chunks of debris fall all around me and bounce off my battle armor. The air in the hallway is instantly saturated with dust, so thick that I can't see half a meter in front of me. I turn on the augmented vision of my helmet visor and look back the way we came. The Lanky is wedged underneath the atrium overhang, blocking all the daylight from the atrium. His massive skull is maybe fifteen meters behind me. More debris is falling with every movement of the Lanky's head. With my M-80 out of my grasp, I reach for the M-66 fléchette rifle on its sling, punch the fire-control selector all the way down to "FULL AUTO," and fire an entire 250-round magazine at the Lanky's head at maximum cadence, one hundred rounds per second. The alien recoils and lets out another wail, but this one sounds a lot more strained than before.

"Fucking die already," I shout, echoing Halley's sentiment from a few minutes ago.

Behind me, some of Sergeant Fallon's squad join in with their own weapons, the low booming reports from the M-80s making the dust jump on the concrete floor. The Lanky wails and pulls its head back, away from the gunfire. Then it lurches forward and rams its cranial shield into the hallway opening again. There's a tortured groaning sound from overhead, and an avalanche of debris crashes down between us and the Lanky. I cover my head as the hallway turns completely dark.

"Holy hell," Sergeant Fallon says into the squad channel with a cough. "That thing is pissed. Go augmented, people."

I turn on the vision augmentation of my helmet visor, and the interior of the hallway comes into view again in the ghostly green-and-amber glow of night vision.

I switch frequencies on my comms suite and toggle into the drop ship's support channel.

"Halley, do you read?"

"Barely," she sends back. Even with my suit's power cranked up all the way, the connection is horrible, too much ferroconcrete filling the space between us.

"We are on the ground floor," I tell Halley. "The Lanky brought half the floor down on us. He's hurt badly, but he's still moving around in the atrium somewhere. If he gets out of there again, you'll need to finish him off."

"Second Squad is engaging the other Lanky three blocks down from where you are," Halley replies. "I'm flying fire support. Stand by."

I hear the staccato of cannon fire in the background of the transmission. A few seconds later, Halley's voice returns.

"I have almost nothing left in the guns. Hold that Lanky in the atrium and finish him off. That one's all on you. Don't let him get away. These guys can do a ton of damage out here among the civvies."

"No shit." I cough out some dust. "We'll do what we can."

I toggle back into the squad channel.

"They're tussling with the other Lanky three blocks away," I tell Sergeant Fallon. "We're on our own with this one. Can't let him get out of here and into the streets."

"Let's go, then," Sergeant Fallon says, and comes over to help me to my feet. "Gotta find a way around this rubble."

On the other side of the rubble pile, in the direction of the atrium, the small-arms fire has started again, the irregular cacophony of gunshots from dozens of different weapons. The civvies are shooting at the Lanky again from the safety of the upper-level concourses, but if we can't bring it down with our guns, they might as well be pissing on it from above.

I pick my M-80 rifle up, eject the bases of the empty shells from the barrels, and load the chambers with two fresh rounds. Then I follow Sergeant Fallon and the rest of the squad down the dark corridor, away from the wall of concrete debris that's blocking our way back to the atrium.

Whatever the Lanky did knocked out the power in this part of the building. We rely on our augmented vision to traverse the hallways. Sergeant Fallon and her squad seem to be very familiar with the layout of a fifth-gen residence tower, because they never stop and check for directions as we make our way back to the atrium through unblocked corridors.

The atrium is still noisy with the sound of sporadic gunfire. The Lanky is nowhere in sight from my vantage point of the hallway, but there are chunks of concrete raining down onto the atrium floor from above.

"He's up on the wall," Sergeant Fallon says. "Didn't know the bastards could climb."

"Me, neither," I reply.

"Five left, five right," she says, and points to the covered space beyond the hallway entrance, where we will still be sheltered by the second-floor overhang.

I dash out of the hallway and to the nearest cover, a hip-high set of planters holding artificial flowers that have a thick frosting of concrete dust on them. Behind a nearby column, there's a pair of armed civilians. They have weapons pointed toward the atrium. One of the civilians sees me and recoils a little in surprise. For a moment, it looks like he's thinking about swinging his rifle toward me, but then he holds up his hand and points across the atrium.

"He's out there on the wall," he shouts. I dash over to their position and skid to a stop on my knees.

"You're fleet," he says.

"I am," I confirm. "Followed the Lanky in. Brought some friends."

Both civilians are dressed in olive-drab fatigues that look like they're straight from an old history show on the Networks. They have rank insignia on their collars, the old pre-reform United States ranks we used before the services got unified four years ago. One of the civvies wears the three chevrons of a sergeant. The other wears the single chevron of a private. Their guns are a mismatched pair of antique cartridge rifles—a hundred-year-old M4 that has most of the finish worn off its metal parts, and a scoped rifle with a handle for manual bolt operation.

"Friends," he says, and eyes the nearby HD troopers. "That kind usually ain't friendly around here."

"You got more people here?"

"One more fire team, up on the tenth-floor balcony. About twenty volunteers. No big guns, though. We called in for reinforcements, but they'll be awhile yet."

"Who are you with?" I ask.

"Lazarus Brigade," he says.

"What the fuck is that?"

"We are the militia," he replies, as if the answer is self-evident. "Ask those guys there. We do the job they ought to have done all these years."

"Stop socializing over there, Andrew," Sergeant Fallon says on the squad channel. "We have work to do. Get me eyeballs on that alien son of a bitch."

Two of the troopers dash out to where the overhang ends and peer upward. Instantly, our TacLink feeds update with a three-dimensional representation of the Lanky, hanging on to the wall of the atrium ten floors above us. The rest of the squad follow, and we hurry out into the open, dodging rubble and falling debris.

"Not so much fun now, is it," I say when I spot the Lanky with my own eyes. It's crawling—or rather trying to crawl—up the inner wall of the atrium, using the overhangs of the concourse levels as hand- and footholds. But its size and mass work against it. We watch as the Lanky claws for purchase and breaks loose big shoals of concrete, which fall to the atrium in front of us with dull crashes. There's concerted rifle fire coming from one of the higher concourses—probably the militia squad—and sporadic, random gunfire from the other balconies. The Lanky is slow and sluggish, and there are many holes and scorch marks on its hide.

"MARS launchers," Sergeant Fallon orders. "Shoot him down, and for fuck's sake, stay way clear. Fucker's gonna make a splash when he hits the ground. On my mark."

She cranks up the amplification on her suit's PA system and shouts into the hundred-story void above us.

"Cease fire, cease fire. We are shooting rockets. Step back from the atrium. Fire in the hole!"

The civilian gunfire ebbs. Sergeant Fallon jabs an arm upward at the Lanky.

"Three, two, one, fire!"

Four rockets burst from the launcher tubes and shoot upward to where the Lanky is scrambling for purchase on the wall like some gigantic cave spider. This time, nobody misses. Four armor-piercing warheads plow into the Lanky's torso from below and pluck the creature off the wall like the world's biggest flyswatter.

"Back off!" Sergeant Fallon shouts, but nobody needs the encouragement. We dash back to the overhang on the opposite side of the atrium. The Lanky screams, and the sound amplifies and reverberates in the giant hollow concrete tube of the atrium until it seems to come from every direction. It flails for purchase and manages to hook a spindly hand into a concourse ledge maybe twenty floors up, but all that mass hanging off it is too much for the concrete, and a ten-foot section of it breaks loose. Then the Lanky and the concrete slab tumble to the ground in a terrifying display of mass in motion.

When the Lanky hits the concrete of the atrium plaza, it feels like we're at the epicenter of an earthquake. Everyone in the squad is swept off their feet and sent tumbling. The crash from the impact sounds like the explosion of a thermobaric warhead. I feel the ground buckling underneath me. All over the residence tower, windows shatter and things pop out of place noisily and violently. The Lanky lets out one more wail, rolls over, and lies still.

Soldiers don't leave things to chance. We get to our feet, and everyone unloads whatever weapon they are holding into the bulk of the prone alien fifty meters away. After a few moments, the civvies from the upper floors join in with their own guns, and for a good ten or twenty seconds, there's a cacophonic fusillade of uncoordinated gunfire, a mad minute with no direction and no other purpose but to put rounds on target. The Lanky in the center of the storm never moves.

"Cease fire," Sergeant Fallon orders over the squad channel. "Cease fire. He's done."

The military gunfire stops immediately, while the civilian fusillade ebbs bit by bit.

"Halley, strike two," I pant into the air-support channel. "We took out the one in the atrium. What's your situation?"

It takes a few moments for Halley to reply to my hail. She sounds very stressed when she does.

"Third one's down, too. Second and Third Squads have casualties, and I'm all out of cannon rounds. Get out here if you can."

"Affirmative," I reply. Then I toggle over to Sergeant Fallon and the squad channel. "The other squads need a hand with wounded. Let's regroup outside."

"First Squad, grab your toys and let's go," Sergeant Fallon says. "We take the east exit."

Outside, the night is chaotically loud. The security alarms of the tower block are sounding their unpleasant ascending klaxon. On the plaza between the four residence towers, people are streaming out of buildings to either flee or witness the spectacle. I hear gunshots in the distance, the familiar rolling booms of M-80 rifles firing their heavy armor-piercing shells. Overhead, Halley's drop ship circles above the block, engines roaring, and her searchlights are painting bright streaks across the broken hull of the Lanky seedpod nearby. The sight of so many civilians surging onto the plaza, many of them armed, fills me with more dread than the idea of taking on another Lanky. The last time I was here, fifteen or twenty kilometers to the east, a mob like this fought a battle-hardened squad of Territorial Army troopers to a draw and damn near killed us all. If this crowd decides that we aren't welcome here despite the Lanky presence, we are about to have a very unpleasant evening.

I turn around to tell Sergeant Fallon to retreat back to the building and go up to the roof for pickup, but there's another group of civvies pouring out of the high-rise behind us. They're not as numerous, but most of them are armed as well, and we can't just bull our way through that crowd without starting a fight.

Then there's a loud, tortured rumbling groan in the air. It's an organic sound, not a mechanical one. It sounds like someone has taken a gigantic chicken bone in both hands and is slowly breaking it apart.

"There's movement at the wreckage," Halley sends to the platoon. "Oh, shit. There's more of them coming out."

From our vantage point on the eastern side of the building, we can only see the nose of the crashed Lanky seedpod. The bulk of it is around the corner from our perspective. But the sound of material failure is coming from there, and that doesn't foretell happy news.

Halley turns on the public-address system on her ship, and her voice booms across the plaza, amplified by thousands of watts.

"Everyone get clear," she bellows. "Everyone get off the plaza and under cover. The wreckage is not empty."

A murmur goes through the crowd like a wave. Some people heed the warning and try to stream back to the buildings, only to push against the stream of people who decided to stick around and get closer for a look.

We start running toward the corner of the building, toward the spot where the nose of the seedpod has ground a furrow into the concrete plaza. We're not even halfway there when a chunk of the seedpod's flank ejects from the hull forcefully and sails through the cool nighttime air. It lands on the ten-meter concrete dam that forms the outer wall between the residence towers and glances off, leaving a deep gouge in the concrete and crashing onto the ground just on the edge of the plaza.

Another Lanky climbs out of the wreckage and onto the plaza, and the mood of the crowd tips from curiosity and concern to full-blown panic in the span of three or four seconds. The crowd surges back, this time in only one direction—away from the Lankies.

Then the hull of the seedpod shudders, and another Lanky emerges, unfolding its limbs and clambering off its broken ride like a giant bug leaving a used-up garbage receptacle. It slides down the hull and lands feetfirst on the plaza with a thud.

Gunshots roll across the plaza as some of the armed civilians start firing at the Lankies. I can't tell them it won't do much good because they have no comms gear, and I doubt they'd listen even if they could hear me. The gunfire increases in volume as more and more people join the fusillade. The Lankies look indecisive, like they just woke up from a nap and aren't quite all there yet, or maybe they are intimidated by the unusual sight of so many human beings right in front of them. The lead Lanky lets out its trilling wail and starts walking forward into the plaza, and the one behind it follows after a moment.

"MARS rockets," Sergeant Fallon bellows.

I know we brought maybe two rockets per launcher, and we used up most of our supply on a single Lanky already, but there's nothing else left to do other than run away and let the Lankies wreak havoc down here.

I shoulder my M-80, which seems ludicrously inadequate for this scenario. Then I grab a new pair of shells and stuff them into the barrels. Next to me, our four MARS gunners take a knee and aim at the closest Lanky, fifty meters away. The noise and chaos all around us are apocalyptic.

"On my mark. Three, two, one, *fire*!" Sergeant Fallon shouts. Four launchers disgorge their payloads, and the closest Lanky is blown off its three-toed feet by the impacts. It goes down in a flailing tangle of limbs.

I hear the thundering staccato of a heavy machine gun. Tracers streak across the plaza and over the heads of the crowd. They lay into the Lankies and deflect off their tough hides in puffs and sparks. I look for the source of the fire and see a machine gun mount on a tripod, set up on the low roof of one of the administrative buildings in the center of the plaza. The people manning the gun are wearing the same olive-drab fatigues as the militia soldiers I met in the atrium of the tower. *Lazarus Brigade.* I have a brief flashback to a hot summer night five years ago, when a gun mount just like that hosed one of our drop ships out of the sky and killed half my squad when we went out to rescue the pilot.

Everyone is firing at the Lankies now—HD troopers, armed civilians, and the uniformed militiamen with the canister-fed automatic cannon. I load and fire, load and fire, again and again, until the ammo loops on my armor are empty. The Lankies are backing away from the volume of fire that's getting thrown their way. They cluster in front of the barrier wall, safety in numbers and proximity. Then they start climbing the retaining wall, which is only half as tall as they are.

"Coming in hot," Halley shouts over the platoon channel.

"I thought you have no cannon shells left," I shout back.

"I don't," she says. "But I have seventy tons at five hundred knots."

I almost drop my rifle in shock. "Don't," I say. "Don't do this."

The distant wailing of the Dragonfly engines increases in pitch and volume. It's coming from the east, a drop ship at full throttle and well above the speed of sound. Then it appears in the sky between the two eastern towers, engines aglow. Halley banks the ship smoothly and elegantly and shoots right through the space between the towers. Then there's the muffled sound of a low explosion, and Dragonfly Delta Five streaks across the plaza like a huge missile and plows into the barrier dam the Lankies are climbing onto.

The fireball that blooms into the sky and outward from the barrier dam illuminates the whole plaza in a furious shade of orange. The Lankies disappear in the inferno, crushed and flung aside by the impact force of millions of joules, far more punch than all the MARS rockets we are carrying on our backs combined.

I can't even find the strength to shout, or cry, or do anything but stare at the fireball and the enormous gash the drop ship has torn into the top of the barrier wall. The heat wave from the explosion washes across the plaza and over me, and I don't even flinch when my helmet lowers the face shield automatically to protect my eyes.

"Good chute," I hear Sergeant Fallon over the squad channel. "Good chute. Hot damn, that was some warrior shit."

I look up and see the white triple canopy of a fleet emergency parachute in the sky beyond the damaged tower. From the chute's suspension lines dangles the cockpit-escape module of a drop ship.

The sudden relief I feel makes my knees buckle, and I sit down on the ground, hard. Sergeant Fallon walks up to me, rifle still at the ready and pointed downrange. Then she takes one hand off the gun and pats me on the shoulder.

"Relax, Romeo. She's fine."

"Can we just please stop killing shit tonight by flying into it?" I shout, and Sergeant Fallon laughs as she walks off.

The capsule goes down in the no-man's-land between the PRCs, where the old Detroit was never fully razed and the new Detroit just went up around it in fortified islands. We find the chute and the escape module five hundred yards past the barrier dam between the towers. When we reach the capsule, Halley has already popped the explosive bolts that separate the halves of the module. She's sitting in the rubble in front of the capsule on a section of the parachute that saved her life.

"This is the lousiest honeymoon ever," she says when I come running up to her.

"I want to fucking punch you for that," I say.

She looks at me with a tired smile. "'Don't do this,'" she says, repeating my last statement to her on the radio in a gently mocking tone. "I know how and when to work an ejection-seat handle, Andrew. I am not a moron."

I hold out my hand to help her up, and she takes it.

"I guess we're even now," I say.

When we get back to the plaza, there are armored vehicles in front of the administration building, and at least a hundred of the militia troopers in OD green fatigues are securing the site and managing the flow of civilians. The other squads of Sergeant Fallon's platoon are nowhere to be seen. Some of the green-clad militia spot us as we walk up the access ramp to the plaza, and two armored vehicles with heavy-machine-gun mounts on them come toward us.

"Oh, sure," Sergeant Fallon says. "Now they show up. After we've done all the work."

The armored vehicles stop in front of us, and their remote-controlled gun turrets swivel to cover us with their muzzles. We raise our hands slightly and keep them away from our weapons.

The tail hatches of the armored mules open, and more militia troopers file out and form a semicircle around us. Then the passenger hatch on the lead mule creaks open, and a tall black female trooper sticks her upper body out of the hatch to address us.

"Put your weapons and helmets on the ground, please," she says.

Halley pops the retention strap on her leg holster, pulls out her pistol, and chucks it onto the ground in front of us. Then she looks at me and shrugs.

"Their turf," she says.

"Homeworld Defense don't just give up their guns," Sergeant Fallon says. "I have no interest in getting hog-tied and shot like a dog in a dirty basement somewhere."

The female militia trooper nods at Halley. "Guess it's true what they say about selection," she says. "All the smart ones go fleet."

Something about her face rings a bell in the back of my head. It's still dark, and she's thirty meters away, but I can see tattoos on her face. An unusual tribal pattern. I've seen it once before, almost five years ago.

"Corporal Jackson?" I say. She startles.

I remove my helmet and drop it at my feet.

"Grayson," I say. "We were in the 365th together."

The woman I knew five years ago climbs out of her vehicle and comes trotting over to us. She is wearing the same fatigues all the other militia troops are wearing. Her collars bear the gold-leaf insignia of a major.

"Yes, we were," she says to me, and smiles a very sparing little smile. "Yes, we were. Seems this night is full of surprises."

"Oh, you ain't seen nothing yet." Sergeant Fallon removes her own helmet and flashes a grin. "Kameelah fucking Jackson. Still got that big stupid knife you were hauling everywhere?"

Jackson laughs out loud. The teeth she flashes are still perfectly straight and white. "I do, Master Sergeant. It's in the truck." Then her smile fades a little. "I'm still going to have to collect your weapons and your comms gear, please."

"Are we POWs now?" Halley asks. "We just saved your bacon down here, you know. Should count for something, shouldn't it?"

"You're not POWs," Jackson says. "You are making a donation to our cause. And no," she addresses Sergeant Fallon. "We're not going to hog-tie you and shoot you like a dog in a basement somewhere. So unsling your goddamn weapons already, and we can have our little reunion sitting down."

The militia troops lead us to the back of one of the armored vehicles. They're courteous and surprisingly professional about the whole thing. We surrender all our comms gear and weapons, and Corporal Jackson—I have a hard time thinking of my old squad mate as a major despite the rank insignia on her collars—gathers everything and deactivates the electronic stuff expertly.

"How on Earth did you end up falling in with this lot?" Sergeant Fallon asks her as we file into the armored troop transport.

"Long story," Jackson says. "After Detroit a few years back, I went looking for the people who sprung that ambush on us. And I found them."

She waits until we've all taken our seats and then straps herself into the jump seat closest to the door and its control panel.

"Funny thing, too. I was going to find them and kill the whole lot of them. For Stratton and Paterson, you know?"

I nod when she looks at me. Stratton and Paterson died the night Sergeant Fallon lost her leg and I got wounded. That was my last drop with the Territorial Army before I got to join the fleet, and hardly a week goes by where I don't revisit the battle in my dreams, and sometimes my waking hours.

"But you didn't," I say.

"No," she replies, and smiles that enigmatic smile of hers I remember well. "I didn't. Was going to, for sure. But then I got captured and met the general. He was a colonel back then."

"And he talked you into joining? You, Kameelah Jackson, the baddest corporal in the 365th?" Sergeant Fallon chuckles. "The man sure can talk, I'll give him that."

"Turns out we've been shooting at the wrong people all those years," Jackson says. "Ain't ashamed to admit I was wrong. About a bunch of things."

"So you're the general's right hand now?" I ask. She looks at me and flashes a quick grin.

"Among other things," she says. "Among other things."

The armored troop transport rumbles along for the better part of an hour. Deprived of all our technology, we are blind in the windowless back—not that I would know my way around Detroit even if I had a view. When the transport finally comes to a stop, Sergeant Fallon is asleep, or pretending to be. I am bone-tired after the last few days of constant fear of death and combat, and I want to fall asleep, but my anxious brain won't let me. The last time I was down here, among the same people, I didn't get to leave under my own power. I was airlifted out, with two fléchettes in my left side.

The back door of the transport opens and reveals a large underground garage, stuffed full of equipment and vehicle parts. More militia troops in their olive-drab fatigues are milling around or working on gear. We file out of the armored transport and stretch our legs.

"This way," Jackson says, and gestures toward one end of the hangar-like garage. Halley and I hesitate for a moment, and Jackson rolls her eyes.

"Ain't no underground execution chamber around here," she says. "I give you my word we won't just shoot you in the back of the head."

"I wasn't worried about that," I lie.

"Locking you in for the night," she says. "For your safety. Don't want to be walking these streets, in those uniforms. Shower and sleep, and tomorrow we'll talk."

"I want to stay with my husband," Halley says, and moves closer to me. "You separate us now, we're going to have a problem."

"Of course you can stay together," Jackson says. "We're not uncivilized down here, you know."

CHAPTER 26

LAZARUS BRIGADE

I wake up on a military folding cot. Halley is on the cot with me, and she's still asleep, drawing air in deep and even breaths. The room we are in is not in a basement. There's a window on one wall, and light streaming in and illuminating the dingy flooring and tired paint on the walls. The blindfolds we were wearing when they led us here last night are on the floor next to our cot. I've spent enough time in welfare housing to know that I'm in a PRC apartment somewhere.

I carefully extract myself from Halley's embrace and climb out of the cot. The only thing I took off last night was my CDU jacket, which is hanging over the back of a chair nearby. The chair is screwed into the floor with lag bolts.

I put my jacket on and look around. The view from the window shows a sunrise over a nearby river. The morning sun is reflecting in a thousand windows out there, all fifth-gen PRC residence towers, clustered in groups of four along the riverbank.

Corporal–Major Jackson's militia troops frisked us expertly last night and removed all weapons and everything that can be used to communicate, but they left me my personal document pouch and the simple little aluminum ring in it. My dog tags are missing from my neck for the first time in years, confiscated for their locator-beacon function that could trigger an SAR mission if a fleet unit got close enough to this place to pick up the signal.

The kitchenette is bare except for some plastic mugs in the cupboard and half a packet of soy coffee next to them. I draw some water in one of the mugs, add coffee powder, and heat the whole thing up in the food-processor unit for thirty seconds, just like I did back home when I still had to make do with soy-based everything.

When the coffee is ready, I take the mug over to the window and look over the river again while I take a sip. The PRC looks almost peaceful. The coffee is truly awful, but there's something soothing and familiar about its perfect awfulness.

Halley wakes up a little while later and stretches on the cot like a cat after a nap in the sunshine.

"That smells pretty bad," she says.

I walk over and sit down on the edge of the cot. She reaches for the mug, and I hand it to her to take a sip.

"Tastes bad, too," she says, and makes a face.

"Lousy honeymoon," I say. "Terrible wedding night. Worst bed-and-breakfast ever."

"An auspicious start," she says, and we both smile at each other like idiots.

Thirty minutes after I finish my coffee, there's a knock on the door.

I look at Halley and raise an eyebrow.

"Come in?" she says toward the door.

There's the mechanical snap of a heavy-duty lock, and the door opens. Outside in the hallway, I can see two militia troopers standing guard, sidearms on their belts. A tall black man steps into the room. He wears the same fatigues, unflattering and baggy OD green, and the rank insignia on his collar tabs are that of a one-star general—the old-school general's star with five points, not the new post-reorganization rank with a gold wreath and a four-pointed star in it. His bearing carries authority more so than the stars on his collar. He wears his hair in a very short military-regulation buzz cut, and there's quite a bit of gray flecking his temples, but he looks lean. A warrior, not a pencil pusher. There are no insignia or badges on his fatigues, only a name tape that says "LAZARUS."

"Good morning," he says. "I hope you're at least a little rested. Last night was pretty eventful."

"Good morning," Halley replies. I merely nod.

"I'm General Lazarus," he says. "I'm in charge of what the men have come to call the Lazarus Brigade." He smiles curtly. "I was against that because of the personality-cult aspect and because it limits our growth by definition, but I have to admit that it has a nice ring to it. May I sit down?"

"Your place," I say, and gesture at the chair. Lazarus isn't armed, at least not visibly, but something tells me that it wouldn't be wise to offer him violence, even disregarding the armed men standing in front of the door. He has the bearing of a veteran. There's an efficiency to his movements, the sense of a tightly coiled spring underneath a deceptively smooth surface, that tells me this man used to do dangerous things for a living when he wore the uniform.

"Let me start by expressing my thanks for your defense of our PRC last night," Lazarus says when he is sitting down. "You took a great deal of personal risk, and you bought us the time to muster our own forces and get the situation under control."

"Then why are you detaining us?" Halley asks. "Stripping us of our weapons and gear. We couldn't tell the rest of the fleet where we are even if we wanted to."

"That is standard procedure, unfortunately. We need the weapons for our own use, and we can't let you communicate with the fleet or the HD and give away our location. But you are not prisoners, just guests."

"So we can leave?" I ask. "Right now?"

"You can," Lazarus says. "We'd have to blindfold you and take you to a safe pickup spot, but yes, you can leave. I would, however, ask that you consider hearing me out before I let you go."

"If this is an interrogation, it's the weirdest one ever," Halley says.

"It's not an interrogation," Lazarus replies. "It's a job offer. A chance to switch career paths."

I laugh and fold my arms in front of my chest. "Oh, man. And here I thought this week couldn't possibly get any weirder."

"We've had a complicated relationship with the government of the PRC," Lazarus says. "At first, they clamped down on us with the Territorial Army. Then, when we got too big to get stepped on, they backed off, let us run our own affairs. As long as we kept things quiet and orderly, you see."

"Didn't look so quiet and orderly from orbit last night," I say.

"The PRCs are in full rebellion," he says. "The ones without a Lazarus Brigade or its equivalent are eating themselves and each other. What was left of the fleet after Mars just disappeared from orbit a few days ago without warning or explanation. Homeworld Defense—well, I think we know what they've turned into in the last few years. They never worked to defend us anyway. The NAC government has all but abandoned us to our fate. You could stay with your respective services and get used up to feed what's left of the machine, or you could serve the Commonwealth here, at home, directly and without a self-interested bureaucracy. I can't promise you a retirement bonus, but I can promise you food, a place to hang your hats, freedom of movement, and a purpose."

Halley and I look at each other. She looks as bewildered as I feel right now.

"Lazarus Brigade is made up of veterans," the general says. "Not exclusively—there aren't that many of us around—but most of the leadership positions. Almost all our officers are veterans, and about half our senior enlisted. The rest are recruited and trained locally from the PRCs. We do the job the Homeworld Defense battalions have ceased to do a long time ago. We perform police duties and external defense. We run the infrastructure and network with other PRCs. But we are never enough people for the job, and we always need experienced veterans with desirable skills."

Lazarus gets up from his chair and walks over to the window. Outside, the PRC has come to life with its day-to-day business, millions of people surviving by the slimmest of margins every day and week, living from ration day to ration day.

"The Lankies will be back sooner or later. I can't count on the Homeworld Defense troops to defend us. They were absolutely no help last night, even though they have three bases within thirty flight minutes from here. When—not if—the enemy comes back, we are all that we have. I need people who can train others how to fight these things."

He looks at Halley.

"Lieutenant Halley, you are a drop-ship pilot and a senior flight instructor. We have a small drop-ship fleet and very few pilots. If I could persuade you to stay with us and become head of our combat-aviation school, you could build your own program from scratch."

Then he looks at me.

"You, Staff Sergeant Grayson, are a combat infantryman, and we always have a need for those. You are also a trained combat controller, and we have nobody in our ranks who's qualified for that job. You would both be officers, if that sort of thing holds any importance to you. Lieutenant Halley, you would be a major in the brigade. Staff Sergeant Grayson, you would be a lieutenant. Or a master sergeant, if you would prefer to remain an NCO. Some do."

"Where did you serve?" I ask. "You were a combat grunt, weren't you? Marines?" I wager a guess.

"Marines," Lazarus confirms with a smile. "2080 to 2106. I was a lieutenant colonel of infantry."

"Who made you a general in this outfit?" Halley asks.

"The men did," Lazarus says. "I was more honored by that than by those silver oak leaves the corps bestowed on me."

Halley and I look at each other again. She gives me the tiniest of smiles and then shrugs. *Hell if I know*, the shrug says.

"Can we think about it?" I ask.

"Of course you may think about it," Lazarus says. "My offer is good until you ask us for a ride back to the safe pickup point."

Lazarus straightens out the front of his tunic with a sharp and short tug.

"Are you hungry? Maybe you can discuss this better over breakfast."

"I'm starving," Halley says. "Yes, please. I'd like something to eat."

"Have you made the same offer to Sergeant Fallon yet?" I ask, and Lazarus smiles.

"I have," he says simply, and from the look he gives me, it's clear that's all he's going to say about that particular negotiation.

Lazarus and the two guards with him take us down to the basement level, and then out into the fresh air of a residential PRC plaza. It's not the same we defended last night—the barrier dam is intact, and there's no seedpod hull wedged into the corner of one of the towers here. They all look identical from the air, and without my suit's navigation gear, I couldn't even begin to guess which of Detroit's many PRCs we are in.

Lazarus leads us to the admin center in the middle of the plaza. The admin centers usually hold public-safety personnel and food-distribution stations. We see ration booths open, but no public-housing cops. Instead, we see olive-clad brigade troopers milling about among the civilians, and nobody's shying away from them or cursing them from a distance.

The chow hall is moderately busy. There are a few dozen brigade troopers sitting at tables and eating breakfast. General Lazarus deposits us at a table in the corner of the room, where two familiar faces are talking over barley porridge and coffee.

"The lovebirds slept in this morning, I see." Sergeant Fallon takes a sip of her coffee and nods at the bench across the table from her. Halley and I sit down with our own meal trays.

"You met the general," Jackson states matter-of-factly.

"We did," I say. "And we just had the strangest conversation I've had since I left the PRC and put on a uniform."

"I've had stranger," Sergeant Fallon says.

"Did we win?" Halley asks. "I mean, I know we kicked the shit out of our Lankies down here last night, but there were a bunch more pods coming down."

"Can't tell from the PRCs without a brigade unit in them," Jackson says. "But the ones we control, they won theirs. Took some fierce fighting, though."

"I don't doubt that," I say. "How many did we lose last night?"

"Three," Sergeant Fallon says. "Sanborn, Cameron, Bardo. Eight more wounded."

"Hell of a bill," I say. "But they did all right. Considering they had shit for training against Lankies."

"Ah, hell. It's all infantry combat. Shoot the bad guys until they drop. It's just bigger bad guys, that's all. Even the local guys and girls did okay, for a bunch of barely trained civvies and a handful of out-of-shape vets. Imagine what they could do with some training and better weapons than those antiques they have to use. They sure as hell aren't short on motivation here on their home turf."

I look at her, and she returns my gaze passively and with a little bit of amusement in her eyes. Something about Sergeant Fallon's demeanor tells me precisely which decision she made when the general presented her with the same offer he made us.

"You're staying," I say. "You are staying with the brigade. You're not going back to Homeworld Defense."

"Ah, hell," she says. "Homeworld Defense practically kicked me out even before they dumped us on that ice moon." She takes another sip of her coffee and puts the plastic mug down again gently. "Besides, I think I have some shit to atone for anyway. Might as well do it here, where I know my way around."

"So what rank are you going to hold in the brigades?" I ask. "You have got to be their first Medal of Honor winner. I figure Lazarus offered you at least colonel's eagles."

"Fuck, no," she says. "Do I look like a goddamn officer to you? I'm staying master sergeant."

"Good." I grin. "Because I really can't picture you as anything else in my head."

"What about you two? I thought for sure you'd be on a boat back up to the carrier already. Especially you, Lieutenant," she says to Halley. "No offense."

"None taken," Halley says neutrally.

"We haven't decided yet," I say. "No real rush. If the world ends tomorrow, it won't matter. And if it doesn't end tomorrow, it won't matter, either."

"Then stop the chatter and eat your porridge," Corporal-now-Major Jackson says. "Shit tastes awful when it's cold."

She winks at Halley and me and gets up from the table.

"Don't be late for your first day of orientation, Master Sergeant," she says to Sergeant Fallon. Then she walks off, crossing the dining facility with that peculiar bouncy little swagger she's always had.

"Outranked by one of my former squad nuggets," Sergeant Fallon grumbles around her coffee mug, but there's the hint of a smile at the corner of her mouth. "Well, Major Unwerth always warned me that would happen to my insubordinate ass one of these days."

EPILOGUE

The air up here is fresh and clean, or as fresh and clean as it ever gets in a PRC. The drop-ship landing pad on the rooftop of the residence tower looks like it hasn't seen any landings in years. We sit on the edge of the pad and look east across the river. The sun is climbing up into a gray sky, the ever-present pollution denying us the blue skies we should be seeing with the sparse cloud cover overhead. But the city has a rough and brutal sort of beauty to it—rows and rows of fifth-gen residence blocks, hundreds of towers lining both sides of the river and dozens of square miles beyond. It may be a rough patch of earth on the ground between all those blocks, but up here, it's almost serene. There's a vitality to all these warrens of streets and alleys, teeming with people every hour of every day.

"I think it's nuts," Halley says. "But so are all the other picks on the table. You said it—the fleet tucked tail and ran. We're on our own now. What's one drop ship going to do up there?"

"I can't believe you're even considering staying with the brigade," I say. "You of all people."

"I don't hate the idea altogether." Halley shrugs. "It would be interesting to get a pilot school off the ground in this place. Can't say I wouldn't like the challenge. What about you? What are you going to do if we go back up there to rejoin what's left of the fleet?"

"Report to *Regulus* or *Midway*." I shrug. "Put on another bug suit. Do combat drops. Probably die horribly and senselessly on some unimportant rock out there."

"You make it sound so appealing," she says with a laugh.

"They'll retrieve *Indy*'s stealth buoys and try to figure out where the fleet went with all the good shit. I wouldn't mind being a part of the ass-kicking that's going to follow when the joint task force shows up wherever they went and reclaims whatever they ferried out of the system."

Thinking about *Indianapolis* and Colonel Campbell is like a small, sharp knife in my chest. I wonder how many of the crew went into the escape pods before *Indy* made that last desperate attack run, and I'd love to be able to find out. But with *Indy* gone, most of my friends are dead, and those who are left are almost all down here on Earth. Fighting the Lankies on Earth, as terrifying as it is, feels right. It feels like I'd be doing what should have been my job all along. But what's left of the fleet will need every hand on deck if we want to keep the Lankies away from Earth in the future.

"I don't want to decide this right now," I say. "I don't want to leave again and go wherever some pencil pusher with stars on his shoulder boards tells me to go. But I don't want to just piss on my oath of service."

"'I solemnly swear and affirm to loyally serve the North American Commonwealth, and to bravely defend its laws and the freedom of its citizens,'" Halley recites. "Doesn't say where and how. Just says to bravely defend. You can do that down here just the same. Maybe better. Fewer pencil pushers."

I look at the pale and diffused sunlight glistening on the river. Down below, on the waterfront, the ever-resilient seagulls are circling in the breeze and diving for scraps, white specks in the distance.

"You got the letter," I say. "The one you punched me for."

"I did," she says. "Came in the interstation mail."

"I wonder if my mom got hers. I sent it with the same guy, on the same day."

"They were still doing mail runs from and to Luna until the relay went on the fritz," Halley says. "That was only two days before you got there. I'm pretty sure she got it."

She puts her hand in mine—her right hand, my right hand, not the one that's half-gone and wrapped in trauma gel. *I wonder how many doctors Lazarus has recruited*, I think.

"What did you tell her?" Halley asks.

"I told her I love her," I say. "Told her thank you for bringing me up and getting me away from that shit-sack of a father."

I look east, where I know the Green Mountains are somewhere in the distance past the horizon, beyond New York and Lake Champlain.

"I told her to get out of Boston and to the place where we last had coffee," I say. "And that I'd come see her there if I made it back."

"Well," Halley says. She holds her ring up next to mine and clinks them together lightly. "Then let's not decide right this second. The fleet has no idea where we are. If we decide to stay here with the brigade, the fleet's never going to know. And if we decide to go back, a few weeks aren't going to make a difference. Not to them, anyway. I want to spend some time with my new husband without having to check schedules or look at a damn chrono. I want to live life for just a little while. Let the world go to shit after. We'll deal with it then."

"I bet we could ask General Lazarus for a week or two of thinking time and a ride out to the Green Mountains or Boston," I say. "He needs us more than we do him. He can throw in some incentives."

I take her hand into mine. She's tall, only three inches shorter than I am, and her hands have long and nimble fingers that mesh perfectly with mine. The air carries the scent of water from the Great Lakes. I don't know how much time we have bought ourselves with what we did yesterday—with Colonel Campbell's sacrifice—but I know that I can choose how I get to spend that time, and I know what the colonel would say about that.

"I owe you a honeymoon anyway," I say. "Let's go talk to the general."

Her content smile is all the affirmation I need.

ACKNOWLEDGMENTS

The number of people who have had a direct or indirect hand in making the book in your hands (or on your Kindle in front of you) is big enough that it causes me sweaty-handed anxiety at the prospect of forgetting to mention someone.

First and foremost, a big thank-you to the fabulous crew at 47North, who have worked with awesome efficiency (nay, *efficient awesomeness*) to get this thing on wheels and down the road: Britt, Ben, and Justin, my editor Jason Kirk, and everyone who's toiling behind the scenes to make things run smoothly in Seattle. I'd also like to thank David Pomerico, who isn't at 47North anymore, but who is the guy who got the Frontlines series a home there and shepherded me through three novels.

Thanks to Andrea Hurst, my developmental editor, who once again made sure that the novel has as little suck and as much awesome as possible.

Thanks again to Marc Berte, my scientific sounding board, who makes sure that my science is not completely and ludicrously impossible.

As always, thanks to my Viable Paradise posse of regular rogues and ruffians: Claire Humphrey, Katrina Archer, Julie Day, Chang Terhune, Jeff Macfee, Curtis Chen, Steve Kopka, and Tiffani Angus. Your company and camaraderie over the years has kept the fire under my butt lit, and our little network is handily the best thing about this new career other than the royalty checks.

Thank you to John Scalzi, who is always generous with his time and advice, and Elizabeth Bear and Steven Gould. You guys are the Jedi Masters to our little VP Padawan posse.

Thanks to my agent, Evan Gregory, who keeps looking out for my interests in the dog-eat-dog world that is publishing, and who makes sure I don't just sign any old thing people put in front of me.

Thanks to the Camp Daydrinker gang, Team Pantybear: Claire, Julie, Erica Hildebrand, Al Bogdan, Mike DeLuca, and Katie Crumpton. I didn't get the novel finished on our retreat, but I got to recharge the Writing Energy Meter to where I could, and making new friends and traditions is always awesome.

And last but not least—a big thank-you to my readers. You keep buying these books and spreading the word to others, and I keep writing them, and it's a racket that seems to work out really well for everyone involved. I appreciate every e-mail, review, and kind word in person, and I feel incredibly fortunate and grateful to be able to do what I am doing for a living.

ABOUT THE AUTHOR

Photo © 2013 Robin Kloos

Marko Kloos was born and raised in Germany, in and around the city of Münster. In the past, he has been a soldier, bookseller, freight dockworker, and corporate IT administrator before he decided that he wasn't cut out for anything other than making stuff up for a living.

Marko writes primarily science fiction and fantasy, his first genre love ever since his youth, when he spent his allowance mostly on German SF pulp serials. He likes bookstores, kind people, October in New England, Scotch, and long walks on the beach with Scotch.

Marko lives in New Hampshire with his wife, two children, and roving pack of vicious dachshunds.